"KATIE, YOU'RE ONE HELL OF A WOMAN," O'Brien said, then he burst into laughter.

Katherine countered with a brief smile. They had been walking up the street toward the edge of town. Now they stopped and she tugged on the sleeve of his jacket for emphasis. "You must understand something, Jim," she said seriously. "What these men did to me, my child, my husband—it is not forgivable. Nor is it forgettable. It is not as though I can bring back the dead, but I have a debt to their memory. I am dedicated to it and nothing on this earth can stop me. Can you understand that? It is as if my life will remain at a halt until I have done this thing. When it is done, my life can begin again."

Other Avon Books by
Trevor Meldal-Johnsen

ALWAYS

THIS CRUEL BEAUTY

TREVOR MELDAL-JOHNSEN

AVON
PUBLISHERS OF BARD, CAMELOT, DISCUS AND FLARE BOOKS
A BERNARD GEIS ASSOCIATES BOOK

THIS CRUEL BEAUTY is an original publication of Avon
Books. This work has never before appeared in book form.

AVON BOOKS
A division of
The Hearst Corporation
959 Eighth Avenue
New York, New York 10019

First Avon Printing, March, 1983

AVON TRADEMARK REG. U. S. PAT. OFF. AND IN
OTHER COUNTRIES, MARCA REGISTRADA, HECHO EN
U. S. A.

Printed in the U. S. A.

WFH 10 9 8 7 6 5 4 3 2 1

*This book is for Marcia,
as indeed they all are.*

ACKNOWLEDGMENTS

My thanks go to the many people in South Africa, both white and black, who provided me with information and insight into that beautiful land. They are too numerous for me to single out, but they know who they are.

My apologies for certain factual liberties, but my allegiance went to the story.

Finally, my gratitude to those who read and enjoy this book. Although it is dedicated to my wife, it is also for you.

Chapter One

THEY WERE a family of four. The woman sat stiffly beside her husband in the front of the wagon. She was concerned about her children. The older boy, the five-year-old, was ill, suffering from a three-day fever that had stubbornly refused to break; although it worried her intensely, she had mentioned it only casually to the man. It was, she had decided earlier, her burden to bear.

They were at the top of a pass, usually a place of hope and promise. The land ahead of them rolled back in slow, even waves, a greener, more welcome land than that they had passed through. But in spite of the view, she felt gripped more by a nameless dread than by excited anticipation. From the hills of tangled vines and twisted trees on either side they could hear the hoarse barking of baboons, or perhaps it was only one of the animals futilely answering its own echo. There was no way to tell. The bush was as impenetrable as a stone wall.

There was another wagon coming up the mountain from below, and they were waiting for it to pass.

"Good thing we saw him before we started down," her husband said. "If we had met him halfway I don't know what we would have done."

It was fortunate, for the narrow track down hardly justified the name. If the wagons had met, one would have had to retreat. They had heard the progress of the other traveler first, shouts, the crack of the whip,

1

and the wheels thumping over loose rock, and then they had caught a brief glimpse of him a few hundred yards away.

"Just a few minutes more and then we can start down," the man said. He was large, this Englishman, with thick forearms and big hands that would be more at home in soil than with quill and ink. During their journey the sun had reddened his good-natured face and lightened his sandy brown hair. The flabbiness he had developed over the past two years had hardened since leaving Cape Town, and he seemed more fit than ever before.

The woman did not answer him, however. The wagon and its steady progress forward to their destination was his responsibility. Hers was the care of the children.

An eagle wheeled lazily overhead, scanning the area in great circles. She lifted her narrowed eyes to the soaring bird and wondered how far it could see. If one could get high enough, she thought, perhaps one could see the future.

"Don't worry," the man said. He placed his hand gently on her knee. "It's going to be all right. You'll see."

She looked over at him, surprised by the tenderness of his words, fighting back the sudden prick of tears. Her concern had insulated her from him, blinding her to the depth of his caring.

She took his arm. "It's just that I don't know what else to do," she said. "It's been so long and the fever hasn't broken yet."

"Don't worry," he repeated. "He's a game little fellow. Tougher than he looks, too."

There was a cry from inside the wagon. Colin, the two-year-old, had awakened. A few seconds later he stuck his head through the canvas behind them, and the woman picked him up.

The other wagon came into view, lunging around a

clump of rocks like a frightened beast. It was driven by a small dark man with prominent features and a pointed beard. Obviously he was a trader. He had bright and alert black eyes, and when he smiled his teeth were as white as ivory.

"How is the track down the mountain?" the Englishman asked after they had greeted each other.

"Not too bad," the trader said cheerfully. "You will have to put on chains and *reims*, those leather thongs, and slide much of the way, but it will not be difficult. Your oxen look to be fine animals."

The trader asked them to join him for coffee before continuing. They were making good time, but they had wanted to reach the valley below well before dark. "He will have news of the north," the man said to his wife, a question in his voice.

"He may also have some kind of medicine," she said dully, fiddling with a golden tendril of hair that had escaped from below her bonnet. She was growing increasingly terrified by her inability to help Timothy. Even now he lay inside the wagon, mumbling incoherently to himself, his body burning.

"We'd be delighted," her husband said, clambering down from the wagon.

"I am Cohen," the trader said, shaking his hand.

"Alan Carson." He waved to his wife and the baby she was holding. "My wife Katherine, my son Colin. The other boy is in the wagon with a fever. We were wondering if you had anything that would help?"

"We shall see," Cohen said. He shouted orders to his Kaffir servants, and a man began to unload a box from his wagon. The other servant began to build a fire. "Come on, *mevrouw*," he gestured with a comforting smile to Katherine. "Let us sit and talk for a while."

Cohen's rickety wagon was drawn by sixteen donkeys. There were four more of the animals trailing, each heavily loaded with goods. The two black ser-

vants wore only tattered khaki pants and walked
without shoes. Katherine thought that Cohen himself looked like something from one of her more ex-
otic dreams. His striking appearance was made more
colorful by a broad-brimmed green hat, a bright red
shirt, and pin-striped pants more suited to a Cam-
bridge garden party than the African veldt.

Cohen sat on his haunches and placed two tin cans
of water on the fire. "Don't worry, missus. I have
something that will fix your boy right up," he said
with a wink. He took an assortment of leaves and
roots from a small box brought by his servant and
threw these into one of the cans.

"What is that?" Katherine asked suspiciously.

"It's a Kaffir remedy for fever," Cohen said. "I
have used it myself and it works like magic."

Katherine looked apprehensively over at Alan. He
just gave a slight shrug as if to announce his unwillingness to interfere.

"Believe me, it will work," Cohen protested, noticing her discomfort. "It was given to me by a Kaffir
wizard after I saved him from drowning in a flooded
river. He swore it would save me from evil spirits.
When I was in the Low Veldt last year I came down
with fever and used it. In an hour the spirits were
conquered and the fever broke. There's no doubt that
it works."

He grinned throughout his little tale and Katherine didn't know whether to take him seriously or not.
She found it hard to tell if he even believed what he
was saying. The twinkle in his eyes seemed to belie
his words. This talk of wizards and evil spirits!
Surely no white man would take it seriously.

"At the very worst, I promise it won't harm the
boy," he consoled.

He threw a handful of coffee into the other can and
stirred it quickly with a burning twig before the
froth could overflow. Placing it on the ground to set-

tle, he cautiously eyed the other can. "We will let this one boil a few minutes more," he said.

He looked frankly and appreciatively over at Katherine while he spoke. It wasn't every day in the bush that one met a beautiful woman with blue eyes and golden hair and a fine, strong body. Some of the younger Boer women were pretty, of course, but they grew old quickly out here. Like flowers, you had to catch them in their season. This one, he could see, had dark circles under her eyes from fatigue, but it did not diminish her attractiveness.

"Where have you come from?" Alan asked, not reacting to the man's obvious appraisal of his wife. He had been married to her long enough to grow used to the effect Katherine had on men.

Cohen waved his arm vaguely. "North," he said. "I have been trading at the Boer farms and settlements. The ladies all need pretty things and needles to sew with; the men need powder and tobacco. It is lucky for me that men use their powder and smoke their tobacco and that the ladies can be depended upon never to be satisfied with how they look. In return, I have come back with a few trinkets, some gold, a little ivory, a few skins."

Alan cast a disbelieving eye at the man's wagon. If he loaded it any heavier it would collapse. "It seems you have done fairly well, Mr. Cohen," he said in his slow, even way.

"The Boers appreciate me," Cohen said with satisfaction. "I don't cheat them, you see, not like some of the people that come out here. They know my merchandise is good and they know my word is good. Besides, as a bonus I bring them news from other places on my route. I tell the men about the crops, the hunting, the Kaffirs, and the women about the new babies and the latest scandals. I bring a little light into their lives."

He carefully poured their thick, black coffee and

handed it to them. "You are both English, I see," he said, sipping slowly and smacking his lips. "What brings you to the heart of Boer country?"

"We are going to settle and farm," Alan said. "Are the natives giving much trouble up this way?"

Cohen chuckled. "Being English, you might get more trouble from the Boers than the Kaffirs."

Katherine's lips tightened. This constant Boer-English antagonism irritated her. "We're now South Africans," she said. "We are starting off with no more than anyone else, and we're willing to work as hard as anyone. I'm sure that being English counts for little during Kaffir raids and times of hardship."

"True, missus, true," Cohen allowed. "But there is still strong feeling among the Boers. Remember, it was only two years ago, in 1848, that the British called the land between the Orange and Vaal rivers theirs, and Potgeiter led his people north to the Transvaal. Less than fifteen years since the Great Trek from British rule. Feelings still run high here."

"We will deal with that when we come to it," Katherine said sharply.

Alan was determined to get an answer to his earlier question. "What about the Kaffirs?" he asked. "Is there trouble? You seem to travel without firearms."

"Oh, I am just a *smouse*, a trader," Cohen said. "A friend to everyone. If I have to pay a little tribute here and there, I do. Nobody bothers with me. But there is still trouble, especially in the north, where settlers are few. Raiding parties. The murder of isolated settlers. But no real war now, thank God."

The can of herbs still bubbled ferociously over the fading embers of the fire. The water had turned a dark, sullen green.

Cohen asked where they were planning to settle.

"I hear the land around the Magaliesberg Mountains is fertile," Alan replied.

"Yes, it is," Cohen said, his face lighting up with pleasure. "One of the best spots. It is a wild land, but beautiful, with lovely valleys in high mountains. It is watered well, lots of rain, and still alive with game."

"And there's still land to be had?"

"Oh, *ja*. There is always land, particularly if you are willing to settle for a small valley, smaller than the usual Boer farm."

Alan nodded thoughtfully. It was heartening news. Traditionally, the Boer sized his farm by riding for two hours in each direction. At each change of course he would dismount and make a crude beacon, then return to the point at which he had started. The farms, measured this way, were roughly sixteen miles in circumference, varying from ten to twenty thousand morgen. They were enormous pieces of property by English standards, but the Boer, with his passion for privacy, felt confined if he could see his neighbor's smoke. Alan decided he would willingly settle for a smaller portion if he had to. It would still be plenty of land for him.

Cohen took the can of herbs from the fire and placed it on the ground. "It will cool in a few minutes and then you can give it to the boy," he said.

Katherine gathered her skirts and stood abruptly. She placed Colin, who had been sitting on her lap, beside his father. "I must see how Timothy is," she said, and hurried to the wagon.

She stood in the gloom of the interior and looked down at her son on the bed. His firm mouth, normally quick to smile, was now moving in silent recitation, and his breathing was as short and quick as that of a cat in the sun. His hair was light brown, the color of his father's. She brushed it aside and felt his burning forehead. No trace of moisture; it was as dry as cracked leather. She wished fervently that she could pray, but it was something she had never been able to do with any conviction; she felt, almost super-

stitiously, that to pray without conviction was worse
than to do nothing at all. If anything happened to
Timothy she didn't know what she would do. He was
more precious to her than her life. She loved little
Colin, of course, but Timothy was older and she had
loved him longer.

"Don't let him die," she said aloud to nobody in
particular. There, she had said it! The unspoken
words, the true fear that gripped and twisted her insides. If he should die she could never bear it.

She looked around as if to escape the vision in her
mind. The inside of the wagon was tidy but crowded,
without an inch of free space. Their worldly belongings filled it. There was the bed in the center and
then the chests, cupboards, and shelves lining the
walls. There were boxes of sugar and flour, barrels of
powder, oil, water, and brandy for emergencies.
There was grease and tar and salt and tobacco, which
neither of them used, to trade. One of the drawers
held a treasure, their supply of seeds for wheat, oats,
vegetables, tobacco, and Indian corn, and the pits of
apricots, oranges, peaches, and other fruits. In the
center of the wagon a lantern hung from a chain, and
on one wall she had even found space for a mirror.
The guns were kept loaded on wall racks—three
rifles and a pair of silver plated pistols, a present
from Alan's wealthy uncle in Cape Town. Many of
their supplies had, in fact, been purchased at wholesale cost from him, for he liked his nephew and
wished him well in his new enterprise. Here within
the rounded canvas walls were the components of
their new life, the foundations upon which they
would build and grow.

She wondered if there wasn't something missing,
sensing that material things alone could not with-
stand the pressures of this strange, enigmatic land,
that survival was perhaps more a matter of spirit
than anything else. She had not always felt this way

about the country. At times, she thought she loved it. But in the last few days this feeling of antagonism had grown along with a vague sense of alarm, as if somehow this land of unparalleled opportunity also declared itself to her as an enemy.

She heard her husband laugh loudly at something the Jewish trader had said. How could he laugh while their child lay here like this, she thought hotly. Then she shook her head at her own unreasonableness. He never worried when it was useless to worry, and she had always admired him for that—the steady, phlegmatic part of his character that remained calm and resourceful in spite of everything. He was right not to be worrying now. In truth, she was worried enough for both of them.

"How is he?" Alan asked when she came back out.

She shook her head. "The fever is still high."

Cohen stuck his finger into the can. "It is still warm, but cool enough to swallow now." He handed the can to her. "It will help. Make him drink every drop. Then let him sleep."

After transferring the liquid to a tin cup, she held it up to Timothy's lips. He gulped at it greedily, his body craving the moisture, then fell back to the pillow. Within seconds he was asleep again, his breathing still shallow and irregular. She drew the covers up around him and stroked his hair.

It seemed so unfair that children who had not been on earth long enough to commit a single evil deed should be visited by such travail. But then she had never been convinced of any real fairness in life. Her father, a Church of England clergyman, had attempted to teach her that God always rewarded the good and the just, but she had not been persuaded. Too often she had seen the good suffer on equal terms with everyone else.

When she went back to the fire, Cohen was talking about the Boers. She took Colin on her lap and sat with the men, only half-interested in the conversation. It was following a path not too far from that of her own thoughts. The devout Boers typified for her the type of religious acceptance she had never been able to achieve. In Cape Town they had met Boers, of course, but their acquaintances were for the most part English. Also, they had been told by knowing friends that the Cape Boers were different from those who had headed north on the Great Trek, the hard-liners.

"They are an easy people to misjudge," Cohen said, shaking his head. "Ach, yes. Very easy. People think that because they are slow, they are stupid. True, they are slow to speak, slow to anger, and slow to act, but once they have decided upon a course of action they are as fierce as a buffalo, and just as dangerous. They believe in their God, their Bible, and their destiny. Sometimes this makes them difficult to deal with. Try telling a Boer that the world is round and he will know you for a liar."

Alan laughed, but Cohen held up his hand. "No, no. You must understand. They are also a practical people, these Boers. Here's an example. I know this Boer, Kruger is his name. Very devout. His Bible is his life. One day he was out hunting with a party of his neighbors and the veldt was bare. Not a head of game in sight. They had disappeared into the earth. The next day, it was the same. Nothing. Well, Kruger came up with the solution. He would go into the bush and pray for game. He demanded not to be disturbed, no matter how long he took. God would hear his prayers. So Kruger went into the bush to wrestle in prayer, and no doubt he did. But he also went to a nearby Kaffir *kraal* where there were many people and told them that unless they beat up the game and drove it in the direction of their camp, he would bring a Boer commando down on them. The power of Paul Kruger's prayers was much talked about."

They all laughed at the story, but Cohen felt it necessary to explain. "The point is," he said, "that although the Boers believe themselves to be God's chosen people, they also believe that God helps only those who help themselves. It is very practical."

"I've heard that they are a cruel people," Katherine said.

"Perhaps," Cohen said. "Indeed, they are harsh. But you cannot be soft and survive out here. Their God is not the forgiving Christian God of Jesus. It is the God I am familiar with, the God of Israel, a terrible God, one who does not suffer the foolish. Perhaps it was necessary for them to choose that God, hey?"

Cohen stood up, throwing the remains of his coffee on the fire. "I must go," he said. "I want to be through the pass by nightfall."

"Us too," Alan said. "Is there much game in the valley down there?"

"*Ja*, there should be. I saw a herd of buck yesterday."

"Well, it has been a pleasure meeting you, Mr. Cohen," Alan said, holding out his hand. "Perhaps we will meet again."

"I shall be back in a few months, like a bad penny. Cohen is the Wandering Jew. He always returns." He gave a small, gracious bow to Katherine. "I hope you will be happy in your new land, missus."

"Thank you. And thank you for the medicine," she said. Looking down, she saw that Colin had fallen asleep in her arms. "Do you think we should go down the mountain now?" she asked Alan. "It might be better if we stopped here and watched Timothy's progress."

"It will be cold up here tonight," Cohen interrupted. "Better you go down. There is a small river at the bottom and you will be able to make him more comfortable there."

"Right," Alan said. "Don't worry, my love. We'll take it carefully on the way down."

"I suspect you don't believe in my Kaffir medicine," Cohen said to her. "But I promise you, missus, by the time you reach the valley you will be happily surprised."

"No, it's not that," Katherine said, embarrassed, for indeed she had little hope that the leaves would do anything. "I'm just worried about moving him. He should be resting as much as possible."

"He will rest," Alan said. "We will move very slowly."

"Well, *totsiens*," Cohen said, using the Boer word for good-bye. "Good luck on your journey."

He turned and went back to his wagon, shouting good-naturedly to his servants. Climbing up to his seat, he gave the English couple a last wave and cracked his long leather whip, stirring the donkeys into jerky motion.

"Nice fellow," Alan said, putting his arm around her. "An interesting character."

"We had better put chains on the wheels and get started," Katherine said curtly, surprising even herself with the tone of her voice. Yes, she had liked the little trader, but her son's life was in danger. The sooner they reached their stopping place the sooner she could care for him.

Every turn of the wheel had been a trial and a test since leaving Cape Town. Familiarity had made some things easier to bear during the two months of travel, but this uncompromising country had a talent for providing unexpected hardships with remorseless regularity.

Katherine crouched inside the wagon, kneeling beside the bed, her arms braced against Timothy's shoulders in an attempt to cushion the violent movement. Clouds of red dust rose like fog from the rough track, clogging her nostrils and irritating her eyes as the wagon swayed and skidded precariously down the steep hill. Her knees were separated from the rough plank floor by only a thin blanket, and they painfully protested every bump in a path that seemed to consist of nothing but endless ruts. Timothy continued to sleep, however. Colin was in front with his father and, as usual, she found herself worrying about him. One unexpectedly large bump and over Colin could go. A silly thought, she told herself; yet Alan's hands would be fully occupied with the reins, and a span of sixteen oxen was not easy to control. She could hear the animals bellow and snort, complaining against the weight of the yoke and the wagon pressing them from behind. Alan's voice had grown hoarse shouting commands at the beasts. "Whoa-up! Slow down! Left, left! To the right, to the right! Pull up there, pull up!" It seemed a waste of energy to her, yet it provided a bond of a kind between man and oxen, and perhaps, after repetition and time, the dumb animals even understood.

She heard him call back into the wagon's interior: "Not too much farther. We're almost at the bottom. Just a few hundred yards." Thank God! Her arms were ready to fall from her shoulders.

What little Katherine could see of the valley ahead suggested that it was lushly verdant. They would outspan the oxen there, and then both men and beast could rest and eat. Thank God for the Trekboers who had begun going north fifteen years earlier, she thought. At least there were rough tracks of a sort now, and there were passes through the mountains so that they did not have to take their wagon apart and carry it piece by piece over the rugged ranges as their predecessors had done. Also, they knew where they were going. They had been able to purchase a map in Cape Town; crude as it was, it was still a boon as long as they used it with caution.

She saw the river that Cohen had mentioned, a dappled ribbon of brown and silver. Perhaps they would all be able to bathe. Safety was the prime concern, as usual. What with crocodiles and snakes, and even bigger animals, one had to be careful in this God-forsaken country. There were dangers everywhere, dangers such as she had never dreamed of in the soft green and drizzle of England. Here, an inviting patch of grass could be concealing a nest of mambas, or boomslangs, or rinkalses, or pythons, and puff adders. There were snakes for every season, she thought. If the grass were longer, it might conceal larger beasts: lions, or leopards, or even the gigantic buffalo that attacked anything that moved with a blind, insane fury. The river banks too were not without danger; there was quicksand in places and innocent-looking logs could suddenly become crocodiles with jaws big enough to snap a child in two. And if that were not enough, there were always wild Kaffirs willing to burn and kill defenseless settlers. Disturbed by these thoughts, Katherine found herself wondering for the hundredth time what she was doing here, the genteel daughter of an English vicar.

"We're almost down now," Alan called. She could feel the wagon begin to level.

There was the reason: Alan Carson. His family had always been farmers. She should have known he would never be happy doing anything else. Sitting in Cape Town after six months there, little more than a clerk in his uncle's trading company, the opportunities had been as alluring as gold.

"There is land, land for the taking," he had told her, his enthusiasm overcoming his usual placidity. "Thousands of acres of land, rich and fertile. Game in such quantities it blankets the veldt. A chance to create exactly what we wish to create for us and our children."

She had finally agreed, even though she was aware of the dangers and knew Alan was often blinded to the point of irrationality once he had an idea. But she

loved him wholeheartedly and would follow him to
the center of Africa if need be. His happiness was all-
important, for she was wise enough to know that if
he were unhappy they would all be unhappy. They
were, above all, a family, a unit, and they belonged
together in spite of any adversity. Besides, her agreement wasn't totally unselfish. Cape Town had begun
to bore her with its rigid social structure, its endless
tea parties and lawn parties and its formal dinners.
She was annoyed with the smug superiority that per-
vaded the place. She hadn't been able to make close
friends, not real friends with whom one could share.
Alan was really the only friend she had. Other than
that, the children were her life.

The grass beside the river was tall and green and it
undulated in long ripples before the gentle breeze.
Large shade trees surrounded a circular clearing
that had apparently once been used as a camping
site. Well-blackened rocks formed a rough square, a
receptacle for the ashes of many previous fires.

Miraculously, Timothy's fever had broken. He was
sweating profusely now and his body temperature
was dropping. When Katherine went back to the
wagon he looked up, even managing a weak smile,
and said, "I'm thirsty, Mother." She ran down to the
river and came back with fresh water that he gulped
greedily.

Katherine almost cried with relief. Silently, she
thanked Cohen for his potion, whatever it had contained. Perhaps the fever would have broken anyway, perhaps not. It didn't matter a shred. All that
mattered was that Timothy was on the mend. Soon,
she knew with a mother's certainty, he would say he
was hungry.

The oxen were outspanned so that they could fill
themselves on the rich grass and rest in the shade.
Strong, sturdy animals, they nevertheless needed to

stop two or three times daily, depending upon the terrain. This had limited their progress since leaving Cape Town to about fifteen miles a day, and that only on good days.

After quickly cooling himself down in the stream, Alan took the horse they kept tethered to the wagon and announced that he was going to hunt for fresh meat. They had not seen much game since leaving the small Boer settlement of Bloemfontein, but while coming down the mountain Alan thought he had spotted a herd of antelope a few miles into the valley.

"Why don't you rest? You look exhausted," Katherine said. "We can go without fresh meat for another day or so."

"If I look exhausted it is only from lack of meat." Alan laughed at his own joke. "All day I've been thinking about a thick and juicy wedge of tender venison. I'll only be about two hours. We will feast and camp here for the night. We deserve the rest and we'll all sleep better on a full stomach."

The prospect of meat appealed to her too, and she did not again try to dissuade him. He took one of the Brunswick rifles and powder and left with a cheerful wave. For a man who had spent years slouched over a desk, he had hardened remarkably since they had begun the trek, she thought admiringly as she watched him ride off.

She took Colin down to the water and stripped off his clothes. The river widened and slowed at a bend and she let him play in the shallows there. After washing the grime from her own face, she sat on the bank and watched the child play, hitting the water with his hands, entranced by the splashes, laughing with delight. He was oblivious of the cold. She closed her eyes for a moment and imagined the laughter being carried on wings through the clear dry air, alighting somewhere on the veldt miles away.

The worst *was* behind them. Alan had promised

her that only a few days earlier, and she believed him. Nothing could be worse than those first few weeks, anyway. They had closely approximated her conception of hell. The only consolation was that her ability to survive that ordeal showed she could survive anything.

After leaving the mountains of Wellington, northeast of Cape Town, they had entered a plain of such dull horror that she found herself fighting an urge to ask Alan to turn back. There was nothing there but sand and pebbles and brittle gray bushes. But it was Eden compared to what lay ahead: the Karoo Desert. They came upon it after leaving the tiny settlement of Karoo Port; it consisted not of the sandy windswept dunes associated with the Sahara, but a flat unbroken sheet of ugliness with nothing, plant or mineral, more than a hand high. There was only dry, drab sand beneath a hot yellow sun. It was a place of mirage and deception, promising great lakes of shining water and relief in the distance. But there was no relief. The vegetation, for lack of a better name, was bracken and gray and grew in small pathetic tufts. Thin, cracked roots escaped the ground, as if trying to raise themselves from the dead. Skeletons, both human and animal, lay on either side of the trail, serving as warning to the careless traveler. And although there was no trace of a breeze, mysterious pale clouds of dust rose around them and circled lazily before falling back to earth.

Katherine had discovered then that there was no speech in hell, for they found themselves virtually unable to say anything in this oppressive atmosphere. She could only clutch the children to her side and stare blankly with red-rimmed eyes at the vast emptiness, her thoughts as dull and repetitive as the landscape.

Even so, it was not a totally predictable environment. In the open country one day, a dust storm had

struck as suddenly as lightning. One minute there
was nothing but the vacant horizon, and in the next
came a tempest of palpable clouds of dust that filled
every open cavity of the body and wrapped around
them like a second skin. The oxen stumbled to a halt;
although only a few yards ahead of them, the beasts
were almost invisible. When the family sought shelter inside the covered wagon they found the dust
there as thick as anywhere. They were overcome by a
terrible thirst, but water was in finite supply and
they doled it out a half-cup at a time, two to the children for each one of theirs.

And then, as suddenly as it had come, the storm
disappeared, replaced once more by the pitiless heat,
the monotonous landscape, and the swarms of black
flies that seemed to follow them wherever they were.

They had been traveling about two weeks—they
lost track of time, for each day was the same as the
one before—when they finally arrived at Beaufort
West, their spirits as flat as the land they had passed
through. Probably the only thing that kept them
from even discussing a return to Cape Town, Katherine realized, was the thought of having to go back
through that desolate hell. It seemed far better to
face wild animals and even the spears of Kaffirs than
that domain of Beelzebub again.

Luckily, the country began to change at that point.
Although still dusty and hot, it was also green, and
with this sign of life, their spirits lifted again.

Now, as Katherine sat at the bank of the river
watching Colin play in the water, the land looked
positively lush. Yes, the worst was definitely over.
Soon they would reach the Vaal River, and across it
they would come to the land the Boers called the
Transvaal. There they would find a home, a farm
with rich soil where they could grow their own food,
a house they would build with their own hands, a
place to put down roots and prosper.

She went back to the wagon, one eye still on Colin, to gather soiled clothes and linen. It was her chance, maybe the last for days, to wash their belongings. There was a large smooth rock at the edge of the water near where Colin played. She could rub and pound the clothes against it, kneading them like dough.

Timothy was asleep on the large bed in the center of the wagon. He was relaxed and calm now, his breathing deep and slow. Normally they all four slept on the bed. When she and Alan needed their privacy they left the children in the bed and slept under the wagon. She listened again to the sound of Timothy's breathing, then leaned forward for a closer look.

The world tipped crazily to one side. The blood drained from her face.

There was a snake on the bed.

It was curled in a rumpled circle beside Timothy, not six inches from his head, as sound asleep as he was.

Katherine realized she was holding her breath and slowly exhaled, not daring to move. The snake was long, predominantly green, its body covered with small, repulsively oily scales. She had no idea when it could have entered the wagon, but it had obviously been attracted to its present position by the heat of her son's body.

If he moved! The thought was too horrible. She looked wildly around for some kind of weapon. There was a gun on the wall not far from her, but there was no possibility of using it. The snake was much to close to Timothy. There was a sharp-edged hoe on the wall as well. Perhaps she could sweep it down at the reptile's head. And if I missed? she asked herself. What if she just wounded the snake—what then of Timothy? It was too high a risk. The mattress was too soft to provide enough resistance for a fatal blow.

Timothy groaned and moved his leg. She stopped breathing again and even inadvertently closed her

eyes for a second, the picture flashing unbidden into
her mind: his body moving; the hiss; the strike swif-
ter than vision at the boy's face. But when she
opened her eyes, things were just as they had been.
He had relaxed again and the snake had not moved.

There was a broom about two feet away from her.
It was the only alternative. Cautiously she moved
one foot over, then the other. She reached out and
clasped the wooden handle, lifting it off the ground,
careful not to bump anything. Turning the broom
around, she held the handle with both hands just
above the straw.

She leaned forward, the broom handle outstretched in front of her. Slowly, carefully, she lowered it down toward the snake. Her heart was
thundering now, and she could feel perspiration drip
down her forehead into her eyes.

When the handle was only an inch away from the
center of the pile of snake, she tightened her grip on
the wood and took a deep breath. Quickly, without
further thought, she jabbed down, feeling the pole
slide through the coiled center of the soft mass. Using all her strength, she swung the handle of the
broom up and across to her right. The snake was
lifted off the bed. It hissed and writhed against the
broom handle but it was too slow. It flew through the
air and out the back of the wagon. She watched with
a mixture of horror and relief as the snake landed
with a soft thud in the dust.

Katherine was suddenly too exhausted to do anything more about it. Now that the reptile was out in
the open, she knew she should take the gun from the
wall and kill it. Instead she used the broom as a support and leaned her forehead against the rough
straw bristles. Gradually her breathing returned to
normal and the color came back to her face. She saw
the snake slither away, disappearing into the grass
far beyond the wagon.

Timothy was still sleeping, undisturbed. Looking down at the boy, she suddenly felt helplessly angry, not at the snake or any other specific target, but more at this land that could bring into play circumstances which could place her child's life in jeopardy. She hated this need for endless vigilance. One wrong step, a casual lowering of your guard, and the dangers sprang out at you. She had not bargained for this, not in the beginning when they had decided to come here. Oh, she had heard of the dangers, but without experience to back them up, warnings of that sort lacked any sense of reality. Now it was real. Now she knew. Well, she told herself firmly, I'll fight it every inch of the way. This land will not take my children from me. I will not let it get the better of me. If there is a fate written here, if the cards have already been dealt, I will play my hand to win.

Katherine heard the sound of hooves carry through the still evening air, and a few minutes later Alan rode into the camp, an antelope slung over his saddle. It was a pretty animal, a dark chestnut color, with a long narrow head.

"It's a hartebeest," Alan said proudly as he dismounted. "I came across a whole herd, thirty or forty of them. Only had to use one shot."

When he had first gone out hunting after leaving Cape Town, he had wasted four shots and returned empty-handed, so his pride in his improved marksmanship was justified. Powder was one of their most valuable commodities. They had only as much as they could carry. Later, when it ran out, they would have to depend upon traders like Cohen for additional supplies. After he butchered the antelope, Alan would dig out the lead bullet and put it in a can with others to be melted and remolded later. They were learning to waste nothing.

"How is Timothy?" he asked.

"Better, much better. Perhaps he will even be able to eat with us."

"Good, good," Alan said. He picked Colin up and swung him high in the air. "And you, my little one. Have you been helping your mother?"

"He helped me wash the clothes," Katherine said. Her mouth suddenly watered for the taste of meat. "If you're going to butcher that animal I had better build the fire up now."

Alan hung the antelope by its tendons from the branch of a tree and began to skin it, whistling a country ditty. It was the best humor he had been in for days and Katherine began to feel the contagion of it. She decided not to tell him about the snake just yet.

"How is the land yonder?" she asked, stoking the fire with a long branch.

"Ah, Katie, it's improving," he replied expansively. "Beautiful, as a matter of fact. The grass is long and sweet, and there is game enough to satisfy any man. I saw a herd of zebra, pretty as punch, like striped horses."

"Did you see any people?"

"No, not exactly. There was a farm a few miles farther on, though. I saw the smoke from their fire. We will pass by tomorrow. It looked like they've irrigated and planted some land. Been there some time. Maybe we'll be able to trade for some fresh vegetables and fruit. We'll see."

"Oh, that would be excellent," she said. "Especially for the children. I worry about their diet."

"You worry too much, Katie," he said with a smile. "They'll do fine."

As if to prove him right, Timothy called from inside the wagon. Katherine hurried over to him immediately.

The boy was sitting up in the bed, stretching and yawning. Katherine asked how he was feeling.

"I'm hungry, Mommy," he complained. "I want something to eat."

Katherine took his head in her hands and pulled it to her breast. "I'll bring you some food in a few minutes, Timmy. I'll bring you something to eat." To her surprise, she found she was crying, the victim of an overwhelming sense of relief.

That night, their appetites sated by the plentiful fresh meat, Katherine and Alan drew another kind of nourishment from each other as they lay on the ground beneath the wagon.

But just before she fell asleep, Katherine was disturbed by an unwelcome thought. In spite of the lucky escape with the snake, in spite of Timothy's recovery, and in spite of the tenderness and joy when she and her husband had joined their bodies together, nothing had really changed. The foreboding had not disappeared. The feeling of dread that had bothered her for days was still with her.

Chapter Two

A MIRACULOUS PERIOD of time divides African day
and night. It is a time when the colors of the landscape change from a brilliant orange to a soft, tender
mauve, passing through all the gradations between,
a time of profound silence and awesome stillness
when every beast and bird seems to stop whatever it
has been doing to listen to the sound of a world that
has ceased its turning. It is a peaceful time, one of
truce between predator and prey, hunter and hunted.

It lasts no more than five minutes, this moment of
dropping sun and lengthening shadows when even
the breeze dies and the leaves no longer rustle. Yet,
brief as it is, ever since they had started their trek,
Katherine had grown to love this interval and even
come to depend upon it. To her it seemed magical, as
if a spell had descended over the land, blanketing it
with a tranquillity intense enough to quiet even the
bustling minds of men. Fancifully, she imagined it
actually soothed the savage land and its equally
untamed inhabitants, cleansing and renewing the
spirits of both.

Alan laughed at her thoughts, calling them a leg-
acy of the superstitious Celt in her blood, but both he
and the children seemed no more immune to the
moment than she. He would sit and doodle with a
stick in the sand, just as intent upon the silence as
she, while the children would appear somnolent in
comparison with their activity of just minutes ear-

lier. Always, the spell would be broken by just one
sound, like the snap of a hypnotist's fingers. Sometimes it would be the startled cry of a bird, sometimes the lowing of an ox or the roar of a lion.
Whatever it was, whenever it came, it was like a signal, and all activity would suddenly resume as if by
common agreement. The creatures of the veldt would
busy themselves in preparation for the darkness of
the night less than an hour away.

On this night, the spell was broken by the sound of
hooves. There were horses on the trail behind them,
probably about a mile away.

One of the oxen began to snort and paw at the
ground. A hoopoe bird swooped out of a nearby tree
with a shrill cry and flew in the direction of a distant
thicket.

"Horses are coming," Timothy said.

"I hear them," Alan replied. He went to the wagon
against which his rifle was leaning and picked it up.
They had already lighted their evening fire, and the
travelers would have seen the smoke. He sat on a
rock beside the fire and faced the trail, placing the
gun on the ground beside him. One never knew. Even
Kaffirs sometimes had horses these days. It always
paid to be careful. He waited for the riders to come
into view.

They had made good progress since Timothy's ill-
ness, crossing the Vaal only the day before. With the
crossing came a sense of accomplishment, but also a
renewed awareness of danger. They were now offi-
cially in the Transvaal, still more than a hundred
miles from their destination but far from British
jurisdiction in this wild and virtually uncharted
country.

There were three horses on the trail, three men
riding single file on small, sturdy Boer ponies. They
had slowed almost to a walk and looked frail and
miniaturized in the distance, although in the clear

evening light Katherine could make out that the man in front had a dark beard.

When they were about thirty yards away the leader raised his hand and shouted, "*Hoe gaan dit?*"

"Hello!" Alan shouted back. He got to his feet, leaving the gun on the ground. There was little to fear from fellow white travelers in this country.

The man reined to a halt. "You are English?" he said in a surprised tone. His voice was guttural and deep.

"Yes, my name's Carson. Traveling north with my family to settle."

The man dismounted, holding the reins of his horse and shaking Alan's hand with his free one.

"I am Klaus Wohlman," he said.

"German, are you?"

"*Ja,*" he said. He gestured at the two men still on their horses behind him. "That is Dieter. He is also German. And that is Tommy, who is an Englishman like yourself."

Wohlman was a big man in his late twenties, almost as tall as Alan, yet broad enough to somehow look squat. Above the gray-flecked goatee was a tanned face, one that had obviously seen much of the outdoors. He had pale blue eyes and crooked teeth. He exuded an air of rough authority, probably, Alan thought, gained in military service. He was obviously the leader of the group. The other two men were younger. Dieter, tall, thin as a pole, hard-faced, and silent, looked to be in his mid-twenties. The Englishman was more boy than man, not yet twenty, with red hair and freckles, the sharp pointed features of a ferret, typical of some London slum. They all wore long greatcoats and looked as if they had been riding hard for days.

"Will you join us?" Alan asked.

"*Ja*, thank you," Wohlman said. "We are ready for a rest."

"Good. We can offer you some coffee," Alan said.

The other two men dismounted and led their horses over to a patch of grass. Wohlman walked over to the fire with Alan and met the family.

Katherine passed out coffee and then began her evening chores, leaving the men to their conversation.

"Your wife is very beautiful," Wohlman said, looking after her.

"Thank you," Alan said. "She is a good woman."

The men sipped their coffee in silence for a moment. A crow cawed from the tree above their heads, then flopped away in graceless flight.

"It is not usual to see an English family out here," Wohlman said. "What brings you?"

Alan shrugged. "The same as everyone else. We are looking for land to farm."

Wohlman nodded. "*Ja*, there is plenty of land for those who want it."

"What are you doing here? You don't look like farmers."

"No, we are not," Wohlman said, smiling widely at some private joke. "We are prospectors, hunters when need be."

Alan kept the thought to himself, but they did not look much like prospectors to him. There was no sign of prospecting equipment on their horses. Perhaps they were hunters; at least they carried guns, but where was the profit in hunting unless one ventured to the far north, where elephants were more plentiful and ivory the reward? In truth, they did not look particularly well equipped for hunting, either. Still, he thought, Africa was filled with adventurers, and three more were no skin off his nose. Live and let live.

"Have you had any luck?" he asked politely.

"A few nuggets here and there," the man said noncommittally. "The Boers do not like prospectors up

here. In fact, you will find that they do not care for
strangers at all."

"It's understandable," Alan said, for he happened
to share the Boer concern. "If anyone finds gold in
any quantity up here they know it's the one thing
that will bring the English north. And that's what
they've been trying to get away from. Even though I
am English, I can understand it. Besides, from what
I've heard, the Boer has little use for gold himself. He
places his value in his farm and his cattle. Gold does
not feed cattle."

"They are a stupid people," Wohlman said in a
surly tone. "They are ignorant and uncivilized and
can see no farther than their noses."

"That's hard to believe of a people with the daring
to trek a thousand miles and more into the wilderness," Alan said.

Wohlman grunted and sipped at his coffee.
Throughout the conversation, the man Dieter had
remained silent and unmoving. An unpleasant-look-
ing fellow, Alan thought, noticing the dissatisfied
twist to his mouth, his hard black eyes and smooth,
uncallused hands. He looked the type who would suddenly explode in a tavern fight after a certain
amount of ale. The boy had not spoken, either, just
following the conversation with protruding frog eyes
that gave him a continuous expression of surprise.
Alan wondered what the boy was doing with the others. He was mismatched and out of his depth, that
was for sure.

"Where are you from, Tommy?" he asked.

"London," the boy replied in a low, unwilling voice.

"And what brought you to Africa?"

"I dunno," Tommy said, speaking to the ground. "I
just wanted some adventure, I s'pose." The accent
was from somewhere near the docks. Alan recognized the whine in the vowels.

Tommy paused, then his head jerked up. "I wanted

to be where a man's a man," he said; "where there weren't no betters lookin' down at me all the time and givin' orders and—"

"South Africa is a land of opportunity," Wohlman interrupted. "It is what brings us all here, is it not?"

Alan rubbed his nose, suddenly realizing that the boy must be an army deserter. There were a few of them around, men who for one reason or another took off from the British garrisons in Natal or the Cape, and headed for the wildness and freedom of the north.

"Yes," Alan said carefully. "There is opportunity aplenty here for an honest man who is willing to work for it."

"Exactly," Wohlman said. "And are we not all honest men?" Briefly he bared his crooked teeth in a tight smile.

It was a question Alan had actually been considering for the past few minutes. He was uncomfortable with these men and had begun to regret their encounter. Perhaps it took hard nuts like these to conquer the interior, but there was something about them that disturbed him, some lack of equilibrium, even of humanity. Responsibility was a word that meant something to Alan. These men, he suspected, believed in nothing except the opportunities that were presented to them.

Just then Katherine walked back to the fire. "Would you gentlemen join us for dinner?" she asked, the perfect and polite hostess even in the middle of nowhere.

Alan groaned to himself while Wohlman assented. It was not what he had wanted. Something told him that it would be better if they parted from these men right now. Still, he decided, he had no wish to antagonize them and he would have to make the best of it. There was an unwritten rule in the interior, one that he as a newcomer here could not afford to violate:

when you met another white man you extended the
hand of hospitality. It was, he well knew, a valuable
rule of social conduct, one almost necessary for survival in a hostile environment where the help of another could mean the difference between life and
death.

"I want the children in bed early. I don't want
them around these men," he whispered to Katherine
as he helped her bring some supplies from the wagon.
She nodded without speaking, her eyes flicking over
to the group around the fire as if seeing the men for
the first time.

Later, when they ate dinner around the fire, Katherine continued the role of hostess, however, keeping
the conversation alive.

"Are the Kaffirs dangerous around here?" she
asked. "Is there really a problem with them?"

They had seen their first really wild Kaffirs only a
few days before, a small group of tall and impressive
black men who wore only loincloths and beads. They
leaned on their long sharp *assegais* and impassively
watched the wagon pass from a distance of about
fifty yards. Alan had kept his gun on the seat beside
him, but the men made no overt move.

"*Ja*, there is a problem, a big problem," Wohlman
said with a wolfish grin. "There are too many Kaffirs."

Something close to a chuckle came from the man
Dieter.

"You cannot trust these Kaffirs," Wohlman continued. "One minute they are as quiet as sheep, and
then without warning they are sticking their spears
into your back, burning your farms and raping your
women." He looked over at Katherine and took another bite of meat, letting the fat run into his beard.

"Surely they're not all like that?" she asked.
"There are good and bad men in every group."

"How can you tell the difference?" he asked. "They

are all as black as sin, they all look the same. No, they are all savages and the only good Kaffir is a dead one. When I see a Kaffir I shoot him. They keep their distance from me."

Alan was incredulous. "You mean you murder innocent men on sight?" he asked, his voice rising.

Wohlman laughed, a harsh, coarse sound. "They are not men," he said. "You have a misunderstanding here. They are savages, little better than animals, good only for slavery. And believe me, none of them are innocent. If you expect to survive out here you would be wise to do the same. Shoot them on sight. They will understand that."

Katherine clenched her fists, color rising to her cheeks. "That's a despicable attitude. No wonder we have these endless wars with them. It is men like you who create them." She stood up and beckoned to the two children. "Timothy. Colin. It's time for you to go to bed." She took them each by the hand and led them to the wagon.

"I have upset your missus," Wohlman said. He added thoughtfully, "She has a temper, but she is a handsome woman. You don't see many women like that out here."

All three of the visitors followed her with their eyes.

"She is a courageous woman and a woman of principle," Alan said curtly. Damn these men, he thought. He had known they would not be pleasant.

"She does not understand how it is here," Wohlman said, turning back to Alan. His eyes looked red in the light of the flickering flames. "You English have always been too easy on the Kaffirs. It is one of the reasons the Boers left the Cape and came north. They may be stupid people in many respects, but they do understand that only the strong survive out here. The weak must die, otherwise they can drag the strong down with them. That is their fate."

"And so you would have the strong prey upon the weak?"

"That is the way it has always been," Wohlman said. "Who am I to change it? It is the way of both beasts and men."

Alan shook his head. "There are differences between men and beasts. If you believe this, how can you talk of savages? It seems to me that there is not much of a line between them and civilized men like yourself."

Wohlman snorted derisively. "You refuse to face the facts. The strong have always overcome the weak. Your British Empire is founded on that fact and that fact alone."

"Aye, that is partly true," Alan admitted. "But we always give something in return. Education, organization, our religion, a civilizing influence."

"While you drain the wealth from the country like any pirate."

"Sometimes. And I am not proud of the fact. I intend to put my labor into this land. I will live here and become a part of it. If I am lucky enough to create any wealth it shall stay here."

Wohlman smiled grimly. "Be careful. The only way a white man can become a part of this God-forsaken land is to be buried under it. Six feet under."

Dieter made a sound again. It could have been a giggle or a chuckle, or he could have been choking on his food. He did not look up.

"If you feel so about this country, why are you here?" Alan asked the German.

Wohlman lifted a mug of coffee to his mouth. "I have my reasons. It is not so bad."

The boy Tommy giggled. "They won't 'ave 'im anywhere else, mate. That's the truth of it."

"Your tongue will end on the blade of a knife if you do not control it," Wohlman said softly.

"It was only a joke," Tommy protested. He

sounded like a sulky boy captured in a transgression. But he dropped his eyes.

Alan leaned forward and threw a log on the fire. A shower of sparks flew up to merge with the blackness that surrounded them.

Katherine came back and sat beside him, her temper apparently controlled now.

"Are the children in bed?" he asked.

"Yes. Timothy wishes to say goodnight to you."

Alan looked quickly around. Tommy was unguardedly watching Katherine, his mouth half open, his eyes as blank as a fool's. Wohlman reached for the can of coffee on the embers and poured more into his cup. The third man sat as still and quiet as he had been all night, his gaze burning back at the fire.

"Yes. Yes, of course," Alan said. "Back in a minute."

Colin was already asleep, but Timothy was lying on his back, staring up at the canvas roof. "I don't like those men, Dad," he said seriously.

Alan bent forward to kiss his forehead. "Neither do I, son. But they will be on their way in the morning and we on ours. You go to sleep now."

On an impulse, Alan took one of the guns from the wall and checked that it was primed and loaded. After placing it on the stepping board at the back of the wagon, he walked back to the fire.

"We do not see too many ladies like yourself out here," Wohlman was saying to Katherine. Obviously he meant the words graciously, but grace was as alien to him as compassion and they sounded harsh and uncomfortable.

Wohlman. Wolfman, Alan thought. The man was like a predator, all teeth and menace.

Katherine began to gather the tin plates. "I must wash these," she said. The boy was still watching her like a love-struck fool.

Was she blushing? Or was it merely the glow of the

fire, Alan wondered. At any rate, she made a pretty picture, blond tendrils of hair falling over her pink cheeks, her breasts pushing down as she leaned forward. Damn! At any other time he would have been proud of her beauty. Now it disturbed him. He wished it hidden from these callous men.

"And I will help," Dieter said, surprising them all by speaking. His English was worse than Wohlman's, more guttural. Words seemed to have trouble escaping his throat.

"No. That won't be necessary," Katherine said quickly. "I will just take them to the spring and rinse them."

"I insist," the German said. He took the cup from Tommy's hands and lifted the plates near him. He stood up and belched. "You have fed us well."

An owl hooted from a nearby tree. It was a forlorn and lonely sound.

Dieter took the plates and walked down toward the copse of trees sheltering the small spring. Katherine had no choice but to trail behind him with the remainder.

Alan picked up a stick and began to stoke the fire furiously. Wohlman reached into his pocket for tobacco and filled his pipe. Casually, he took the stick from Alan's hand and used the glowing end to light his smoke.

The boy began to smile to himself.

Katherine screamed.

It was sharp and piercing and reverberated in Alan's head. It was like the sound of a wild animal in pain, helpless and furious. He grabbed the rifle on the ground beside him and jumped to his feet.

"Stay," Wohlman said.

Alan ignored him and stepped forward. By God, he would kill that German pig.

Silently, without saying anything further, Wohlman took the pistol from his belt. He leveled it for less than a second and shot Alan through the side of the head.

Tommy's smile broke into an uncontrollable giggle.

"Get the gun," Wohlman said.

Katherine's screams were louder now. She had heard the shot and guessed its meaning.

Still giggling, Tommy picked up the gun. He kicked the body on the ground, then turned it over on its back and began to go through the pockets.

"Look out!" Wohlman shouted. "Behind you!"

Tommy spun around. The child, Timothy, was standing beside the wagon. He was unsteadily holding in both hands a gun almost as long as he was, his expression a mixture of fear and confusion.

"Put the gun down, boy," Wohlman began to say, but before he could finish the sentence Tommy fired the gun he was holding at the child.

Timothy fell, his firearm discharging as it hit the ground.

"Alan! Alan!" Katherine's screams of terror came from the darkness of the trees, then stopped abruptly.

Wohlman walked over to the five-year-old boy and dropped to one knee, touching the child's head. "He's dead," he said over his shoulder to Tommy. "You got him right in the chest."

Whatever imaginary world the young Englishman lived in collapsed when he saw the dead body of the child. Reality breached the walls. "My God! I didn't mean—I, I saw 'im with the gun and I shot. I didn't mean to kill 'im." He fell to his knees and began to sob.

Wohlman slapped his face with the palm of his hand. "Pull yourself together, fool. What's done is done. You just saved me the trouble. We can't leave anyone here. I would have had to do it later myself."

"'E's only a child," Tommy said. "I didn't mean it."

The enormity of Wohlman's words sank in. He looked up at the big German, his face white, his eyes bulging more than ever, looking for all the world like a frightened fish out of water. "You mean we will have to kill the woman too?"

"Of course," Wohlman said impatiently. "After we have finished with her. We cannot leave witnesses to this."

"And the other child, the baby?"

"You are a fool. You have no stomach," Wohlman said without answering the question. "Leave everything to me. Just do what I tell you to do. There is no need for you to think."

The young Englishman stayed on his knees. Tears still ran down his cheeks. He began to giggle again. A pocket of gas erupted in the fire beside him, mixing blue flames with the orange.

Wohlman snorted derisively and, leaving Tommy to his private torment, walked toward the spring. The buttocks of the other German were a pale blur in the darkness. He had hiked Katherine's skirts up to her waist and was lying on top of her. She stared unseeing at the stars, her face as empty and forlorn as space itself.

"Hurry up," Wohlman said. "She is not just yours."

Dieter turned his head, his voice a snarl. "Can a man get no privacy? Leave me."

"Bring her up to the camp when you are done," Wohlman said, turning away.

It was unfortunate they would have to kill the woman, he thought as he approached the fire. She was a prime piece if he had ever seen one. A strong, firm body and a pretty face. When the shock wore off, though, she would give nothing but trouble. He had met the type before. Hoity-toity ladies who thought they were too good for you. Still, he thought with relish, he would get his fill before they got rid of her.

Tommy stood at the wagon. The baby was crying. "Ssh. Go to sleep," he was saying. "Stay in bed. Your mommy is busy."

"Never mind him. There is no time for that," Wohlman said. "Get everything of value that we can carry. Put it in a pile so we can load up fast in the morning. We can pack most of it on their horse when we leave. Money, jewels, dried meat, powder, guns. Get them all. We must be away from here before the sun comes up."

He picked up the body of the dead child and dropped it on the ground beside its father. Then he threw two more logs on the fire and rubbed his hands together just out of reach of the flames.

Dieter came from the shadows of the trees. Katherine was walking in front of him, her arms still at her sides, her legs looking as if they were about to buckle. There was a bruise on one side of her face where the German had hit her. Stale tears and dust stained her cheeks.

She dropped to her knees beside her husband and son and touched first the man and then the child on the face. But she did not speak or shed a single tear.

"Go to the wagon and help Tommy," Wohlman said to his partner. The baby was still crying for its mother. Apparently Tommy had been unable to quiet it.

"My baby, Colin . . ." she said softly, lifting her head.

"Never mind him," Wohlman said. "Keep the baby in the wagon," he shouted after Dieter.

He looked down at the woman, put one boot on her shoulder and pushed her back. For a brief moment he showed his crooked teeth, then he began to unbuckle his belt.

The embers of the fire glowed faintly now. Colin had stopped his crying and fallen asleep hours ear-

lier, and even the owl had ceased his mournful hoot-
ing. Katherine lay on her back and looked at the
stars. They seemed to her like chips of ice, ready to
melt at the first sign of warmth.

More than anything else, the night sky reminded
her of Alan. It always would, she decided. Let that be
his memorial. Trekking north, they had sat beside
fires such as this one and looked up. While Alan
talked softly, the sparkling net above their heads
would begin to take shape, and forms would reveal
themselves from the chaos of the darkness. There,
she could now see Centaurus, half man and half
horse, brandishing his spear at Lupus; Orion wielding a club in his left hand; Canis Major and the
dainty Canis Minor. Alan would draw the figures in
the sand: the elongated Hydra; the poisonous tail of
Scorpio; the sadly monstrous Cetus. In quiet, patient
tones he would explain the mythology of each, making them vast in time as well as space. And now,
bruised and aching down to her bones, Katherine
knew only chaos.

Oh, God, that he could be talking again! "Cetus
was a sort of whale," he had said, pointing up at the
figure. "Neptune, the god of the sea, sent him to kill
Andromeda, but instead Cetus was killed by Perseus.
There's a constellation in the northern hemisphere
named after Perseus. Interesting fellow, that. Made
a career out of killing monsters. Best known for cutting off the head of the Gorgon Medusa. He had a
helmet that made him invisible, a handy thing for
any monster-killer to have, you must admit."

And what of Timothy? Timothy would also never
hear his father's gentle humor again. And she would
never hear the voices of either. The urge to sob became almost uncontrollable, but she held it back.
There was still Colin. Still a chance for him.

The three men, the monsters, were sleeping on the
other side of the fire. After taking her, Wohlman of-

fered her to the English boy, but he had refused, stammering that they should sleep if they were to leave at first light. Wohlman had ordered her to stay at the fire. "One move from you and I will wake. Both you and the child will be dead before you can spit," he had threatened. She wondered why he had not killed her then. Probably he intended to have her again when he awoke.

She lifted her head, her entire body hurting with each small movement. Quietly she sat up and took off her shoes. She had to take the chance. There was little doubt that they would both be murdered anyway. Wohlman would leave no witnesses to his crimes. Rather die trying to escape than await slaughter like a sheep.

She sat on her aching haunches for a second, then slowly stood, holding her arms out for balance. There was no movement from the sleeping men, just the sound of one of them snoring. Painstakingly she placed one foot in front of the other, avoiding rocks and dry grass, and made her way to the wagon. She tried to concentrate on what she was doing, tried not to think of Alan and Timothy, or of the violence and degradation she had been subjected to in the last hours, but the ugly pictures clouded her mind. Worst of all, she could still smell the men on her body.

By some miracle, Colin was peacefully sleeping on the large bed. She wrapped a small blanket around him and lifted him to her shoulder, praying he would not wake. With silence and a little luck she could make it to the horse tethered some twenty yards away.

The animal snorted when she approached. "Ssh!" she entreated. "Quiet, boy, quiet."

She stroked the horse along its nose, feeling the warm breath in the palm of her hand. No saddle or stirrups. How would she mount with Colin under one arm, she thought frantically. There was a rock to her left, pale in the starlight. If she stood on that perhaps she could do it. No perhaps about it, she told herself urgently. She *had* to do it. Balancing Colin on one hip, she led the horse over. Already, on the far horizon, she could see the first faint stirrings of light. The men would soon awaken.

She balanced precariously on the rock and tightened her grip on Colin with her right hand. Grasping the mane of the animal firmly with her left, she swung herself up. The horse whinnied at the intrusion and kicked up its rear legs. Its back felt as slippery as moss and she had to dig her heels into its sides to stay on.

Colin finally woke up. It had been too much to hope that he would sleep through her gymnastics. He let out a cry, blasting air from his lungs with the force of a hurricane.

She swung her head around to the dying fire and saw Wohlman sit up. There was no longer any need for silence. "Hup!" she said to the horse, kicking its stomach. "Hup!"

"The woman!" Wohlman shouted to the others.

The horse was not used to a bareback rider. Instead of moving it shook its head and planted its feet solidly on the ground.

Wohlman lifted his pistol. She could see it glint against some source of light. Colin cried louder now. Her chest felt as though it was being squeezed by a metal band, her heart was racing. There was a noise —not the explosion she expected, but the click of Wohlman's hammer as it fell on an empty chamber. He had forgotten to reload his pistol.

Now the English boy stood, befogged by sleep and bewildered by what was happening. But he pointed his rifle at her.

"Fire!" Wohlman shouted. His voice was throbbing with fury. "Shoot her!"

The rifle at his shoulders, the boy was petrified.

Mercifully, the horse began to move. She kicked it viciously in the stomach and it picked up its pace.

"Now!" Wohlman screamed.

The boy fired the big gun, feeling it kick into his shoulder. He saw the woman fall as the slug tore into her. The horse stood on its hind legs for a moment, then broke into a wild gallop and raced away.

"Good," Wohlman said, his anger subsiding. He patted Tommy on the shoulder. "Go and see if she is dead." He turned to Dieter. "We had better pack and move on. If there are any travelers near us they will have heard the shots."

Tommy walked over to the body. His hands were shaking and he felt like vomiting. The baby must have landed unhurt on the ground. It was still crying.

He knelt beside the woman, crumpled like a discarded rag on the ground. Her eyes were closed and blood had colored her dress. The urge to throw up grew stronger. He looked closer and sucked in his breath. The bullet had only hit her arm. It was as good as a miss.

He remained where he was, staring down. Her face was many shades paler than normal, but still as lovely as any London lady he had ever seen. Her eyelids began to flicker tentatively, then opened.

"Is she dead?" Wohlman shouted impatiently from the wagon.

Impulsively, without knowing quite why he did it, Tommy put his hand on her mouth and shook his head at her. "Yes," he shouted. There was a tremor in his voice. "Got 'er right through the back. Must have 'it the 'eart."

He removed his hand and motioned with the palm for her to stay quiet. He rose up and walked back to the other men.

"The baby was not hurt, hey?" Wohlman said. Its cries were growing frantic.

"You want me to shut it up?" Dieter asked.

Wohlman shook his head. "Let us pack what we can and get away from here before daybreak. The animals will take care of the child before the day is done. There is no need to waste powder." He looked over at Tommy. "Good shooting, boy."

Tommy avoided his eyes, his own face almost as pale as the woman's.

Wohlman laughed. "Do not let it worry you. Your stomach grows used to it."

"What about the lead?" Dieter asked from inside the wagon.

"Just the powder," Wohlman said. "Without that horse of theirs we can only take what we can carry." He turned back to Tommy. "Saddle up the horses while I help Dieter. I want us away from here in ten minutes. You never know who may be around."

Katherine lay in the grass and listened to the men talk as they looted the wagon. The ground was damp and she was shivering. It seemed to her that sometimes they were only yards away and at other times a mile or more. She wondered why they were moving around so and realized that the alternately receding and approaching voices were the result of waves of dizziness that were sweeping over her. She was losing consciousness for minutes at a time. God knew how much blood she had lost. She could feel it seeping out of her arm. Colin had finally quieted, probably from exhaustion. He lay beside her on the grass, still holding his blanket and sucking his thumb.

She lay as still as she could, fighting the cold and the pain, keeping her eyes closed in case one of the men should come and check on her. Why had the English boy spared her? She had learned long ago that it was pointless to speculate upon the motives of others, but some female intuition told her that if she were ugly and fifty instead of attractive and twenty-four, his actions might have been different. He would regret his moment of compassion, she told herself.

Her husband and older son were gone, but she would
live. And she would somehow avenge their deaths.

Now she heard the sounds of horses milling about.
A shrill neigh. A shout. Still keeping her eyes closed
she fought a new onslaught of dizziness. She had to
stay conscious long enough to attend to the wound. It
would be ironic if she were spared only long enough
to bleed to death. But with her eyes closed it was like
trying to drink water and speak at the same time.
She could feel herself slipping, the dizziness gaining
control.

Images came like leaves in a wind, tumbling across
her mind. There was Alan on his father's farm in
Sussex, mud caking his leather boots. Rich, brown
English mud. Her father at the pulpit, attempting to
reason goodness into the souls of a docile and disin-
terested congregation. Timothy nursing at her
breast, heavy, pale-blue veins on the surface, the
pressure of his teeth. No more, no more. Brown
English mud...

Slipping away, slipping away...

She opened her eyes, winced, and narrowed them
against the sunlight that pierced with the intensity
of a solid object.

Brown as English mud. Darker even. Gradually
she focused on the feet inches away from her face.

Bare. Brown. Pale on the soles, then darker. A deep
chocolate brown.

Painfully she moved her head and looked up.

An enormous Kaffir stood looking down at her. He
was naked except for a cloth around his waist. He
had wide thick lips, a broad flattened nose, and
brown eyes that carried an expression she could not
read. He stared down at her without moving, as impassive as a statue, leaning on a spear in his right
hand. The blade flashed in the morning sun.

Soon she became aware of another man standing

behind him. Shorter and older, he had tight-curled hair that had grayed. There were beads around his neck, arms, and ankles. He wore what looked like a red blanket and held Colin in his arms.

The older man noticed she was awake and pointed at her. He jabbered excitedly to his companion in a native tongue, but the big man remained silent. Then he took his weight off the spear and twirled it so that the point faced the ground.

Katherine closed her eyes again, overwhelmed suddenly by a deadening sense of apathy. To have survived the death of half her family, rape by two men, a bullet wound, exposure to the elements, to have survived all that only to die at the hands of a savage thrusting his spear into her breast! How could all this be happening to her?

Katherine let her head drop back to the ground, wanting to sob. She wanted to scream and beat her fists against the hard African earth, to hurt it and show her hate for it, this land that had taken those she loved and now claimed her. She wanted to kill it and destroy it.

"God!" she tried to scream. "It's not fair! It's not fair!" But her voice came out a muffled, barely audible croak. Even words had failed her. There was no hope, nothing to be done.

She closed her eyes and waited.

Chapter Three

THE TALL BLACK MAN stabbed his spear hard into the ground. He dropped to one knee next to Katherine and turned her onto her side so that he could see the wounded arm.

"It bleeds still," he said in English.

The incongruity of it left her speechless. This half-naked savage out here in the middle of nowhere spoke English. It was heavily accented, but it was understandable. And it was, without doubt, English!

Ignoring her startled reaction, he went over to a nearby *boom* tree and gathered three or four hand-fuls of dew-laden cobwebs. He rolled them into a ball and then pulled at the edges until they approximated the size of her wound. After taking the sleeve of her dress at the cuff and ripping it up her arm, he slapped the cobwebs on her wound before she could protest.

Katherine finally found her voice. "Those are spider's webs!" she exlaimed with revulsion.

Without answering he tore the loose cloth of her sleeve and wrapped it around the wound, keeping the cobwebs in place.

"The blood will stop," he said.

He turned and spoke to the other man in a language she did not understand, a compendium of strange vowels and clicks. Still holding Colin on one hip, a remarkably contented Colin now, the older man scurried off to the spring, examining leaves and scrub as he walked.

"You speak English," she said.

"Yes," he replied, apparently a man of few words.

She had a hundred questions, but he cut them off by putting an arm around her shoulders and saying, "Sit now."

She pulled her body up with his help, fighting a fresh wave of dizziness. Her arm hung uselessly at her side, nothing but a container for pain, and her head also ached. Realizing suddenly that the bodice of her dress had been torn, she clasped it together with her good right hand. Finally, shifting her attention from herself, she examined her rescuer—or her captor, whichever he was.

He sat opposite her on his haunches, appraising her with calm brown eyes. He was, as she had noticed earlier, a large man, tall and well built, with muscular arms and shoulders. His loincloth was made from the skin of a leopard, its colors still bold. He wore colored bead bracelets on his wrists, two strings of beads around his neck, and a brass bangle on his left ankle. In addition to the long spear he had stuck into the ground beside her, his weaponry consisted of an *assegai*, a short stabbing spear, a *knobkerrie*, a long, carved stick of hard wood with a large knob at its end, and a shield made of pure white skin, probably from an ox.

"Where did you learn to speak English?" she asked.

"From a friend," he said. He flicked a finger in the direction of her arm. "Who did this?"

The smell and feel of the men was still on her, crawling over her body like lice. She clenched her fist and looked down at it, feeling her face flush.

"There were three men," she said with difficulty. "Three white men."

"I have read the tracks and that I have seen," he said patiently. "Tell me of them."

"Two Germans and an Englishman. Actually more

of a boy than a man. One German was named Wohlman, the other Dieter, the boy Tommy. They killed my husband and killed my child. They are murderers. They . . .''

"I have seen your man," he said. "This German, what did he look like?"

Not knowing which he meant, she described both Wohlman and Dieter. The black man's expression changed and he spoke a half-dozen words in his own language with such force that Katherine shrank back.

"What is it?" she asked. "Do you know these men?"

"Yes," he said. "It is the ones I seek."

"What do you want with these men?" she asked.

"To kill them," he said calmly.

The other man came from the trees, Colin tagging along behind him. He carried a wet rag into which he had pounded a soggy mass of leaves and sticks, plants that Katherine realized, as he knelt beside her, were to go onto her wounded arm. She was about to protest but remembered the efficacy of the native remedy Cohen had provided for Timothy and kept silent.

The man untied the bandage on her arm, shooting sidelong glances at her and speaking rapidly as he worked.

"What is he saying?" she asked the younger man.

The big Kaffir grinned, a broad smile that changed his face. He spoke, she noticed, with a deep bass voice that seemed to come all the way up from his stomach, gathering power as it rose.

"He is saying that you are a lucky woman," he said, his voice pungent with mockery. "He says that you are indeed fortunate that the great wizard Kokolo saw your need from afar and arranged to be here at this time."

Kokolo the wizard, as he called himself, examined

the spider webs and clicked his tongue a few times, whether in approval or not Katherine could not guess. She was not totally surprised, however, to notice that the bleeding had stopped. Placing the wet concoction of herbs on top of the webs, he rebandaged the arm. Fixing his eyes seriously on hers, he spoke rapidly.

"He says you must not take it off for three days. The wound will then heal," the tall man said.

"Tell him thank you," she said.

The tall man translated this and Kokolo smiled, his eyes almost disappearing behind folds of creased skin.

Colin began to sniffle and tug at Katherine. She stood unsteadily, but felt stronger than she had expected. "He's hungry," she said. "I shall make some food for all of us."

The wagon had been violated. Clothes were strewn everywhere and kegs of food and supplies overturned. The mattress was torn, the guns gone. The small supply of gold coins she had kept in the cabinet drawer had been taken. The china—fine, delicate china from England—was shattered.

Their lives had been torn, shredded, and overturned. The debacle in the wagon suddenly brought home the loss of Alan and Timothy. The magnitude of what had happened struck her with the impact of a blow. Finally, the tears she had been holding burst through the dreadful dead feeling that had blanketed her since last night. She threw herself face down on the bed and allowed the sobs to thunder through her body.

The strangest thing she had ever experienced happened then: she seemed to find herself lifted out of her body to the roof of the wagon. Looking down, as if from a great distance, she could see her body below on the bed. It seemed a tiny, disheveled thing, racked by grief, the face as white as the sheets it lay on. And yet, disassociated from that body, she felt a sense of freedom and exhilaration more intense than she had imagined could exist. Time ceased to have any meaning in this state. There was only thought, perception, a tremendous sense of power—sensations she could not begin to analyze.

It must have lasted only a few seconds, in spite of a sense of timelessness. At one moment, she was looking at her body with some curiosity, and in the next she was snapped back into it as if on the end of a band of rubber. The experience, whatever it was, was over.

It was like waking from a dream. She stopped crying and sat up, rubbing the tears from her cheeks. At first there was a sense of disappointment, but then a new feeling appeared, minute at first, then growing and growing until it encompassed her. She felt reborn, filled with a vital energy and dominated by a terrible resolve. Where before there was only an emptiness, there was now a purpose as strong and pure as a gleaming rod of steel, one that would sustain her and drive her through the days and months ahead.

Grief would not bring back the ones she loved; they were lost to her. When it was her time, perhaps she would join them. But for now there was a balancing to be done, a justice to be had. She would find the men who had done this, find them and kill them. It was her duty, it was just, and she had the power to do it. She knew this with utter certainty.

They sat around the fire and ate, the woman, her son, and the two black men. While the men buried the bodies of Alan and Timothy, Katherine had gone to the spring and washed. She had scrubbed her body until it hurt, trying to erase the feeling of the hands that had touched her. She had washed her hair and brushed it back, and found a clean dress. Aside from the bandage on her arm and a bruised cheek, she looked almost normal.

The tall black man told her his name was Shandu. He was from east of the Drakensberg Mountains, a Zulu.

"Why do you wish to kill these men?" she asked.

"They came to my village," he said. "They took away the lives of my wife and my daughter. They killed my cattle, they burned my house."

He had been following them for almost two months now, losing the trail, picking it up again. He had been shot at by white men, attacked by other Kaffirs, but he had persisted, never stopping for longer than he had to, never giving up the deadly hunt. This was the closest he had come to the men.

"And him?" she said, pointing to Kokolo. "What is his interest?"

Shandu laughed, a rich bass sound, and pointed at his own chest. "I am," he said. Growing more serious he explained. "He is a wizard who sees things that ordinary men do not see. I met him seven days ago. He said that the spirits had told him to travel with me, to help me with his powers, for there would be milk and honey at the end of the path."

"Do you believe him?"

Shandu shrugged and smiled. "Sometimes I believe him and sometimes I do not. He is both a wizard and a trickster, I think."

She looked at Kokolo with new interest. His face was lined and he was clearly old, but she could not judge his age. He was one of those men who seem to have always been old, wearing his age like a garment, comfortable with it.

He was quite undeterred by her scrutiny and looked back at her with keen, slightly watery brown eyes. Without removing his gaze from her he spoke to Shandu.

"He says that the spirit of your husband is very

powerful and very angry at the men who killed his body. It will help you do what you must do. He says you are very lucky to have such a powerful spirit on your side and that the evil men are most unfortunate to have such a powerful enemy."

Katherine nodded. It was almost as if she had shed the trappings of past thought and behavior. For some reason nothing now struck her as bizarre or unbelievable. Not particularly believable either, she hastily assured herself. It was just the way things were.

"I want to go with you after these men," she said.

Shandu looked shocked. He shook his head. "That is stupid," he said. "You are a woman. What can you do?"

Katherine's lips tightened. "It is my right," she said stubbornly.

Shandu did not answer her. Kokolo cocked his head to one side and asked him a question. Shandu answered, thumping his fist into his left palm, his voice rising. Kokolo closed his eyes and spoke, more slowly this time. Shandu hit his thigh with the flat of his hand, emphasizing certain words and shaking his head.

Katherine watched with interest. Apparently the old man was an ally, speaking on her behalf. Still, she thought, their decision was immaterial to her. She would do what she had to do, whatever their thought on the matter, with or without their help.

Shandu looked back at her, a peeved expression on his face. "Kokolo is like an old woman," he said angrily. "I think you have put a spell on him."

"What does he say?"

"It does not matter," he said. "Listen to me. A day behind us is another wagon of white people. You will be able to travel with them and they will care for you. They are your own kind. It is a man and a woman. You and your child will be safe."

"Safety is not what I seek, nor my own kind," she replied.

He held up empty palms. "What can you do? This is work for a warrior. How will you stand against three men with guns? What will you do in the charge? It is stupid."

"To you it may be stupid," she said. "My husband and my son have been killed. To me it is a matter of honor."

Shandu looked glumly at the ground. This woman had a tongue! Honor was something he understood all too well. But honor was the province of men. In the tribe, in the family, it was men who concerned themselves with honor. Women worked in the fields, bred the children, and did the other things that women do.

Kokolo spoke again to him, persuasively, rapidly tapping a finger emphatically on his own chest. Shandu's voice rose disputatiously in reply.

Katherine became distracted as the argument went on. She had put Colin on a blanket in the grass and he had fallen asleep. She leaned back and flipped the corner of the blanket over to cover him. Was she also tired? She had not really taken the time to analyze her condition. The pain in her arm had lessened to a dull, bearable throb. The dizziness had gone and she felt stronger than before. Her body was tired, she supposed, but mentally she felt revitalized by her resolution. Somehow she felt as if she could achieve anything now. It was strange. The last time she had felt this way was as a little girl. When she was eleven or twelve there was a period when she was afraid of nothing. There were no shades of gray in her life, no doubts or reservations regarding her own motives or those of others. Situations were viewed and decisions made, leading to action without effort. It had all been very simple. Later, after her first buffet from life, as she retired to lick her wounds she had come to the conclusion that it had been a false confidence, a childhood illusion. Now, because of her present state of mind, she was not so sure. Perhaps it had not been false; perhaps, she told herself, it was a quality that merely receded bit by bit as one ventured along the road of life, bruising knees and spraining ankles.

Shandu was speaking to her. She pulled her attention back to the present.

"Kokolo says that we must ask the bones," he said. "I have agreed."

"The bones?" she asked, puzzled by the term. She thought perhaps his English had failed him and he meant something else.

"You Christians believe in your Bible. The bones are our Bible. You will see."

Shandu explained further while Kokolo began his preparations. Kokolo had, he said, two sets of bones that he used for divination. "One is called the Father and the other is called the Son. The Father is the larger set and he leaves it at his village. The Son is smaller and he takes it with him on his journeys such as this."

"Where is his home?" She watched Kokolo throw a small blanket gracefully onto the ground before him.

"He is from the Thonga tribe, near the sea," Shandu said with a casual wave to the east.

"And these bones, what do they do?"

"They tell the story of the future."

Kokolo began to take an assortment of objects from a small bag he carried at his waist.

Shandu pointed. "There are bones and those that are not bones. The bones are from the ankles of many animals. From sheep and goats and oxen. From the antelope, the lion, the leopard, the baboon, the ant bear, and others. There are bones of the male and of the female from each kind of animal. Then there are also seashells and stones and other objects with meaning."

Kokolo placed a piece of some type of root in his mouth and began to chew it. Holding all his bones in his hands, he spat the juice on them, threw them on the mat, and said something that sounded to Katherine like "Mhamoo!"

"This is not the throwing, it is only to awaken the bones to make them see," Shandu explained. He was looking at Kokolo with admiration. "We can all read the bones, but the diviner who makes them speak is the power."

Kokolo gathered the bones together and held them in his hands again. Then he selected three or four and rubbed them against Katherine's good arm. He spoke a few words and handed the bones to Shandu.

"He has asked the question, now I must throw," Shandu said.

He threw the bones onto the mat and sat back on his haunches. Kokolo grunted and pointed with a small stick at the pattern that had formed.

Shandu explained there were four elements that one had to look for in the bones: the side upon which they fell; the direction they indicated; their position relative to each other; and the relationship between male and female bones. Each bone had a side that curved in and a side that curved out, the concave and the convex. "If it falls on the side curving out," he said, "it is full, it is standing on its legs and marching forward. If it falls on the side curving in, it is empty, or lies on its back."

She understood from this that the convex side represented the active and the concave the passive. "It is like throwing dice," she said. "It's just a matter of luck how they fall."

"No, no," Shandu said with a frown. "There is a power in the chest of the diviner. Great power. The bones interpret this power in their position, and then we in turn interpret the bones."

To Katherine it sounded like sheer superstition,

but then Shandu might say the same of the symbolic communion of wine and wafer, or faith in the efficacy of prayer. By the same token, her world had changed so drastically in a day that she no longer knew what to believe. The white men had turned out to be savages, the savages were gentlemen. She would not close her mind to anything. Besides, if the bones told them to take her with them on their mission of vengeance, she would be grateful to them.

Kokolo was now pointing with his stick at each bone in turn, commenting in a singsong tone.

Shandu continued his role as translator. "This antelope bone is your husband," he said. "And the position shows that he is angry and vengeful."

The next bone was from a lion, which represented the chief, or in this case a white person because white people are as rich as a chief. "See, the lion is in the foreground. It is leading the way to the three rams that represent the enemy. The rams on their backs show that the three evil men will be killed."

"That means I can come?" she asked.

"Yes," he admitted grudgingly. "It shows there is a need for you."

The leopard bone was Shandu himself. Its position showed that he would become rich and powerful and have many wives and cattle.

A young he-goat bone showed the son who had died. Another, the one who would live. "He is a long distance from his mother, but he is pointed in her direction," Shandu said.

Katherine grew interested in spite of herself. Each bone had its meaning, its own unique story, and yet each seemed to relate to the meanings of their lives. It was, she knew, only a matter of interpretation, but both men seemed without doubt or artifice, and both had implicit belief in what they were saying.

"What about the future?" she asked.

"The bones say you may come," Shandu said.

"They say that we will be victorious over our enemies."

"Yes, I know," she said. "But what then? What of my future?"

A blankness settled over Shandu's face. "We did not ask the bones that question," he said.

The decision facing Katherine was difficult, a classic situation of opposing forces. On one side, there was this driving, single-minded hunger for vengeance, a desire that gave her both impetus and purpose. On the other was Colin. He was all that remained of her life now. He was the seed of the future, and his continued survival gave some meaning and added value to the lives that had been lost. He was the thread that connected them all, living or dead, more precious to her now than he had ever been. And yet, without reservation, she knew that until she rid herself of the self-imposed obligation to avenge her husband and child, she would never be able to provide the support that Colin would need.

Shandu had pointed out that she would not be able to bring the child with her as they tracked the murderers. For once she did not protest, knowing it was true. The journey would be hard and long, its culmination dangerous.

"You have two paths," Shandu said. They stood on the shaded side of the wagon to escape the growing heat of the sun. "There is a town, less than a day from here. You can go there."

"Potchefstroom," Katherine said with a nod. "I saw it on the map."

"You can leave the child there in the care of your own people," he said. "Or you can wait here. The wagon behind will be here before night. They can take the child and care for it."

"Will you wait?" she asked.

Shandu shook his head. "I cannot wait longer. The trail of these men grows cold. I must go now."

"What of your agreement to take me with you?" she said.

"When I have found the resting place of the men, I shall come for you. Together we shall go and do what must be done."

"How do I know you will return?" she asked.

He pushed himself away from the wagon against which he had been leaning and drew himself up to his complete height, looking down at her.

"I am Shandu ka Zukozwayo ka Mancenga ka Tshwaku ka Belesi ka Newama ka Sishi ka Mahlobo ka Qwabe ka Malandela," he said, his voice throbbing with affronted pride. "My father Zukozwayo was of the Dukuza regiment and I am of the Ingulube regiment. If I say I shall come for you, I *shall* come for you."

Abashed, Katherine dropped her eyes. "I am sorry. Please forgive me. You must understand how important it is to me that I do not fail in my mission."

Shandu nodded graciously. "I think whatever you do with your child, we must meet in this town."

"Potchefstroom," she said.

"Yes."

"Good." She made up her mind quickly. "I shall wait for the other wagon and see who they are. If suitable, they can take Colin. Then I shall go to Potchefstroom and report the murder of my husband and son to the authorities, if there are any. They may also have some information about these three men there. While I await your arrival, I'll get what arms and supplies I can."

Kokolo was playing with Colin in a circular area of dirt about twenty yards away. It was a game something like jacks, using large round pebbles. Kokolo, to the delight of the child, would throw one stone in the air and scoop up as many of the remainder as possible before catching the one he had thrown, alternately uttering loud and lengthy exclamations of either disappointment or triumph. It amazed her how comfortable Colin was with the old man. He seldom took to other people and usually fussed when away from her.

"You have been very kind to me," she said, turning to Shandu.

He looked steadily back at her. His eyes, she noticed for the first time, were flecked with gold. "Your enemies are my enemies," he said.

"Still, I'm European. Not of your people, as you say. You owe me nothing."

"You are a woman of great spirit," he said. "I am proud that you have chosen me to help you."

Kokolu interrupted, shouting softly over the distance.

"Your horse has come back," Shandu said. "It is drinking at the spring. We must get it. You will need it when I return for you."

"How will you travel?" she asked as they walked to the grove of trees. It was something she had wondered about. "Those men are on horseback, riding hard."

Shandu smiled. "I shall run. Warriors are able to cover great distances on foot."

"And the old man? Will he run too?"

The tall man chuckled. "He shall run before me and call me a woman and a tortoise."

After leading the horse back to the wagon and tethering it, Shandu asked if she had a saddle.

"Yes," she said. "It must have been too heavy for them to take."

"And the wagon, what will you do with that?"

"I don't know. Either I'll leave it at the town or trade it for other supplies."

"If the people take the child, they may have use for it," he suggested.

"Yes, that's possible. Whether or not they will look after Colin for me, I shall have to travel behind them to the town. I have not had much experience driving oxen."

Katherine went into the wagon and filled a small bag with the Indian corn they called mealie meal. Then she added a supply of the hard, dried strips of venison the Boers called *biltong*, remembering suddenly that Alan had explained the derivations of the word to her one day. It was a combination of two Boer words, *bil*, meaning "buttock," and *tong*, for "tongue." When strips of *biltong* were hung up to dry, they looked like tongues. It struck her as a curious thing to remember and she smiled to herself.

She handed the small sack to Shandu. "I know you cannot carry much, but this little may sustain you somewhat," she said.

He gave a dignified half-bow and thanked her, then turned and spoke to Kokolo. The old man came over, carrying Colin on one hip. He handed the child to her and then peered intently at her, his eyes like bright buttons behind the folds of skin. He spoke, and there was an obvious depth of feeling in his words. Katherine looked questioningly at Shandu.

"He says he has spoken to your man," he explained. "He has heard the spirit voice. Your man is pleased with what you do with the boy and will watch over him. He is pleased at your courage and strength."

"You mean my husband?"

"Of course," Shandu said.

"Ask him how he speaks to my husband," Katherine said.

The old man shrugged at the question, apparently not thinking highly of it, but he answered.

"It is a voice he hears," Shandu said. "It is a sound like any other, but it is in the mind."

"Why can't I hear him? Ask him that, please."

Kokolo pointed his finger sternly at her while he spoke, then laughed, put his hands on his hips, and cocked his head to one side before poking his finger again. He spoke with relish and varied expression.

"He says that you *can* hear him," Shandu translated. "But you do not know how to listen. Your mind is filled with other sounds, like a cage of worthless noise. Your husband has tried to speak to you since he became a spirit, but you have been deaf to his voice. If you would listen for nothing else but the sound of his voice, you would hear." Shandu grinned maliciously. "But he says that you are only a woman and one cannot expect a woman to hear a spirit. It is only a man of superior intelligence and wisdom like Kokolo himself who knows how to listen."

Katherine allowed herself a half-smile. "Tell Kokolo he is so full of himself I am amazed he can hear anything besides the sound of his own voice," she said.

Shandu laughed and slapped his leg. Still chuckling, he came back with Kokolo's answer. "He says that an elephant does not hide its size, nor a lion its strength. The fire does not hide its flames, nor the thunder its loudness. Only people of false modesty seek to hide their superiority."

"Modesty is something he is not qualified to speak of. He has obviously had little experience of it," she said.

Kokolo's next words were accompanied by a woeful expression. "He says he is sorry if he has offended you by showing too much wisdom. In future he shall try to appear more stupid before you. He begs your forgiveness."

"Oh, no," she said. "Tell him I am sorry. Tell him—" She broke off hastily, suddenly noticing the amused gleam in Kokolo's eyes. Snared by a master! She burst into laughter. It was her first hearty, effortless laugh in days, and she allowed it full rein. The men joined in, Shandu buoyant and loud, Kokolo with a soft, self-satisfied giggle.

"We must go," Shandu said finally. "You will be safe here now. The other wagon will reach you before night, and you will travel with them."

"And then I will see you in Potchefstroom," Katherine reminded him.

"Yes, I shall come for you."

"I know it is difficult to judge, but how long do you think it will be before you catch up with these men?"

"How big is Africa?" Shandu asked.

"Yes, I understand," she said. "But I'm not going to wait forever. If you don't come in a reasonable length of time, I am going to seek the men out myself."

"It is better you show patience," Shandu said sternly. "When I find their place, I shall come for you."

Kokolo chucked Colin under the chin and saluted Katherine with an upraised palm. Shandu raised his hand in a casual gesture of farewell. Both men turned and walked away.

Katherine stood with Colin's hand in hers and watched their retreating backs. When they were about fifty yards away they broke into a brisk trot. She lifted her arm and waved, but neither man turned. Her hand dropped, and she stood watching long after they had disappeared from view. In spite of Colin's presence beside her, she felt terribly alone.

Chapter Four

KATHERINE LOOKED for a long time in the direction the men had gone. In truth, she did not know what else to do. The vitalizing energy that had accompanied her "rebirth" was deserting her and a lassitude was taking its place.

Instead of succumbing, however, she took Colin into the wagon and began to gather debris to be thrown out, forcing her body into action, ignoring its protests of pain and fatigue. While Colin watched patiently from the bed, she repacked everything worth saving into drawers and boxes. Each object she saw, each one she touched, carried within it the key to some memory. The first thought was to scurry past it with head averted, but she decided instead not to resist. The memories were now a part of her and they would always be there. She could not escape them any more than she could evade life itself.

She delved through a pile of clothes and broken stoneware and came upon her Wedgwood vase, a favorite piece. Miraculously it had escaped intact. She lifted it gently and ran her fingers over it. Alan had bought it for her a few days before they had left London, an extravagant gesture to be sure, but he saw how much she liked it. "It will always remind you of our last days in England," he had promised. And so it did. It was blue and white jasper, decorated with white relief figures. She placed it carefully on a shelf.

Poor Alan. He had never backed away from anything in his life and she had loved him for his tenacity and courage. Once in London she had seen him fearlessly charge three robbers who were attacking a defenseless clerk on his way home from work. While others stood and watched, Alan bowled over two of the men and fought the other with his fists until the man turned and ran. Marching forward, he called it. A man must always march forward, he said. Look where it had got him, buried beside his oldest son in the earth of a strange land. Katherine tasted the bitterness in her mouth, then shrugged at her thoughts. If he had been any other way he would not have been the man she loved.

Colin sat on the bed and looked at her curiously as she worked. For a while he was content and silent, and then he asked where his father was.

"He has gone away, dear," she said absently.

The answer was incomprehensible to him, and a minute later he asked the question again. She began another evasive answer, but his persistence reached her and she realized that it was not an idle question.

She laid down the clothes she had been folding and sat beside Colin on the bed. Placing him on her lap, she wondered what to tell him, going through a number of alternatives in her mind. He looked up at her, his blue eyes wide and expectant, and she knew it was the truth he wanted.

"Your father is dead, Colin," she said. "Bad men came and hurt both him and Timothy. Now they are both dead. Dead means that you will never see them again. It is like going away. You will not see your father again. Never again."

Colin began to sniffle, then to cry. "I want my daddy," he said. "I want my daddy."

Katherine grasped his shoulders and turned his body, forcing him to look into her eyes. "You will not see your daddy again," she said firmly. "He has gone. You must accept that, just as I have."

She wondered how she was going to tell him that she too was leaving, if only for a while. She reminded herself not to use the words "going away," to avoid any association with what she had just said about his father.

Either her words satisfied him, or he grew bored with the subject. He reached for the necklace around her throat, his tiny hand grabbing it and pulling, and said, "Mine."

It was an old game, but this time, instead of removing his hand, she took the locket from her neck and fastened it around his.

"Yours," she said, to his great delight. It had belonged to her mother and had been given to her when she left England. Now seemed the right time to pass it on to him. Once again, she opened the locket and showed him the two miniature paintings depicting Alan on one side and herself on the other, facing each other and seemingly gazing into each other's eyes. She closed the locket with a firm snap and turned away to hide her tears.

After cleaning up as best she could she fed them both and then put Colin on the bed to sleep. There was nothing to do now but wait. She walked aimlessly outside, checking the oxen, moving the horse to a greener patch of grass, unproductively fussing. She hated to wait at the best of times, and now more than ever. The killers would be miles away by now, Shandu and Kokolo padding in bare feet miles behind them. What if they lost the trail? What if the men disappeared forever? No, it was impossible, she told herself. No country, no continent even, would be large enough to hide those men from her forever. She would never give up, never rest until she found them. They owed her two lives, and she would collect, even if she had to spend the rest of her life alone in this wilderness.

She sat below a large tree and leaned her back

against the gnarled trunk. It was an ancient tree and had probably grown there for centuries. The sun had passed its zenith and the afternoon was at its hottest now. All that moved was an ungainly black crow in the branches above her, and the only sound was its occasional disconcerting caw. Under different circumstances it might have been pleasant sitting here this way, as in the somnolent aftermath of a picnic when the food and drink had been consumed and the children sent to play, leaving nothing to do but partake of idle chatter or slip into a languorous doze. She sighed heavily and closed her eyes, wondering if life would ever be that casual and carefree again. It was a portion of her past now, and it seemed a lifetime away. Boating on the Thames during their courtship, picnicking in the foothills of Cape Town's Table Mountain, dancing in moonlight at the Governor's Ball, the men resplendent in uniforms and suits, the women dazzling in their gowns and jewels. How inconsequential it all seemed to her now. It was like the games of childhood, a childhood long gone and only faintly remembered.

Her eyelids grew heavier and she allowed them to relax. Why struggle? she asked herself. There is nothing to do now but rest. Nothing to gain . . . Soon the other wagon would come and from that point she would know her course.

She must have fallen asleep then. In one moment she was idly observing the passage of her scattered thoughts, and in the next she was telling herself that she was dreaming.

A familiar voice was calling. "Katherine! Katherine!" It rose and fell in the arms of a whistling wind that had come from nowhere. She floated toward the source of the sound, as light and nebulous as a breath, and found herself standing in a small, sheltered grove.

She was not at all surprised to find Alan waiting

there for her. He sat leaning forward on a log, his arms on his knees, dressed exactly as he had been when she had last seen him.

"I am so glad you heard me," he said, the gentle voice unmistakably his.

She took a step forward, wanting to hold him, but he held up his hand. "No," he said sadly. "You cannot. We only have a few minutes to speak."

She stopped then and waited for his message. "My dear, you are embarking upon a course of vengeance. I want you to know that there is no need to do this on our account. Timothy and I are both beyond hurt now. You might even say that we are happy."

"I must do it," she said.

He nodded slowly, as if he had expected her answer. "Yes," he said. "It was my duty to say that, just as you feel your duty. The men you seek, they are going north to a mountain of caves. You will find them there, burrowing like moles in the earth." He broke off and lifted his head, as if listening. "I must go now," he said.

"Will I see you again?" she found herself asking.

He smiled at her, the warm, gentle smile she knew so well. "Aye," he said. "There is nothing more certain."

Inexplicably, as happens in dreams, a wagon had appeared beside him. It was drawn by four white horses with red bridles and its canvas was blue. He climbed lightly into the seat and took the reins into his hands.

"Farewell, my love," he said.

His voice and image grew fainter and fainter in her mind. She stood there in the clearing and listened to the sound of the wheels as he left. There was a steady rumble, the creak of the wagon frame, the crack of a whip, the rhythmic clatter of hooves.

Slowly she opened her eyes and saw that a wagon had pulled up twenty yards behind hers.

For a moment she teetered undecidedly between reality and fantasy, and then she realized that the dream was over. The wagon of the travelers that Shandu had told her about had arrived.

James McPherson was one of those men who appear larger than their actual physical dimensions. Although stocky and muscular, with strong, work-hardened hands, he was not a tall man, at the most an inch taller than Katherine's five feet seven inches. However, behind the rural red face and sky-blue eyes was a restless energy. He appeared in constant motion, even when sitting. Eyes, mouth, hands, or feet, something was always moving, reaching out, or drawing back.

His wife Anna was just the opposite: slight of build, sweet-faced, quiet and shy, a perfect counterpart to his robust heartiness. Whereas he was a native of Glasgow, she was a Cape Boer of French and Dutch descent. She was pious, he was free-thinking and irreverent to a point approaching agnosticism. They were as far apart as north and south, yet their devotion to each other was obvious and touching. Anna was not awed in the slightest by her husband's restless vitality, but she obviously adored him whole-heartedly, smiling at his jokes, clucking her tongue fondly at what she considered his foolishness. He, on the other hand, was as attentive of her as a mother hen, always including her in his conversations and catering to her every need, almost to the point of fussiness.

They both now hovered over Katherine and Colin, deluging her with contradictory advice. Anna offered tea. McPherson insisted that what she needed was a "good, stiff drink."

They had both been shocked and horrified at her story, consoling her fervently over the loss of her husband and son. They had also generously and emotionally offered to help her in any way they could, and their offer brought her to the focal point of her plan.

"You should turn back to Cape Town as soon as possible," McPherson said, for the second time. "This is no place for a woman to be without her husband."

Katherine shook her head slightly. "I must find someone to look after Colin for a time—while I attend to other matters. I need someone responsible, stable, someone I can trust him with. Maybe in Potchefstroom there will be someone. It is a lot to ask, I know, but at present I have no other choice."

She felt rather than saw Anna McPherson's eyes slide covertly over to Colin and guessed the thoughts in the woman's mind. The couple had been married three years, but for whatever reason, they were childless. The chance of having a child, even for only a short period of time, was not to be thoughtlessly discarded.

"What is it that you have to do?" McPherson asked bluntly.

"I must bring the men who killed my husband and son to justice," she said.

"That is a matter for the authorities." McPherson took a pipe from his shirt pocket and began to stuff it from an old leather tobacco pouch.

"I shall go to Potchefstroom and report it to the authorities, if there are any authorities there," Katherine said. "If they are willing to help bring these men to justice, I shall be grateful. If not, I shall do what has to be done."

McPherson lit the pipe with long, strong pulls. When he spoke, his head was wreathed in smoke. "Begging your pardon, but you are only a woman. What do you expect to be able to do?"

"Thank you for pointing that out, Mr. McPherson." She regretted her reaction immediately and apologized, explaining the roles of Shandu and Kokolo.

"When they return for me, we shall go together and hunt these men," she added. "I shall not be a woman alone."

McPherson shook his head doubtfully. "You seem to be placing a lot of trust in these two Kaffirs. How do you know they will come back? And how do you even know that they themselves will not harm you further? It sounds a risky venture to me." He bit down on his pipe as if to stop himself from saying more.

"I know it's risky, but the risk does not lie in Shandu and Kokolo," she said emphatically. "You forget that these men saved my life. I know they will return, and I know I can trust them."

"But they are only Kaffirs!" Anna McPherson interjected suddenly, her face flushed. "Godless savages! How can you place your faith in—" Her voice subsided as quickly as it had risen, and she looked down at her lap, as if ashamed at her outburst.

Katherine restrained a flash of anger. "No," she said quietly. "I have seen savages, and they were white. These blacks are men of honor, and compared to the European murderers, they are civilized people."

"Now, look," McPherson said. "Be sensible. Why do you not go to Potchefstroom, report the matter, and then go back to Cape Town with your son? Probably the best thing you could do then would be to return to England. Get away from the memories. It may not seem possible now, but in time you will forget this horrible experience."

"I do not want to forget," Katherine snapped. "The past can only hurt me if I do forget it. Now, today, at this minute, I have my honor to live with. If I follow your advice, forego my principles and allow these men to escape unpunished—*that* is something I will never be able to live with. I shall do what I must do."

Giving the impression of stillness for once, Mc-

Pherson looked at her silently, his eyes narrowed against the sun. He began to puff thoughtfully at his pipe, as if consulting it for wisdom. "Would you excuse us," he said finally. "I wish to discuss this with my wife."

"Of course," Katherine said, rising. She took Colin by his hand and walked back to her wagon, her mind already racing ahead. She had no doubt that McPherson would offer to take Colin. They were good and decent people and would do the good and decent thing. (They were going to farm at some place northeast of Potchefstroom; she had forgotten the name of the nearest *dorp*, or town, but it was a destination that did not conflict with her plans.) As long as they were not going a thousand miles out of her way, there would be little difficulty in meeting up with them after she had completed her mission. At any rate, they had planned to bypass Potchefstroom and turn east just a few miles on. They were close to their destination now and wanted to avoid unnecessary stops. She remembered with a pang that she and Alan had felt the same way when they crossed the Vaal. The thought of a stable location, perhaps even a home, after weeks of wagon travel was enticing. Perhaps, in exchange for the favor he would do, McPherson would take her wagon. It was not without value. They had a servant traveling with them, a tall, thin half-caste woman with yellowing skin and a permanently mournful expression on her face. She could drive Katherine's wagon behind theirs if need be. If McPherson did not want the wagon, perhaps he would be willing to trade a gun and powder for some of its contents. Wohlman had taken their arms and she needed to obtain a rifle, even a pistol. She would see.

Colin nuzzled at her breast. She had stopped breast-feeding him about four months earlier, but sometimes he forgot.

"Are you hungry?" she asked. She took a piece of dried fruit from its tin and handed it to him, smiling as she watched him tear it with his small, sharp teeth. Thank God she had decided to wean him before leaving Cape Town. The separation would be easier to bear for both of them.

"Mrs. Carson."

McPherson called from outside the wagon, and she went out to stand beside him.

"My wife and I have been thinking it over," he said, clearing his throat. "About your wee one, that is. We have decided that we would like to look after him for you, if you approve. We can't have him going to strangers none of us know, people who may not even speak his language."

"Thank you, Mr. McPherson," she said gravely. "I was hoping you would say that. I would not feel at all concerned for his safety, knowing he was with you."

McPherson cleared his throat again. "I want you to know, however, that we do not agree with what you are doing," he said, looking directly at her. "I do not want you to interpret our offer as encouragement for your plan. But you are a strong and determined woman, I see, and it is obvious that no matter what I say, you have your mind set. If it were not us to look after the boy it would be someone else, and we would rather it be us." He broke off and looked at his boots, kicking at a clod of earth. "Also, we are unable to have children and it would do Anna's heart a world of good to have a wee one running around her skirts."

"I understand your feelings," Katherine said. "I appreciate your telling me what you think, and I respect your opinion. But you are right. My mind is made up."

When they reached McPherson's wagon, his wife came up to Katherine and held her hands tightly in hers. "I want you to know that we will look after the boy as if he were ours," she said in her stilted English. "He will be safe and happy with us, I promise you." Her eyes glowed and she looked more alive than before. If McPherson had needed persuading, she had obviously been the one to do it.

"I know he will, and I appreciate it with all my heart," Katherine replied.

"You must tell me all his likes and dislikes, so I can know what to do for him," Anna said, releasing Katherine's hands. "All children are so different, even at this age."

"Well, you may begin by holding him now," Katherine said, holding Colin out to her.

Anna lifted him up before her and shook him gently, clicking her tongue. "Oh, *ja*, you will be happy with us. You will be happy with us," she crooned to him.

Colin smiled back at her, not displeased by the attention. Katherine felt an ache of loss as she watched Colin in the other woman's arms, as if a limb had been torn from her body, but she steeled herself against it. "There's something you must take into account," she said, speaking to both husband and wife.

"Yes," McPherson said. His wife lowered Colin and held him on her hip, eyes watchful now.

"There is a possibility I may not return," Katherine said. "Something may happen. I may not be able to come back and you must be aware of that, for it will change your responsibilities."

"I think we are more aware of that than you are," McPherson said pointedly. "Otherwise you probably would not be going." He filled a long pause with a puff on his pipe. "If such an unhappy event occurs . . . does the boy have relatives you would wish him sent to?"

"He has relatives, but none I would wish him sent to," Katherine said. "If I don't return I would wish that you raise Colin as your own. Would you both be willing to do that? I must know."

"It is something we have already discussed," McPherson said calmly. "We would not be taking the lad unless we were willing to face that possibility."

"Good. Then it is settled."

"I would still dissuade you if I could," McPherson said.

Katherine smiled sweetly. "We both know that you cannot."

"I will take your wagon and oxen only on the understanding that I am just keeping them until you return," McPherson said.

They were drinking coffee and making the last-minute arrangements.

"I shall not need it again, even upon my return," Katherine said. "We are not a large family anymore. Colin and I will never need more than a horse-drawn Cape cart. I want you to have the oxen too. You can use them for ploughing or barter, as you wish. I cannot ask you to do this without giving something in return."

"Well, they certainly will come in useful," he said uncertainly.

"It is done," she said, clapping her hands. "All I ask from you is a gun, if you have one to spare."

"I can give you an old flintlock that I have as a spare. It is not an ideal gun for a woman."

"It will do," she said. "I'll learn how to use it."

"Do you have everything else you need for your journey?" Anna asked.

"I shall take very little. A change of clothes and some food. The other food, the flour, sugar, and, of course, the seeds are yours to do with as you wish."

"Don't burn your bridges too completely, lass," McPherson cautioned. "We will hold your belongings in trust for you."

Back in her wagon, Katherine gathered some *biltong*, dried fruit, and biscuits. She stripped off her petticoats and put on a simple, gray cotton dress. There would be no need for laces and girdles and fancy scents on this journey. Another dress, a blouse, two blankets, and she had all she needed.

All that remained was Colin. She sat on the bed with him again and tried to explain. "I am going to leave you with Mr. and Mrs. McPherson for a time," she said. "They are nice people and they will look after you. I have to go and find the men who hurt your father and brother, and I cannot take you with me. Do you understand?"

Colin stared back at her without speaking. All she could do was assume he understood. It was no time for baby talk. She plunged on. "There is a possibility I will not come back, if something happens to me. In that case, the McPhersons will be your mother and father. Trust them in all they do, for they are good people."

His continued silence almost struck her as a rebuke.

"I must do this," she said. "I must do it for your father and for Timothy." She held him to her breast. "Perhaps one day you will understand my reasons and also how much I love you, even though I leave you now," she said, her voice muffled against his head. She wondered if she was doing the right thing. If it was right, why did it hurt so? But she consoled herself with the thought of the dullness that would live in her heart forever if she turned back now and went to Cape Town, imprisoned by unfulfillment. She blinked at the tears in her eyes and kissed Colin on the forehead. "You will understand," she whispered. "You are my son and you will understand."

McPherson had saddled the horse for her and she stood in an uneasy silence with Anna and Colin as he tied the blankets on.

"There," he said, slapping the animal's hind end. "You're all ready."

She kissed Colin for the last time and handed him to Anna. "Remember me," she said, and mounted.

Colin began to whimper, as if realizing for the first time that a separation was imminent.

"Here," McPherson said, handing her a small bag. "You are willing to give away too much. Your oxen alone are more valuable than this. I'm thinking you may be needing it."

The bag held a dozen gold coins. She slipped it into her pocket, for he was right: she would not be able to depend upon charity.

"For a Scotsman you are the soul of generosity, Mr. McPherson. I thank you."

"Go with God," Anna said.

Colin began to cry loudly now. It was time to move on.

"Good-bye," she said, and flicked the reins. She rode off without looking back, the cries of her son piercing the back of her skull like arrows.

Chapter Five

THE HORSE HALTED at the top of the rise, and Katherine looked down at Potchefstroom, the oldest settlement north of the Vaal River. There were almost a hundred houses, dominated by a reassuring church steeple. The town had been founded in 1838 by the original Trekboers, but she had heard there were more than five hundred people living there now, a veritable metropolis in comparison to the surrounding wilderness.

Katherine dismounted and then got back on the horse again, this time sitting sidesaddle in a bow to civilization's demand for modesty. Since leaving the camp she had ridden through the deserted countryside with her long dress pulled over her knees, her legs bare and sun-warmed to mid-thigh. It had given her an extraordinary sense of freedom. The ride, however, had not been entirely pleasant. It had taken almost four hours, and now every muscle in her legs and posterior ached. She made a mental note to ride at least once a day until Shandu returned. Her muscles needed hardening. Chances were that this would seem like a Sunday outing compared to the ride that lay ahead once the criminals were located.

The horse began to pick its way downhill, placing its feet carefully among the tumbled rocks. Katherine's thoughts returned again to Colin. Their parting had been harder on her than on him, she realized now. He would cry at odd moments during the next

few days when he thought of her, but that would pass
and he would soon settle into a routine with the Mc-
Phersons. But she would think of him constantly.
She was truly alone now, disconnected entirely from
her past, and it was a curious feeling. Her only real
mission in life was to find Wohlman.

She reached a wagon trail and picked up speed. On
the outskirts of the village two small boys playing in
a tree beside the road saw her and greeted her in
their own Dutch dialect.

"Do you speak English?" she asked the larger of
the two, a lad of about ten.

The boy's eyes widened with surprise and he almost lost his hold on the branch. He shook his head
silently at her and said a few quick words to his companion. They both slid down the tree and took off at a
run ahead of her. It had not occurred to her how
strange it would seem: a lone Englishwoman on
horseback appearing out of the veldt.

By the time she reached the town center, a small
crowd of seven or eight people had gathered to watch
her arrival. She dismounted forty yards away from
them and walked with the reins in her hand.

A portly, clean-shaven man stepped forward. He
wore a black waistcoat, and below it she could see
striped braces holding up his trousers. He greeted
her in English, a trifle pompous in his role of spokes-
man. "Welcome to Potchefstroom, *mevrouw*," he
said.

"Thank you," she replied, adding calmly, "I wish to
report a murder. To whom do I speak?"

The man's poise deserted him. "A murder?" he repeated, his voice rising to a squeak. A buzz of conversation broke out in the crowd as someone else
translated. "Who has been murdered?" he asked.

"Actually, it is two murders. My husband and my
son," she said. "Three men came to our camp the
night before last, killed them, and robbed us."

"Two murders?" he said, shifting in excitement from one foot to another. "White men? White men killed them?"

She nodded slowly. Her legs were hurting and her arm had begun to throb. More than anything, she wanted to sit. The ride had been harder on her than she had realized.

"You must report it to the commandant," the man said. He had recovered his composure now and looked at her more closely. "You are hurt. Your arm. Are you all right?"

"Yes," she said. "Where would I find him? This commandant."

"His farm is four miles out of town, but I think he is here today. Come. We will go to Tante Sara's store and see if he is there." He took her good arm. "My name is Piet Marais. I am the schoolteacher here."

"There is no school today?"

"It is Saturday."

"Oh," she said dully. She had long ago lost track of the days.

Many of the people followed them to the store, but waited outside while they went in.

"There he is," Marais said as soon as they entered the dimly lit room. He pointed to a tall, gaunt man standing at the end of the counter. "Mr. Pretorius."

The man turned and looked at her. His gray-bearded face was dominated by keen brown eyes. There was a sense of authority and competence about him, and she could see why he was the leader of the people in this area. He had been talking to the woman behind the counter, an enormous lady, wreathed in fat.

Marais bustled up to him and spoke in his own tongue. The commandant came immediately toward her and pulled over a chair. "Please sit down, *mevrouw*," he said in heavily accented English.

She sank down gratefully.

"Your name is . . . ?" he asked.

"I am Katherine Carson."

He nodded and leaned against the counter. "Tell me everything that has happened to you."

Katherine hesitated, her mind going back over the previous days. She looked down at her hands. So much had happened. She would have to stick to the essentials.

Pretorius spoke to Marais, who went back out to the street; the fat woman disappeared through a door in the back of the shop.

"I asked them to leave us," he explained. "This must be painful for you, and I am sure you would desire privacy."

"Yes. Thank you," she said. "I hardly know where to begin."

"Your husband . . . he is also English?" he prompted.

"Yes. Yes. We came from Cape Town where we have been living for six months. We wanted to settle near the Magaliesberg. Alan, my husband, wanted to farm . . . "

She told him of the arrival of the three men at their camp and the murders of her husband and Timothy, describing the men and giving their names.

"And you, *mevrouw*?" Pretorius asked. "Did the men harm you?"

"Yes," she said. "Two of them raped me. Later one of them shot me. But as you can see, I am somehow still alive."

"Indeed," he said drily. "But you are wounded?"

"It's nothing," she said. She touched her arm and felt the bandage through the sleeve. "I am alive. My husband and son are not. I was fortunate enough to receive help."

She explained about the two black men who had found her and the fact that they were now tracking the murderers. "They will return here to tell me

when they have found them." She spoke defiantly, as
if expecting him to contradict her. McPherson's
disbelief had left its mark.

Pretorius did not comment, however, but asked
more questions about the men. "No such men have
passed this way," he said finally. "I would have
known of it. They must have turned to the east."

"I think they're going north," she said.

"Why? Did they say anything else, something you
have not told me?"

She shook her head. What could she say? That her
husband had appeared in a dream or vision and told
her that they would be found in a mountain of caves
to the north. "No," she said. "It's just a feeling I
have."

Pretorius pursed his mouth. "I don't think so. As I
said, I would have heard. Still, I shall mount a commando and follow their trail from your camp. I know
of the place you describe."

It was foolish, Katherine thought. She had no
doubt that Pretorius was an exceptional man, a
tough man. He had not blanched while she told her
story, offered no expressions of sympathy, just listened with a quiet attentiveness. Still, she doubted
that he would be a match for the cunning of Wohlman.

"Why don't you wait until the two natives return
for me?" she said. "They are tracking these men and
will know exactly where they are. By now you will
probably just be wasting your time trying to pick up
their tracks. The trail will be cold."

"Perhaps," Pretorius said with a nod. "But we cannot wait on two Kaffirs who may or may not come
here, who may or may not even be following the men.
No. Too much time has passed already. I shall take
some men and follow them now."

Katherine suddenly felt too tired to argue. Not
that there was much point to it, anyway. Pretorius

was the type of man who would change his mind only on direct orders from God Himself. At least she was grateful for his zeal in wanting to track down the murderers, however futile his efforts might prove to be. But right now she could think only of sleep. Sleep in a bed was what she yearned for.

Pretorius must have read her mind. "You must rest now. Do not worry further about these men. We will take care of them." He called out and the fat woman came back into the room.

They spoke to each other in *Taal*, as the Boers called their language, and then he turned to Katherine. "Tante Sara will look after you," he said. "She has a spare room in her house, and you can be her guest there."

Katherine hesitated, wondering if she should go with the commando. She wanted to be there if Wohlman was caught. She had her own plans for him. She felt almost certain, however, that Pretorius would not find them. She could use this time to regain her strength and await the return of Shandu and Kokolo.

"When are you leaving?" she asked Pretorius.

"There is not much daylight left now, and the men need to stock up with supplies and arms. I think we will go early in the morning tomorrow."

Katherine nodded. It was too late, much too late. Wohlman could already be a hundred miles away; by tomorrow, even farther.

"Come," Tante Sara said in English. "You must lie down and rest and let me look after your arm."

"I shall see you upon your return, then," Katherine said to the man.

"Yes, *mevrouw*," Pretorius said with a slight incline of his head. "I hope we will have the men who abused you. They shall hang by the neck as an example to all who think our country lawless."

"Come," Tante Sara said again, taking Katherine's arm and leading her through the back door of the shop into the house beyond.

"Sit," she commanded, pointing to a large, over-stuffed couch. "You need some good strong coffee."

Katherine sat as ordered and listened to the rattle of cups in the kitchen. She looked around the large room. The sofa on which she sat faced an apparently well-used fireplace that had slightly blackened the whitewashed wall around it. Tante Sara's wagon must have been loaded to the hilt on her northward trip. The shelf above the fireplace and every other available shelf in the room was loaded with knick-knacks, mainly of china. There were plates, saucers, cups, human and animal figurines, many of them probably family heirlooms. The overall effect was chaotic, making the room look smaller than it was. Katherine looked out the window at the far side of the room and saw fruit trees through the snowy lace curtains, perhaps peaches and plums.

Katherine sighed under the weight of it all, searched for a descriptive word, and chose "normal." This was how people lived. This was probably how she would have lived if the past had not buckled into a different shape.

The Boer woman came back into the room and interrupted her thoughts. She carried a silver tray with coffee, milk, and sugar on it, which she placed on a small hardwood table in front of the sofa. Then she sat down heavily beside Katherine, wheezing and short of breath.

"I will take some coffee with you, and then I must go back to the shop," she said. She poured the coffee and stirred in milk and sugar. "There is hot water on the stove for you to wash with and a clean bed in the back room."

"You are very kind," Katherine said. *Tante, tante?* "Aunty," she realized. It was a sign of respect and affection toward elderly Boer women. She remembered hearing the word in Cape Town. *Oom* was the word for uncle, and it was used in the same manner for men.

"*Ach*, it is nothing," the woman disclaimed. "You have been through a terrible thing."

Her innumerable chins trembled when she spoke, but Katherine noticed that her pale blue eyes were sharp and attentive. She was assuredly a formidable woman in this town.

"Tell me," she continued. "To where were you going with your family?"

"We were going to the Magaliesberg."

Tante Sara shook her head and clucked her tongue sadly. "It is good land up there," she said. "I have often thought that we should have gone on instead of stopping here when we did. That was our plan. But my Janse was tired of traveling and wanted to dig into the soil and begin growing, *Ai jai!*" She shook her head again.

"You have a family?" Katherine asked.

"*Ach*, poor Janse is gone, God bless him. Killed five years ago by Kaffirs. He was a good man, that one. A good husband." She paused to shake her head again. Her jowls rolled from side to side. "Now there is just myself and the two boys. Men! I must remember that they are men now. Piet runs the farm just a few miles out of town; Jannie is married with his own farm in the Lydenburg district to the northwest. How the times change! When we came here they were nothing but little *skelms*, causing mischief and doing the things that boys do. Now they are men, respected in the community. Brave men, and good commandos, too. *Ach ja*, how the times do change. When I came here there were a handful of us and thousands upon thousands of blood-hungry Kaffirs. Lions roamed the veldt a mile away and the game was like a moving cloud. Now there are five hundred and more of us. The buck have scattered, and the Kaffirs too."

"I'm sorry you lost your husband," Katherine said.

"*Ach*, that is an old wound," Tante Sara said, dismissing it. "Your wound is fresh and bleeds still, hey? To lose a young child, I think it is even more dreadful than to lose your man. To lose them both . . ."

"What is done is done," Katherine said firmly. She was not seeking sympathy.

The old woman blew on her coffee and then sipped at it. She peered over the rim of her cup, her eyes as bright as buttons. "Did those men touch you? Did they harm you?" she asked.

"Yes," Katherine replied. She gave no details. In a community as small as this, the story would not need embellishment to spread. She leaned her head back on the sofa and closed her eyes for a second.

"*Ach*, shame!" Tante Sara said. "Here I sit, my tongue wagging like the tail of a dog, and you are almost asleep." She put her cup down on the tray. "Come, let us go to the kitchen and I will look at your arm."

Kokolo had told her to leave the herbs on the arm for three days. So far it had been effective, and there was no point in disturbing it now. "I think I should just like to wash and then, perhaps, sleep a little," she said. "The dressing on my arm can wait until tomorrow."

"Of course, of course," the woman said soothingly. "I will take you to your room."

Katherine followed her along a narrow passage. Tante Sara rolled her bulk from side to side, rather than directly forward. She was so wide, her hips brushed the walls as she moved.

The room was small but comfortable enough for one person. The walls were bare, but there was a bed, a commode, a chest of drawers, and a window facing out into the garden. To Katherine, the bed looked wonderful.

"I will bring you water," the woman said.

Katherine sat gingerly on the edge of the bed, feeling frail and ragged. If she lay down, she would probably be asleep by the time the woman returned. Slowly, she unlaced her boots.

Tante Sara staggered back carrying a large bucket of steaming water. She set it down beside the commode.

"You may not feel like it, but if you wash before you sleep you will feel better," she said. "There is soap and a cloth. I shall leave you now. Sleep as long as you wish. I shall not wake you for anything."

"Thank you," Katherine said. "You are very kind. I am a stranger, imposing in your home. It is very nice of you to take me in like this."

"*Nie, nie*," Tante Sara protested. "I am an old woman with no family now. I am glad to get company. Now you sleep." She backed out of the room smiling and closed the door.

Katherine examined herself as she undressed. There were soft, blue bruises on the insides of her thighs and at the tops of her arms near the shoulders. The makeshift bandage was still firmly in place over the wound, and no new blood had seeped through. She looked impersonally down at her body, as if it belonged to someone else. The legs were long and slender, the hips curved, the stomach flat; her breasts were large, but still firm and well shaped in spite of the greedy mouths of two children. It was, Alan had often told her, a beautiful body, in spite of being a trifle thin for the fashion of the day. Looking at it now, however, nothing struck her as attractive about it. It seemed as plain and functional as any other utensil, but one that had been beaten and mauled beyond all reason.

She dipped a washcloth into the hot water provided by Tante Sara and rubbed it over her face. The warmth rejuvenated her skin. Quickly she rinsed the rest of her body, lingering over the bruises and allowing the heat to seep into every pore. After drying herself, she slid into the bed and lay on her back. Her eyes closed with a will of their own.

A wagon rumbled by on the street outside. There was the shrill nervous neighing of horses and the shout of a man. The sun slanted through the thin lace curtains at an odd angle, splitting the wall with its light.

This is the world I live in, Katherine thought in one of those odd, luminous moments that appear from a place beyond sight or intellect. No matter what happens now, I know there is a pattern to it.

The thought dwindled into the obscure haze of sleep.

The position of the sun confused Katherine when she awoke. It illuminated the room with a brilliance that forced her to close her eyes again. She lay there and moved her limbs, one at a time. Everything worked. Her left arm felt stiff, but there was hardly any pain around the wound.

She opened her eyes more slowly this time, allowing the light to strike them gently, then sat up. The clothes she had been wearing were neatly folded on a chair beside the bed. They had been washed and ironed. The hot-water bucket had been taken from the room. A vase containing one large sunflower sat on the chest. Originally it had faced her, she could see, but now the flower had twisted toward the sunny window as if curious.

After dressing, she walked through the house to the shop. There was nobody there but Tante Sara, who sat in a large rocking chair, her hands busily knitting a gray garment, her lips repeating the numbers like a litany. The chair squeaked as she moved and the needles clinked against each other in rhythm.

"Oh, you have finally risen from the grave," she said when she saw Katherine. "You are looking better than when I first saw you, that is for sure."

"How long have I been sleeping?" Katherine asked. She had no idea of the time.

"Almost twenty hours!" Sara exclaimed. "*Magtig!* I thought you were dead. But then I saw you breathing."

She put her knitting down on the floor beside the chair and rose with a grunt of effort. "I will get you coffee. It is time I took some as well." She pointed to another chair behind the counter and told Katherine to sit.

The shop was typical of country stores. It had something of everything in it, although the quantities were pathetically small. Bolts of material, sewing and knitting supplies, animal feed in small barrels, lamps, candles, matches; all the essentials of survival and very few of the luxuries—except for some jars of brightly colored sweets that no doubt attracted children as honey did bees. On one wall were saddles, on another hung an assortment of tools. The larger, utilitarian items must be where she made her profit, Katherine thought.

"You are wondering where it all came from," Tante Sara guessed. She put down the tray and poured their coffee. "After Janse passed away I did not know what to do with myself. Jannie was about to marry, and the farm was safe in the hands of Piet. Farming is hard work for an old person like me. What was a woman to do? It was fortunate that Janse was a frugal man and we had some money put away.

"It was lonely on the farm, even though I had Piet there. He is a young man, with a young man's blood. I am an old woman and my blood has thickened in the veins. It flows slower now. I cannot keep up with the pace of the young and need the company of others of the same pace."

The woman paused and breathed deeply, her eyes clouded with a half-forgotten vision of youth, a time

when she was pretty and slim and bright, a spring-
time when laughter rose to her lips as readily as did
sighs now.

"Oh, that man could dance," she said half to herself. "He had feet as nimble as a goat, and he could
spin me as fast as a top. At *nachtmaal* the musicians
would gather with their fiddles and concertinas and
harps and play. The old people sat in their chairs and
watched us until we dropped from exhaustion. Janse
would sometimes sing. He had a deep voice that
made both men and women cry. I was so proud to
have him then, so young. Now it is my turn to sit in
the chair and watch the young ones dance."

"What is *nachtmaal*?" Katherine asked.

"It is when our people come together to take communion," she explained softly, still entranced by her
memories. "Every quarter, the people come from far
and wide. On Thursday, dozens of wagons begin to
gather in the town. Friday is a time of news and
trading, when friends who have not seen each other
for months can sit together and take coffee. There
are meetings and the singing of hymns, and on Sunday the Holy Communion. For many who live in the
bush, it is the only time they can get to a church. *Ach*,
it is a great gathering. It is—"

She broke off suddenly, as if realizing for the first
time that she had an audience. "I am sorry," she said.
"An old woman's fancy sometimes . . . "

"No, no," Katherine said anxiously. "It's quite all
right." This was a life she knew nothing about, and it
fascinated her.

"No. I was telling you about this store and how it
came about," Tante Sara said firmly. "After Janse
passed on I decided to move from the farm into the
town. There are old friends here, people of my own
kind. At any rate, a *smouse* came through. A wagon-
load of goods he carried, and donkeys so laden they
could hardly walk. But he was ill, this *smouse*, his

body hot and cold and shaking like leaves in the wind, and all he wanted to do was go back to Cape Town. So I bought everything he had at a good price and opened this shop. It is not a very busy shop. Still, it keeps me occupied, which is as God wills. Now that Janse is gone, I make the best of my life."

The woman's words were further proof to Katherine that life consisted of a series of gains and losses: hopes, aspirations, loved ones, possessions. Until finally one lost life itself. "It seems so unfair," she said aloud.

Tante Sara took the comment as perfectly natural, almost as if her thoughts paralleled Katherine's. "It is God's will," she said. "He works in mysterious ways."

God's will be damned! Katherine wanted to exclaim. But there was no reason to upset this devout woman's beliefs. It would only antagonize her. Instead, she kept silent.

"It is said that the English are people of little faith," the old woman said with a shrewd glance at her. "Is that true, *mevrouw*?"

"It is true of some and not true of others."

There was a short silence, and then Katherine asked, "Did Mr. Pretorius leave?"

"*Ja.* He and six others rode out before dawn this morning. They will be on the trail of those men by now."

"They will not catch them," Katherine said.

"Oh, he knows what he is doing, that one," the old woman said confidently. "He has tracked many men in these parts before. Criminals, Kaffirs, he has tracked them all. Very seldom do they escape."

"He will not catch these men," Katherine said.

Tante Sara looked at Katherine's face, and something she saw there made her stop the words on her lips. Katherine was staring out the window to the street beyond. It is not faith, Katherine told herself.

It is a *knowing*. Pretorius will not catch those men because they are mine.

"I think I shall go for a walk," she said.

"There is not much to see in our little town," Tante Sara said. "I suppose you could walk to the river."

Katherine went to the door and stood looking into the street. Soon the hunters would straggle back, she thought. They would say they had lost Wohlman's trail and look apologetic. She would thank them for trying and say that they did all that was expected of them. She would not tell them that they had failed because Wohlman was hers. But he was hers. As sure as rain fell from the sky, he was hers.

Chapter Six

KATHERINE LIFTED the heavy saddle onto the horse's back, almost losing her balance. Breathing hard from the exertion, she began to strap it on. Since Pretorius had left three days ago, she had been out twice, each time riding for two hours on the northward trail, familiarizing herself with both the terrain and the feel of the saddle beneath her. Her arm had healed well—all that covered it now was a thin layer of gauze—and generally her strength had been recovered. But riding was not yet comfortable. She hoped another three days would sufficiently harden her to handle the long ride she was certain lay ahead.

"There you are, boy," she said, finishing the job and patting the horse's neck. The animal had a mind of its own, but they seemed to be gaining a wary mutual respect for each other.

The sound of hooves drummed through the street in front of the store. Katherine ran through the house and saw Tante Sara in the doorway of the shop.

"Is it them?" she asked.

"*Ja.* It is Pretorius."

She stood beside Tante Sara and watched the men ride up. Pretorius looked as stoic as ever, but exhaustion lined his craggy face. It had obviously been a long, hard grind. Men slouched wearily in their saddles and sighed heavily and stretched when they dismounted. They were dust-covered and heavy-eyed, and those who had left clean-shaven now rubbed the rough stubble on their faces. She did not understand what they were saying to each other, but she could guess: they had done their duty and now they were glad to be home.

"You did not find them," Katherine stated unnecessarily.

"No," Pretorius said, and shook his head.

They went into the shop and Tante Sara brought him coffee. He gulped at it and smacked his lips.

"We followed their trail northeast for fifty miles," he told them. "It was easy. Three men on heavily laden horses. They did not bother to hide their tracks. Then the tracks disappeared. Just like that." He snapped his fingers, a disgusted twist to his mouth.

"Well, I thank you for trying," Katherine said. She had known it would happen like this. It confirmed her estimate of Wohlman's cunning.

"*Ja*, we tried, but it was not good enough," Pretorius said. He was angry at himself, she could tell. "It was hard, rocky land. A stream. They went down it, but we could not find where they came out. All of us searched for a full day. They were too clever for us."

"I told you they were not fools," Katherine said. "They knew that someone would follow them soon."

"They will be found," Pretorius said. "Every settlement for a hundred miles around knows what happened and who to look out for. In a week it will have spread five hundred miles. News travels fast. Soon somebody will see them and word will come back."

And if they are a thousand miles away . . . Katherine thought to herself.

"Sooner or later, they will be found," Pretorius said. He drained his coffee and stood. "I must return to my farm now. I am sorry, *mevrouw*, that we did not catch your men."

Katherine thought she might have sounded ungracious and hastily corrected herself. "I am grateful for your efforts," she said. "I realize your sacrifice to do this."

"Our sacrifice was not as great as yours, *mevrouw*, and for that I am truly sorry."

"All I want is justice," she said.

"I shall do my best to see that you get it," Pretorius said grimly. "We must have law. Men like this do not stop after one time. If they escape, others come after them. This is not a godless country anymore."

"*Ach*, there is a man," Tante Sara said after he left.

"Yes, he seems . . . well, capable," Katherine said, at a loss to describe the formidable Pretorius.

"Capable!" Sara said. "He is a leader of men, that one. A good, God-fearing man."

"Well, I'm going for my ride now," Katherine said. She walked toward the back of the room.

"This riding?" Tante Sara said from behind. "Why do you go running around the country like this? It is not womanly."

"It's good exercise for me. I need to build my strength up again," Katherine said. She had not spoken of her plans to the woman and did not intend to. In her overwhelming desire to do what was best for Katherine, Tante Sara would surely try to stop her. "I shall return in two or three hours."

Katherine took her usual northward route from the town. In spite of mottled blue clouds on the horizon, the sun shone brightly—a perfect day for riding. The buildings of the town soon gave way to scattered farmhouses and then even wider stretches of emptiness. It was hard to think of this land as settled once one left the town. The only clues were occasional fields of crops, an isolated herd of cattle, and wisps of smoke from distant farmhouse fires.

When Trekboers had first arrived to settle the

area, it had swarmed with game. Great herds of antelope roamed the plateau as they had for hundreds of years. There were dozens of varieties: gemsbok, eland, sable antelope, roan antelope, kudu, hartebeest, wildebeest, blesbok, the bushbuck families, springbok, and many others. There was big game too —elephant, hippopotamus, rhinoceros, zebra, giraffe, and crocodile. Amid this abundant food supply, the lions reigned as undisputed rulers. Also in the cat family were leopard, erroneously called "tigers" by the colonists, cheetah, red lynx, and the small wildcat. There were three varieties of hyena and more of jackal to clean up the lion's leftovers. And these were only the relatively large animals. Rabbits, wild pigs, and scores of other noncarnivores were plentiful. Of course, there were also snakes, as many as thirty varieties, and most of them venomous. There was nothing as multitudinous as the birds, however. Countless species filled the skies and waters with their color and their songs. It had been a veritable Eden then. Now, just a few years later, man had already begun to make his mark upon the land. There was still game, and plenty of it, but the wholesale slaughter had reduced the amount drastically from the infinite abundance that had once existed.

Katherine rode for almost an hour before she caught her first glimpse of animals, a small herd of antelope grazing on new green grass in a clump of trees. The animals had learned to keep their distance from human settlements. Soon, those that survived would leave the open lands altogether and take to the mountains and areas of denser bush, as yet uncleared by man. In time, she thought, the flora and fauna of South Africa would disappear altogether, for man was a resourceful hunter with an insatiable appetite for blood. It seemed impossible now and, indeed, many said it was, but one did not have to be a genius to know that if you drew often enough from the well it would dry up.

She reined her horse on the crest of a hill and examined the strange landscape. She was farther from town now than she had ever ridden before. Ahead was a long, tubular valley, and far away, at its end, she could see the blue haze of large mountains. She could spot only one farm, a small house about three miles from where she stood. Trees covered the slopes of both sides of the valley, and in the distance she saw the silver glint of a narrow river.

It was a peaceful scene and she felt an urge to visit the farmhouse in the valley; but gray clumps of cloud scudded across the sky, and she realized that a strong breeze had come up. Judging from the sun's position, it was now midafternoon, somewhere around three o'clock. Potchefstroom was a good two hours behind her. She pulled the horse around regretfully and gave it a sharp tap on the flanks with her heels.

The startled horse took off back down the hill at a gallop. Katherine dug her legs into its side and held tightly onto the reins. At first she was nervous, but after a minute, when she knew she would not fall, she found herself exhilarated by the sensation of speed. Her long golden hair flew back, and the rushing air pressed tears from her eyes. She gave the animal its head then. She felt the sleek muscles move beneath her and saw the pounding hooves miraculously avoid the scattered stones in their path. She willed it to go faster, leaning forward until her face touched the mane, hearing the animal's every breath. It was like flying on the back of Pegasus. It was freedom.

The horse continued its pace for about a mile past the bottom of the hill and then reluctantly slowed to a jog-trot, tossing its head and whinnying. Katherine's face was flushed. She was breathing as hard as the animal, more from excitement than exhaustion. She had never galloped so fast on a horse before, especially over terrain as rough as this. Only then did she become aware of the risk she had taken. One stumble, one loose rock at that speed, and she could have been killed. It was uncharacteristic of her, and yet she felt relieved, as if she had broken out of yet another constraining pattern. She laughed out loud and patted the horse's neck.

Suddenly, the sound of a man's voice broke into her thoughts. The man was singing, his voice strong and clear, a baritone that reminded her of some of the Irish singers she had heard. She listened disbelievingly.

> *Good-bye, Moysheen Durkin,*
> *Sure am sick and tired of workin';*
> *No longer I'll dig praties,*
> *No longer I'll be poor.*

A horse popped into view from behind a tumble of rocks just ahead of her on the trail. Its rider was a slim, wiry man with an untidy mop of sandy brown hair and a disarming grin.

"*Goeie dag, mevrouw,*" he said.

"*Goeie dag,*" she said.

He leaned forward and peered at her. It might have been rude, if not for the widening grin. "Well, I'll be," he said. "I'll bet you're English."

Katherine found herself smiling back at him. "How did you know?"

He scratched his head. "Well, apart from the atrocious accent, I can tell by your clothes. They're a mite too fashionable for a Boer girl. There's also something different about the way you sit a horse. And finally, you're prettier than any Boer girl I've seen in these parts. Why, you're a picture to warm the heart of any man."

Katherine realized her skirt was pulled up to her thighs. She flushed and pushed it down to cover her knees as best she could.

"If I judged by your blarney I would say you were Irish," she said, recovering her composure. "But I have heard the accent before and I will pick you for an American."

He laughed delightedly. "Not only beautiful but clever too! What luck! You're more right than you think. I'm an American of Irish descent."

"What on earth is an American doing here in the middle of Africa?" she asked curiously. "You are only the second I have met here."

"Prospecting," he said expansively. "I seek gold and precious gems. I seek the riches of Africa. The bounty. The spoils."

She noticed then that his horse was laden with equipment: shovel, pick, and metal pans. "And have you found it, sir?"

He put a morose expression on his face. "Not yet, my lady, but give me time. I must warn you that I am not a man to give up easily."

"I shall remember that," she said.

"Are you riding to Potchefstroom?" he asked. When she nodded, he said, "Then I shall ride with you and grace you with my charming company." He pulled his horse beside hers.

"My name is Katherine Carson," she said.

"And I'm James O'Brien at your service, ma'am. Jim O'Brien, to be a bit more brief." He leaned forward on his horse and flourished his hand. "Late of Boston, Massachusetts, and now a child of the wind."

"A child of the wind?"

"To be sure. I follow the wind. Like a child, I go where it would take me. I fly on its soft wings, like a bird, alighting where the grass is green and the water tumbles in the sun. Free as a bird. Happy as a lark."

Katherine could not help smiling at his pretensions. "I assume that what you mean by that lyrical outburst is that you are an irresponsible adventurer and opportunist," she said.

O'Brien struck his forehead with the palm of his hand. "Such hard words from the mouth of one so beautiful. Sacrilege! You've no sense of the poetic, no appreciation of skillful metaphor. You're a cold and heartless woman with a frigid English heart." He added dolefully, "Of course, you're also essentially correct in your appraisal."

Katherine laughed at his performance. In some ways he was a younger version of the Jewish trader Cohen they had met, a man with a quick, cheerful tongue and no attachments, one who lived to a large degree on his wits. If her appraisal was correct, he was a man with his own standards of honor and integrity, a romanticist at heart, but not a man considered one of society's stalwarts. The American looked to be about her age, in his mid-twenties, but somehow she felt older by a generation. Of course, her husband had been eight years her senior, and that contributed to the feeling. Having a family had also added maturity. The responsibility of children, the careful allocations of time, energy, and money they necessitated, had combined to add a seriousness to her outlook on life. It was an attitude obviously not shared by the young American. His boyish foolishness felt like a welcome breeze. Compared to the dour stiffness of the Boers she had met recently, it was delightful.

"Oh-oh. I see it's *Mrs.* Katherine Carson I'm speaking to," O'Brien said. He was looking at the wedding ring on her left hand.

"I'm a widow," Katherine said. She twisted the ring with her right hand. It was the one thing Wohlman had overlooked in the confusion of the shooting, apart from the chain and locket she had given Colin.

"I'm sorry," O'Brien said. "When did your husband pass away?"

"A few days ago," she replied.

O'Brien looked startled. It was not the answer he

had expected. She did not have the appearance of a widow in mourning. "May I ask what happened?" he asked in a more subdued tone.

She gave him an account of her experiences as they rode. He listened without interrupting, a fact she felt grateful for. His manner was courteous and interested, and every now and then he would nod his head to acknowledge that he had heard. He was easier to talk to than anyone else she had known, for some reason, and she found herself giving details omitted in her other accounts. The overall effect was strangely cathartic, and when she concluded she felt a deep sense of relief.

"And so I came to Potchefstroom. I'm staying in the home of Tante Sara, the shopkeeper. There I wait for the next chapter to unfold," she said.

The muscles of O'Brien's jaw worked furiously. "God, what scum!" he exclaimed finally, and then grew silent. They rode quietly for a minute, and then he asked, "Did anybody from town go after these men?"

"Oh, yes. Mr. Pretorius took a group of men and went out for three days, scouring the countryside. Today they came back—empty-handed, of course. I predicted that."

"He's a good man. If he couldn't find them, I doubt anyone can."

"Shandu will find them," she said. "I told Pretorius to wait for him, but he would not. He seems to have little faith in his darker brothers."

"Your Zulu?" he said thoughtfully. "You might be right. I must say the Zulu is the best of the lot. A savage fighter, but a man with a code of his own. Sometimes I think their behavior is more admirable than our own civilized customs. As for Pretorius, I wouldn't worry about him. The Kaffirs in this country are the Boers' one blind spot. They are determined, I think, to either annihilate them or condemn them to slavery. You'll see; in generations to come this attitude will return to haunt them." O'Brien shrugged carelessly. "In America there is a similar situation with the Indians of our plains and the black slaves of the South. It seems to be a problem our race is condemned to repeat wherever it is. Like America, this land is big enough for everybody to live in peace. It's pure folly."

Katherine looked at him curiously. "You're a man of many parts, Mr. O'Brien," she said.

"Of course." His tone changed back to a light-hearted lilt. "I'm part scoundrel, part poet, part philosopher, and always a lover."

Katherine did not comment. O'Brien apparently liked to keep the thoughtful part of his character hidden from the view of others.

"What are you planning to do now?" he asked. "Go back to England?"

"When Shandu comes back, I will go with him to apprehend the killers of my family."

His mouth dropped. "Apprehend the killers?" he asked incredulously. "I thought you were just going to report their whereabouts. Are you wanting to make sure they finish you off this time?"

Katherine's mouth tightened. "I'm not helpless. And this time I will not be the one who is unprepared."

"And what will you do after 'apprehending' them? Bring them back to justice?"

"No," she said. "I shall kill them."

O'Brien narrowed his eyes at her. "My God, I think you mean it!"

"Of course I mean it," she said impatiently. "I think I have the right to avenge the death of my husband and son, don't you?"

"I'm not arguing with that. Nobody could argue that point after what you've been through. I just question your ability to do it, that's all."

"Because I'm a woman?"

"I suppose so. Yes, because you are a woman. I see that you can sit on a horse without falling off, but can you shoot? Can you fight? Are you as strong as that German—what's his name—Wohlman? I'm not doubting your courage. I'm just talking of physical liabilities."

"I shall manage," she replied.

O'Brien shook his head in wonder. "God damn!" he said. "I've known you less than an hour, but already I say that if anybody can, it's probably you."

Katherine looked up at the glowering sky. The scudding clouds had formed a black mass. "We had better pick up our pace, Mr. O'Brien. It could rain soon now."

O'Brien peered up, much as he had originally peered at her, as if noticing the sky for the first time. "No doubt about it," he said. "We're going to get wet. Now let's see how well you can really ride."

He flicked his reins and his horse picked up the pace. Katherine gave her animal a kick in the flanks and shouted. "Yup!" she cried as she passed him. "Yup!"

O'Brien laughed in the background and let out a wild yell. "Yeeup! Yeeup!"

Both horses broke into a gallop. Katherine bent low, maintaining her lead. She could hear the pounding hooves of his horse just behind her and grinned with excitement. The sound grew closer and after a minute O'Brien's horse drew up beside hers. She looked sideways to see O'Brien with a broad smile that matched hers. Neck and neck they thundered across the veldt, creating their own storm of dust, the wild-eyed snorting horses straining forward.

"You can ride! You can ride!" O'Brien conceded in a shout. "But we'd better slow down or we'll wear these beasts out."

She pulled at the reins and relaxed, slowing the

horse to a fast trot. "Are you sure it was the animals you were worried about?" she asked mockingly.

O'Brien let go his reins, felt his backside, and groaned. "To be sure. I could have kept that pace up all day. It was only kindly consideration for the horses," he said. "Truly though, we have half an hour to go, at least, and we should keep their strength for the last mad rush if it rains."

They dropped down to a walk. Katherine's legs hurt, but not nearly as much as they would have just a few days before. She was pleased with her progress.

"You live in Potchefstroom now?" she asked.

"I just use it as a base. I stay with Marais, the schoolteacher. He's not a bad sort. Good enough to give me a bed whenever I need it, which is more than I can say for most around here."

"I've found the local people most hospitable," she said, slightly surprised.

"Ah, but you're a lady in distress. The Boers may not have the polished manners of an Englishman, but they are gentlemen toward women," he said. He frowned and added, "But the main thing is that you're not prospecting for gold. If our friend Pretorius had his way, he would throw me out of the country today. Luckily I have a few friends."

"Why on earth would he do that? Surely the Boers don't have anything against Americans?"

"Gold. The yellow metal. Treasure, m'lady. Do you have any idea what would happen if gold was discovered here in the Transvaal? There are now probably ten thousand Boers scattered throughout this territory. A month after the discovery of gold, there would be a hundred thousand people cluttering up this lovely veldt. Prospectors, gamblers, women of debatable repute, bankers, criminals like your friend Wohlman. I've seen it happen before. And the Boers know it. I don't blame them a bit."

Katherine remembered her husband talking in a

similar vein. "Then why are you prospecting here?" she asked.

"I do it because that's what I do," he said. "I've told Pretorius that if I find gold here, no one will ever know. I mean that. I'll not even sell it here. But, of course, he doesn't believe me, and I can't say I wouldn't feel the same way if I was in his shoes. It's asking a lot to place the fate of your country in the word of a stranger."

"So you are consequently not the favorite son of the locals?" she said ironically.

"Just not all of them," O'Brien corrected. "I do have some friends here. After all, I'm a charming fellow, am I not?"

"Indeed, Mr. O'Brien," Katherine conceded. "You have all the charm and no doubt much of the blarney of your Irish ancestors."

"Ah, what a suspicious mind you have." O'Brien shook his head sadly. "My life is an open book. It's written on my face for everyone to see."

Their repartee was interrupted by a large drop of rain. It immediately became a dozen and then a flurry.

"Are you ready to ride, Mrs. Carson?" he asked.

"Yes, Mr. O'Brien. I am ready to ride."

Within minutes the rain came down in torrents, a solid sheet of water as hard as pebbles, drenching them to the bone. Puddles quickly formed on the path ahead of them, and the horses splashed through, spraying water in all directions. Katherine lifted her face up to the sky and felt the sting of the rainfall. Lightning ripped the sky and thunder boomed around them.

In ten minutes it was over. The rain moved off into the distance, streaking the land with gray pillars of water. The town was just below them, about two miles away.

"Another ten minutes and we would have been safe," O'Brien complained.

"I don't care," Katherine said. She wiped her face with her sleeve. "It was welcome. After so much heat and dryness it was welcome."

Her hair had turned into a long, sodden mop, and she reached back with both hands to wring the water out. O'Brien was looking at her with a curious expression on his face. She looked down and saw that her blouse was soaked almost to transparency. It clung to her body like a second skin, outlining her breasts and stomach. Embarrassed, she pulled at the material, trying to make it hang instead of stick.

O'Brien reached to the back of his horse for his roll and unwound a blanket. "Here," he said, handing it to her. "Modesty is next to godliness among these people. You'd better wear this when we ride into town. Keep you warm, too."

Katherine took the blanket and wrapped it around her shoulders. She should have noticed the condition of her blouse. He shouldn't have looked at her like that. She didn't know whether she was angry or flattered. Still, a new realization had come: for the first time since Alan's death she could see that even in the area of relationships with men life would go on. The future did not have to be barren.

O'Brien smiled innocently at her. He was handsome enough, she admitted. And he had a dashing air about him that was attractive in its way; a tongue that could talk monkeys out of trees. Probably the veldt was dotted with broken hearts left in his wake. No doubt something could develop if she allowed it to. It wasn't for her, however. Alan was still in her heart, and she had business to settle on his account.

O'Brien began to sing again, unabashed by her presence.

> *Good-bye, Moysheen Durkin,*
> *Sure am sick and tired of workin';*
> *No longer I'll dig praties,*

No longer I'll be poor;
Sure as me name is Carney
I'll be off to Californee
Instead of diggin' praties
I'll be diggin' lumps of gold.

When I was young and sportin'
I was never tired resortin'
In alehouse or in playhouse
And many the house besides;
I told me brother Seamus
I'd be sure and be right famous,
And I never would return again
Till I roamed the world wide.

They exchanged quiet smiles and rode into Potchefstroom together without further conversation.

The next day O'Brien visited Katherine at Tante Sara's shop.

It was ten in the morning, and she was sitting in the store with Sara, sipping coffee as usual. The old woman drank countless cups of thick, black, heavily sugared liquid viscid enough to stand a teaspoon in. Katherine, who took milk in her coffee, usually nursed the same cup until long after it had grown cold.

"Good morning!"

She looked up to see O'Brien standing in the doorway. Clean-shaven and dapper, he was smiling cheerfully. "Mrs. Carson. Tante Sara," he said.

Tante Sara grunted an unenthusiastic greeting.

"Good morning, Mr. O'Brien," Katherine said. "I trust you have become dry."

"As good as new," he said blithely. He did not seem at all taken aback by Tante Sara's reception. "Tante Sara, my dearest one, you have grown more beautiful since I last saw you. How can this happen in just a few weeks? What's your secret? Tell me and I'll package it. We'll sell it to thousands of women around the world and make our fortunes. We'll both become rich."

Tante Sara smiled in spite of herself. "I work hard, think good thoughts, and praise the Lord," she said. Then she added critically. "Not like some, who worship only money and wander about the countryside hoping to find it under their feet instead of working for it like honest men."

O'Brien touched his heart. "Tante Sara, how can you speak to me like this? You know I worship the ground you walk on, and I would do anything for you. I'm despondent. If there were a bridge near here I would go and throw myself off."

"*Ach, voetsak* you *skelm*," she said, flicking her hand at him. But she smiled as she spoke, more flattered than anything. She broke into a smile and said, "If you did that you would probably charge the whole town admission to watch you."

Katherine laughed, and O'Brien turned his attention back to her. "She has the tongue of a serpent and the beauty of Sheba," he said. "May I take you for a walk, Mrs. Carson? The sun is beaming and the birds are singing."

"I would be delighted, Mr. O'Brien," she replied. The small shop tended to grow oppressive after a while. She took his arm and they walked out, the disapproving clink of Sara's knitting needles behind them.

"You are a silver-tongued devil, Mr. O'Brien," she said.

"What? For bringing a little light into an old woman's dreary life?"

They walked through the deserted streets of the town toward the Mooi River.

"Tell me something about yourself," she asked. "I still find it curious to see an American here searching for gold. I thought all the gold was in California, and like that song you were singing, that all the Irish went there too."

"Much of it is, but so is half the population of the world," he said. "Including a lot of Irish, I must admit. I was there for a time in '49. Did all right too, I suppose. At least I made enough to pay my way over here. Anyway, California was too crowded and wild for a sedate young man with tastes such as mine."

Katherine looked disbelievingly at O'Brien.

"The truth you'll be wanting? I wanted to discover new fields. Not for me the pickings of others," he said intensely. "I wanted to go where men had not yet looked for gold, to find it there and have my name in the history books. A more solitary adventure. Anyway, gold is only the half of it. Little more than excuse, really."

The river was high, a rushing dirty brown stirred up by the rains of the day before. They sat on a pile of stones and watched it sweep angrily past them. A log, part of some dead tree, rushed by, twirling in circles.

"What do you mean, an excuse?" Katherine asked.

"Well, when I was a youngster . . ."

"Where was that?" Katherine asked quickly.

"Boston. Boston, Massachusetts. The Irish section of the city. Anyway, all the kids I knew, all my friends, at least those with the slightest sense of adventure, wanted to go West to seek their fortunes. Out to the plains where the buffalo and Indians roam. All the land in the world and adventure enough for anyone.

"God knows why, but I was different. Probably it was the stories I read as a kid. I never really wanted to go West. Oh, I wanted adventure like any other young man, but for some reason my heart was set on Africa. More than anything else in the world, I have always wanted to come to Africa. Even when I was young, six or seven years old, I had a feeling, a premonition that Fate demanded it. It was very strange, I guess. Nobody understood it. My preoccupation with the African continent was very un-American. My father thought I was crazy. Still does, I guess."

"And is it what you wanted? Are you happy here? Or was it not happiness that you were seeking?" Katherine asked.

"What a strange question," O'Brien said. He looked at her for a long moment. "I don't know what I'm looking for, if the truth be known. Maybe it isn't happiness. I haven't yet found my end of the rainbow, but I love this country. There's nothing I like more than going out by myself in any direction. God, it's so splendid, so filled with life and variety, so beautiful. Don't you agree?"

"Sometimes I think I feel the way you do, at others I think I hate it, this cruel beauty."

"I understand," O'Brien said with a flash of insight. "It seems so cruel and impersonal at times. But then so does God, doesn't He?"

They fell into an easy silence, each following a passage of thought.

"Is there gold here?" Katherine asked finally.

O'Brien drove his fist into his thigh. "I believe the biggest goldfield in the world is here, waiting to be discovered. It will make California look like a mere nugget. The land is perfect for it. Besides, I've found enough to know that it's here. All I have to do is figure out where it's coming from." He waved his hand. "Somewhere out there. Somewhere in the north is a lode to end all lodes, the mother of the mother."

"And that has become your purpose, to find it?" Katherine asked.

O'Brien grinned, his intensity dropping like a discarded garment. "I don't know. Sometimes I think there is more pleasure in the looking than the finding. Do you know what I mean?"

"I suppose so."

"It's like courtship," he explained. "The thrill and intoxication of pursuit, the edge of anticipation, the titillation of the promise. It's all far more exciting than the culmination. It grows ordinary and predictable then."

Katherine laughed at the analogy, then stood and dusted her skirt. "I think I would like to walk back now."

"Are you still waiting for your Zulu?" O'Brien asked with a smile.

"I shall wait until he comes," she said.

When they got back to the store, O'Brien talked to Sara while Katherine went to get his blanket. She had hung it in the backyard to dry. She handed it to him and thanked him. He raised a quizzical eyebrow and looked as if he was about to speak, but thought better of it.

At the door Katherine asked him how long he would be staying in town before leaving again.

"A few days. Stock up with supplies again and visit a couple of people," he said. "I may stay a little longer this time, though. I must admit your company provides a very pleasant change from the usual."

"Thank you," she said. "I enjoy your company too."

"I shall call on you again," O'Brien said. He tossed the blanket over his shoulder in cavalier fashion and walked out into the street.

When she went back inside Sara asked where she had been with O'Brien.

"We walked down to the river," she said.

The old Boer woman did not look up from her knitting, but she gave a formidable sniff of disapproval. "It is not right," she said.

"What? What is not right?" Katherine was puzzled.

"You are a widow of only a few days. It is not right for you to walk unescorted with a man so soon. People will talk."

Katherine suppressed a sharp retort. "I appreciate your concern for me," she said instead.

"I know it is not my business," Tante Sara continued. She lowered her knitting and looked up. "People in these parts do not act that way. It is important that we show respect for our dead. There is a long period of mourning, and only then is it proper to see other men. You are English and cannot be expected to know these things. Still, this is not England."

"That is true," Katherine said. "I shall bear your advice in mind."

She realized then how she probably appeared to the townspeople. It hadn't even occurred to her before. Why, she wasn't even wearing black! Her husband's body was barely cold, and there she was, walking alone on the street with a handsome young man, smiling for all the world to see. Shameful! Even in England it would be shocking to most. Why wasn't she mourning? Because, she told herself, mourning would not bring back the dead. Nothing would. There seemed to be no purpose to it now. She had cried once and that was enough. God knew Alan would not want her to be weeping and wailing forever. How dare they judge her by their own prejudiced standards? No, she thought, it was not fair to be angry with them. Custom was the lubricant on society's wheels. She was the one out of step. She would have to live with that.

The only thing that angered her about her own behavior was that she was wasting time in this town. There was a job to be done and she should be out there doing it instead of frittering away her time here. Where was that Shandu? She would give him only five more days, and then she would take to the trail by herself. Pretorius had been led northeast, but she knew Wohlman had gone north, probably toward the west, not the east. It would be difficult, but she would ask questions until she found somebody who had seen the three men. It was a big country, but not big enough to hide a band of three white men for too long. The decision lightened her mood. The seductive rhythm of life in this town had dulled her. It was too easy to fall into a comfortable pattern and obscure the goal. In the meantime she would continue her riding practice. She would be ready when the time came.

"I'm going riding now," she told Tante Sara.

There was a loud sniff and the sound of knitting.

During the next few days Katherine discovered that she was becoming a capable horsewoman. There was a bond developing between her and the animal, something she had not experienced before. There was a growing familiarity that enabled both horse and woman to anticipate each other's actions, a degree of telepathy if one felt fanciful enough to call it that.

There was a bond growing between her and O'Brien as well. They walked often—down to the river, through the orchards on the outskirts of town, and on trails that led into the hills. O'Brien never spoke of this increasing affinity; he carefully observed the proprieties of recent widowhood, but she could tell he was aware of it. She saw it sometimes in his glances and heard it in the subjects he avoided. There were moments when he accidentally touched her and withdrew as sharply as an embarrassed schoolboy. When speaking to her, he would sometimes forget himself and allow his gaze to linger too long on her eyes. Suddenly he would become aware of what he was doing and look away with a stammering loss of composure. O'Brien was no stuttering schoolboy; he was an intelligent, sophisticated, and handsome young man who had doubtless had more than his share of conquests. There had been a subtle change in his earlier flirtatious attitude. She suspected that his reversion to patterns of adolescent

courtship might be due to the fact that he was falling
in love with her.

It was flattering and not unpleasant, but it was
certainly not what she wanted. She liked O'Brien
immensely and was grateful for his company and his
friendship, particularly at this time; but in her mind
it was nothing more than platonic. Thoughts of love,
a relationship of that kind with anyone, lay in a distant future, a time when she was absolved of obligation. She had been able to submerge her frequent
thought of Colin and the McPhersons only because
her resolve to avenge her husband and her son held a
higher priority. In comparison, her relationship to
O'Brien was surely one of no more than casual
friendship.

On Friday, Katherine and O'Brien walked down to
the river for lunch. Katherine had packed some
bread and soft cheese and they sat on a patch of lush
green grass.

While she attempted to spread cheese on the
bread, O'Brien explained why the Irish had a difficult time in America. "We're a minority and we're
Catholic," he said. "Many of our people were little
more than peasants at home, and were uneducated
and ignorant when they left Ireland. We came to
America to escape famine, grinding poverty, and the
heels of the English."

"Well, the Irish are not particularly loved in England, either," Katherine said playfully.

"Katie, you have a way of putting things," O'Brien
said. "Not that I care for that particular remark. Are
you sure you have no Irish blood?"

"I have a thimbleful of Celtic blood in my veins.
Perhaps that accounts for it."

"I knew it!" O'Brien exclaimed. "Of course it does.
It gives you your intelligence and your beauty."

"What about my admirable character and my
many other attributes?"

"None of that is English. It must have come—" O'Brien cut the sentence off. There was the sound of a horse on the road above the river. They heard a shout as the rider urged his mount on.

"He's riding hard," O'Brien said. "Something's up."

There were more shouts from the direction of town. Katherine began to wrap the bread back in its cloth.

"What are you doing?" O'Brien asked. "I was just beginning to enjoy myself."

"It might concern me. I want to go back."

"It's probably nothing," he said. "And even if it is, it doesn't have anything to do with us."

Katherine stood up. "I'm going," she said. The bell in the church began to ring, a signal for the townspeople to gather.

"Well, it must be serious," O'Brien said resignedly. "I suppose we might as well see what it is."

By the time they reached the main street a crowd of people had gathered. An excited murmur rose like a cloud around them. Marais, the schoolteacher, was standing at the perimeter and O'Brien asked him what was happening.

"A number of farms to the east have been attacked by Kaffirs," Marais said tersely. "People killed. Houses burned to the ground."

The buzz of conversation died down and Katherine recognized the voice of Pretorius rising above it.

"What is he saying?" she asked.

"The men will form a commando and go and fight the Kaffirs."

"Come on," O'Brien said, tugging her arm. "This isn't our business. Let's leave them to get on with it."

"Wait," she said. "If Shandu arrives when Pretorius has gone, what will happen?"

"If that event ever occurs, you will just have to wait for Pretorius to return."

"No. I must speak with him."

The crowd began to disperse to carry out Pretorius's orders and Katherine went up to him. "Mr. Pretorius," she said.

The Boer commandant tipped his hat and greeted her distractedly.

"What if the Zulu returns with news of the whereabouts of the men who killed my husband and child?" she asked.

Pretorius looked disturbed. "I am sorry, but we must ride," he said. "There are twelve people dead now. If we do not avenge this there could be many more."

"But what will happen if he arrives?" she insisted.

Pretorius shrugged. "He will have to wait until we all return then."

"There may be no time to wait!" she said angrily. "Those men may be on the move. Beyond reach. Any number of things."

"I am sorry," he repeated. "But he is not here now. There is no guarantee that he ever will be. You would do better than to depend upon the word of a Kaffir. They have just murdered twelve of our people, three women and six children among them. You think I will wait?"

Katherine did not know what to say to that. Pretorius's expression was more grim than she had ever seen it.

"Besides, *mevrouw*," he added. "I would think that you would understand revenge as well as anyone."

"Very well," she said. "When he comes I shall go after the murderers myself."

"Do not do anything foolish, *mevrouw*," he warned, his face stern. "There is a season for all things. Those men will be caught in time. It is just that now is not the right time for it. Have some patience."

"You do what you have to do. I shall do what I have

to do," Katherine said. She turned and walked back toward O'Brien, who had remained some yards back.

"O'Brien," Pretorius said over her shoulder. She heard his heavy footfalls behind her and saw the American look back. He did not speak.

Pretorius passed her and stopped in front of O'Brien. "Are you going to ride with us?" he asked. "We need all the able-bodied men we can find. It is a large Kaffir force this time."

"No, I'm not," O'Brien said, looking squarely at the Boer. "My feelings are still the same."

"Are you white or not?" Pretorius said harshly.

"I am not Boer," O'Brien said levelly.

"Sooner or later you must decide whose side you are on," Pretorius said. "The one who sits on a fence in a war is liable to be shot at from both directions."

O'Brien nodded and did not answer.

"You have no right in our country," Pretorius said, and walked away.

"What was that all about?" Katherine asked.

"A difference of opinion." O'Brien took her arm. "Come. I'll walk you back to the shop. I guess the picnic's over."

"Why wouldn't you go with him?" she asked.

"I can't let myself be a part of these endless wars between white and black," he said with an air of weariness. "There is a constant cycle of vengeance. The only end in sight is destruction of one or the other. I can't contribute to that. It's not a case of right or wrong. Both sides have too much right and too much wrong for it to be clear anymore. I just stay out of it. It is not worth fighting for."

"What would you find worth fighting for, I wonder?"

O'Brien looked down at the ground as they walked. "I think that perhaps you would be worth fighting for, Katie," he said.

Later that evening Katherine wondered about

what O'Brien had said. They were both willing to
fight for people, not for ideas. If that was considered
a selfish attitude she was just as guilty as he. To her,
a Kaffir war was nothing but a distraction. It did not
touch her in the same place as the deaths of members
of her own family. Well, she told herself, that was
how she was. She had her job to do and, if necessary,
she would do it alone. Two more days, that was all.
She would give Shandu two more days to arrive with
news from the north. If by that time he had not come
she would take matters into her own hands and go
north alone.

North! The word lay in her mind like a beacon. Up-
country. Everything that had happened to her had
pointed her in that direction. It was an awesome
thought. Her fate would culminate in the north.

Chapter Seven

TANTE SARA WAS SHAKING Katherine's shoulder.

"Wake up!" she said. "Wake up!"

"What is it?" Katherine asked. Weak light was just beginning to seep into the room. She groaned and struggled to keep her eyes open.

"Wake up!" Tante Sara repeated, her voice agitated. "There is a Kaffir here to see you. A big, ugly Kaffir."

Katherine sat up abruptly. The sleep cleared from her head like smoke in a wind. "Shandu? Shandu is here? Now?"

"I do not know his name, but he wishes to see you and says that it is important. He is outside at the shop door."

"Please! Invite him in," Katherine said as she got up. "I'll be there immediately."

Tante Sara snorted disparagingly. "God forbid! He stays where he is. Two women alone in the house and he with a big spear! All the men out on commando! You come and see if he is your Kaffir."

Katherine hastily pulled a dressing gown over the nightgown provided by Tante Sara and ran down the narrow passage, through the shop, and on to the front door.

He was sitting on his haunches, his back resting against the wall, his eyes half-closed.

"Shandu!" she shouted joyously. She had begun to fear that he would never come. There was a mixture of relief and joy in seeing him.

He rose to his feet and loomed over her. She had forgotten how tall he was. She wanted to throw her arms around him, but Sara was standing behind her and the woman's heart would probably have stopped dead. Instead she took his hand and pumped it vigorously up and down, a foolish grin on her face.

"I'm so happy to see you. Are you all right? Come in. Come in." She pulled at his hand.

Shandu smiled, apparently a little taken aback by the fervor of Katherine's greeting. He wore the same clothes she had last seen him in, although he now carried a red blanket she had not noticed before. His face and legs were covered with streaks of dust, but he showed no signs of exhaustion.

"You must be thirsty and hungry. Come into the kitchen," she said.

Tante Sara looked as if she were about to protest. It was one thing to take a Kaffir into her shop, but her kitchen was another matter. This was the Kaffir, though, who Katherine said had saved her life. She said nothing, but followed the two as they walked through the shop.

"It's all right, Tante Sara," Katherine said. "You can leave us alone if you wish."

Sara looked undecided, then said, "I shall be in the shop. Just call if you need me."

They went into the kitchen, and Shandu sat on a stool while Katherine poured coffee.

"Well," she said, handing him a cup of steaming liquid. "Did you find them?" Her voice thickened with the words, and the hand holding the cup trembled slightly. This was the question she had been waiting to ask, and suddenly she knew that whatever answer he gave, it would terrify her.

Shandu gulped his coffee appreciatively and let out a sigh of satisfaction. "Yes," he said finally. "I have found them."

"Where? Where are they?" she asked. Her voice sounded strained in her own ears.

"In the north. Three, maybe four days."

"Are they still all together?"

"Yes. The three men. They are still together."

"Well, tell me what happened," Katherine said impatiently.

The bell at the front of the shop rang. They heard Sara move from where she had been standing in the passage, listening to them.

"That woman does not like me," Shandu said.

"Don't worry about her. Her disapproval is unimportant," Katherine said. "Tell me what happened. Did you see Wohlman? Did he see you? You didn't do anything, did you? Tell me everything."

Shandu started to tell her his story. His face impassive for the most part, he spoke soberly and undemonstratively, without elaboration.

"Where is Kokolo?" Katherine interrupted.

"He is still there."

Shandu went on to say that he and Kokolo had picked up the trail easily enough, but they had lost it at the same point Pretorius gave up. Kokolo had found it again after a lengthy search, and they had continued to track the men.

"How did he find it?" Katherine asked.

Shandu allowed himself a quick grin. "He said he entered the body of an eagle and used the bird's eyes to see the track."

"Do you believe that?"

Shandu shook his head, smiling again. "He was lucky and saw the tracks before I did. They had covered them by the dragging of a bush behind them, but one of the horses strayed to the side and left marks for us to see. Kokolo must always show his powers, even if they do not exist."

They had followed the trail for almost three days, skirting the edge of arid land for most of the time. "The murderers did not want to be seen by any of the Boer farmers, so they traveled a long way to avoid them," Shandu explained. Finally, after entering a more verdant area, they had come to a small native village below a range of mountains.

"Kokolo went into the village alone. If they heard of a Zulu warrior they would wonder about it," he said. "I waited in the hills, and at night he came back to tell me what he had found there."

The men were indeed in the village, and they were firmly established there, Kokolo had told him. In fact, they had as good as taken over the village, plying the chief and elders with liquor and threatening the dissidents with their guns. "These villagers are not warriors," Shandu said, a touch of disdain in his voice. "They have been beaten many times by other peoples from the north. They are a clan of the Kgalagadi people, I think."

Each day the white men rode out of the village into the neighboring areas. One of the villagers told Kokolo that they were "searching," but he did not know what for. They would go into the hills and follow the rivers.

"Perhaps they're looking for gold," Katherine said. "Wohlman said they sometimes did that."

"Yes, that is what I think," Shandu said.

At night the village was quiet. Apart from the headman, whom they supplied with copious quantities of liquor, the rest of the village was allowed only to imbibe on one day a week.

The next morning, satisfied that he could learn little more by staying there, Shandu had left, traveling almost without stopping in order to reach Katherine quickly.

"What shall we do now?" she asked, suddenly at a loss. "The commandant here, Pretorius, is away for a long time. I don't know when he'll return. Most of the men went with him."

"There is fighting?" Shandu asked.

"Yes, but it doesn't concern us except that they are not here."

"True," Shandu said, quickly dropping the subject and yawning. "I must sleep. I have slept little these past three days."

Katherine put her hand up to her mouth, abashed. "Oh, of course. How thoughtless of me. I should have realized how tired you are. Please wait here and I'll make arrangements."

Tante Sara was alone in the shop dusting the counter. "Shandu is tired. He has hardly slept for three days," Katherine said. "Is there a bed he can use? He needs sleep more than anything right now."

Sara's reaction was violent. Her face grew livid and her chins trembled. "Sleep!" she cried loudly. "Is it not enough that I let this Kaffir into my kitchen? That he drinks from my cups? Now you ask me if he can sleep in a bed! Not so. Not so. He can sleep outside where he belongs. He cannot set foot in my house again. I will not have it."

"He's a fine man. A man who saved my life," Katherine ventured, setting off another bout of rage.

"He is not a man, he is just a Kaffir! As for saving your life, I would wonder why and worry at what he wants. These people are nothing but murderous, godless savages. He has no right to be with civilized people. Have you no shame! These are the people who killed my husband and you ask me to take him into my home as a guest. How can you ask such a thing? How can you?"

She was close to tears and it seemed pointless to discuss the subject further. To her, all Kaffirs were murderers.

"This is your home and I shall respect your beliefs," Katherine said. "But I shall not agree with you."

She turned to leave the room, but as she reached the door, Sara spoke. "There is the woodshed outside," she said resentfully. "It is dry and he can sleep in there."

Katherine was distressed to relate the conversation to Shandu, but when she reached the kitchen she found it unnecessary. He had heard.

"I said that woman did not like me." He grinned, attempting to ease her discomfort. "I shall sleep in the shed. It is good. You should not have asked what you did. It is not the custom here."

"Oh, I am so sorry, Shandu," she said, touching his arm. "I'm so ashamed."

"The shame is not yours," he said. "It is nothing to be concerned about. People see only what their own deeds allow them to see. They cannot help themselves."

"You don't want anything to eat now?" she asked.

"Now I must sleep," he said. "Afterward I will eat. And then we must go."

"Yes," she said. "We must."

She took a blanket from her bed, praying that Tante Sara would not notice, and led the way to the woodshed. It was made of slatted board and had a dirt floor, but at least there was a relatively clean space more than long enough for his body. He spread the red blanket on the floor and assured her that the other was enough of a cover, saying it would soon be warm.

"How long do you wish to sleep?" she asked.

"Six, seven hours. No longer," he said. "Kokolo was not able to say how long the men would stay in the village. I cannot waste time here. If we are to catch those men, we must go back soon."

"We shall have to forego the help of Mr. Pretorius, or anyone else for that matter," she said. "I shall gather provisions and prepare myself for the journey while you sleep."

"That is good," he said.

She looked into his gold-flecked eyes and felt a rush of affection. "I'm so glad you came back, Shandu."

"You doubted?" he asked.

"A little. Only a little."

After dressing and then eating breakfast in the frigid atmosphere provided by Tante Sara, Katherine took the small sack of gold coins that McPherson had given her and went to another store to purchase supplies. The fact was that Sara's shop was hopelessly inadequate. There was a larger store in town that stocked the merchandise Katherine would need.

As she crossed the street, mentally running over the essentials she required, Jim O'Brien stepped out of a doorway.

"Katie! Where are you off to in such a hurry on a beautiful morning such as this? A day like this is meant for leisure, preferably in my company."

"I'm leaving here today, Jim," she said.

For once the voluble O'Brien was at a loss for words. In spite of her obsession, as he thought of it, he had never anticipated this moment.

"Your Zulu has come," he said finally. He looked as though he had been slapped in the face, but Katherine was too excited to notice.

"Yes, he has," she said enthusiastically. She took his arm. "Jim, he's found them. He knows where they are. It's exactly as we planned."

"And where is it that they are?" he asked, regaining his composure.

"They're in a native village, three or four days to the north."

"The name of the village?"

Katherine looked puzzled. O'Brien's attitude was strange, almost antagonistic. "I don't know the name. Shandu never mentioned it. I don't think he knows, either. Or perhaps it doesn't have a name." She shrugged it off, the frown leaving her forehead. "It doesn't matter anyway. It's north and Shandu knows where it is. That's what matters."

"Aren't you going to wait for Pretorius? You can't mean to go by yourself against these killers. Christ, woman, you don't even know where you're going!"

"I have no time. Can't you see that, Jim?" She looked at him as if he were a fool. "There's no guarantee that Wohlman will stay there. I must leave immediately."

"And what will you do when you get there?" he asked. "Ride into the village and ask them to surrender in the name of the law? Or perhaps you plan to sneak into the village at night and bind them while they sleep. Grow up, Katie. This is no storybook adventure. This is real, and these are hard, callous men you're dealing with—murderers. Last time you escaped with your life. Don't you prize it? What's wrong with you?"

He saw Katherine's mouth tighten. "Look, Katie," he said more quietly. "Let's at least talk more about this. You can't just go rushing off into the wilds without thinking it through."

"O'Brien, I've been thinking of nothing else," she said.

"All right, all right. What are you going to do when you get there? What's your plan? What's your Zulu's plan? Tell me that."

"We don't have one," she said bluntly. "If Shandu does, he has not told me. But we will think of something. When we get there we will observe what's happening and make a judgment based upon what we see. It would be foolish to do otherwise. Any plan made now may well prove to be worthless in reality."

O'Brien threw up his hands in exasperation. My God! You couldn't argue with this woman. She had a mind of her own and an answer for everything.

"Here's another alternative," he suggested. "Suppose you wait for Pretorius. He should be back in a day or two, no later than that. Three at the most. Even if Wohlman has left the village where they were last seen, they will be easy enough to track. They won't be expecting pursuit at this stage and won't be covering their tracks as they did before. You won't be rushing into something. You'll have numbers on your side and what passes for law in these parts. It is a much more intelligent alternative."

Katherine looked at him and shook her head. "No, it's not," she said emphatically. "It is actually one of the least intelligent alternatives. I have no idea when Pretorius will be back, or even if he will be back. I have told you Wohlman is three or four days away, correct? Now, by my judgment, that could be about two hundred miles. Do you really think Pretorius will drop everything and ride two hundred miles to apprehend them? I think he may just be happy to hear that they're out of his area, and that will be that."

For a moment O'Brien bristled, then he burst into laughter. "Katie, you're one hell of a woman," he said.

Relieved to see one less impediment in her path, Katherine countered with a brief smile. Without being aware of it, they had been walking up the street toward the edge of town. Now they stopped and she tugged on the sleeve of his jacket for emphasis. "You must understand something, Jim," she said seriously. "What those men did to me, my child, my husband—it is not forgivable. Nor is it forgettable. It is not as though I can bring back the dead, but I have a debt to their memory. It is not just for them, though. I have a debt to myself and to Colin. I am dedicated to it and nothing on this earth can stop me. Can you understand that? It is as if my life will remain at a halt until I have done this thing. When it is done, my life can begin again."

"I don't know if I ever will understand you, Katie, but I admire the hell out of you," O'Brien said fondly. "And I'll tell you one more thing. I'm going to come with you. Somebody has to protect you from yourself."

"You?" was all Katherine could say.

"Yes, me. Don't look so surprised. I'm no babe in the woods, and obviously you need a man of experience to go along with you. Who else but me?"

Surprise hardly began to describe her feelings. She had never expected the American to commit himself to anything beyond words.

"What about your independence, your unwillingness to get involved?"

O'Brien looked puzzled, then he beamed. "Oh, you mean my conversation with Pretorius. That's different. For philosophical reasons, it goes against my grain to attack Kaffirs. They kill to defend their homeland. These men killed out of greed."

"Why are you willing to do this?" she asked. "There's no need for you to get involved in something that doesn't concern you."

O'Brien looked at her with a broad smile. "You don't know, Katie?" he said. "You must know how I feel about you, even though I haven't spoken of it. My feelings for you make it something that does concern me."

Katherine was flustered. Yes, she knew, but she had not expected this declaration now, however indirectly phrased.

"Jim," she began carefully. "I value you immensely as a friend, probably above anyone else right now. Also, I admire and like you. But—"

O'Brien put a finger on her lips, cutting off her words. "There's no need for you to say it, Katie," he said softly. "I know how you feel, and I wouldn't expect you to feel otherwise with the death of the man you loved so recent. But you said a few minutes ago that your life has stopped; that you would not begin to live again until this was over for you. I want to help you do that, Katie. I'm looking to the future."

"As long as you understand . . ."

"I understand. Truly, I understand," he said. "I expect nothing from you, nothing at all. I want only the opportunity to be of service to you."

Katherine's throat thickened and tears pricked at her eyes. She felt deep emotion unrelated to her main purpose for the first time since Alan's death.

A Boer farmer and his wife rode by in a small horse-drawn cart. They looked curiously at the foreign couple as they passed.

"I thank you with all my heart," Katherine managed to say.

"Good," O'Brien said cheerfully, rubbing his hands together. "Now that's settled, we need to make some plans. What supplies were you about to buy? No. First tell me more about where these men are. That will help me judge the situation better."

They stopped walking then and leaned against a tumbled fence of rock while Katherine told him what she had learned from Shandu. She reached the point about Wohlman's "search" and asked what he thought they could be doing. "Is there gold in that area, anything valuable?"

"I haven't been up that way, but there could be gold anywhere in this country," he said. "As for other precious stones, I don't know. Occasionally the odd traveler or Kaffir has turned up with a stone or two—agate, an amethyst. I think some hunter came back a year or two ago with garnets from a tribe up north. But this is gold country. Wohlman is probably prospecting for gold."

"Well, I suppose we'll find out in time," Katherine said, dismissing the subject.

"True," he said. "So what were you going to buy?"

She ran down her list, which included powder, food, blankets, and the curious addition of a pair of men's pants.

"What for?" he asked.

"To ride in. There's nobody in the bush to shock."

"Yes, but there is here," he said. "You'd better let me buy those for you. God knows what they'd think if you went in and asked for men's pants. You're a suspicious enough character here already. What I really wish I could add to your list, however, is some extra men."

"There are none," she said. "Everyone that was able to leave went with Pretorius."

"Not quite," he said vaguely. He pushed himself off the wall. "You go and do your shopping. Leave the trousers to me. I think I can judge your size. Meanwhile, I'm going to see a man about a hunt."

He turned and walked in the opposite direction from town.

"You're not coming back to town now?" she asked.

"No, I have to see someone who lives out this way. You go and do your shopping. I'll meet you back at Tante Sara's. What time does your Zulu wake up?"

"About five hours. And I wish you would stop calling him 'my' Zulu," she said sharply. "He's not mine, and his name is Shandu."

"So be it," O'Brien said, unabashed. "You be ready to go. I'll be there before then."

With that he turned again. Katherine looked after him, not sure how much she liked this new, purposeful, and domineering O'Brien.

Waiting for Shandu to wake up was the worst part for Katherine. After packing the supplies, there was little for her to do except chat with Sara, who acted as if the morning's argument had never happened. She even pressed some supplies on Katherine, refusing to accept any payment. If the woman insisted on being a fool, the least she would do was help. "These are *boerewors*," she said, handing her a packet of the local sausages. "They are made from springbok and pork and seasoned with vinegar. It is the best sausage in town. The secret is that you do not mince it, but pound it with a stamper. That keeps the flavor. Grill it on a stick over your fire and you will have a delicious meal."

Sara also gave Katherine a dozen long strips of the dried meat, *biltong*, something Katherine had forgotten to buy. She would have given her more, but Katherine stopped her.

"You've been very kind to me," Katherine said. "I have much to thank you for."

"It is nothing," Tante Sara said. "I remember when my Janse died. If it had not been for the people here, the true friends who helped me, I might have soon gone on to join him. Where are we if people cannot help each other, I ask you?"

"Well, I thank you, anyway," Katherine said. "Perhaps one day I'll be able to repay you."

O'Brien bustled through the front door of the shop then. He opened his eyes wider against the darkness and peered around.

"He's not here yet," he stated finally.

"Who?" Katherine asked.

"Koos du Toit. He was supposed to meet us here."

Tante Sara gave one of her most disapproving sniffs and clicked her tongue. "You are taking that *skelm* with you?" she said. "He is no good, that one. He will give you nothing but trouble."

"He may not measure up to your high standards, Tante, but he can ride and shoot as well as any Boer in Africa," O'Brien said.

"He is a wastrel and a drunkard who has not done an honest day of work in his life," she said flatly.

Katherine began to frown, and O'Brien hastily reassured her. "Don't worry, Katie. He'll be an asset to us. He knows this country like the back of his hand, and you couldn't want a better man in a fight."

"Who is he?" she asked.

"He has a small farm just out of town. Sometimes

he hunts. He's also come prospecting with me a couple of times."

"He sounds a rather shiftless character," she said.

"He is. He is. I'll be the first to admit it. He's somewhat of a rebel by Boer standards. But he'll be useful to us, I promise you."

"Why didn't he ride with Pretorius?" she asked.

"Well, he never rides unless there's something in it for him," O'Brien said. "At least, he—"

"Then why is he riding with us?" Katherine asked.

O'Brien looked sheepish. "Let's go outside and see if he's coming," he said.

Katherine stepped outside with him, a questioning look on her face. Apparently he did not want the Boer woman to hear his answer.

"So, tell me," she said. "What's in it for him to come with us?"

"Well, Katie," he said, lowering his voice, although there was nobody else there to hear. "Actually, I paid him to come with us."

"Oh, Jim," she said. "You shouldn't have done that."

"It's all right," he protested. "I can afford to do it. Anyway, it wasn't very much." He looked embarrassed again. "I—I kind of led him to believe that there would be some booty involved when we caught Wohlman."

"Oh, Jim," she said again in dismay.

"Well, there may be," he said defensively. "Those men have probably been plundering innocent people like you all the way up from Cape Town. Koos can have whatever we find, except of course anything that belongs to you. Listen, Katie, he's a tough, hard man and that's what we need, more than anything else. We don't need men with good character references at a time like this. For God's sake, there are three of them. Who knows, they may even have the villagers fighting for them. We need all the help we can get. You can't argue with that."

"No, I don't suppose I can," she said resignedly. "I don't like it, but I can't argue with it."

O'Brien considered the matter closed. He walked over to his horse, which was tethered at a post a few feet away, and picked up a small package that was sitting on the saddle. "Here are your clothes," he said, handing the package to her.

He took another package from his saddlebag, this one wrapped in cloth. "That old blunderbuss you carry around with you won't do much good in a fight," he said. "I brought you this instead. It's an American invention."

She took the cloth and opened it. "Why, it's a Colt revolver," she exclaimed. She had been shown one in Cape Town.

O'Brien looked surprised at her recognition of the weapon. He took it back and showed her how it worked.

"It has a revolving cylinder that aligns the loaded rounds with the barrel each time the hammer is cocked. It's not like the musket. It's loaded from the front of the cylinder instead of the muzzle. Each chamber is separately loaded with a charge of powder and a bullet, and then each chamber is capped at the rear with a percussion cap. Now watch carefully. To keep it safe while loaded, you lower the hammer between two caps, like this. It's loaded right now, so be careful. Six shots instead of the normal one. And the barrel is rifled, so it's accurate for a good distance."

"Is it easy to fire?" she asked nervously.

"Not bad when you know how," he said. "Once we're on our way, I'll give you a few lessons. You should be able to pick it up in no time at all."

Katherine was relieved. Although she had diligently practiced riding every day, she had been derelict in her shooting practice. Both times she had fired the musket McPherson had given to her, it had almost knocked her from her feet, bruising her shoulder. The pistol seemed a far easier alternative.

"How shall I carry this?" she asked, taking the pistol back from him.

"Either like it is, in your saddlebag, or you can stick it in your belt."

"I don't have a belt," she said.

"When you open the package I gave you, you'll find that you do," he said. "If you're going to wear trousers you had better have a belt or it could be embarrassing."

Katherine laughed. She looked up at the sun. "It must be after midday now. I'd better go and awaken Shandu. He'll probably want to eat something before we go."

Only then did she notice the other horse tethered beside O'Brien's. She had seen it, of course, but it had not registered.

"That's for your Zulu," he said, noticing her stare. "We can't have him running all the way while we ride in comfort."

"Do Americans always throw money around this way?" she asked.

"Only for someone special," he said.

She was saved a response by the arrival of a man on a gray pony. He reined up a few feet away and looked down at them. "O'Brien," he said with a quick nod.

"Koos! Glad to see you," O'Brien said. He gestured toward Katherine. "Koos, I want you to meet Mrs. Carson. Katherine, this is Koos du Toit."

"How do you do," she said.

The man touched his broad-brimmed hat and said, "Good day, *mevrouw*. I am pleased to meet you."

He dismounted then, a man of medium height, but broad and solid, with a neck half the length and twice the thickness of O'Brien's, a physically powerful man. His face and arms had been browned and roughened by years of sun, but his most striking feature was his nose, which was twisted and bent to one side. It had probably been broken half a dozen times, Katherine thought. Judging from his scars and the sullen set of his mouth, she decided that he was a quick-tempered, surly man, his general attitude dominated by some bitterness.

"I'm grateful for your help and I'm glad you are joining us," she said, although she was not certain she was.

He nodded to her and said to O'Brien, "Are we ready to go?"

She realized that he was uncomfortable with women and probably had little to do with them. Almost certainly he was a bachelor.

O'Brien looked questioningly at her.

"If you'll saddle my horse, I'll prepare," she said. She went back into the shop and left the two men outside.

The man worried her. O'Brien's judgment was an unknown quantity. For now she would just have to take on faith his claim that the man would be of help. For that matter, the benefit of O'Brien's presence was questionable. She had no real knowledge of how he would react under pressure.

She went through the house and out the back to the woodshed. Shandu was curled up on his side with his hands between his knees, his breathing calm and untroubled, as peaceful as a baby. She touched his shoulder and drew her hand back quickly, shocked by the warmth and softness of his dark skin. She did not know what she had expected, but it was not that velvety softness.

Shandu opened his eyes and adjusted them quickly. "It is time?" he asked.

"Have you rested enough?" she asked.

He sat up and stretched, the large muscles in his back moving fluidly below the satin skin. "Yes. It is

good," he said. "A little food in my belly and I shall
be ready to go."

"Come to the kitchen and I'll get something for
you." She turned and walked back on the path, leaving him to gather his belongings.

A large pot of beans simmered on the stove. She
ladled some into a bowl for him and placed it on the
counter. She found some bread and spread a thick
layer of butter on it. Shandu came in, put his shield
and other items in the corner, and handed her the
blanket she had given him.

"Sit and eat. I'll dress and then we will leave. Oh,
by the way," she added over her shoulder. "Two men
are coming with us to help. O'Brien and du Toit are
their names. I think that we need all the help we can
get."

"If they can fight, that is good," Shandu said.

"We shall see," she said.

She went into her bedroom and opened the package O'Brien had given her. It contained men's pants,
a shirt, socks, and a leather belt. The pants looked
too small, the shirt too big, the socks a mystery. She
discovered that the socks were all that fit. After
dressing, she looked with dismay into the bureau
mirror. The trousers clung to her hips and thighs like
a second skin, outlining every curve of her lower
body. The shirt, thank God, was baggy and long. Instead of tucking it into the pants, she let it hang to
the middle of her thighs. Most untidy, but more mod-
est. What a sight she made! She couldn't help smiling
at the image facing her. Knowing O'Brien for the
Irish devil he was, she suspected that perhaps he had
bought the pants in this size on purpose.

She recognized that with nothing to do but wait
and think during the past few days, she had re-
gressed from what she thought of as her "new self."
The inactivity had sat on her like a weight. Now, the
prospect of imminent action revitalized her and she

felt a renewal of the energy she had experienced back at the campsite. Once again that overwhelming sensation of being able to accomplish anything she set her mind to infused her. She was going and she would succeed. It was all that she wanted and all that was real in her life at this moment. Nothing else mattered. No future, no past. She would live in "now" until she accomplished her mission.

After a cursory tidy-up of the bedroom, she went back to the kitchen. Shandu was just finishing the bowl of beans. Thankfully, Sara had been occupied in the shop.

While Shandu looked silently on, she went into the shop and said good-bye to Tante Sara, thanking her again for her hospitality and refusing offers of further supplies. Sara shook her head critically at Katherine's dress, but admitted the practicality of it. "One could expect no less from an Englishwoman, so I suppose it will be all right," she said with a heavy attempt at humor. She reached up to a shelf and took down a man's hat. "Here is one thing you must take. You will need it in the sun." It was large, but Katherine's abundant hair kept it in place. "Now you really look like a man," Tante Sara said, tucking Katherine's hair in at the back.

They went outside to where O'Brien and du Toit were waiting.

Katherine introduced them and O'Brien came forward. He shook Shandu's hand warmly. "I have heard a lot about you," he said. "Of the fact that you saved Mrs. Carson's life, for which I am grateful, and of your promise to return for her. I see you are also a man of your word."

"And this is Koos du Toit," Katherine said to Shandu.

Du Toit nodded and did not speak, his eyes hard and unfriendly. He did not offer to shake the black man's hand. Shandu looked back at him with an equally stony expression, meeting his gaze and holding it. To Katherine, it looked like a confrontation of enemies, intuitively recognizing each other and silently drawing the lines between them. She shuddered to herself and mentally cursed O'Brien in a most unladylike manner. Dammit! A Kaffir hater! He had brought a Kaffir hater along with them and as sure as hell it was going to cause problems.

She stepped forward casually between the two men and said as brightly as she could, "Well, gentlemen, shall we go?"

"Here's your horse, Shandu," O'Brien said, walking over to the animal.

"Horse?" Shandu said, apprehension on his face for the first time since Katherine had known him.

"He's a good animal," O'Brien said. "I've ridden him myself often."

"I do not like horses, nor do they like me," Shandu said, unpersuaded.

"He's all right, I promise you. He's a strong beast, well trained and obedient."

"A horse is obedient only so long as it suits his purpose," Shandu said stubbornly. "I shall run beside you."

Katherine added her weight to the argument, for that was what it was rapidly becoming. "Shandu, we're going to be riding hard and fast. There's much territory to cover, many miles. I know you can run, but wouldn't it be better to conserve your energy for the battle that lies ahead?"

"I am a warrior," Shandu said. "I can run and then fight when the time comes."

"A warrior who is afraid of a small horse?" du Toit said with a nasty smile. "Are all the mighty Zulu warriors as women around animals?"

Shandu acted as if he had not heard the comment, but he drew himself upright to his full height and walked over to the horse, a brown Boer pony. Tentatively he reached a hand forward to touch the bridge of the animal's nose. The horse snorted and drew its lips back over its gums, showing large yellow teeth. Shandu pulled his hand away.

Du Toit laughed and Katherine shot him a dirty look.

"Here, let me show you," O'Brien said. He took a block of sugar from his pocket and put it in Shandu's hand. "Hold your palm flat, like this," he said, demonstrating. "All right, now hold your hand out and give it to the horse."

The horse took the sugar from Shandu's hand and neighed for more. The big Zulu looked distrustfully at the animal.

"He'll love you like a brother now," O'Brien said. "Just remember, you're the boss. Never let the horse know that you're nervous. They can sense it and take advantage of it."

He helped Shandu tie his shield and spears to the side of the saddle and then showed him how to mount and hold the reins. Finally, Shandu sat in the saddle, his back straight and stiff while at the same time he tried to appear nonchalant. Katherine felt like clapping her hands, but she did not want to embarrass him further. Still, it was an impressive sight. With his spear jutting up beside him as he sat there, he looked as regal as Shakespeare's Othello.

O'Brien held Katherine's horse while she mounted. "I knew you were beautiful," he said softly enough for only her to hear, "but I had no idea you were beautiful in so many places."

O'Brien mounted his horse and doffed his hat at Tante Sara, who was standing in the shop doorway.

"Tante Sara," he shouted. "I know you will pine for me, but I promise to be back soon. Be faithful to me while I am gone."

With a last good-bye, they wheeled their horses around and took the east road out.

Chapter Eight

THEY RODE EAST through a rolling land of knee-high grass and short, stunted thorn trees. When finally, after hours of travel, the veldt before them turned crimson as the hot red sun dropped behind the far horizon, they decided to stop.

While O'Brien and Koos unsaddled the horses and tethered them near a patch of green grass, Shandu gathered wood and built a large fire. Katherine unpacked some food and waited for the flames to die down. By the time the coals began to glow in a perfect pile for cooking, the stars had appeared.

The four of them sat around the fire, protected from the evening chill, while Katherine cooked the *boerewors* that Sara had given her. Pork fat splashed into the coals, causing small bursts of flame, while a delicious odor mixed with the rising smoke.

They had not talked much while riding, and the relative silence continued until after they had eaten and wiped their greasy fingers in the grass. Koos du Toit pulled a pipe from his pocket and lighted it. O'Brien began to question Shandu more specifically about their destination.

He wanted to know the name of the village where Wohlman had been seen, but Shandu did not know it. Earlier Shandu had explained that they would have to ride east before turning north in order to avoid a number of native villages. Their only hope lay in surprise, so it was important that they not be seen, this strange troupe of white men, a white woman, and a Zulu.

"How far east do we still have to go?" O'Brien asked now.

"Another day, I think. Maybe more," Shandu said. "We go up behind some mountains and then cross them to the place where the village is."

"Have you been this way before?"

"No," Shandu said. "Kokolo told me of the way. He has traveled here before and told me of the landmarks to look for."

"That will take us through the dry country," Koos said. "There is no water and the heat's strong enough to kill the flies."

"Yes, but Kokolo said it is only for a short while," Shandu said.

"I don't like it," Koos complained. "Why don't we stay east of the mountains, where there is water, and travel in the foothills."

"We will be seen and the messages about us will go out before a day has passed," Shandu said.

"He's right," O'Brien agreed. "You know how the news travels out here. My God, with a party like ours we might as well have a military band marching along with us."

"I still don't like it," Koos said sullenly. "Why should we trust a Kaffir? For all we know, he could be leading us all into a trap. Why should we put our lives in his hands?"

"If I wished to kill you, I would do it now," Shandu said derisively. "The first thing I would do is stick your tongue into the ground with my *assegai* to stop its prattle."

Koos stuck his jaw forward belligerently. "If you want to try it, Kaffir, then just—"

"Shut up, both of you," O'Brien said. "There's no need for this kind of quarreling. We have an enemy waiting for us. If we fight among ourselves we might as well give up right now and go back."

"I have never trusted a Kaffir before and I'm still alive. I do not trust this one," Koos said resentfully.

"You can trust this one," Katherine said. "The only reason I'm still alive is because of the help he gave me. He's an honorable man."

"All right. Let's end the subject," O'Brien said. "Katie, will you put some water on for coffee?"

She filled the tin can from a bottle and placed it directly on the coals. Within minutes it bubbled and she threw in a handful of coffee, stirring it with a charred stick.

"You do that very well," O'Brien said. "Where did you learn?"

"My husband taught me," she said.

"Oh." He lapsed into an uncomfortable silence.

"It's all right," she said after a minute. It was not the first time this had happened between them. Generally, O'Brien avoided talking about her family. She couldn't have him continue to be fearful of bringing up the subject. It placed too much of a barrier between them.

"I don't mind talking about my husband," she said. "He was a fine man and I wish to remember him."

"Tell me about him, then," O'Brien said. Katherine had never looked so beautiful to him as she did at that moment. She had taken her hat off earlier, and now her golden hair tumbled down around her shoulders. Her eyes sparkled like sapphires in the moonlight, and the flames of the rebuilt fire moved red shadows across her face, softening the skin and accentuating her high cheekbones.

"He was a simple man," she said, "a good man, more of a farmer than anything else. He loved the soil, loved to watch things grow and to care for them.

"His family was well-to-do. They owned one of the largest farms near the town where I was brought up, in Sussex. I used to see him often in town and at church, but he was older than I was and I did not think he ever noticed me. Later, he told me that the reason he was still single at twenty-five was because he had seen me when I was fourteen and had determined to marry me."

Katherine stopped and smiled at the memory. At fourteen she had been knobby-kneed and gangly, uncomfortable with the present and unaware of the future. Alan had seemed to her the ultimate in sophistication. She would occasionally see him drive a cart into the town market, but more often saw him on Sundays at church. He sat with his parents and two sisters, adorned in suit and top hat, sometimes even carrying a gold-tipped cane. The congregation would sing "Onward, Christian Soldiers," and she would fix her eyes on the back of his head and sing with all the fervor she could muster, dedicating the words to him and surprising her mother with her uncustomary enthusiasm.

By the time she was seventeen and he had started courting her, things had changed on the surface. There had been other suitors by then, of course, many of them, far too many for her father's sense of propriety, but they seemed callow and immature compared to Alan. She dropped them without a twinge of hesitation. Her father was overjoyed at the prospect of marriage between them. It would not only finally rid him of all the other suitors, but, loath as he was to mention the fact, the Carsons were one of the wealthier families in the area and strong supporters of the church. The thought of his daughter becoming a member of that family was pleasing to him and, in fact, he went so far as to say that the marriage was "blessed in Heaven."

Alan's family, in turn, adored her, and indeed, the union did seem blessed. They went to live on the farm with his parents and both of their children were born there. At first they were happy, but Katherine discovered that secretly Alan had more than a little of the pioneer in his heart. Africa had called to him since childhood. There had been no more avid listener in his family when his uncle's letters arrived from Cape Town with news of life in the colony. Wisely, or so she had thought at the time, she had encouraged him. Shortly after Colin's first birthday, they had embarked for Cape Town and a new life.

"He loved this country so much," she said to O'Brien. "It was love at first sight for him. When we sailed into Table Bay and saw the white clouds sitting like a tablecloth on Table Mountain, he said that he was finally home. Cape Town was just a beginning, though. He used to tell me that there was a voice in his head. It would repeat, over and over, 'Go north. Go north.' It would never rest until he obeyed it."

"I know the voice and I know the words," O'Brien said quietly. "I think we have all experienced it, or something like it, at one time or another."

Katherine looked at him and nodded. "I encouraged him again, of course," she continued. "I believed it was a wife's duty to encourage her husband. I believed in the power of dreams. I used to think that if I had not encouraged him, first to come to South Africa and then to journey north, he would still be alive today, and Timothy too, but that sort of guilt no longer rests comfortably on my shoulders."

"True," O'Brien agreed. "If we regretted our yesterdays, the present would be unbearable. I've made many mistakes in my life. I'm not proud of them and don't wish to repeat them, but I refuse to dwell on them."

Shandu had been staring silently into the fire. Now he spoke, surprising them with the interruption. "Courage is the attribute of the warrior, but it is not courage in war alone that is needed," he said in his soft, deep voice. "Courage is walking forward, no matter what is ahead, and not looking back, no matter what is behind."

"My husband used to say that a man must always march forward," Katherine said.

"I have seen the courage of the Zulu people," Koos said. "Women and children put to the spear."

"We are a great people, but one fault is large," Shandu said calmly. "When a man who is stronger than the others comes, we follow him and do not think for ourselves. If the leader is a great man, such a people can do much. If he is an evil man, they can do great evil."

"You sure have had some leaders to remember," O'Brien said. "I've heard stories about Tshaka and Dingaan that I can't believe."

"Tshaka made us a nation of great warriors, but the price was high for this. One time Tshaka wanted to see how many it would take to fill the Tatiyana *donga*. He had half a regiment of men killed and thrown into the *donga* to see how many it took," Shandu said.

"What's a *donga*?" Katherine asked.

"A split in the ground made from rain."

"A ravine," O'Brien added.

"My God! He did that just to satisfy his curiosity?" she said.

"He was the king," Shandu said simply. "One time he wanted to see how a child lies in the womb and had a woman heavy with child killed. Another time, he asked a woman who was drawing water for a drink from her earthen pot, and she said, 'Drink by lapping the water as other dogs do,' not knowing who he was. He then ordered that she be put to death and cut open to see what kind of heart so rude a person had. It was found to lie close beside the lung."

O'Brien shook his head. "I heard that when he became chief Dingaan killed all his brothers except one who was simple-minded."

"I was born near the end of Dingaan's time," Shandu said. "One time he thought the vultures were hungry and had many people killed for them." He stopped, as if that explained it all.

"And yet they had great fighters, those men," O'Brien said.

"They gave our people discipline," Shandu said. "Tshaka showed his men how to use the *assegais* in the battle against the Ndwande *impi*. He said, 'Do not throw your *assegais*. Use only one *assegai* and stab with it from a close distance.' After he had won the battle he picked out all the warriors who had thrown their *assegais* and called them cowards. Each one had his left arm held up and was stabbed under the armpit like a goat. Tshaka said, 'Let them feel the *assegai*.' After that, his warriors did as ordered."

"It is evil that men should be treated that way," Katherine said.

"It was the way," Shandu said.

Koos grunted and emptied his coffee grounds into the sand. "I am going to sleep," he said. "We have a hard ride ahead of us tomorrow."

"That's not a bad idea," O'Brien concurred with a yawn. "We should be on our way by sunrise."

"Late tomorrow we will reach the dry country," Shandu said. "There will be no water and it will be hot. We must look for water in the morning and fill our bottles."

"Is there any nearby?" O'Brien asked.

"Kokolo said there is a stream in the next ten miles. We shall look for it." He wrapped his blanket around his shoulders. "Now I sleep," he said.

Katherine lay on her back near the fire with Shandu on one side of her and O'Brien on the other. Koos obviously thought it improper for a native to sleep near them and made his point by moving to the other side of the fire.

The stars were obscured by clouds now and Katherine felt a pang of regret. She had looked forward to sleeping with them overhead. An owl hooted nearby and then, from across the veldt, there was a roar.

Katherine sat up. It was the first time she had heard a lion. It was a powerful, filling sound, one that unreservedly announced the dominance of its owner.

"It's only a lion," O'Brien said sleepily. "Don't worry about it."

"Are we in danger?" she asked.

Koos's voice came from the edge of darkness. "It is at least a mile away. In any case, it will not bother us. It has just made a kill."

The lion roared again and a moment later they heard the yipping of hyenas. Katherine fell asleep uneasily, wondering how scavengers were able to learn of a kill so quickly.

The landscape began to change drastically the next day. The stubby thorn trees, adapted to survive with their long white thorns and knobby haphazard branches, were at best caricatures of normal trees, but here even they were sparse. The grass became shorter and browner and the heat more intense. Katherine began to feel she was repeating her nightmare journey through the Karoo Desert.

To distract herself, she rode beside Koos and attempted to draw him into conversation. Their relationship had not begun auspiciously; she felt that if perhaps they talked she could find some way to heal the breach between them. The breach, however, was Shandu, and it was not an easy one to overcome. The Boer had his own ideas, and no desire to change them.

She told him how Shandu had saved her life after the attack by Wohlman, but all Koos said was that he must have had an ulterior motive. "These people are savages," he maintained. "Mercy is not one of their traits. There must have been some other reason. I would watch out if I were you."

"What experiences have you had to make you feel this way?" she asked, trying to understand.

"I am an Afrikaaner. I was born in this country. I have fought Kaffirs and killed many," he said, an edge of pride in his voice. "Ten years ago, when white men were fewer here, the Kaffirs were bolder. I have been to farms they have attacked and seen what they have done. Women, children, dogs, chickens even! Never do they leave anything alive. Nor do they just kill. They torture and maim like beasts! These were just ordinary Kaffirs; the Zulus are more blood-thirsty."

"But, Koos," she tried to explain. "It was white men who attacked me and killed my child. They would have killed me too if they could have. But because of what those men did, I don't feel that all white men are evil. One has to approach people by what they do, not by what one expects them to do."

Koos snorted derisively. "By expecting treachery from Kaffirs at every opportunity I am still alive to-day. Listen," he said. "All white men are not saints, I admit, but you cannot tell me that all Kaffirs are not devils. They have no God, no morals, no reading. They are little better than animals. I, for one, will keep my gun primed and my eyes sharp. It is more likely than not that he is leading us into some kind of trap. Where is this water he is leading us to, I ask you? From what he said this morning we should have reached it two hours ago. Believe me, he has nothing good in mind for us."

"Why?" she said patiently. "What could he want from us? What could he gain?"

"Our death, *mevrouw*. Our death. What more do these people want?"

Katherine shook her head in frustration. There was no reasoning with this man. Logic: if Shandu had saved her life, why should he now want her dead? Koos would shrug and answer, "Who can read the minds of Kaffirs. They think differently from us." It was hopeless.

She caught up with O'Brien, who was riding slightly ahead, and confided her feelings. "O'Brien," she said, reverting to use of his last name. "What on earth made you bring this man? He's nothing but trouble."

"Koos?" he said. "Look, he can fight and he knows how to look after himself in the bush," O'Brien said. "That's what we need."

"I don't like him. I think we should send him back now before it's too late."

O'Brien looked at her incredulously. "Send him back? You must be joking. You want me to say to him, 'Please turn around, Koos. The lady thinks it would be better'?"

"Yes. That's exactly what I want."

"Well, I'm not about to do that," O'Brien said. "Even if you can't see it, we need him. When the going gets rough and we're facing three armed killers and a tribe of Kaffirs, you'll realize that I'm right."

Katherine's voice sweetened. "Jim, you seem to be under the impression that you're in charge of this expedition," she said reasonably. "I want to assure you that is not the case. Furthermore, if you remember, you volunteered to come with me, I didn't ask you Shandu and I were prepared to do this by ourselves and we still are."

O'Brien laughed in amazement. "God! What a woman you are! Listen, Katie, let's not get into a fight over this. Just give the man a chance to prove himself. I'll talk to him about his attitude, if that's what's bothering you. If there's any trouble later on, I'll be responsible for him and handle it. Just trust me on this." He raised an eyebrow at her and said, "You do trust me, don't you?"

"Of course I do," she said. "It's just your judgment I'm not sure of."

"It will be all right, I promise you," he said persuasively. "Besides, I've already paid him his money. You wouldn't want to see me lose that now, would you?"

It was probably a good idea to reserve judgment for now, Katherine decided reluctantly. She would keep an open mind, but at the first sign of real trouble with the Boer she would insist upon a parting of the ways.

"Very well, Jim. We'll give him a chance," she said.

"There's my girl," he said with a smile. "I don't think you'll regret it."

"If I do, you will as well," she warned.

"You're a tough lady, Katie," O'Brien said cheerily. "But now that we have that settled, let's go back to your shooting lessons. I've shown you how to fire at stationary objects. Let's see how you do from a horse. The objects will still be stationary, but you won't be."

Katherine took the revolver from her belt and began to fire it as they moved. She chose as her targets trees and sandy little hillocks where she could see the bullet by the spurts of sand. The pony was well trained and, impervious to the loud noises, didn't break its stride at all. The revolver kicked upward each time she fired, but she quickly adjusted to that. By the fourth shot, she was able to hit what she aimed at.

"Excellent!" O'Brien said enthusiastically. "You're a natural, Katie. Now let's practice reloading while you ride."

Katherine groaned. That was harder.

"Now, now. Students should never complain," O'Brien said, enjoying his teacher role. "Remember, an unloaded gun is absolutely no use at all. A revolver is not even long enough to use as a club. Always keep your gun loaded. That's one of the most important rules."

"Yes, sir," Katherine said. "Yes, sir, teacher."

The water hole was nothing more than a small, muddy pond. They reached it before nightfall and allowed the thirsty horses to drink.

"Do you think it's safe enough for us to drink from?" Katherine asked. Her mouth curled with distaste.

"I don't know," O'Brien said. He looked as worried as she was. "It doesn't look too appetizing. But if the horses can drink it . . ."

"Here," Shandu said. He was standing about thirty feet away on the other side of the pond. They all walked over.

"This is the source," he said. He pointed down at a thin ribbon of water, not more than two inches wide, that led into the pond.

"A spring!" Katherine said. She dropped to her knees and put her mouth down where the water passed over a smooth rock. "It's wonderful. As sweet as sugar," she said.

They each drank their fill in silent gratitude. This trickle of water was the sole source of life in God knew how many miles. The thought encouraged reverence. Using a cup, they transferred water to the bottles. It was a time-consuming job.

"Is this where we turn north?" O'Brien said to Shandu.

"Yes. Forty or fifty miles up and we should reach the edge of the mountains."

"Is it dry like this all the way?"

"Kokolo said there is no more water until the mountains and then there are more springs."

Katherine looked around. The land was flat as far as she could see, and to the west the country seemed even drier.

"This is the edge of the Great Thirstland," Shandu said, narrowing his eyes into the setting sun. "Few men can live there."

"Go in there and you are dead," Koos said. He pointed into the sky. "There is the proof."

Katherine followed the direction of his finger and saw the circling vultures, four of them, dropping lower and lower into the reddening sand.

"I wonder what's there?" she said.

Koos shrugged. "Probably a dead buck. Leftover meal from a lion."

She turned to O'Brien. "We might as well spend the night here."

He nodded agreement. "Might as well. It's a long ride tomorrow. We should start with the horses fresh and watered."

After gathering wood for the fire, they sat silently around it while O'Brien cooked the last of the *boerewors*. The awesome strangeness of the terrain overwhelmed the desire for conversation. It was as if each man had first to find his place in order to be comfortable enough to talk. The utter silence had something to do with it. There were no birds, no sounds of game, nothing but a velvet stillness. In a sense, it was a scene of great beauty, but the beauty was shot through with menace, for the quiet was not natural.

"We probably scared the animals away," Koos explained. "Normally they would come to the water hole in the evening."

"How they must resent us," Katherine said. "Here we sit, drinking their water while they watch in thirst from the darkness."

"Africa is big enough for all of us, isn't it, Shandu?" O'Brien asked in his normal cheerful tone.

"I do not know," Shandu said carefully. "Is Africa big enough for both white man and black man? I fear it is not."

"We can live together. Surely our friendship proves that," Katherine said.

"We are only two," Shandu said. "I fear that the great days of my people are over. There are many of you and all the time you come, more and more of you.

You want our land, and you have the guns to take it. My people will fight, but I fear that in time they will not win."

"Your land!" Koos exclaimed derisively. "We both arrived in this land at the same time. When van Riebeeck landed at the Cape, your people were not there yet. It was only when we went north and you came south that we met. This land belongs to those who can take it, and to those who can use it."

"It is not that simple," O'Brien said. "Regardless of who arrived at the Cape first, when you talk of anywhere north of the Orange River, you're talking about land the Kaffirs consider theirs. You're drinking their water, killing their animals, tilling their land. What do you expect them to do? Stand idly by and watch you take it from them? They're too brave and honorable a people for that."

"*Ach*, you Americans are as bad as the English with your love for Kaffirs," Koos said disgustedly. "Brave! Honorable! You are mad! These people do not know what the words mean. You talk of their bravery. Have you ever seen a Kaffir fight by himself? They are like dogs, they fight in packs. Cowards!"

"There are those who use their tongues instead of their spears," Shandu said. "You use yours instead of your brains as well."

Koos clambered to his feet, his face red. He stood and flexed his powerful hands. "No Kaffir talks to me like that. Stand up like a man and say that to me."

Shandu got to his feet in one fluid motion and faced the angry Boer.

Katherine and O'Brien rose as well, consternation on their faces. "Stop it!" Katherine commanded. "I will not have this."

Both men ignored her. Shandu stood with his arms relaxed at his sides. Du Toit leaned forward from the waist, his hands open.

"Come on," O'Brien said. "There's no need to get excited."

"I am going to kill this Kaffir," Koos said.

Shandu waited, not moving or speaking.

Koos moved forward one step, let out a roar, and propelled himself across the distance separating him from the Zulu.

"Oh, my God," Katherine said, her hand rising to her mouth.

Koos's head took Shandu in the stomach. Shandu stepped back a pace under the impact, but did not even grunt. Koos straightened up and swung his right fist. It hit Shandu on the side of the head. Shandu shook his head once, then stepped forward and put his arms around the Boer's waist. He bent his knees and came up, with the Boer on top of his shoulders. He spun around and then let Koos fall. The Boer landed on his back, the air leaving his lungs in a bellow.

Shandu did not press his advantage. He stood back and looked at Koos, a small smile on his lips.

The Boer got to his feet. He swore once and then charged again, both fists swinging. His timing perfect, Shandu turned to the side, bent his knees slightly, and stuck his right arm straight out with the palm open. It caught Koos on the chin. His head jolted back; his feet continued to move forward. It seemed for a moment as if he were suspended in the air, and then he landed on his back again with a terrible thump.

Stunned by the fall, he got up more slowly this time. Shandu stood in the same relaxed position, the small smile still on his face. A look of comprehension dawned on the Boer's face; he knew he was no match for the big Zulu. He dropped his hand to his belt and brought it up with a knife. Slowly, he moved forward.

"I will cut your heart out and feed it to the vultures," he said.

"No, you will not!" Katherine said. She spoke with such authority that all three men turned and looked at her.

She held her revolver in her hand. It was pointed at Koos. "That's quite enough now," she said. "You will put away the knife."

The Boer stared at her, then looked at Shandu and back at her, trying to judge if she meant what she said.

"I mean it," she said. She pulled back the hammer of the gun.

Koos glanced at her for a second and then put the knife back in its sheath. Without looking at Shandu, he turned and went back to the fire and sat down.

Shandu walked slowly back and sat down as well. With a bored expression on his face he picked up his *boerewors* and continued eating.

"You will leave us tomorrow," Katherine said to Koos. "I don't want you with us any longer."

"You are taking this Kaffir's side before mine?"

"You will leave," she said.

"What about our agreement?" he asked, turning to O'Brien. "Who is in charge here? You or this woman?"

O'Brien shrugged helplessly. "She is, I'm afraid."

"But she is making me leave for a fight with a Kaffir!" Koos said, unable to believe it.

"I'm sorry," O'Brien said. "But it doesn't look as if it will work out."

"We had business," Koos said vindictively to O'Brien.

O'Brien shrugged again and looked down at the ground.

"You will be sorry," the Boer said. "When things get rough and I am not there to help, you will be sorry."

"We will manage quite well, thank you," Katherine said.

"So be it," Koos said, and then repeated the words for ominous emphasis.

He finished eating in sullen silence and then picked up his blanket and moved a few yards away from the fire. He lay on his back and stared up at the sky.

Katherine too looked at the sky. The clouds had passed and the stars were visible. It was like the return of old, welcome friends. They sparkled against the soft black backdrop, sending messages of light she could not read.

"I'm sorry for what happened," she heard O'Brien say softly to Shandu.

"It is nothing," Shandu said. "A man with hate in his heart is like a river that is dammed. When the rains come it overflows and breaks."

"I wish things could be better between the peoples of this country," O'Brien said wistfully. "It's such a damn waste."

"Things will be better when my people are truly conquered," Shandu said.

"You can't mean that!" O'Brien protested.

Shandu chuckled. "No. But they will be better for the white people, will they not?"

O'Brien shook his head. "The same thing has happened in my country with the Indians. The same shortsightedness."

"What are these Indians?" Shandu asked curiously.

"They are the people who were first in America," O'Brien explained. "It is a situation much like it is here, even though the question of who was here first is disputed."

"The black man has been here since Umkulunkulu, the first spirit of the Zulu nation. What is there to argue about?" Shandu said, dismissing the subject. "Tell me, these Indians, are they black like me?"

"No. They are a kind of brown color. Much lighter than you."

"Huh!" Shandu said. "But they are not white?"

"No. They are a different race. A fine people, I think, with many great warriors among them. They ride horses, shoot bows and arrows, hunt buffalo on the plains of America."

"Buffalo! You have buffalo in America too?"

"On the plains; once they abounded as far as the eye could see. Soon, like the red man, they will be gone. They are different from your buffalo, though."

"Red man? You said these Indians are brown."

O'Brien held out his hands. "I know. Still, they call them Red Indians to distinguish them from another, different kind of people that is found in a country called India. They are called Indians too."

Shandu was fascinated. He crossed his legs and leaned forward. "Tell me more about these Indians of yours. What are their customs?"

By the time Katherine fell asleep, Koos was already snoring. But the other two men, one white, the other black, were still energetically discussing the Indians of America.

Katherine woke everyone with her scream.

There was a flurry of confused activity as the men sat up and grabbed for their weapons.

"What is it? What did you see?" O'Brien asked.

"I don't know," Katherine said. "I opened my eyes and saw a face. I thought I saw a face over there."

She pointed to a small hillock covered by stubby, gray bushes. The three men scanned the area.

"I don't see anything," O'Brien said. "Koos?"

Koos shook his head. He held his rifle pointed in the direction Katherine had indicated.

"Shandu?"

"I see nothing yet."

"Maybe I was dreaming," Katherine said uncertainly. "I swear I saw something that looked like a gnome. A small little man with brown skin."

O'Brien laughed and stuck his revolver back in his belt. "A gnome! Katherine, you should be careful what you eat before you sleep. Maybe it was Tante Sara's *boerewors*."

"Bushmen!" Koos said, as if uttering an oath.

O'Brien reached for his revolver again, the smile disappearing from his face. "Bushmen? Here?"

"We are on the edge of their territory," Koos said. "They probably use this water hole. We had better saddle up and keep a sharp eye. They are treacherous little bastards."

"God! I always wanted to see a Bushman," O'Brien said. "I didn't think they wandered this way."

"They go where there is food," Koos said. "They were all over this country before we came."

"Even as far east as my country," Shandu said. "Still you can see their paintings in caves in the Drakensberg Mountains."

"Where are they?" Katherine asked. She had recovered from the shock. "I see nothing now."

"If a Bushman does not want to be seen, you will not see him," Shandu said.

"If I see him I will shoot," Koos said.

"No. Don't do that," O'Brien said. "They have done nothing to us. Perhaps they mean no harm."

"Your 'perhaps' is the difference between life and death," Koos said. "They carry arrows tipped with poison, these people. I am told that a man dies in agony if scratched by them. The poison is strong enough to kill an elephant."

"If the little people wanted to kill us you would be a dead man already," Shandu said. "We cannot see them, but they can see us, of that I am sure."

He stepped forward, stuck his spear into the ground beside him, and held the palm of his hand up in the traditional Zulu greeting.

Nothing moved on the landscape before them. Already the rising waves of morning heat were making everything shimmery and insubstantial.

"There are still Bushmen in the Orange Free State, but they're hard to find," O'Brien said to Katherine. "I've always hoped to encounter one."

"Who are they?" Katherine asked.

"Nomads. The most untamable people in Africa," O'Brien said, admiration in his voice. "They hunt or eat what grows around them. Always move. I've heard that after they shoot an animal with one of their poisoned tips, they can run after it for three days until it drops dead, either from the poison or exhaustion."

"They also steal cattle and kill people with those arrows," Koos said. "Our people shoot them whenever they see them."

"There's to be no shooting until I say so," O'Brien said with a sharp look at the Boer.

"There," Shandu breathed.

A shape rose from the ground. It was magical. One second there was nothing; in the next it was as if the ground had opened like the palm of a magician's hand to reveal the form. It was a small apricot-colored man, less than five feet tall.

He was the strangest being Katherine had ever seen. It was not only his size, although to see a midget in the desert was bizarre enough; the shape of his body was even more curious. His stomach hung in folds around his middle as if waiting to expand, and his buttocks were extremely large, dwarfing the rest of his body. He was naked, except for a small flap of covering in front that barely hid his genitals. He held a bow in front of him like a staff, and on his back he carried a small quiver of arrows.

Yet there was something beautiful about the little man. He stood as straight as a rod, as if trying to gain every inch of height possible. His bones were slight and fine, giving him a graceful appearance in spite of his stomach and buttocks. His features seemed more Oriental than anything else.

"There you see the true inhabitant of Africa. The first one here," O'Brien said under his breath.

The man stood at the other side of the pond on the slope of the hillock and stared at them as intently as they watched him. He said something to Shandu, more clicks in his words than in the normal Bantu language.

Then came the shot.

As she spun around to see where it had come from, Katherine saw the Bushman fall. Koos stood behind them, a grin on his face, his rifle still smoking.

"I got him!" he said triumphantly. "You see that? I got him."

They stood in stunned silence. Shandu was the first to act. He broke into a sudden run, directly at Koos. About eight feet away from the Boer his feet left the ground and he flew through the air, a terrifying scream transforming his face. He hit Koos with the impact of a falling tree, knocking the breath from the man and sending him to the ground. Almost in the same motion he struck Koos on the head, stunning him further. He lifted the rifle up with two hands and brought it down across his knee with an animal roar.

Just as he lifted the splintered butt to bring it crashing down on the Boer's head, O'Brien broke out of his trance.

"No! Shandu, no!" he shouted, and jumped forward, grasping the Zulu's right wrist with two hands.

The two men struggled for a few seconds, and then Shandu released the wood, letting it fall to the ground.

Ignoring the dazed Koos, they all turned to look back at the dead Bushman. His body had disappeared. In its place were four more Bushmen. Silently, another rose beside them from behind the hillock. The puzzled look in the Bushmen's eyes indicted them all.

"We'd better get the hell out of here," O'Brien said. "Saddle up, all of you."

"No. Shandu, tell them we are sorry for what happened," Katherine said.

"Sorry, hell!" O'Brien said. "Saddle up before they figure out what to do."

The Bushmen were talking excitedly among themselves now. They had seen the one who killed their fellow attacked by the others. In fact, even as the others saddled their horses the evil one still sat on the ground.

O'Brien finished saddling his horse with record speed and lifted Koos's saddle onto the back of the Boer's pony. There was a whistle beside his ear, and an arrow thudded into the leather.

"I guess they made up their minds," he said coolly. Taking the revolver from his belt, he fired it once over the heads of the Bushmen. They scattered back behind the hill.

"Mount up!" he shouted. He quickly tightened Koos's saddle and then walked over to the stunned Boer. He slapped his face twice. "If you want to live you had better get on your horse now," he urged.

Koos shook his own head to clear it. "I am all right," he said, rising to his feet unsteadily.

He reached for the pistol in his belt. "First I must kill the Kaffir," he said.

"You will do no such thing," Katherine said. She held a revolver in her hand, pointed at Koos's chest.

The Bushmen reappeared, slowly raising their heads up over the hillock.

"Don't be a fool," O'Brien said to Koos. "We don't have time to fight among ourselves."

The Boer looked uncertain, then swung himself onto his horse, pistol still clutched in his hand. Katherine kept her revolver pointed at him.

"It is all right," Koos said to her. "I am not going to do anything."

"Yes, you are," she said. "You're going to turn your horse to the east and ride back the way we came. We go north."

The blood left Koos's face. "You must be mad," he said. "They will come after me and kill me."

"Katie, he's right. You're sentencing him to death," O'Brien protested.

Shandu watched silently, his spear in one hand.

"He's on a good horse," she said, her tone pitiless. "If he's lucky, he'll succeed. If not? What is it your Bible says, Koos? 'An eye for an eye, a tooth for a tooth'?"

"You cannot do this to me. I am a white man, like you," Koos said.

"Dead men have no color," she said bitterly.

"Katie, you can't do this," O'Brien said.

"You're welcome to join him if you wish," she said.

"I will not go," Koos said, moving his horse forward. "You will not shoot me in cold blood."

She pulled the trigger. The bullet whistled past his head, not more than two inches away.

"East," she said.

The Bushmen had ducked down at the sound of the shot, but they did not move behind the hill this time, realizing that it was not meant for them.

Koos looked into her eyes. Whatever he saw there decided him. He turned his horse east.

"All right now, move!" Katherine shouted. She fired a shot over the heads of the Bushmen and, as they ducked back behind the hill, wheeled her horse around. Shandu took off at a gallop beside her. O'Brien hesitated for about three seconds, then shouted, "Good luck, Koos!" and followed them. Koos was left with no choice. He dug his heels into his animal and took off the way they had come.

Katherine lay low on her horse, urging it on. She had no idea how far the Bushmen could shoot their arrows. The best thing was to put as much distance between them as possible. She heard the hooves of Shandu's horse pound the earth just behind her and, a little farther back, O'Brien urge his horse on with a colorful mixture of oaths.

Finally, after about a mile, she allowed the horse to slow down to a walk. O'Brien and Shandu pulled up beside her. She looked back over her shoulder at the water hole.

"It appears we've made our escape," she said.

They all looked. There were no Bushmen following.

"They will not follow us," Shandu said. "If they are not too hungry and tired from their march, they will go after the one who killed one of them."

She turned to O'Brien. "I am sorry, Jim, but I did what I felt had to be done."

The American still looked unsettled by the experience.

"I suppose so, Katie. I suppose what you did was right, but—"

"But you are too decent a man," she finished for him.

"And you, Katie, are a driven woman," he said warily.

"Not really," she contradicted. "I just know what I must do."

"It's a good thing we filled our canteens last night and didn't wait till morning," he said. "What now?"

There was no doubt that the leadership had changed hands. "Now we ride north," she said.

There was something she had to know. "What did he say to you?" she asked Shandu. "The Bushman. The one that Koos shot?"

Shandu stared ahead, his face unreadable. "It is their greeting. He said, 'Good day. We saw you from afar. We are dying of hunger.'"

"God damn that Koos!" said O'Brien.

The desert was not as bare and lifeless as it had

looked from a distance. In fact, it was replete with life, something they had not expected. They first passed a small herd of several dozen steenbok. The animals just moved aside, not bothering to run, still inexperienced in the ways of man's destructive nature. Later they saw some graceful gemsbok, long horns tilted back as if for speed. There were also ostriches—tall, long-necked, comical, and nervous. They ran as soon as they saw the humans, as fast as horses, heads bobbing up and down. Most plentiful of all, however, were the snakes. The desert was drier than normal, and there was little cover for the reptiles. They saw puff adders, small silvery vipers, black mambas, and golden cobras. For the first time Katherine felt no fear. The reptiles even seemed beautiful to her. Their sinuous movements and their many-hued skins gave them a unique loveliness shared by no other creature.

The sight that took their breath away was a herd of kudu that filled a plain slightly below them. There were thousands of the fine-looking bucks milling about. They sniffed the air and pawed the ground, raising clouds of dust; they nibbled at the few sparse thorn trees, oblivious of the presence of men.

"There must be five thousand of them," O'Brien said in an awed whisper. "I've never seen that many animals in one place at a time."

"They are traveling for food, like everything else in this desert," Shandu said. "Once all Africa was like this. Giant herds of many kinds filled the land. It was a time before men took too much."

O'Brien recovered his good spirits quickly. Later, when they saw a small herd of duiker run in the opposite direction from them, he shouted out joyously, "See how they move! The way they keep their heads down and their backs bobbing up like that. Aren't they wonderful. 'Duiker' is Dutch for 'diver.' See, they look like porpoises. Difficult to hunt because they never stop to look back."

To Katherine it was a natural wonderland. This was a facet of the Africa she had pictured in her mind while still in England. This was a land where nature was still supreme. The bowl of blue above was unmarred by cloud or smoke; the land, as far as the eye could see, was devoid of any trace of man. If it were not for the heat, she thought, it would be an Eden. But the heat was there and it could not be ignored. The fiery ball in the sky dominated the entire landscape.

O'Brien placed things in perspective for her. "Don't be lulled into a false sense of security by what you see around you now," he cautioned. "The rains have not come here yet. These animals that you see, they are all desperately searching for water and food. The weaker of them will die here, victims of this cruel beauty. Nor can men survive long in this place."

By midday, the heat was overpowering. It sat on them like a weight. Their eyes hurt from the constant glare, and all three were exhausted. Luckily, they found a small grove of camel thorn trees. Usually found much farther south, these were a remnant of older times, some period of forgotten history when perhaps they covered the entire desert.

They dismounted wearily and leaned against the tree trunks. Soon they were seated on the ground. Sipping carefully from their canteens, they tried to conserve water they knew would be needed later. It was ten minutes before anyone generated the energy to speak.

"They say it is so hot here that when it rains the water evaporates before it even hits the ground," O'Brien remarked dully. "It has to drop buckets full of water to have any impact."

"Thank you for that cheerful news," Katherine said. In spite of her riding practice, her legs and buttocks were beginning to hurt after two days in the saddle. She looked at her hands and saw they had swollen. Her feet felt puffed up as well. She tugged at her boots and pulled them off.

O'Brien managed a grin. "Ah, the charming and beautiful Katherine Carson. Once the belle of the ball, her face is now powdered with dust, her shirt stained with perspiration, and her hair caked with dirt. If only your friends in the Governor's Mansion could see you now."

Katherine smiled at the image, remembering how those Cape Town ladies, settlers in the colonies, an ocean away from the comforts of home, had prided themselves on their adventuresome spirits. When acquaintances heard that she and Alan were traveling north to the Transvaal, they had been shocked. A little adventure was fine, but that was too much. Indeed they should see her now. In their attempts to dissuade her from the journey they had warned her of the hardships and perils of the bush. The worst of their tales paled beside the reality of what had occurred and was happening even now.

She took some pieces of *biltong* from her knapsack. "Will these make us thirstier?"

"For a short while," O'Brien said. "We can have another drink before we leave, though. I have heard that the salt will actually help us."

She handed them each a piece and took one herself.

They chewed silently for a while, and then O'Brien wet his finger and held it up in the air. "Not a breath of wind. We're walled in by heat."

"We must stay here for a few hours until it grows cooler," Shandu said.

Katherine looked dismayed. "We'll lose time. We should press on."

"How long can your horse travel in this heat, and at what speed?" Shandu said logically. "It is better to wait until the sun is on its way down and the air is cooler. The horses will go better and we will go faster."

Katherine looked out into the distance. She could not refute his logic, in spite of her desire to keep moving. As far as the eye could see, the air looked like distorted glass, twisted by the undulating waves of heat. Suddenly she pointed. "Look! Water! A lake!" she said.

Blue water shimmered near the northern horizon. There was a smudge of violet mountains behind the lake.

"It's just a mirage," O'Brien said. "Reflections in the sky." He added wearily, "I think Shandu's right. We could sleep for a couple of hours, if it's possible in this heat, and then travel in the darkness when it's cool."

"Yes," Katherine said, her voice meek. She felt diminished by this land. "I suppose it's best. No matter how little, this is shade of a kind. We might as well take advantage of it."

Too exhausted to move, they lay where they had been sitting. Within minutes they were asleep, while the air danced in shimmering waves around them.

It must have been four o'clock when they awoke. The heat still pounded the earth around them, but the glare of the sun had lessened.

"It will be cooler in an hour, and it will be cold in three hours," O'Brien said jauntily. He looked more like his old self, revitalized by the sleep. The dark moons that had begun to appear under his eyes had diminished, and when he walked to saddle his horse there was a spring to his step.

Katherine's body still ached, but she too felt better, a lifting of the spirit more than anything physical, although she noticed that the swelling of her hands had gone down. Shandu looked as fresh as he had at the start of the journey.

After another ration of water, they mounted and continued their northward journey.

O'Brien found himself thinking of Koos as they rode. "I wonder if he made it out of there okay," he said.

"I'm sure I don't care," Katherine said. "If there is any justice, they caught up with him."

"Are you serious?" O'Brien asked, shocked by her bluntness.

"He killed a man," she said simply. "There are consequences to every action."

"He was a friend of sorts," O'Brien said. "I can't share your sentiments. We've ridden together before, never with any rancor between us."

"Perhaps now you will choose your friends with greater care," were Katherine's last words on the subject.

They rode in an uncomfortable silence for an hour, and then Shandu spoke. "I see the mountains," he said.

O'Brien and Katherine narrowed their eyes into the light ahead and saw a blue haze.

"It is not another illusion?" she asked.

"No, it is not. It is the mountains," Shandu said. For the first time since leaving Potchefstroom, he smiled. "Just as Kokolo said, the mountains are there."

"How far do you think?" O'Brien asked.

Shandu looked uncertain. "Twenty, maybe thirty miles."

"If we ride fast, we could make it shortly after nightfall," Katherine said.

"Well, what are we waiting for?" O'Brien asked. He let out one of his American yells and his horse broke into a canter. The hardy Boer ponies would be able to maintain that pace for hours. The end of their journey was in sight.

Chapter Nine

THE LAND BEGAN to change as the mountains grew closer. Small tufts of pale green grass blotched the rocky sand, and the thorn trees were more plentiful. The land also began to slope slightly upward; looking back, they could see the desert at a lower elevation.

They reached the true foothills of the range shortly before dark. The mountains ran in a north-south direction, and the party decided to continue along the western slopes. "It is green on the other side, but there are people there," Shandu explained. "We go on maybe ten or fifteen miles. Then there will be a cut through the mountain where we can go without being seen. There will be no guards, for they do not expect people ever to come from this direction. Only madmen travel in the desert."

They saw bigger trees now, tall ancient survivors with green leaves and red flowers. With the increased foliage came a new profusion of birds: bulbuls, orioles, cuckoos, and the carrion-eating black crows that seemed to thrive in every area of Africa. Herds of antelope dotted the desert plain below them.

The land was rougher on the slopes, however, with many eroded hollows and *dongas*, and as the darkness grew they decided to stop to avoid accidents. A lame horse was something they did not need at this stage, let alone an injured rider.

One of the hollows was full of water, and the first

thing they did was to lead their horses to it and let them drink their fill. Then they tethered the animals in a patch of short green grass and began their nightly preparations for making camp. It was becoming a ritual, comforting in its familiarity. While Katherine took food from the saddlebags, the men would gather wood for the fire. Then, in a show of ceremony, O'Brien would take out his precious box of lucifer matches, drawing one through a piece of sandpaper to light it and putting it to the dried grass they used for kindling. While warm shadows leaped and danced around them they would eat and talk, usually of the past and present, seldom of the future. It was as if the present and past were contained in the trembling ring of light around the fire. The future was somewhere beyond the perimeter, a dark unknown they were unwilling to pierce with eye or mind.

That evening O'Brien was talking about his experiences in California. Katherine was growing used to his mercurial moods. Now he was in good spirits again, as if the events and arguments of the day had never happened. "I don't wish it on this country. If gold is discovered in any great quantity here, it will mean the end of the Boer way of life, and there is much to admire about them," he said.

"The veldt will be littered with shanties and tents at first, and then there will be towns. In California, towns appeared overnight, and they were beehives of anarchy and disorder. Within months, people had come from all over the world. The miners themselves were a rough lot, by any standards, but they were not the worst of it. Thieves, murderers, confidence men, ladies of ill repute—they all flocked there like animals around a water hole. There were gunfights in the streets—I saw them with my own eyes. Many miners had their claims jumped. Fortunes were made and lost in a day. Men went mad in the excitement of it all. This was all just a few years ago, and it is still happening as far as I know. God forbid it happens here."

"You once said that there was more gold here than they dream of in California," Katherine said.

"I know there is. Don't ask me how, but I do. One day the biggest goldfields in the world will be here in the Transvaal. Maybe farther north, but somewhere in this country."

"I don't think you will ever find it," Katherine said.

O'Brien was surprised at her remark. "Why do you say that? Why not me? I know more about prospecting than most. Certainly more than anyone around here now. Beyond that it's largely a matter of luck, and I have never been short on luck."

Katherine smiled. "Because you will not let yourself be the one. I think you love this country too much as it is to see it become another California. Oh, I know you promised the Boers to keep it a secret, but really, how long can a secret like that be kept? The Boers know it, and so do you. No, Jim, I think you'll always search the stream right beside the one with the gold in it. You'll find just enough to keep you happy and keep you looking. That's what you really enjoy, anyway, isn't it?"

She stopped talking then and watched him, a small smile on her lips. Shandu chuckled, amused by her evaluation.

"My God!" O'Brien exclaimed. "Katie, you're a witch. No doubt about it. To come up with a theory like that!"

"Well, admit that it could be right," she said.

"It could be. It could be. But if I really feel that way, what am I doing here? Tell me that, if you can."

"You're doing what you enjoy," she said. "You have a life of little or no responsibility, and all you do is travel around a country you love. You said you

would not wish the discovery of gold on these people,
but you would not wish it on yourself, either. It
would change things too much. You would have to
find yourself another place to love."

"You could be right, Katie," O'Brien said, serious
now. "I think I told you once before that I felt at
times as if Fate had brought me here. Well, all my
prospecting and talk of gold . . . sometimes I think
that it is all a way to kill time until I see what Fate
has in store for me. Somehow, since I have met you,
that fate seems much closer."

Katherine did not acknowledge his last remark.
She threw a log onto the fire. Shandu hummed softly
under his breath.

"Shandu, what of you?" she asked. "When this is
over and we have done what we set out to do, what
will you do? Your wife and daughter are dead, your
cattle gone. What will you do?"

"I shall find a new wife and more cattle and I shall
live on," Shandu said philosophically. "It will not be
difficult. The future is only hard when one is a pris-
oner of the past. When one is able to learn from the
past and not live it again, one is truly free."

"And you with all the questions, Katie?" O'Brien
said. "What about you? What will you do?"

"Why, I shall get my son and begin anew," she said
without hesitation.

"By doing what?" he persisted.

Her certainty deserted her. "Ah, that's another
matter. I have no answer, for I haven't decided.
When it's time, I shall make the decision."

"Well, I hope I figure in your decision, whatever it
is," O'Brien said.

"You'll always be my friend, whatever happens,"
Katherine said, adding: "As will Shandu."

It was not what O'Brien wanted to hear, but he did
not pursue his point as he gazed into the fire.

Although well aware of the significance of the interchange, Shandu was not uncomfortable. He continued humming softly to himself, his features relaxed, his eyes half-closed, looking to Katherine like a large cat.

She sipped her coffee thoughtfully, sneaking a sideways glance at O'Brien, who was still staring into the fire. He had clean features, a wide, firm mouth, long, almost feminine eyelashes. A handsome man, and no doubt he would be an exciting and sensuous lover. But that was not enough. It never was between man and woman. One could take Shandu as an example. His firm, muscled body was close to the epitome of classical beauty. No doubt, he too was a fine lover. But quite apart from the impossibility of such a union in society's view, he and Katherine were worlds apart. With O'Brien, even though he was an American, she shared some common realities, some similarity of background. It was all a matter of degree, however. Did she share enough with O'Brien to create a successful relationship? What would her decision be? She had no idea. And now was obviously not the time to decide.

There was a clatter of falling rock from the darkness of the hill below them. O'Brien and Shandu both sat upright, eyes tensely searching the gloom. Katherine's hand moved to the pistol on the ground beside her.

"Did you hear that?" O'Brien whispered.

Shandu silenced him with his hand.

"Maybe it's just an animal," O'Brien said.

More rocks tumbled down the hill, and then came the clear sound of a man, at least one man. There was a grunt of effort, a muffled voice.

Shandu gestured with his hand again and they rose silently, backing into the shadows beyond the light of the fire. Shandu held his throwing spear on his shoulder, while Katherine and O'Brien pointed their revolvers in the direction of the sounds.

The noises came closer. Whoever it was, he was approaching the fire.

They waited in quiet suspense. Katherine found she was holding her breath and released it slowly. A figure stepped boldly out of the darkness, walked up to the fire, and casually lowered himself to the ground where they had been sitting.

Katherine and Shandu spoke in unison.

"Kokolo!" they exclaimed.

Kokolo insisted, of course, that he had found them through magical means. They soon learned, however, that he had been waiting for them on this side of the range since the previous day. Shortly before dark he had seen the first stream of smoke from their fire and set off to meet them. Kokolo explained that he had deliberately made a great deal of noise because it would be more dangerous to come upon them suddenly and by stealth.

Katherine had a thousand questions, but she assumed that Shandu's were similar, so she sat patiently with O'Brien, waiting for the translation, while the Zulu interrogated Kokolo.

The two black men talked for almost half an hour. Kokolo's face went through a confusing array of expressions, ranging from woe to hilarity. With his twinkling eyes and urchin grin he even had Shandu laughing at times.

Finally Shandu turned to the others and said, "You must understand that Kokolo makes more of things than they are."

"Is he lying?" O'Brien asked.

Katherine understood perfectly what Shandu was trying to say. "He exaggerates," she explained to O'Brien. "You'll see what Shandu means as we hear the story. Go on, Shandu."

The first thing they learned was that Kokolo had narrowly escaped with his life.

"At first everything was good," Shandu said. "The people thought he was a great magician and listened to his words and sought to be his friends. All the people in the village loved him like a wise father except one. That one was the chief, a drunken dog who licked the feet of the white men. He learned that Kokolo was asking questions about the white men, and so the chief ran to his masters, the white men, and told them. They were very angry.

"Kokolo says he changed himself into a mouse and crept into the hut to hear the conversation between the chief and the white men," Shandu explained, and added with a straight face, "I think a person who was there told him about it.

"They ordered the chief to kill Kokolo, saying that he was a spy sent to their village by another tribe who wanted to steal their women and cattle. Although a drunken fool, the chief was still wise enough to be afraid of Kokolo's magic. He told the men that he did not want to kill Kokolo, and asked if he could just send him away from the village. At this, the white men grew even angrier and one of them struck the chief, calling him a coward and asking who he was more afraid of—them or Kokolo. They said if he did not kill Kokolo they would do it themselves. Then they would kill him.

"At this point, Kokolo left the hut. He turned himself into an eagle and flew to the mountains, where he has been waiting for us," Shandu concluded.

"What have Wohlman and his friends been doing at the village?" O'Brien asked.

"Each day the men have ridden out into the mountains. They have been looking, he thinks, for the yellow metal, gold. The day before he left it was different. The white men were interested in a stone one of the villagers wore around his neck. The three men rode off with this man, and stayed away that night. The next evening, the evening that Kokolo left,

they came back, without the man. He thinks that
they killed him. The white men were very excited and
talked a lot among themselves."

"What could it be?" Katherine asked.

"Maybe some kind of gemstone," O'Brien guessed.

"Kokolo tried to find out but was unable to,"
Shandu said. "He says that the white men live like
kings. The chief has provided them with wives who
cook and clean for them and sleep in their hut with
them. They have their choice of maidens. Nobody
else is allowed into their hut. Kokolo talked to one of
the maidens and tried to find out more about the
stone and what the white men were doing, but the
girl was afraid of the white men and would not talk
about it."

A picture flashed into Katherine's mind of Wohlman's crooked wolflike teeth and of the quiet menace
of Dieter. Yes, she could understand the fear of the
woman.

"What else is there?" she asked.

Shandu smiled. "Kokolo is most anxious to return
to the village. While he was there he performed certain miracles for the people, such as healing the sick,
ridding the chief's second wife of evil spirits, and in-
suring a good harvest. For this they were to give him
one dozen cattle and two maidens for wives. By
threatening to send him away or even kill him, they
have not honored this debt. He feels that he has been
cheated and wishes to return, to claim what is right-
fully his."

"He's quite a businessman, our Kokolo," O'Brien
said with a grin. "That's not a bad haul for a few
days of work."

"How does he think we should approach the problem?" Katherine asked. "He's been there. He should
have the best idea."

Shandu had not asked this question but put it to
the old man now. Kokolo made a show of thinking

about it before answering. He cleared his throat and
cocked his head to one side. After scratching his gray
head, he launched into a lengthy reply.

"He says that he will consult his ancestor spirits
and obtain the solution to your problem," Shandu
said. "He thinks that the answer is in the mountains.
That we will best be able to defeat these men there.
There are too many others who will help them in the
village. Even though the villagers do not like these
men, they are afraid of them. They will do what their
chief tells them to do, and what the white men
order."

"Basically that means he has no idea," O'Brien
said with a shrug of his shoulders.

"What is the best time to attack the men?" Katherine asked.

"He says that on Sundays the village celebrates
with drinking and dancing, and that would be the best
day. It is possible that the men will go into the mountains that day since they do not observe the holiday."

"What day is it today?" Katherine asked.

"Friday," said O'Brien. "That gives us a day to get
there and prepare ourselves. Can we do it?"

"If we rise early tomorrow and begin, we can be
through the mountains before it is night," Shandu
said.

"Good. Then we shall do it," Katherine said.

Kokolo was looking intently at O'Brien. He pointed
to him and spoke to Shandu.

"What is he saying?" O'Brien asked.

"He says that you have traveled a great distance
across great water to reach this place," Shandu said.
"He says that all your life, your footsteps have
brought you in this direction. The spirits have
brought you together with her for this time."

"For what? What does he mean?" O'Brien asked.

"That is all he can say," Shandu translated. "He
says he can only tell you what the spirits tell him.

Perhaps in time his ancestors will tell him more. He says also that he is honored to know you, that you are a brave man."

"Tell him thank you. And likewise," O'Brien said. He was surprised by the black man's remarks. They were indeed close to the mark.

Kokolo grinned and spoke again. He seemed to be enjoying his role of oracle. This time he addressed himself to Katherine and lightly touched her hand once while he spoke.

"He says that you have changed much since he saw you last," Shandu said. "You have grown stronger, like a tree that has withstood many storms and now can stand against anything. The spirits have been kind to you. Now you have much lion in you."

"Thank you, Kokolo," she said. "I am happy to see you again, faker that you are."

Shandu translated it faithfully. Kokolo decided to accept the epithet as the ultimate compliment and grinned happily.

Kokolo refused to ride on the back of Shandu's horse.

"Ask him if he's afraid?" Katherine joked.

Shandu took great pleasure in asking the question, and he laughed heartily at Kokolo's barked reply. "He says he is not afraid of the horse but afraid of how badly I would guide him."

Although they made relatively slow progress over the rocky terrain, Kokolo surprised them with his endurance. He ran alongside them at a steady trot, carrying on a conversation with Shandu while he moved.

They reached the pass shortly after noon. It was a natural east-west fold in the mountain and consisted, Kokolo assured them, of a path created over the years by hunting parties who went to the desert when game was short in the valley beyond.

It was really little more than a narrow trail, a line where brush had been pushed aside and earth patted down by the passage of many feet over the years. The horses had to proceed in single file, and Kokolo took the lead. As they traveled up toward the summit of the pass, the vegetation began to change. The brush grew thicker and greener and the variety of trees increased. Massive rocks began to appear on either side of them, some of them many tons in weight. They were scattered around the hills, as if tossed there by some titanic force in a moment of anger.

They reached the summit after three hours. The difference in the land that lay ahead of them was astounding. The valley below was as green as an emerald, a jewel of gently rolling hills, spliced by the silvery glint of streams. This side of the mountain was riotously lush with vegetation, altogether different from what they had seen before.

"So this is where all the rain goes," said O'Brien.

"The range of mountains must stop it from reaching the desert," Katherine remarked. She pointed down to their left. "Look, a stream! How wonderful. Is there time to stop and wash?"

Shandu consulted with Kokolo and said, "We can stop there for a short time, but he says that from now on we must be careful how we move. At places it is possible for them to see us from the valley. We must continue down before we stop for the night."

They dismounted where the path intersected the stream and drank their fill. After washing their faces, arms, and feet, they unsaddled the horses and rubbed the dusty animals down with fresh water. It was pure luxury and both man and beast reveled in the sparkling stream. Finally, Kokolo had to order them to hurry if they wanted to reach his chosen campsite by nightfall.

The winding path descended now in sharp leaps and bursts. The air grew visibly thicker, and Kather-

ine could feel it on her skin, unlike the ghostly thin
atmosphere in the heights or the dry vacuum of the
desert. Beneath the high shrieks and whistles of the
birds was the intimate hum of clouds of insects. Gray
monkeys leaped through the trees around them,
chattering obnoxiously at the passing caravan.

Katherine fixed her eyes on O'Brien's back. A huge
pool of perspiration stained his shirt and he swayed
easily from side to side like a drunk, unresistingly
matching the movements of his horse as it picked its
way down. Every now and then he would glance back
at her without speaking, as if to make sure she was
still there.

It was so near now, so unavoidable, she began to
feel doubts about her ability to succeed in what she
wanted to do. Soon she would come face to face with
Wohlman again, and her revulsion at the thought
almost choked her. She half closed her eyes to picture
the moment of meeting, the shock on Wohlman's face
when he first saw her, facing the revolver in her
hand and knowing he was about to die. Yet even as
she formed the picture in her mind, she knew the
way it would actually happen would be quite different, something quite unexpected. She did not doubt
that she would exact her revenge in some way, but it
was the manner of it that now concerned her. In fact,
if she admitted the truth to herself, it was her companions that worried her. O'Brien and Kokolo in
front of her and Shandu riding behind. What would
happen to them? These men had all become her
friends and, in a way, her responsibility. Where was
she leading them?

A long, hanging branch whipped at Katherine's
face, reminding her to pay attention to the path. The
stream was on their right now and she caught
glimpses of the valley through breaks in the thick
brush. She guessed that they were moving along the
side of the mountain and not directly down as before.

"How much farther?" she asked Shandu, and he
called the question to Kokolo.

They were near, Kokolo said. A half hour at the
most. He drew from his apparently bottomless reser-
voir of energy and picked up the pace, his thin legs
churning rapidly. It was dusk now, and the air was
alive with birds returning to their nests for the
night. A huge bat, its wings the length of Katherine's
forearm, flitted across the path in front of them.
There were more of the furry primordial creatures in
the trees around them, hanging from the branches,
blissfully content in their upside-down world. There
was a sudden steep descent over a precarious stretch
of slippery gravel, and then they found themselves in
a small hollow, sheltered by a grove of tall, vine-
encrusted trees.

Kokolo signaled for them to dismount and tether
their horses, then he made them walk behind him up
the facing hill. It was a rough ascent through thick,
pathless brush, and Katherine and O'Brien were
panting by the time they reached the top. Kokolo
cautioned them to remain behind cover and pointed
out the terrain.

They were almost in the valley here, in the last
foothills of the range. The mountain they had descended loomed behind them like an ogre. They could
see a rising pall of smoke about a mile or two into the
valley.

"That is the village," Shandu said.

They looked more intently and saw the thatched
roofs and mud walls of the huts. People moved about
the village as precisely as ants. The sound of a herds-
man bringing his cattle into the *kraal* for the night
drifted up to them.

There was no sign of Wohlman or the other white
men.

"They may be in their hut," Shandu guessed. He
spoke to Kokolo and then said, "It is the largest hut
over there."

It was set back a little from the rest of the village on the southern side, a large round building. There was no smoke coming from it, although all the other huts had fires burning. A figure moved from the large hut; it was too distant to tell whether it was man or woman, but it did not appear to be a white man.

Kokolo looked worried. He muttered something to Shandu.

"He says that there is usually a fire burning there at night," Shandu said. "He does not know why there is no fire now. He thinks that later tonight he should go down and look. Maybe the white men have gone away again, as they did a few days ago."

"Is it safe for him to go down there?" Katherine asked anxiously. "They do want to kill him there, you know."

"He says that you must not worry. He will use magic to make his enemies sleep."

"Well, we might as well go back and make camp in the meantime," Katherine said regretfully. As she had watched the scene below them her heart pumped furiously. She was more than ready to act, but now it was a time to be patient.

"They won't be able to hear the horses?" she asked anxiously when they were back in the hollow.

"Too far," O'Brien said. "Sitting in this hollow, the brush will smother any sound we make."

"What about our smoke? Perhaps they'll smell it."

"They have their own fires filling their noses. Stop worrying," he said.

He went to gather firewood, eager to ward off the increasing chill. Katherine took out the remnants of their food, while Shandu unsaddled the horses. Kokolo sat like a prince and watched all the activity, a benign smile on his lips.

After they had eaten Shandu suggested that it was time to make a plan.

"Has Kokolo been inspired by his ancestor spirits yet?" O'Brien asked with a grin.

Shandu must have communicated the tone of the question to Kokolo. The old man gave O'Brien a disapproving look before answering.

"He says that tomorrow when the men leave the village we must follow them to where they go. Then we must trap them when they return along the path. But this plan is no good if the men are not there. First he must go to the village tonight and find out if they are there."

"I suppose that's the first step," Katherine said. "If they've gone on another two-day trip we'll just have to wait for them to return, unless we can find out exactly where they are. That may be difficult."

O'Brien looked down. "I assume from what you said earlier, Katie, that you still intend that Wohlman and the other two be killed? You have nothing in your mind of capture?"

"Of course I'm still of the same mind," she said, as if surprised by the question. "Wohlman is to be killed. Anything else would be impractical anyway. We're not a sufficiently large force to be able to apprehend them and take them back to town. Do you have qualms?"

"Of course I do," O'Brien said. "The idea of shooting men down in cold blood is—well, it's not something I've done before and not something I like."

"I promise you that if you don't shoot them down, they will have no qualms about killing you. Besides, O'Brien, you knew when you came what I intended."

"Yes. Yes, I did," O'Brien admitted. "It's just that now, faced with the actual prospect, it's somehow different."

"Perhaps you should not join us when the moment arrives," Katherine said quietly.

O'Brien flushed. "No. I came to help you. And make no mistake, you need my help. I don't have to like what I have to do, that's all."

"So be it," Katherine said. She turned to Shandu. "How much trouble can we expect from the villagers, once Wohlman is disposed of?"

Shandu consulted with Kokolo. "He thinks they will run without a leader," he said disdainfully. "They are not warriors, these people. As it is, they do not like the white men. They will not fight for them unless forced to."

There was a long silence, and Katherine found herself thinking unexpectedly of Colin. Was he being well cared for by the McPhersons? Right now she had no alternative but to think he was. She must be free to concentrate on her mission—the death of Wohlman and his accomplices.

O'Brien seemed to sense her thoughts and came out of his silence. "Katie," he said, "I want you to understand that if I question you it's because I care for you so much. If I am critical, it is because I care." His voice was thick with emotion. "I have seen your resolve change you to what you are. I have no quarrel with that. But I do not want to see you destroy that which is fine in you, and that is why I caution you. It is my own fear. Accept it in the spirit I give it, Katie."

His plea touched her. Unconsciously, she smoothed her hair with her hand. "Ah, Jim, you are a true friend, and I value you for it."

O'Brien took her hand in his. They sat in fragile silence. Katherine promised herself that she would not hurt him. If she decided that she did not want him as he wanted her, she would somehow find a way of releasing him without hurting him.

Shandu and Kokolo sat on the other side of the fire, talking comfortably to each other in soft, musical tones, the rhythm of their voices as much a part of the land as the song of the birds and the roar of the lion. Their brown eyes looked as if they had been polished to a soft glow in the firelight, and they touched each other freely while they spoke, their white teeth gleaming with their frequent smiles.

Katherine withdrew her hand gently from Jim's and reached for the can of coffee warming on the coals. She poured the coffee for both of them, and then she asked Kokolo the question that had been sitting on her lips for hours. "Shandu, please ask Kokolo if he has spoken to the spirit of my husband again."

Shandu received the question without surprise and relayed Kokolo's answer back to her. "The ancestor-spirit is waiting to see what will happen," he said.

Had Kokolo spoken with him? she asked. No, came the answer, he had not. Then how did he know? How do you know it is morning? You see the sun rise. How do you know it is night? You see the darkness. How do you know you are awake and not sleeping? You know. That was how he knew. He knew, that was all.

Slightly chastened by the implication that she was querying that which was obvious to anyone with the intelligence of a child, she became silent.

"Do you believe that stuff?" O'Brien asked in a voice just above a whisper.

"I believe nothing and hope for everything," she said.

Kokolo must have felt that his sharp words needed clarification, for he began to talk directly to Katherine, pausing every now and then to allow Shandu to translate.

"It is apparent to me, he says, that you are a child in these matters," Shandu repeated. "You have powers, but you do not yet know what they are. He wishes to tell you something about ancestor-gods.

"When a man or woman dies, he at once becomes a god, a *shikwembu* or ancestor-god. He enters that which does not reach the point where it ends. Where there is no beginning and no end. For gods, there is no such thing as distance; they are everywhere present. They are like heaven, the sun, the moon. There is no place where it can be said that the sun and moon are not. They know at all times what their descendants do, and in many ways control the lives of their descendants.

"Each family has two sets of gods, those of the father's family and those of the mother's, *kweru* and *bakokwana*. There are also gods of *assegais*, those who have been killed in battle, and the gods of bitterness, the ones who have been killed by beasts, or drowned, or even killed themselves. Your ancestor-gods can protect you against the other gods, such as Gods of the Bush. They are ones who have not been properly buried, and they wander through the bush, attacking innocent travelers. There are also other gods, but they do not concern you.

"The gods appear to their descendants in many ways. Sometimes they are in the form of animals. The Mantis, and the little green snakes called the *shihundje*, are messengers from the gods. Sometimes they appear as puff adders. At other times they will appear to you in your dreams. Most people, however, talk to the gods through the bones. It is through the bones that the gods make their wishes known. The gods can bless and they can curse. Beware when the ancestor-gods are angry. That is why one must make offerings to them. Kokolo says that he knows there are different gods where you come from, but these are the gods that are here. When one is thirsty in a strange place, one must drink the water that the people there drink, or die of thirst."

Kokolo now spoke more quietly, leaning forward in a confidential manner. Shandu translated for him. "He says that that is the lore. That is what most people think is truth. What they do not know is that the gods talk to them all the time. He can hear his ancestors whenever he wishes. He does not need to use

bones or the other devices. All one has to do is listen
for the sound of their voices. This is something very
valuable he is telling us, he says. It is not known to
most others. Listen for the sound of voices. When you
hear them, you can talk to them with your thoughts.
Listen, he says."

Kokolo had been leaning forward on his haunches
while he spoke, his eyes burning as hot as the coals of
the fire. He seemed younger and more powerful than
before. Now he rolled back and sat, apparently finished, once more the charming old charlatan.

Katherine sat quietly, her expression remote, her
thoughts racing. What did Kokolo really mean? "Do
not ask if I have spoken to your husband, woman. He
is speaking to you." She remembered that earlier,
when she had first met him, he had spoken about listening. She had not paid heed then. She was too intent upon her own thoughts to listen to his.

Katherine stood up and walked away from the fire.
She stopped just beyond the ring of light and stood in
the dark, her arms folded across her chest to ward
off the chill. The icy stars glittered through the lat-
tice of leaves. There was a dog's bark in the distance
and the answering howl of a jackal.

She closed her eyes. The sound of voices. Where
were they? How could they penetrate the barrier of
her thoughts? She tried to listen, but all she heard
were her own musings.

Alan! she called in her mind. Talk to me!

And then the answer came. It stood out, true,
strong, different. It was not her thought.

*Katherine! I am with you, my love. I will always be
with you. Listen to my voice and you will hear it. Listen and you will hear.*

She stood motionless in the darkness, her back to
the others, the tears rolling down her cheeks.

Chapter Ten

THEY WAITED for Kokolo until the coals in the fire turned gray, the radiance to ash.

He had gone into the village, as planned, shortly after they had eaten, promising to be back within the hour. Three hours had passed.

"He must be in trouble," O'Brien said gloomily for at least the third time. He gathered some sticks and logs and threw them onto the dying fire.

"You will put out the fire that way," Shandu said. He scraped together some dried grass and twigs and pushed them under the pile that O'Brien had made. Kneeling on all fours, he blew into the brush until a flame leaped out of the embers. "That is better," he said.

"Wohlman must have captured him," O'Brien said. "I think it's time for us to do something."

"What do you suggest we do? Go and ask them?" Katherine said.

Shandu held his hands close to the fire to warm them. "I shall go to the village and see what has happened," he said.

"No. Then we'll have two of you to worry about," Katherine said.

"I will be careful not to be seen."

"It's too much of a risk," she said. "We must be cautious. If they've caught Kokolo, they could be waiting for us."

"Kokolo would not talk about us," Shandu said. "They cannot know we are here."

"Something is wrong," Katherine said doubtfully. "I feel it in my bones."

"We can wait here till morning to see if Kokolo returns," O'Brien said, "but sooner or later, if he doesn't, we are going to have to go in and look for him. Better do it now under cover of darkness."

"He speaks the truth," Shandu said. "We must act."

"Don't you see, this puts us on the defensive," Katherine said vehemently. "Our only chance all along has been that we go in and surprise Wohlman."

"When in doubt, one must act," Shandu said. "Every true warrior knows that. To do nothing is fatal. A warrior who stands still can be stabbed with the *assegai*."

Katherine rubbed her forehead. She couldn't argue with their logic. "There's no moon tonight," she said, looking up at the sky. "Shandu, do you think we can get into the village without being seen?"

"We?" O'Brien said. "I thought Shandu was going to go down by himself."

"If there's a trap, we might be able to fight our way out of it," Katherine said. "If Shandu goes in by himself, we could lose half our force in one day."

"And if we all go in, we could lose our entire force in one day."

"I know," she said. "I think that's the risk we have to take. We can't leave Kokolo there."

She repeated her question to Shandu, who nodded confidently. "Yes. If there are guards, we can avoid them. It is very dark."

"Kokolo apparently couldn't," O'Brien said dubiously.

"Kokolo was not expecting a trap," Katherine said. "He may have been careless."

O'Brien shrugged and stood up. "All right. If we're going to do it, let's do it now."

"Your white faces are like torches in the night," Shandu said. "We must darken them."

He mixed some water into a mound of loose earth until it reached a thick consistency. Katherine and O'Brien patted the mud on their faces, spreading it around their eyes and mouths and covering every inch of exposed skin. Katherine pulled her hair up into her hat.

When they had finished, Shandu inspected them carefully, plastering a few places they had missed. "Now you look like Zulu warriors," he said, appraising them with his hands on his hips.

They went down the hill to the village, avoiding the path. Shandu guided them into a *donga*. It was twenty feet deep, eroded by decades of storms. Filled with debris, the branches of trees, and the bones of slaughtered animals, it led down to the village. The villagers had apparently used it as a dump.

They moved as quietly as possible, but in the darkness it was hard to avoid loose rocks and logs, and they often fell, suppressing the exclamations that rose to their lips.

After about twenty minutes, O'Brien asked if they were near the village. Shandu motioned for them to stay where they were and clambered up the steep sides of the *donga*. A few minutes later he slid back down, sending a hail of pebbles before him.

"We are there," he said. "We must cross a clearing and go past a cattle *kraal*."

"How will we know which hut Kokolo is in?" O'Brien asked.

"It will be the one with guards outside," Shandu said. "Come. When you get to the top, lay flat on the ground."

Katherine went first, pushed from behind by Shandu. O'Brien came last. When he reached the top, Shandu extended a hand and pulled him over the lip of the gully.

They lay on their stomachs and looked at the village. The first houses were less than fifty yards

away, and the land ahead of them was devoid of
cover, except for a *kraal* with walls built of piled-up
brush, mainly the branches of thorn trees.

"We can take cover behind the *kraal*," Katherine
said.

"Yes," Shandu agreed. "First we must stay here
and watch."

They lay for ten minutes without moving and
watched the village. There was no movement, no sign
of life.

"What about dogs?" O'Brien asked nervously.

Shandu tapped the head of his spear. "This will
take care of any dogs we see. You must not shoot
your guns unless you have to. We must do this in
great quiet."

Finally, Shandu decided it was safe. Leading the
way, he proceeded in a crouch, his body bent forward,
his hands almost touching the ground. They halted
behind the shelter of the *kraal* and listened. Apart
from their own ragged breathing and the stirrings of
a few cows, all was quiet.

"Wait here now," Shandu ordered. "I will go and
see where Kokolo is being kept." He slipped silently
into the darkness, soon merging with it.

Katherine and O'Brien waited quietly, their ears
attuned to the noises of the night. There was the monotonous music of crickets, a flap of wings, the hoot
of an owl, the howl of a jackal in the distance.

If there was a trap in this place, it was diabolically
clever, Katherine thought. The village was as quiet
as death, its inhabitants apparently sleeping
soundly.

There was a rustle in the gloom and Shandu appeared. "I have found him," he whispered. "There is
a hut over there on the other side of the *kraal*. He is
inside it, I am sure. There are two guards outside the
door."

"Are they standing or sitting?" O'Brien asked.

"Sitting," Shandu said. "I think one of them is sleeping. It should not be difficult to overcome them. You go around one side, I the other, and then—" He pounded his fist in his palm to illustrate the point.

"What do I do?" Katherine asked.

"I think you wait. It will only take two of us," Shandu said.

"No. I will come behind you. I may be of some help," she said.

Shandu inclined his head in resignation. He knew better than to argue with her. "Let us go. Follow," he said.

He led the way around the *kraal*, past one hut to the back of another. It had thick mud walls and a conical thatched roof.

"The one on your side is asleep," Shandu said to O'Brien in a barely audible whisper. He motioned with his hands for the American to go around the circular building.

Shandu moved in the opposite direction and Katherine followed, her body close to the wall. Shandu stopped suddenly and she bumped into him. She could just see the side of the guard's body. He sat cross-legged, his head lowering and jerking up every now and then. This one was falling asleep as well.

Shandu moved quickly then. He jumped forward around the curve of the building, landing in a crouch beside the startled man. Before the guard had time to react Shandu slid one arm in front of his neck and the other behind. The man grunted once, and then there was a loud snap as his spine broke.

Katherine followed quickly, just in time to see O'Brien come around the other side. He hit the second guard once on the head with the butt of his revolver. The man toppled to the side without a sound.

Shandu moved into the open doorway of the hut. There was a scuffling noise and a thump, and Katherine and O'Brien entered in time to see a man fall to the floor. There had been a third guard stationed inside the hut.

Kokolo sat against the far wall. His hands and feet were tied with leather thongs. He spoke to Shandu, his voice angry. The big Zulu dropped to his knees and untied the bindings.

"He wishes to know why we took so long to come and get him," Shandu said over his shoulder. "I told him that we thought a powerful magician like him would be able to take care of himself. He did not say anything to that for once."

Kokolo rubbed his ankles and wrists and then allowed Shandu to help him up. He looked unsteady on his feet but otherwise unhurt.

"Let's get the hell out of here," O'Brien said.

They went back outside. Everything still looked peaceful. Katherine stopped briefly to peer at the two guards.

"Come on," O'Brien said, pulling at her arm. The two black men had already gone ahead.

They ran to catch up, back to the *kraal* and across the clearing to the *donga*. Katherine slithered down the side, scraping her hands and arms on the rough gravel. Kokolo was already moving up the ravine, but Shandu stood there and motioned them ahead. They moved up the gully at a trot, not as careful to be quiet as they had been on the way down. Katherine sucked at the palm of her hand and tasted blood where she had grazed it. O'Brien ran into a log and swore.

They had gone about two hundred yards when the village erupted. The night silence was shattered first by one cry and then by a chorus of shouts joined with the barking of dogs.

"They've found the guards," O'Brien said. "We had better hurry now."

"They will not follow," Shandu said from his position in the rear. "Better we slow down now and be quieter. They do not know which way we have gone."

"What about their dogs? Can they follow us?" Katherine asked.

O'Brien chuckled in the darkness. "I doubt it. These aren't English hunting dogs."

"They will be afraid to follow," Shandu said scornfully. "These men are not warriors. They do not know how many were there. All they will see is Kokolo gone and three dead guards. They will not hasten to follow."

"Wohlman will not be afraid," Katherine cautioned.

"Wohlman has gone," Shandu said. "Kokolo told me that the white men have left."

They sat around the dead embers of their fire, more out of habit than for any practical purpose. Shandu decided not to relight the fire, just in case his appraisal of the villagers had been inaccurate. Fully recovered from his ordeal, as self-assured and cocky as ever now that he was safe, Kokolo told them what he had discovered.

"The white men left yesterday very quickly," Shandu said. "Kokolo learned that in the afternoon another white man arrived in the village. He spoke to Wohlman and within the hour they all left, taking eight or nine warriors with them."

"I wonder what that could have been about?" Katherine asked.

"Probably some friend they'd arranged to meet up here," O'Brien ventured.

"Why the warriors?" Katherine asked.

"Kokolo says that they wanted the men for work. The chief gave them to the white men in exchange for liquor," Shandu said.

"How did Kokolo get caught?" Katherine asked.

"He says that they were waiting for him. It was a trap. He says that a wizard cannot be trapped, but that they were waiting for us, not him, and that is why he was caught."

"Waiting for us?" Katherine repeated stupidly.

"When Wohlman left he told the chief that a white man, a white woman, and a Zulu warrior would be coming. He told the chief that if he killed them, he would be rewarded upon their return."

"My God! How did he know?" O'Brien said.

"Obviously the man who rode in had something to do with it," Katherine said.

"Maybe he rode through Potchefstroom on his way up here and heard about us there," O'Brien said. "It's a much shorter route directly up than the way we came. He might have ridden through on the day we left. He would still have been here before us. I'll bet that's it!"

"It was Koos du Toit!" Katherine said suddenly.

"Koos! How could it be?" O'Brien said. "The last we saw he was riding back to Potchefstroom with a gang of Bushmen at his heels. It couldn't have been. Why would he do something like that, anyway?"

"It couldn't have been anyone else," Katherine said. "The natives were expecting the three of us. If it was someone who rode through town just after we left, he would have known that Koos was with us, that there were four of us. Wohlman would have told the chief to expect four of us."

"My God! You're right," O'Brien said.

"Instead of going back to Potchefstroom, he could have gone east a little way and then gone up this side of the mountains while we traveled on the other side. It would have been faster and he would have been here before us. As to why, I would consider revenge as a motive. We left him to what could have been his death. He wanted to kill Shandu and he probably was not particularly fond of us, either, by that time. Perhaps he thought Wohlman would reward him if he warned him we were coming."

"Well, I did lead him to believe that Wohlman would have a lot of booty," O'Brien said uncertainly.

"I think you are right," Shandu said to Katherine. "There is nobody else who could have seen us while we were traveling up here. Even if they did, how could they know where we were going?"

"Damn me for a fool!" O'Brien said vehemently. "I never figured Koos for a turncoat. Never. How could I have been so wrong?"

"When people are angry, they do things that are out of character," Katherine said kindly. "It's not something you could have known."

"I should have," O'Brien said. He held his hands out helplessly. "I'm sorry. I'm truly sorry."

"The thing we have to realize now is that the situation has changed," Katherine said. "The element of surprise has gone. Wohlman knows I'm alive and that we're after him."

"Why didn't he wait for us?" O'Brien said. "He could have set the trap himself. Why run off?"

"Perhaps he had more important business elsewhere?" Katherine said. "Taking the men with him for work. Maybe he has found his gold." She shook her head thoughtfully at her own guess. "It's not like Wohlman to leave loose ends behind, though."

Kokolo spoke to Shandu. "He says that we interrupted his sleep by rescuing him," Shandu said. "He is now going to sleep."

O'Brien laughed. "Grateful fellow, isn't he? It's not a bad idea, though. We can attack this problem fresh in the morning." He looked over at Katherine's set, dogged expression. "Come on, Katie. It's not the end of the world. We'll come up with something. Don't worry about it."

"We have no choice," she said. "We have to follow Wohlman."

"There's always a choice," O'Brien said. "Let's get some sleep, and I'm sure in the morning we'll be thinking more clearly."

O'Brien was right. Katherine awakened in the

morning feeling refreshed, her mind no longer
clouded by the bitter, self-deprecating thoughts that
had filled it until the welcome final veil of sleep. The
sun had already risen and Shandu had made a fire. A
tin of coffee exuded its invigorating smell.

"The fire," she said. "They will see it."

"It does not matter," Shandu said. He poured her a
cup and handed it to her. "Kokolo and I have been
talking."

The coffee scalded her throat, but she gulped it
gratefully. O'Brien walked over to the fire. Cheerfully he wished her good morning. "You looked so
beautiful asleep, I didn't have the heart to wake
you," he said.

Katherine's hand automatically went up to her
hair. She must look a mess, she thought. The mud
still caked her face.

"I must go to the stream and wash," she said. "I
understand you've all been making plans while I was
sleeping."

"Not me," O'Brien said. "Shandu and Kokolo have
been cooking something up."

Overcoming her curiosity, she fought her way
through the brush to the small stream. Kneeling on a
rock beside it, she washed the mud from her face
with the icy water. She used the tail of her shirt to
dry herself and realized for the first time how rank
the cloth smelt. Her clothes needed washing, and her
body could use some hot water as well. All in all, she
was a mess. She couldn't understand how O'Brien
could still find her attractive in these circumstances.

When she got back to the camp, O'Brien was sitting beside the other two men, drinking coffee. After
filling her cup again, she sat beside him.

"So, what is your plan?" she asked Shandu. "I hope
there is a good reason for letting the entire world
know where we are."

"We must know where the white men have gone to

be able to follow them. Is that not so?" Shandu
asked.

"Of course," she said.

"How do we find that?"

She hesitated before answering. "I assume that
we'll follow their trail, or—" She stopped, realizing
his point. "Of course, if Kokolo was unable to find out
even in which direction they went, that will be difficult."

Shandu nodded. "He does not know. They could
have gone north or south. The only way to know is to
ask at the village."

"I suppose you're right," she admitted. "But how
can we do that? We've killed two of their people and
they would kill us on sight. Wohlman has already
promised the chief a reward in return for our lives."

"Kokolo and I have talked. He knows these people.
He says we would ride into the village, bold and un-
afraid, as if nothing has happened. They will not expect that and will be afraid."

"But . . ." she began. Her voice trailed away as she
tried to grasp the idea.

"They are not warriors, these people," Shandu continued. "Kokolo says they are afraid of his magic."

"A bold plan, Katie," O'Brien said.

"A risky one," she said. "What if Kokolo is wrong
in his estimation of the villagers."

"I think he is right," Shandu said. "He believes
enough to chance his life. Kokolo does not value his
skin lightly, that much I know."

"We should press the advantage and go now,"
O'Brien said. "Let's not give them too much time to
think about it."

"Kokolo should be mounted on a horse like a visit-
ing dignitary and, Shandu, you should be walking in
front with your shield and spear," Katherine suggested.

Shandu laughed. "It is good. But we shall have to

see if we can get Kokolo to go on a horse. He likes them even less than I did."

They broke camp quickly, rolling their blankets and packing utensils. After saddling the horses, Shandu approached Kokolo with Katherine's suggestion. The old man rolled his eyes up and shook his head, but Shandu continued in a low persuasive voice accompanied by flattering gestures, obviously telling Kokolo how fine he would look on the back of a horse. Finally Kokolo spread his arms out in a gesture of submission. Shandu turned to Katherine. "He will do it. He does not like it, but he admits that it is a good idea. He says that as it is your wish, he will do it."

Getting Kokolo onto the horse was almost as difficult as persuading him to do so in the first place. He gingerly touched the animal on the neck, then jumped back when it moved its head. He patted its flank, then jumped back when it lifted a leg. He finally insisted upon speaking to the horse at length.

"What is he saying?" Katherine asked.

"He is telling the horse that he is a wizard and that if the horse is bad to him he will turn it into a mouse. He will become a hawk and catch the mouse. He will fly into the clouds with it and drop it to the earth." Shandu broke into hearty laughter, unable to maintain his normal sober translator's tone. Kokolo glowered at him, but continued to talk to the animal. "Now he is saying that if the horse is good it will have green grass for the rest of its days, and many wives."

Satisfied that he had reached an understanding with the animal, Kokolo gestured imperiously to Shandu and asked him to lift him onto the horse's back. Shandu declined, showing him instead how to mount by using the stirrups. Grudgingly, Kokolo did as shown. Finally he sat up on the horse, his back as straight as a rod and a disdainful expression on his face.

"It's wonderful," Katherine said, clapping her hands. "Perfect. He looks as if he was born on a horse."

Shandu told Kokolo what she had said, and he allowed himself a quick smile before resuming his regal pose. While the others mounted up, Shandu showed Kokolo how to use the reins.

They set off down the hill to the village, an imposing procession. Shandu took the lead, shield in one hand, *assegai* in the other, as tall and impressive as any royal attendant. Kokolo followed with no signs of nervousness in his bearing, his head held high, an aura of majesty surrounding him. Katherine and O'Brien rode side by side in the rear. The American carried a rifle across his knees with one hand.

About half a mile from the village, they began to see signs of frenzied activity. People ran from hut to hut and a crowd began to gather in the square before the chief's residence. They could hear the shouts of men and women as they grew nearer.

"Look neither left nor right. Just straight ahead," O'Brien said to Katherine, taking Kokolo's lead.

As they rode into the village the noise died down. The people surrounding the square parted to let them through, leaving Katherine with a peripheral impression of frightened eyes and shuffling feet.

The chief stood in front of his hut and watched them approach. Twelve armed warriors stood beside him, six on each side, but they looked more afraid than threatening. The chief himself was imposing only because of his size. He was a big man who might once have been strong. Now his muscles had degenerated into fat. He had the drooping breasts of an old woman, and enormous, flabby jowls. His eyes were as small and furtive as a pig's. He looked sideways at his warriors for reassurance, his fear evident.

Kokolo, his eyes never leaving the chief, rode directly up to him. He reined his horse only a few

inches away from the man, forcing him to move back
a step. Katherine and O'Brien drew level with
Shandu, stopping about five yards behind Kokolo.

Kokolo began to speak, his voice high and musical,
evidently making sure that everyone in the square
could hear his words.

"Tell us what he is saying," Katherine said to
Shandu out of the corner of her mouth.

"He is telling the chief that he is as foolish as an
old woman to keep the wizard Kokolo shut up in a
hut. He says chains could not hold him if he did not
want to be held. The chief has allied himself with the
white *baloyi* —that is someone who is evil, who has
the evil eye, a criminal, one who eats human flesh—
but he cannot win against the magic of the mighty
Kokolo."

Shandu coughed, whether from embarrassment or
suppressed laughter was uncertain. "Nor can he win
against the mighty Zulu warrior Shandu, the personal favorite of the Zulu King Mpande, or these
white people who are representatives of the Queen
Across the Sea."

Judging by the gasps among the audience, Kokolo's
words were having an effect. High on his horse, he
shook his finger at the chief.

"He says that if he were an evil man, a vengeful
man, he would cast a spell that would make every
person in this village die of a terrible disease, or one
that would kill all the cattle in the *kraals*, or one that
would multiply the chief's fatness so that he would
finally burst into a thousand pieces. But he is not. He
is a kind and forgiving man, and he will give the chief
and his village a chance to make up for the wrongs
they have done. He says he will not even have me call
the *impis* —regiments—of Mpande into this country
to slaughter all the people, although after what they
have done to my friend Kokolo that would be very
understandable. No, being a kind man, he will do

none of these things, although he could if he wished. No, he shall treat them like civilized people, even though they may well not be. If they do not take this chance he so generously gives them to become good people again, terrible things will come to pass. The earth will open up and swallow their cattle, the waters will rise and drown their children, the heavens will open and spit fire."

Kokolo lifted up his right hand on the last words. He held it in the air for the count of three and then there was a bang. Gray smoke rose in a plume from his outstretched hand.

The crowd gasped and one person moved back from where they had been standing. A few women began to wail. The chief looked stunned.

"Most impressive," O'Brien murmured to Katherine.

Shandu stepped forward then and stood beside Kokolo. He glared ferociously at the chief, who took another step backward.

Kokolo spoke again to the chief in a sharp tone. The man answered him in a stammering rush of words and bowed from the waist. Shandu turned and marched back to the horses, looking directly at Katherine and O'Brien, ignoring the crowd.

"The chief says that it has all been a mistake. He was bewitched by the evil *baloyi* and did not know what he was doing. He begs Kokolo's forgiveness."

Kokolo spoke again in his high, artificial voice. For a moment Shandu looked surprised, but he quickly masked his expression. He began to curse under his breath in Zulu.

"What is it?" Katherine asked. "What is he saying?"

Shandu lifted his eyebrows. "He is asking the chief who the strongest warrior in the village is. The chief says it is the man on his right. Kokolo says that I, Shandu, will now give a demonstration of my power as a warrior and challenge him to a fight for the amusement of the people."

"Why on earth is he doing that?" Katherine said angrily. "He has won his battle."

"He is now just having his fun with me," Shandu said with a sour smile. He stepped forward and stood beside Kokolo again.

The great warrior of the village did not look honored by his title. He stood his ground in line with the others, a look of wild apprehension on his face. Finally, after a tirade by Kokolo and a few sharp words from his chief, he stepped forward, a shield in his left hand and an *assegai* in his right.

He was almost as tall as Shandu, but where the Zulu was all hard muscle, this man was already sprouting a belly and his legs were flabby. Apparently he had been resting on his laurels for a long time. He and Shandu moved off to the side and faced each other.

Shandu stood with his shield lowered in disdain, his *assegai* loosely held in his right hand, as relaxed as a cat. They might have stood and faced each other until sunset, for the other man was in no mood to begin hostilities. Finally, Shandu grew bored, took a step forward, and contemptuously tapped the man's shield with his *assegai*. The man immediately took a fighting stance and began to circle around Shandu, looking for an opening. This too might have continued indefinitely if Shandu had not drawn a gasp from the crowd by throwing his shield on the ground behind him. Far from giving him fresh heart, this action made the warrior even more dubious of the outcome.

He circled some more and then stabbed at Shandu with his spear. Shandu struck it with his spear and flicked it harmlessly aside. Again the man stepped in, lifting his *assegai* above his shoulder and bringing it down fast. Shandu's relaxed pose dropped. Almost

faster than the eye could follow he moved in beneath
the man's spear. With a quick swing of his *assegai,* he
knocked the spear from the man's hand. Swinging it
around, he used the blunt end to smash his shield.
The force of the blow sent the warrior tumbling back
onto the ground. His shield fell to one side and
Shandu pounced forward, landing lightly beside the
man, his *assegai* pressed against his throat. He held
it there for a moment and then stood and walked
away, his back to the fallen warrior.

The crowd reacted with a chant the whites did not
understand, although it was apparently flattering to
Shandu. Throughout the bout and into its aftermath,
Kokolo had maintained an attitude of stoic disinter-
est, as if the outcome had never been in doubt. Now
he spoke again to the thoroughly cowed chief.

Shandu, who had walked back to stand beside the
others, translated in a tone of admiring resignation.
"Now he tells the chief that perhaps he will let me
train his warriors to fight like men. He will get me
into trouble, that one."

"You didn't look like you were in trouble," O'Brien
said.

"I will let him have his joke," Shandu muttered.
He put his hand over his mouth to hide a smile as
Kokolo continued his speech to the chief. "He is now
reminding the chief that he is owed one dozen cattle
and two maidens for the good deeds he did." Shandu
spluttered out the next words. "He says that now the
chief must give him two dozen cattle and four maidens. All this for his kindness in forgiving the chief
for his wrongs, and also for restraining us, as we had
wanted bitterly to punish the village for treating
Kokolo badly."

"What gall!" Katherine exclaimed.

"The chief agrees," Shandu said. "We are to be his
honored guests for as long as we wish to stay here.
He promises to treat us as royalty."

Kokolo managed to get off his horse without falling and stood in front of the chief, suddenly smaller now that he was on the ground.

"Kokolo is telling him that there are important matters to discuss," Shandu said.

The chief nodded at Kokolo and waved his arms at the assemblage, shouting out orders. The crowd began to disperse, a hum of conversation accompanying them as they discussed the wonders of the morning.

"The chief told them to go back to their duties and said that there would be a celebration this evening to welcome his honored guests," Shandu explained. "We must now go into the chief's hut to talk."

Katherine and O'Brien dismounted and Shandu led their horses to a post beside the chief's hut. The chief then led the way into his hut, followed first by Kokolo and Shandu.

It was a round hut, like the others in the village, but larger than all of them except for the one Wohlman had occupied, one that they later learned was used for tribal meetings. The skins of wild animals adorned the walls and floors, there was a pit for fire in the center, and low wooden benches covered by more skins for seating.

They sat in a semicircle facing the chief. Smiling blissfully, he reached into a box at his side and pulled from it a half-empty bottle of whiskey. He poured some into small red clay cups and handed them to his guests. Kokolo and Shandu declined, but out of the corner of his mouth Shandu told Katherine and O'Brien to accept.

O'Brien downed his in one gulp and smacked his lips loudly. "My God, that Wohlman travels in style!" he said.

The chief nodded his head, still smiling.

"He probably stole it," Katherine said. She took a small sip and had to restrain herself from coughing.

"Well, let's find out where Wohlman is," she said to Shandu.

"One must not hurry these matters," he said. "We will find out what we need in time."

The chief poured another cup for O'Brien, less enthusiastically this time, and offered more to Katherine. Taking another small sip, she declined, already feeling slightly light-headed.

"I'm curious," O'Brien said to Shandu. "I thought each village had its own witch doctor. How is it that the local fellow didn't challenge Kokolo?"

"I asked Kokolo that," Shandu said. "The magician here was killed by Wohlman. He shot him on his second day here. The man tried to warn the chief against him."

"How could Wohlman get away with this?" Katherine said. "I mean, the chief does have warriors. Surely they could have put up a fight."

"This is a small clan," Shandu explained. "They have been beaten many times in battle and broken apart. This man is a small chief with power only over this area; he is not a king. They have no stomach left for battle. What we did here today with threat, Wohlman did with deeds. At the same time, he gave the chief liquor and other rewards."

Kokolo, who had been making small talk with the chief, now began to question him seriously. The others stopped their conversation and watched silently. After about ten minutes, Kokolo told Shandu the essence of what he had learned.

"Wohlman has gone north," Shandu said. "He took with him the two white men who came here first and the third who came later. They also took six warriors with them. The chief does not know where they went, but estimates that it is within two days' journey. They would not say what they were doing, but they asked him questions about a shining yellow metal. Some days ago, they became interested in a man, one of the villagers, who wore a necklace made of rocks around his neck. After talking to this man, they took him with them for a couple of days. When they came back, the man was not with them. They said he had been killed by a lion. The white men were excited and talked much among themselves. They began to make preparations to leave the village. Then the other white man arrived. There was much shouting between Wohlman and the others, and then they all rode off."

"What was the rock that they were interested in?" Katherine asked.

"He does not know. He has never looked at it. He thought they were just rocks."

"It could have been gold," O'Brien said excitedly. "A nugget, a rock with a vein running through it. It must have been important for Wohlman to rush off like that, and then kill the man who knew where it came from."

"North," Katherine said glumly. "That covers a lot of territory."

"We shall follow their trail," Shandu said confidently.

"I assume that nobody else in the village has any idea where they could have gone?" Katherine said.

"The chief was curious and questioned his people. They did not know. The wife of the man with the necklace said only that he found the stones somewhere in the north."

"We should waste no time," Katherine said. "We should leave now while the trail is warm."

"We should wait here tonight and leave in the morning, I think," Shandu said. "The horses have traveled hard. If they must travel hard again they should rest and eat. You too." He hesitated at a fresh thought. "Perhaps it would be better still if I travel alone on the trail. We spoke earlier of an ambush. Wohlman must know we will follow. If I go by myself, I will not be seen. It will be easy for him to see all of us together."

"And easy for him to kill you alone," Katherine said. "Now we must go together. O'Brien and I have guns. In an ambush we can fight. You and your *asse-gai* will be helpless against their guns."

"He will have to find me to shoot me," Shandu said.

"No. We go together," Katherine said.

"We go together," Shandu said, surprising them with his acquiescence. Apparently he had no wish to continue the argument.

The chief's eyes were growing red from the whiskey. He spoke to Kokolo.

"He suggests that we go and rest now," Shandu said. "In the evening there will be a celebration for us. He has given us the big hut where Kokolo was held."

"Can we trust him?" Katherine asked.

"Of course not," Shandu said. "We shall have to watch him at every moment. What he said about the men going north is true, and I do not think he will trouble us while we are here. But if Wohlman returns, then he will change. He is one of those who will always bow to the strongest. While we are strong, we are safe."

"What is the chief's name?" O'Brien asked.

"Nkupu."

O'Brien stood and bowed at the chief. "Nkupu, I thank you for your generous hospitality. Your whiskey was made by the gods themselves."

Shandu translated the compliment and Nkupu bobbed his head gratefully. When they left the hut he was pouring himself another cup of the drink.

"He'll be asleep in an hour," O'Brien said when they were outside.

"And you?" Katherine asked.

O'Brien beamed warmly. "Just enough to take off the chill," he said.

As they tethered the horses outside their quarters,

a young man came up to Shandu. They spoke together for a while and then he left.

"What did he want?" O'Brien asked.

Shandu smiled. "He is the oldest son of the chief.
He is not like his father. He wishes me to teach him
how to fight. I said that maybe I would at some later
time."

"A friend in the court," O'Brien murmured. "Just
what we might need."

They entered the large hut, this time examining it
at their leisure. It was sparsely furnished, with just a
few cattle skins for a bed, a long wooden table, and
some foot-high benches; but it was cool and clean. On
one long bench beside the wall was a collection of
clay pots, some large enough for cooking, and smaller
bowls for serving. There were also some straw baskets on the floor, attractively rendered by interweav-
ing dark and light straw. The floor was hard and
shining.

Katherine rubbed her toe on the surface. "What is
this made from?" she asked Shandu.

"It is clay and cow dung," he said.

"Oh."

"It is very good. Hard like a rock. You cannot put a
hole in it. In most villages, the women put a new
layer on it every week, to keep it clean," he said.
"Here they must get the clay from the river. Into the
clay they mix fresh cow dung and then spread it very
thin on the floor. It dries quickly and becomes very
hard."

"The pottery and baskets are made here too?" she
asked.

"Yes, that is also a job for the women. They tend
the fields and cook the meals."

"And the men?" she asked.

"The men in a village work hard," Shandu said.
"They build and mend the huts and that takes much
time. They care for the cattle and goats. They hunt
for meat. They make all the tools that are used."

"Ask Kokolo how he did that trick with the smoke," Katherine said.

"You will not get an answer," Shandu warned, but he asked the question.

Kokolo acted as if he had not heard. He stared down at the floor impassively, studying the hairline cracks as if they were a map of the universe. Shandu repeated the question.

The old man looked up and spoke to Katherine. Shandu shook his head at the words, but relayed them to her.

"He says that you cannot ask about his magic. 'If the people who live in the desert mountains have never seen the ocean, how can you explain it to them? So it is with magic that requires great understanding.' That is what he says."

"It was just a trick," Katherine protested.

Kokolo leaned forward and asked Shandu what she had said. Shandu translated and Kokolo answered at length, in a somber voice.

Shandu grunted and turned to her. "He wishes me to tell you exactly what he has said in his words," Shandu said. "It is this: 'I am Kokolo the Magician. When I trick, it is only for a joke. When I do magic, it is a serious business. It is my life. You may laugh at my tricks and you may even laugh at my magic, if you wish, but the first step on the path to wisdom is to be able to see true magic.' Those are the words he said."

They looked at Kokolo in silence. Even O'Brien was at a loss for a reply. Somehow the words had seemed so personal that they were all touched, although they could not have explained why.

Chapter Eleven

TWO YOUNG WOMEN brought them food late in the afternoon. The meal consisted of cereals that looked like husked millet and sorghum with a spicy vegetable sauce. The prettier of the two girls—tall, slim, and bare-breasted like all the village women—looked curiously at Shandu as she placed the food on the table.

He smiled at her and asked a question. After she answered he said something that made her giggle.

"What did you say to her?" Katherine said.

"I asked her name. It is Nandi. I told her she was as pretty as the most beautiful Zulu maidens."

Katherine had slept for two or three hours and felt more relaxed than she had in days. The pungent food was surprisingly good.

"Did you sleep?" she asked O'Brien.

"Like a baby," he said. "A little whiskey is the best potion invented."

She noticed that Kokolo was not in the room and asked where he had gone.

"He is with Nkupu, the chief. He is choosing the cattle he is owed," Shandu said.

Kokolo came into the hut then, humming and looking pleased with himself. He joked with Shandu and then sat down, helping himself to a bowl of food.

"He not only has his cattle, but he has chosen his maidens," Shandu said. "Two are young and pretty, to give him pleasure in his old age. One is ugly and hard-working, and the last is fat and ugly and old. It is she who will keep the others from mischief."

"Clever old buzzard," O'Brien said admiringly.

Kokolo nodded, a grin splitting his face. He had understood the tone, if not the words.

Katherine finished her food and then asked Shandu if it was all right for her to walk around the village alone.

"Yes," he said. "For now, we are welcome."

O'Brien looked as if he were about to offer to go with her, but she had stressed "alone" and he thought better of it.

A slight breeze blew outside, but it was warm and pleasant on her face. The village was alive with movement. In the square, some distance away, she could see a large group of men. Laughing children chased one another between the huts. A wailing infant was picked up and comforted by a passing woman. A string of women walked up from the river, balancing large clay pots of water on their heads. They advanced smoothly with straight backs, as graceful as dancers. She missed Colin suddenly. Where was he? How was he? Was he happy with the McPhersons? She strained her mind's eye to see him, to catch just one comforting glimpse, but the barriers of space would not lift for her.

What was she doing here? The flood of doubts assailed her again. It was no good to think this way, she told herself angrily. She had chosen her course and she would live with it. She tried to regain the serenity she had felt just moments earlier, but it was a slippery thing and difficult to grasp.

Katherine approached a group of three huts that formed a semicircle; she stopped there to watch the women. There were four of them, and the sweat ran down their bodies as they worked. Two of the women were sitting on the ground, rubbing the grains off ears of millet. The other two stood and ground the flour. The stone mortars were knee-high and the pestles, made from some hard but light wood, were almost as tall as the women themselves. They were pounding their mortars in perfect rhythm with each other, *gu-gu-gu-gu*.

She became aware that someone was standing beside her and turned to see the girl who had brought their food. She smiled shyly at Katherine and looked away. She was truly beautiful, Katherine thought. Her body was straight and slim and her breasts were small and pointed. She had fine features and brown eyes that seemed to sparkle from some interior source of light. Katherine tried to remember the girl's name.

"Nandi," she said, pointing to her. The girl smiled and put her hand over her mouth.

Katherine pointed to herself and said her name.

"Katrin," the girl said.

They smiled at each other, and then Nandi slowly put out her hand and touched Katherine's hair. Fascinated, she looked at it more closely, exclaiming in words that Katherine could not understand. Soon each of the women there had to feel it and look at it with cooing noises.

Nandi and the other women began a heated conversation, the subject of which, Katherine gathered, was her hair. It ended finally when Nandi smiled and beckoned to Katherine to follow her.

They walked through the village square and Katherine saw that the crowd of men she had noticed earlier were engaged in some kind of game. She stopped briefly to watch and attracted curious stares from the men, but generally they were more interested in the outcome of their game.

There were two rows of men facing each other. In front of each line were two rows of holes in the ground, sixteen in each row. These holes contained the stones of some kind of fruit and the men moved one stone at a time into a different hole. The object seemed to be to capture and confiscate the stones of the opponents.

"*Tshuba*," the girl said, pointing at the game. "*Tshuba*."

It was not a simple game and apparently open to some interpretation, for the men argued loudly among themselves with the vocal and enthusiastic help of a dozen or more spectators. Katherine tried to follow the rules but found the game too complicated.

Nandi pulled her by the hand and urged her to come with her. Soon they were past the village and walking down the hill. Water-carrying women walked in the opposite direction, toward the village, and greeted them politely as they passed, although all stared openly at Katherine. Small boys, no more than seven or eight years old, drove herds of cattle from the green grass below to the safety of the village *kraals* for the night.

Soon they reached the river, a broad body of water joined by streams such as they had seen in the mountains. They walked through slender rushes tipped by rods of flowery white seeds and came to a bend in the river where the water was slow. Nandi pointed to the water and said something. Katherine looked at her in puzzlement, not knowing what she meant. Nandi pointed at her and then at the water again. Still Katherine was baffled. Did she want her to drink it, wash in it?

Nandi must have decided that example was the best instructor. Unabashedly she dropped her leather skirt and walked to the water's edge. She beckoned for Katherine to follow.

Katherine looked around. The opposite bank was deserted, and the bend protected them from observation by anyone on this side. To soak her entire body in water was a delightful thought. She hesitated no longer but quickly took off her clothes and joined Nandi.

The girl looked with amazement at her fair pubic hair and pointed to her own with a giggle, finding the difference a source of amusement. She walked a few steps farther into the water and then, scooping mud from the bed, began to rub it over her body like soap. Katherine followed suit, assuming that Nandi knew what she was doing.

The clay was as soft as flannel. It clung to her body and massaged her, drawing all roughness and discomfort from her skin like a medicinal sponge. She rubbed it over every pore of her body and then dunked herself in the water to wash it off. When Nandi pointed at her hair, Katherine balked, but the girl would have none of it. She scooped up a handful of clay and rubbed in on Katherine's head until her scalp tingled.

When she was finally clean, Katherine stood at the lapping edge of the water, unwilling to dress again. The water dripped from her body and the breeze felt cool on her skin. The late-afternoon shadows were beginning to lengthen now, sapping the strength of the once-powerful sun. Regretfully, she dressed.

Nandi was ready to return to the village, but Katherine sat on a log facing the river and, using grass to demonstrate the process, asked the girl to braid her hair. Nandi got the idea quickly and soon finished the task.

They walked back the way they had come. Smoke from many fires rose into the air above the village. Cattle lowed dissonantly, but somehow the sound blended with the song of a group of women walking behind them. It was a living painting, and so painfully beautiful that, suddenly, Katherine felt like crying.

When it was dark the entire village assembled in

the square for the celebration. Men, women, children, grandmothers who could hardly walk, all sat in a semicircle, the focal point of which was the chief, his family, and the honored guests whom he publicly welcomed with a flowery speech.

One of his wives handed Katherine and the others cups filled with a white liquid. It had a strong odor and Katherine asked Shandu what it was.

"It is something like ale," he said. "Drink sparingly, for it is strong."

She took a sip, and though it had a distinctive taste she had not encountered before, it was not unpleasant. She asked Shandu how it was made, and he willingly explained, saying that he was an expert on the subject.

Apparently it took nine days to brew. The first five were devoted to preparation of the yeast. A grain, either mealies, millet, or sorghum, was used, depending upon what was available. The grain was first softened in water for a day. The next day the water was poured out and the grain covered with leaves to keep it moist. On the sixth day, after the germs had incubated, the yeast was dried and ground. A large amount of grain was then soaked in water and pounded into whole flour. The next day the women who did the brewing boiled many pots of water. Into each they threw flour and a handful of yeast. After it cooled down, they added a little more yeast. At dawn on the eighth day, the pots were all put to boil until the afternoon, when the beer was placed into jars to cool. The remaining yeast was then added. The beer fermented during the night and was strained in the morning.

"It keeps its flavor for only two days, and then it loses its strength and taste," Shandu said. He drained his bowl with a satisfied smack of his lips. "This is good," he added.

Looking around, Katherine saw that the animated

crowd was drinking as fast as Shandu, if not faster. She took another sip.

"Do you like it?" she asked O'Brien.

He was nursing his drink. "Well, it isn't whiskey, but I suppose it's passable."

The square was a pandemonium of noise and laughter by this time. "What are they all doing?" Katherine asked Shandu.

"Some are telling stories of ancient times, others are playing the riddle game, yet others are boasting of their exploits. It is just talk."

Shandu himself was growing louder and more enthusiastic as he talked, his gestures more extravagant by the minute. Perhaps, Katherine thought, it had something to do with the fact that Nkupu's wife filled his beer bowl as fast as he could drain it.

He and Kokolo began to talk together, and then Shandu turned to Katherine and O'Brien and said, "Kokolo says among his people the young men love to smoke the hemp. Their parents cure them by taking the soot from the pipe and secretly mixing it in their food three times. From then on, they hate the hemp."

Katherine found her bowl miraculously filled again and drank some more. "What do you think of these people, O'Brien?" she slurred slightly, leaning earnestly toward him. "Do you think the savage is noble?"

O'Brien looked at her in surprise, then smiled in amusement. "The beer is going to your head, Katie. But I will answer your questions. I am no blind admirer, but they have skills that we Europeans have long forgotten. And you'll find that the native has a remarkable memory. Tell him something and he will repeat it back to you word for word a year later. They are a very honorable people. Relatives, for instance, are responsible for the debts of their own kin. And if a man lends another man a weapon or tool, and the borrower uses it in some criminal way, the fault is equally the lender's. When there are divorces, the relatives must return the *lobolo* money back to the husband. The children then go with the mother."

"I think I have heard of that, *lobolo*. Is that where they pay for the bride?" Katherine asked.

"Yes. They give cattle, or when or where cattle are in very short supply, they give hoes, which are very useful implements."

"But it makes a woman equivalent to a cow!" Katherine protested.

"I suppose that's one way of looking at it," O'Brien said with a grin. "But it is also fair. The wife's family is losing a valuable worker, they should be compensated."

"Shandu told you all this, I suppose," Katherine said.

"Mmm, and a lot more. He told me about some of their sexual customs—the rites of purification and matters like that. Nothing that would interest you, of course."

"Of course," Katherine said. She took another sip of her beer.

"Ah, the dancers will begin now," Shandu said. "Now you will hear music."

The orchestra of five men took its place in the square, and the dancers lined up in a semicircle around them, men in front, women in a second line behind them. The orchestra consisted of an enormous drum that emitted a deep bass sound, four smaller high-pitched drums, and two instruments that looked like xylophones.

"What are those?" Katherine asked.

"That is the *timbila*," Shandu said. "There are ten keys made from very hard wood. They are tied with leather on *sala* shells. The Ba-Chopi people are the best with the *timbila*. We will see how good these people are."

The music began with the sound of the big drum, a

steady rhythm that set the beat for the lines of dancers, which began to shuffle back and forth like two enormous, undulating serpents. The smaller drums darted in like attackers with a sharper, faster improvisation between the beats of the bass. The *timbila* players, each using two sticks, began to chime in with the melody, and the dancers sang in complex harmonies. It sounded strange to Katherine, but it was stirring and powerful, a thing of the blood, not of the brain. The dancers gradually increased their pace until they stomped their feet as if to shake the earth and twirled in frenzied circles. Solo dancers emerged from the lines, and the others clapped their hands around them.

There was obvious significance to the dance. She could tell by the changing expressions on the dancers' faces that this was drama with meaning, but of course it was not clear to her. Shandu and Kokolo were swaying back and forth, clapping their hands in time to the music. She leaned over and asked what the meaning of the dance was.

"It is a story from the history of the tribe," Shandu said. "They sing of the time a powerful enemy came and they fled to the hills. There they regrouped and came back down to defeat the enemy."

And now she could see it was war, for the men mimicked a battle charge, wearing ferocious expressions and pretending to throw *assegais*, as the women urged them on. The battle was won, and then came the victory celebration, where the lines between men and women dissolved and the square became a mass of entangled moving bodies.

The dance ended and another began, and so it went for hours. The copious flow of beer staved off any exhaustion the dancers felt; if anything, the dancing grew more impassioned as the night progressed. Shandu danced, the chief danced, even Kokolo hopped around imitating some animal.

"Amazing, isn't it?" O'Brien said. He drained the beer from his bowl. "I think I am slightly intoxicated, madam."

"I'm slightly light-headed as well," Katherine admitted, slurring the words a bit. They had not drunk much compared to the others, but apparently not much was needed; the beer was strong, as Shandu had warned. "Look at Shandu," she said. He was sitting beside the girl Nandi, and they were both laughing at something he had said. "Are they not beautiful together?"

"Alcohol agrees with you," O'Brien said softly. "Your eyes are sparkling like flames. You would not speak of other beauty if you could see yourself."

"Why, thank you, sir," she said, her smile radiant and her guard lowered by the noise and the excitement as well as the alcohol. "But I have seen much beauty since leaving Potchefstroom. It is so different here. The beauty in England is the beauty of man's creation. Here, there seems to be no order to the beauty until you realize there is a natural order underlying everything."

"America is like that," O'Brien said. "You leave the cities of the East and ride west and you begin to see the immensity of nature, but it is a different nature; it doesn't seem as luxuriant and fertile as nature is here."

"Look at these people, how close they are to their environment," she said. "I think I envy it."

"Who's talking about the noble savage now?" O'Brien said, laughing.

Shandu returned to sit beside them. He still held a bowl in his hands and grinned affably.

"You will be ready to ride in the morning?" Katherine asked dubiously.

"When the sun rises, I shall arise, a new man, with the courage of a lion, the strength of a water buffalo, the speed of an antelope," he boasted.

"You forgot the eyes of a hawk," O'Brien said. He looked more closely at Shandu. "Right now they look like the embers of a dying fire."

"By morning they will once again be the eyes of an eagle," Shandu said pontifically. "While you still snore and dream, I shall be there to awaken you."

Nkupu shouted something to Shandu. "He is asking if you like his beer and enjoy the dancing?" he said.

"Tell him his beer is the nectar of the gods, his men are strong, his women beautiful, and his dancing is the best I have ever seen," O'Brien said grandiosely.

"Huh," Shandu grunted, but he relayed the message and the chief grinned and bobbed his head.

"Where is Kokolo?" Katherine asked.

"He is an old man. I think he has gone to sleep," Shandu said. "Now I too must go."

He rose and stood unsteadily, looking around the crowd.

"Are you going to sleep?" Katherine asked.

"No," he said, and walked away.

Katherine tried to find the girl Nandi, but she had gone. A minute later, Shandu walked off into the darkness. She smiled to herself, guessing his destination.

"Let's take a walk and clear our heads," O'Brien suggested.

They walked from the square on the path toward the river. The moon was out now and cast an ivory glow over the land around them. O'Brien hummed softly to himself as he walked beside Katherine.

"Are you nervous about tomorrow?" he asked.

The question was a surprise to her, more so because she realized suddenly that she wasn't. "No, not at all," she said. "I was far more nervous yesterday. Perhaps I am learning not to try to foresee the future. I don't know if we will see Wohlman tomorrow

or the next day. It could be a week. When we do, we'll
be ready."

"It might be hard to find their trail now," he said.

"I have faith in Shandu. After all, he followed
them here where Pretorius failed."

The river was like a thin sheet of silver moving in
the wind, a flow of shifting shadow and light, a master of disguise, stable below the changing surface.
Here was a true symbol of nature, Katherine
thought. For hundreds, perhaps thousands of miles it
would be a source of life for the land around it. Animals of every variety would come to its banks; birds,
insects, the endless spawn of African life would
drink its vital fluid. Men too would drink from it,
drawing its precious waters and carrying them up
hills to villages like this one. Lives would change,
generations would come and go, but the river would
flow on, changing its course but never its purpose.

Katherine folded her arms and leaned against the
warped trunk of a willow tree, viewing the world
through a veil of drooping branches.

"I was thinking of Colin today. I miss him terribly," she said.

"Well, you left him in good hands," O'Brien said.

"Oh, it's not that. I am sure he is doing well. It's
just... I don't know."

"What?" he prompted.

"I imagine it is like losing a leg. It is something you
take for granted. It is only when you lose it that you
realize how precious it was. A family is like that."

"Well, you'll be seeing your son soon. It won't be
long before this is over."

"I wonder," she said. "Who could have predicted
this? By now Alan and I would have found our land.
We would be building our home now, perhaps even
planting the seeds we brought from Cape Town. The
children... the children would..."

"What is this melancholy tone I hear in the Iron
Lady," O'Brien said, attempting to lighten the mood.

"They are just thoughts, and they will pass," she said. She turned to look at him, her face dappled by shadow. "Is that how you think of me? The Iron Lady?"

"Iron encased in a sheath of silk."

Katherine giggled, an uncharacteristic sound.

O'Brien moved closer. "Katherine, whatever I call you, you must know that I love you."

She faced O'Brien uncertainly. She had never seen him look more serious. "I thought we agreed to let this rest until our business was over?" She glanced away at the moving river.

He put two fingers under her chin and moved her head back to face him. "I've tried, Katie. Believe me, I've tried. Do you have any idea how difficult it has been, beside you like this, day after day, feeling the way I do?"

She felt vulnerable to his words. Perhaps it was the alcohol, or it could have been the beauty and mystery of the setting. "I would prefer that we keep to the agreement," she said, mustering up all her reserves of self-control in an attempt to maintain the distance she had put between them.

He moved his hand to caress her cheek. "I am not talking about agreements, or rules and regulations. I am talking about feelings, of love, of human emotion," he said, his voice soft. "I'm offering my love to you, as I have never offered it to anyone before."

"Jim . . ." she began, but she did not know what she was going to say next and hesitated.

He moved closer, his voice more persuasive. "Katie, listen to me. I've traveled the world to find a woman like you. Men might say that, but in my case it's true. It's obvious that we're meant for each other. Why else would we be together like this in the middle of an unexplored continent? An accident? I don't think so. Fate has brought us together. It was meant to be. Deny that if you can."

"How can you tell that because we have been brought together it is for love? How can you be so—"

"Because I see you. I look at you and I love you." He cupped her face in his hands. "Katie, when I saw you outside of town, sitting on that horse, I wanted to run over and hold you in my arms. I wanted to kiss your lips from the first moment I saw you."

He bent his head and put his lips on hers. She tried to pull her head back, but his hands held her and he kissed her, softly at first, but then more hungrily. She stopped resisting, determined to remain passive, but his mouth was like a flame. How she yearned for the feel of a man's body. It had been so long, so lonely. How wonderful it would be to press her hips against his and feel his burgeoning passion, to fall to the soft ground here beneath the moon and satisfy each other's deepest desire. What harm would there be in it?

For a moment she returned his kiss, opening her mouth beneath his, arching her body forward, but then she stopped and, summoning all her strength, pulled her head back.

"Stop!" she cried. "Stop this now."

He dropped his arms and looked at her, a hurt expression on his face. "In God's name, Katie," he said in a shaky voice. "In God's name, why? I felt your kiss. I know you want me. Why can't we admit this thing to ourselves. How long can you wear your grief like a badge of courage?"

She stepped away. "This has nothing to do with my grief. This has only to do with my mission and how I feel about you."

"How do you feel about me?" he asked, stepping in and taking her arm. "Tell me, then, how you feel about me. For a moment there I thought I knew how you feel about me. Tell me."

Katherine felt tired, confused. What was she doing out here in the veldt arguing with James O'Brien?

"Nothing has changed," she said. "Nothing will change until I've balanced accounts with Wohlman. You're a cherished friend, Jim, and I have no wish to hurt you with assurances of love when I do not even know my own mind."

O'Brien dropped his head in dejection. "All right, Katie. You win again. I have no other choice, do I? Why in God's name didn't I fall in love with a nice normal woman who knows her place and speaks when spoken to?"

Katherine leaned back against the tree, wearied by her empty victory.

"If you were any other way, I wouldn't love you," O'Brien said sadly. "You are really something, Katie. Really something."

She reached out and took his hand. "Friends?" she asked. "Still friends?"

"Of course," he said. "You're a friend still, and I love you. Nothing you say can alter that fact. It's something you're going to have to live with, agreement or no agreement."

Katherine nodded and squeezed his hand comfortingly. "I'm honored by it."

"We had best be going back now," O'Brien said.

She released his hand and they walked slowly back up the hill. The drums were still pounding out their rhythm, and the voices, though fewer now, still sang the ancient songs.

They bypassed the square and cut directly across to their hut. Shandu met them at the door. He took O'Brien by the arm and pulled him inside.

"Where have you been?" he asked. "I have been looking for you both."

"We went for a walk down—"

Katherine interrupted O'Brien's explanation. "What's the matter, Shandu? Has something happened?"

Shandu looked grim. "It will happen. Come, we must talk quickly."

He motioned them farther into the hut. Looking around, Katherine saw that all their belongings were packed.

"Tonight, while we sleep, Nkupu plans to murder us," Shandu said tersely. "Six warriors will creep in here while we sleep and stab us to death."

"My God! How did you find this out?" said Katherine.

"Nkupu's son. He came and told me of his father's plan."

Katherine remembered the young man who had asked Shandu to teach him how to fight. "Why does Nkupu want to do this? I thought we had reached an understanding," she said.

"He has the cunning of a snake, that one. And a venom more poisonous. You remember that the white men took some warriors from here with them when they left. Today one of the men came back. He was sent by the men with a message for Nkupu. The message asked if we had arrived here yet. If so, Nkupu was directed to send back your head with the messenger."

"My head? Literally, my head?" Katherine asked.

"He wished for proof of your death," Shandu said. "What better proof than your head?"

"What happened to Nkupu's fear of us?" O'Brien asked. "The fear of Kokolo's magic, of Zulu *impis*, of the Queen's soldiers? What brought about this change in Nkupu?"

"I do not know if there has been any change," Shandu said. "Maybe all along he planned to kill us. But his son says his father is afraid of Wohlman. More afraid than he is of us. Also, what have we offered him? Wohlman has given him liquor. He has even promised to give him guns later. All we have done is take his cattle and his women, thanks to Kokolo."

"Where is Kokolo?" Katherine asked, noticing for

the first time that he was absent. "Does he know about this?"

"Yes. He told me to pack and he would soon be back. He has gone and become a 'man of the night,' to cast a spell over Nkupu that will bring about his death."

"What's he wasting his time with that for? We have to get out of here," O'Brien said.

"He's also seeing where the guards are posted," Shandu said.

"We saw no guards as we came up from the river," Katherine said.

"Did you look for guards?" Shandu asked.

Katherine shook her head foolishly. Innocents! They had wandered as blithely as children, looking at nothing but the glowing moon.

"What are we going to do?" she asked.

"When Kokolo comes back, we will know better."

"Will the boy help us further? Nkupu's son?" O'Brien asked.

"If it is possible. He will not go into open conflict with his father. That would mean his life. But if there is anything else he can do, he is willing."

"Why is he helping us? He's betraying his own father," Katherine said.

"His hate for Wohlman is greater even than his father's fear," Shandu said. "He says that his father's mind is mixed up by the white man's liquor. He says he is thinking of the village. The white men will destroy the old ways here. He knows that and he also knows that Wohlman is an evil man. He is not stupid like his father, this one."

"When is this attack coming?" Katherine asked.

"He does not know. He heard only that it would be when we slept. I think it will be one or two hours from now, when all is still in the village."

"We can fight our way out if we have to," O'Brien said belligerently. "We have horses and guns, and that should make us a match for six men with *assegais*."

"I agree," Katherine said. "But I have no wish to kill these people. Their only sin lies in the fact that Wohlman has come into contact with them. If they attack us, it will only be because their chief has ordered it."

"This isn't the time to be squeamish," O'Brien said harshly. "Our lives are at stake."

"I like these people," Katherine said quietly.

"The men know that if they attack us some of them will die," Shandu said. "That is the way of these matters."

"I suppose so," Katherine said listlessly. It seemed to her that matters had gotten out of hand. What had happened to her original plan simply to pursue Wohlman and kill him? She had no wish to embroil half the continent of Africa in her quest. Was it all falling apart? Wohlman always managed to be a step ahead of her. Was she no match for him?

"No!" she exclaimed aloud, striking her fist into her palm.

Shandu and O'Brien looked at her in surprise.

"No, what?" O'Brien asked.

"Are we all packed?" she asked Shandu.

"Everything is in the saddlebags." He pointed to the saddles resting against a wall. "The difficulty is getting the saddles onto the horses without being seen," he added.

"I assume the front is being watched?"

Shandu nodded. "There is one man between those huts over there and another on the other side." He pointed in the direction he was speaking of.

"Nothing in the back?" she asked.

"No. I went outside and looked carefully. The horses are tied in the grass behind the hut. But they watch the front carefully and that is the only way out," Shandu said.

"It might be a choice of the saddles or the horses," O'Brien said. "We could leave them and make a run for it. Bareback."

Shandu strode to one side of the door and looked out. "It does not matter what we decide, but we must hurry. Kokolo must come soon."

"We are going to leave unseen through the back door," Katherine said.

Shandu looked at her as if she was mad.

"The back door?" O'Brien asked.

Katherine picked up Shandu's stabbing spear and walked to the back wall. Using all her strength, she stabbed it into the clay. A piece of the dry mud fell to the ground.

"We dig," she said.

Shandu's face brightened. "Yes," he said, "but it will not be easy."

"They pack the clay around a frame of saplings," O'Brien said. "If we're lucky, the saplings will not be too thick and not too close together."

"We'll cut them if we must," Katherine said. She looked around the room and saw a hoe leaning against the wall. "We can use that and the two *assegais*. And you have a sharp knife." She pointed to the sheath at O'Brien's waist.

"It is good, but we must work quietly," Shandu cautioned.

There was no further discussion. They each selected a utensil and began to hack at the wall. Their success or failure would depend entirely upon speed. The horses would have to be saddled and ready to go before their executioners arrived.

Katherine realized she was digging to save her head. She grimaced and redoubled her efforts.

Chapter Twelve

KOKOLO GLIDED THROUGH the hut like a shadow, his face decorated with inhuman streaks of yellow ocher. He looked as if he had risen from a hole in the earth.

They could see through the wall now. Most of the gouged clay was strewn over the floor. The main problem remaining was the wood, which had to be cut on the top and bottom to be removed. Sweat pouring from their faces, O'Brien and Shandu were sawing feverishly at it, the American with his knife and the Zulu with the sharp edge of his *assegai*.

Kokolo understood immediately what they were doing and began to drag the saddles nearer to the hole. His eyes were like black pits against the whitened foreground of his face.

"Where have you been?" Katherine asked. It had been almost an hour since they had arrived back at the hut, and she had begun to wonder if something had happened to the old man.

Shandu repeated the question over his shoulder as he worked, his tone exasperated. Kokolo crouched down and began to clear clay away from the work area. He talked while he worked, speaking in a somber voice.

Shandu stopped work only long enough to say to Katherine, "Ha! He has shown Nkupu with the finger." He began to pull at the post, but it had not been cut enough so he attacked it again with his *assegai*.

"Shandu, what does that mean?" Katherine asked in a strained voice.

"It means that Nkupu is a dead man," Shandu said. "Kokolo has bewitched him." He lifted the index finger of his right hand. "This is the finger that is used. If you wish to bewitch someone you must point this finger at them. That is what he has done. Now, we must go quickly. Kokolo says the warriors will be soon here."

He grasped the pole he was working on with both hands and pulled, his back muscles corded in powerful knots. The pole broke at the bottom. He rose to a crouching position and bent it up, rising as he pushed. It was a resilient piece of wood, but after two or three pushes, it splintered at the top.

O'Brien was still hacking away at the bottom of his pole. Shandu examined it briefly and then began to cut at the top with his *assegai*.

"You must go to the door and watch now," he said to Katherine. "But do not be seen."

Obediently she moved to the door and stood in the shadows to one side. She looked in the direction that Shandu had indicated. Nothing moved in the chalky light. The drums had stopped their pounding and the party-goers had retired. Tomorrow would be like any other day for these people, with work to be done in the fields and cattle to be driven to pastures of green grass elsewhere in the valley. There would, of course, be the bodies of four visitors to dispose of, but that would probably not upset the routine, she thought.

She fixed her eyes on one spot, trying to differentiate between shadow and substance. There! She saw the man Shandu had spotted. He leaned against the wall of a hut and he held his *assegai* with the blade in the air. She would not have seen him if he had not moved the spear from the shade into the glint of the moonlight. Now that she knew what to look for, she moved her glance to the other huts. There was the other man Shandu had spotted. He stood in the alley between two huts, and as she watched he was joined by two more men.

Katherine turned back into the room. "They are gathering out there now," she said. "It won't be long."

"We're almost through," O'Brien said. "Just a couple more minutes."

Shandu pulled at the remaining large piece of wood and snapped it. The crack was quite loud, and Katherine jumped nervously.

"Good work," O'Brien said. "Now stand aside."

He lifted the hoe and swung at the sides of the hole they had dug, chopping out more clods of clay and scooping them away. He stopped to wipe his forehead and Shandu took over, his back glistening in the dim light given off by the dying fire.

"Enough!" O'Brien said. "We should be able to squeeze through there."

They had tunneled through almost eighteen inches of wall. The hole was only two feet by two feet, with jagged pieces of wood sticking out from the walls, but it looked large enough to allow them through.

"I'll go first, and then you can pass the saddles through to me," O'Brien said.

He kneeled on all fours with his back facing the hole and slid back feet first. The splintered remnant of one of the larger stakes caught the top of his pants, but he dropped lower and continued through unimpeded, except for some of the smaller branches that scratched at him. He looked like a subterranean animal returning to its lair after popping its head up to spy out the land.

"Now the saddles," he whispered back through the hole. Shandu took the first saddle and tried to stuff it through the hole, but it would not fit.

"Turn it on its side and put through one end first," Katherine suggested.

Luckily, they were small Boer saddles, well tanned and fairly light. Shandu did as he was told and, with O'Brien pulling from the other side, the saddle slipped through. The other two saddles followed quickly, and then they heard O'Brien scurry away toward the horses.

"Now the two of you," Shandu said, gesturing at Katherine and Kokolo.

"Go, Kokolo," she said.

Smaller than O'Brien, he got through the hole easily.

"Now you," Shandu said.

Katherine backed into the hole and felt wood rip at her hips. The walls pressed against her like a vise. She was larger at the hips than either of the two men who had gone before her. She wriggled and a branch dug into her. There was nothing to do but push past it and grit her teeth. She turned her body slightly and got through with just a few minor scratches.

Still on her knees, she looked back and saw O'Brien hastily saddling the horses. He was working on the second one already. She stuck her head back in the hole.

"Shandu," she whispered.

His face appeared at the other end.

"That was too tight," she said. "You're bigger than I am. I don't think you'll get through."

Shandu grimaced ruefully. "I saw. I do not think so either."

"What are you going to do?" she whispered urgently.

"I looked and saw there are nine men out there now. They will come very soon."

"Nine!" she exclaimed. "I thought there would be six."

"The chosen six might have asked for more. Go quickly and help saddle the horses. Come back and tell me when they are done. I shall have to run out the front."

It meant that they would be seen, but no alternative presented itself to Katherine. She crouched down and ran to O'Brien. She picked up the third saddle and lowered it onto the horse's back. Strapping it furiously, she explained the situation to the American.

"You and Kokolo are the smallest. Double up on my horse," he said. He finished the saddle he was working on and moved over to help her.

He paused to point at his horse. "Kokolo! Up!" he said.

The old man hesitated, unaware of the situation.

"Up!" O'Brien hissed.

Kokolo caught the idea and clambered nimbly onto the horse's back. "I'll be done in a second," O'Brien said to Katherine. "Go and get Shandu. Go! Go!"

She ran back to the hut and whispered through the hole. Shandu looked back at her. "We're ready," she said. He nodded and stood and she could see only his knees.

She remained crouching at the hole and saw him walk toward the door, an *assegai* in each hand. As she watched, a man appeared in the doorway. Shandu reacted quickly, swinging the handle of his stabbing spear and clipping the man on the side of the head. There was a shout.

Without thinking Katherine got up and ran around to the front of the hut. Shandu stood just outside the door, circled warily by two warriors. Another group of six or more were running from the hut across the clearing.

Katherine lifted her revolver and fired it into the air. "Come, Shandu! Run!" she screamed.

Everyone stopped at the sound of the shot except Shandu. The men around him and the ones running in their direction halted in their tracks.

Katherine turned and ran. A moment later she heard Shandu behind her, and then he drew alongside her. Kokolo and O'Brien were already mounted. Shandu vaulted into the saddle of his horse, and

Katherine clambered up behind Kokolo. O'Brien had his revolver in his hand, and she turned to see his shot kick up dust in front of the first man who came around the hut. The man ducked back with a yell.

Katherine reached in front of Kokolo and grasped the reins. She realized he should have been riding behind her, but there was no time for a change now. She bumped him forward with her chest and flicked the reins hard.

"Yeeup!" she yelled and swung the horse around.

They galloped for the hills.

They easily outdistanced their pursuers but did not slow their pace until they came to a coppice of trees in the foothills. There, they dismounted and looked at one another in a combination of relief and triumph. Shandu was exhilarated, O'Brien and Katherine were joyous but more sober, and Kokolo was terrified. He spoke to Shandu immediately after his feet touched the ground, his words sputtering out like a waterfall.

Shandu laughed. "He said he would like to poison that horse, but death is too good for such an animal. He knows now why he has never wanted to ride on the back of a horse. His body aches, his eyes are jumbled in their sockets, and his tongue sticks to the roof of his mouth."

Katherine patted the horse gratefully on the neck. "Tell him the horse saved his life," she said.

"What now?" O'Brien asked.

"Now we should sleep," Shandu said.

Katherine and O'Brien were surprised. "Aren't we still too close to the village?" she asked.

"They'll catch up with us," O'Brien said.

"They will not follow us in the darkness. Look." He pointed at the moon suspended just above the horizon. "Soon there will be no light. They will not have the stomach to follow us in the dark. They know we have guns. They will need the rest of the night to get the courage."

"Well, if you say so . . ." Katherine said dubiously.

Shandu was already untying his blanket. "We must not light a fire, but we must sleep. At daylight they will follow, and we have much riding to do to lose them."

"How are we going to pick up Wohlman's tracks?" she asked. They would be on the run themselves now, zigzagging through the country with warriors at their heels. Ironically, they would be both pursuers and pursued.

"I know the direction Wohlman went," Shandu said. "I spoke to the chief's son." He pointed in a northerly direction. "They went through the end of the valley there; that is all he was able to tell me. But we will lose these men in the mountains tomorrow and then cut across the ridge to the end of the valley. We will find the trail on the other side of those hills."

They took their blankets down and spread them on the ground. Katherine sat with her elbows on her knees, resting her head in her hands. She knew that rest was vital, but she was too excited to sleep. She was gratified that she had not lost her head at the hut and that she had reacted fast enough to save Shandu's life. It was a different feeling from the time in the camp with Wohlman, where she had felt as helpless as a mouse in a trap.

Shandu had been having similar thoughts. "It was good to have you by my side," he said to her. "I was not wrong about you."

"What do you mean?"

"You are a fighter and you have the heart of a lion. A good warrior to fight with." He grinned. "I think I will call you Lionheart from now on. You have earned it. Is that not a good name for her?" he said to O'Brien.

"Yes, that's good," O'Brien replied, then added: "Or Pighead. That would be suitable too."

"Pighead?" Shandu asked with a frown at the mention of that uncomplimentary animal.

"That means someone who is very stubborn," Katherine explained. "Mr. O'Brien thinks that I am pigheaded—obstinate and stubborn."

"True," Shandu said. "But to stay unmoving is to have the heart of a lion. That is why Lionheart is a good name for you."

He turned to Kokolo and told him his decision. The old man nodded sagely.

"Ask Kokolo what is going to happen to Chief Nkupu," Katherine said. "What does it mean to point the finger? I mean, how does it happen?"

"Kokolo says that the chief will die soon," Shandu said after consulting with him. "He has betrayed Kokolo twice, and he cannot let that go unpunished. He does not like to use his powers in this way, but if he does not he will be laughed at by all of Africa."

"How is he going to die?"

"Kokolo says he has let go his power, and it will sweep the chief away to join his ancestors."

"Come on," O'Brien said, joining in. "What exactly did he do to him that will cause him to die?"

Kokolo looked affronted at this persistent questioning, but Shandu finally persuaded him to reply.

Shandu laughed loudly before translating. He was highly amused. "Nkupu will die of alcohol," he said. "Kokolo went unseen into his hut and placed a poison called *tjulu* in a half-empty bottle of whiskey. The next drink Nkupu takes will be his last."

Katherine and O'Brien looked shocked. Poison seemed an alien, not to say criminal, way of dealing death to a man.

"It is one of the ways of the wizard," Shandu said, understanding their expressions. "It is a powder that comes from a bush with pretty flowers that is found in the forest near the sea. Kokolo's people anoint the points of the stakes in elephant pits with this poison.

It is very strong." He added as an afterthought, "Strong enough to kill an elephant—or a fat snake like Nkupu who deserves his death."

Katherine looked down at her feet. She looked up to see Kokolo staring hard at her. He spoke to Shandu, his voice flat, his eyes still on her.

"Kokolo says that you must not judge him," Shandu said. "Death is a simple fact, no matter how it comes. Nkupu is going to find a freedom in his death that he never had in life. He says, Lionheart, that you know little of death still."

Katherine nodded. It was true. She had no right to judge Kokolo. She had come to accept the fact that he was no ordinary man. Who was she to evaluate his actions?

Kokolo spoke again and Shandu sat up, his face interested. "Kokolo says that he will tell you some things about death and spirit if you wish to hear them," the Zulu said.

"Yes, of course," she said.

O'Brien leaned forward as well, attentive.

Kokolo closed his eyes and spoke through Shandu. "Two of the four men that you seek are dead," he said, and opened his eyes to see their reaction.

"What on earth does he mean by that?" Katherine asked, shaken. "He cannot say something like that and leave it there. Ask him to explain."

Kokolo began to talk to Shandu again, without waiting to hear what she had said. Again he looked at her while he spoke.

"One of the men lies dead in a *donga*, killed by the others," Shandu said. Haltingly, with some difficulty, as if dealing with concepts strange to him, he continued to translate the remainder of what Kokolo had said.

"Another of the men is also dead, although he does not appear to be. His body is uninhabited by a spirit, unlike most people. He is only a thing, not a person.

He has no will, no knowledge of good and evil. And yet, like all things without spirit, he is truly evil."

She thought immediately of Wohlman, but then she remembered the blank, lifeless eyes of Dieter and realized with horror that what Kokolo said was true in a sense.

Kokolo smiled at her, as if understanding her shock of recognition.

"I am talking of the spirit," he said through Shandu. "To be wise and free, one must know the manifestations and powers of the spirit. All that is of value in this life is of the spirit."

Kokolo nodded his head vigorously after he finished, to underscore his remarks.

"How does he know a man is dead in a *donga*?" O'Brien asked, unable to contain himself further. "How can he know that?"

"I have seen it," came the enigmatic reply.

O'Brien shrugged his shoulders. He got up and walked to his saddlebag.

"Do you understand all this?" she asked Shandu.

"I understand some, not all," he said, shaking his head ruefully. "He is like a muddy river after a storm, that one. I cannot see the bottom."

O'Brien came back with a book and pen and ink. He sat on his blanket and began to write.

"What are you doing?" Katherine said.

"Writing in my journal. It is time for me to catch up."

"How long have you kept a journal?"

"About five years. Ever since I left Boston. It helps me collect my thoughts. It is just a record of my experiences in this world of wonder."

Katherine woke just before sunrise. O'Brien was sitting up, his blanket around his shoulders. Kokolo was saddling one of the horses. Shandu and his horse were gone.

"Where is Shandu?" she asked. She felt bone tired, as if she had not slept at all.

"I don't know. I just woke up," O'Brien said.

She stood up, enclosing herself in her blanket.

It was a chilly morning.

"There he is," O'Brien said, pointing.

The horse was trotting down from a hill overlooking the valley from which they had just come. Shandu jumped lightly off the animal.

"They are coming after us now," he said. "I have been watching."

O'Brien got up quickly. "How many are there?"

"And where are they?" Katherine added.

"It is hard to tell how many. They are only now leaving the village and too far away to see clearly. Maybe ten, maybe twelve. I think we must go now."

They mounted quickly and rode on up the mountain, soon leaving the open, wooded areas and entering a world of tall trees and thick undergrowth where every plant fought the other for air and light.

It was slow progress. They followed a wide and fairly well-used hunter's path, but at times they had to dismount to avoid overhanging branches and twisted vines.

"We're leaving a trail as plain as an elephant, you know," O'Brien said to Shandu, his voice doubtful.

"We have little choice now," Shandu said. "There are only two ways to do this. We can lose them when we come to a river by going back down in the water, or we will come to a place where we can stand and fight them."

"That is what I was thinking," O'Brien said. "An ambush."

They pressed on. It was easier for Kokolo to trot behind than to ride with Katherine, and he made himself useful while doing this by occasionally dragging leaves across their tracks. It was not enough to lose their followers, obviously, but they hoped that it would confuse them and slow them down slightly.

The forest they were passing through was not, strictly speaking, jungle. There was space to move between trees, and there were clearings at times, but the dense, humid undergrowth and rotting tree trunks in their path made the going difficult. Insects rose like clouds from the mouldy leaves at their feet, and as the sun rose higher the heat added to their discomfort. The only consolation lay in the indisputable fact that their followers were also having a difficult time of it, and there was still no indication that they were catching up.

At about eleven o'clock they stopped in a clearing to rest the animals. O'Brien asked how their food supply was holding out. They had not eaten since the day before.

"It is not good," Katherine said, examining her saddlebag. "All I have left is some *biltong*. Even my water bottle is empty. I forgot to fill it before we left."

"I think I have some water left in one of my bottles," O'Brien said. He shook each of the three bottles strapped to his saddle and took one off. "It's a couple of days old, but stale water is better than none."

They sipped frugally at the water, and Katherine handed them each a strip of the dried meat.

"We need to find water and food soon," O'Brien said.

"There must be a stream near to us," Shandu said. "As for food, there is food in the forest if we look for it."

"I'm worried about the time we're losing," Katherine said. "Wohlman could be hundreds of miles away by now."

"I don't think so," O'Brien said. "This place he's found is not more than two days' ride from the village, remember. I doubt that he'll be leaving it. If he's found gold there he'll be mining it, not moving on."

"It's just that we seem to be moving away from him instead of toward him," Katherine said. The exhilaration of the previous night had worn off. More than anything now she wanted to sleep.

"We will turn and ride north along the side of the mountain," Shandu said. "By now the men behind us will be even more tired than we are. Soon we should come to a place where we can hide our trail."

"Well, let's get going," O'Brien said, standing up stiffly. "The sooner we lose them, the better."

They had gone for about a mile when they heard the water. The stream rushed through a cut in the mountain. It was narrow but moving fast to the valley below. To reach it they rode down a steep hill along a winding game path. When they came to the stream they kneeled beside it and drank their fill of the clear water.

"Fill the bottles. We must hurry now," Shandu said.

Katherine would have liked to rest at the stream, but Shandu was right. If they were going to give their pursuers the slip, they would have to do it before the men appeared on the crest they had just descended. Quickly she filled her bottle and one of O'Brien's.

"You must go down the stream in the water," Shandu told them. "Stay in the water until I catch up with you."

"What are you going to do?" Katherine asked.

"I am going to ride up the water for a little," he said. "When they reach this place, the men will divide to see where our tracks leave the river. Some will go up and some down. I will go up and leave tracks on the side so it looks as if we have left there. That will give us time. I will not go too far. The men who travel up will call those who have gone down and they will all come to the spot where I left the water. It will give us time to hide our tracks lower down."

"But they'll see that only one horse has left the stream," O'Brien protested.

"Do not worry. I will lead the horse back and forth so that it looks like many. Now go quickly," Shandu said.

Kokolo mounted up behind Katherine, and they splashed downstream while Shandu went in the opposite direction. The horses balked at the cold water, and Katherine fought to keep her animal's nose straight ahead. O'Brien's horse did not seem to mind as much; during his prospecting trips he had trained it not to be afraid of water.

The stream was mercifully shallow, though there were three- and four-foot holes and the bottom was slippery with moss, pebbles, and smooth rocks. Twice Katherine's horse almost fell to its knees, and by the time they had gone half a mile, her legs were wet to the thighs. Kokolo muttered to himself throughout the ride.

The river took a sharp turn, and O'Brien, about ten yards in the lead, reined up.

"I think we'd better wait here for Shandu," he said.

On the left, twenty yards farther along, another stream joined theirs. The banks were steeper after the fork, and the water looked faster, creating a funnel effect.

"It does look a lot deeper," Katherine said uncertainly.

"The stream suddenly becomes a river," O'Brien said. "I don't like it much."

"Well, let's wait and see what Shandu says. Perhaps we have come far enough."

A few minutes later, Shandu came up behind them. He reined his horse in beside Katherine and looked downstream.

"Can we get out here?" O'Brien said doubtfully.

The banks at this spot sloped gently up, but they

consisted mainly of soft mud and were almost bare of vegetation. They would leave tracks that would be hard to conceal.

"The men following us know this country. It is their place. This is where they would expect us to leave," Shandu mused. He looked around some more, thinking. "These animals can swim, can they not?" he asked.

"Yes," O'Brien said. "Can you?"

"I can swim," Shandu said. "But I think we must go down farther. One mile down this river and we will be back in the foothills. Our travel north will be much faster then, and we will put distance between us and these jackals who follow."

"You hold on to your horse's saddle and you should be all right," O'Brien said.

Kokolo did not look thrilled by the prospect, but he nodded when Shandu translated the instructions.

Katherine and Kokolo dismounted and walked through the water, one on each side of the horse.

"Keep your powder dry," O'Brien shouted after her, and she quickly lifted the side of the saddlebag holding the supplies onto the horse's back. Grasping the saddle with her right hand, she held her revolver in the left.

The water became deep quickly. One minute the bottom was there, the next it was not. They were in a rushing current of icy water. The horse lifted its head, its nostrils flaring and its eyes wild, seeking the bank. Katherine pushed its head forward and urged it on. Kokolo was no help at all. He simply held onto the saddle with both hands for dear life.

A fallen tree appeared ahead of them on the right. It lay halfway out into the stream, its branches like pointed tentacles. Katherine pulled the bridle to the left as hard as she could. They missed the outstretched branch by about a yard.

Another two hundred yards and they were

through. The river suddenly widened into a placid pond. Katherine led the horse to the shallows at the side, and they stood there and waited for the others.

Shandu came first, clinging desperately to his saddle, his face wet and harried. O'Brien was just a few yards behind him, rifle and revolver held high in one hand, moving with no apparent difficulty.

Shandu mustered a weak smile for Katherine and stumbled up beside her, pulled by his horse.

"Water and horses, water and horses," he said. "They will be my death. When I saw that tree in our path . . ." He shook his head.

"Are you all right?" Katherine asked. She was struck by the thought that Shandu, their pillar of strength, was only human after all, and that he too might crumble in the face of adversity.

"Yes." He patted the horse's flank. "When I saw the tree I did not know what to do, but this animal is smarter than me and it swam to the other side." He patted it again.

"Everybody okay?" O'Brien asked as he came up.

"We're all fine," Katherine said. She turned to Shandu. "What do we do now?"

He scanned both sides of the river and pointed to a rocky portion of bank just ahead. "We leave the river there," he said.

He led his horse downstream to the spot, followed by the others. After telling them to follow as closely in his tracks as possible, he led his horse out. They stopped about twenty yards into the brush and he asked Katherine for a rag. O'Brien took a kerchief from his pocket and gave it to him. They watched as Shandu went back to the river, wet the rag, and rubbed the rocks with it where they had left hoofprints and chips. Then he walked backward, shuffling leaves carefully to cover their tracks on the ground.

"What about all the water on the rocks?" Katherine asked. "Will it dry?"

"By the time they come down this far it will be gone," Shandu said.

They went deeper into the brush then, and for another twenty yards Kokolo covered their tracks. Finally Shandu shouted at him and he ran up to join them.

The river must have carried them quite far down the mountain. The brush here was thinner and there were more clearings. Shandu suggested they get farther away from the water before stopping to rest, and they set off again.

A herd of about half a dozen antelope broke out of the brush just ahead, giving them all a start. O'Brien reached for his rifle, but Shandu shook his head.

"We cannot have a fire yet," he said.

"I'm hungry enough to eat it raw," O'Brien complained.

"You will not need to," Shandu said. He reined his horse beside a tall bush with waxy green leaves and plucked a round brownish fruit from it. He handed one of these to each of them.

Katherine opened hers and found that it contained a green pulp that was sweet and delicious. "What is it?" she asked as Shandu gave her another.

"I do not know the English name," he said. "The girl Nandi described it to me and said it was common in these parts."

"She likes you, that girl," Katherine said with a smile.

"The maiden will be there when I return," Shandu said.

"You think we'll be able to go back there?" Katherine asked.

"With the chief gone, his son will become the leader. He still wants me to teach him how to fight. I think he would like me to train his warriors if he is chief."

"If I ever thought of settling, that valley would be

a better place than most," O'Brien said. "Good earth, water, grass. You could grow almost anything there. Raise cattle too."

"It's hard to think of you as a farmer," Katherine said.

"Stranger things have happened," O'Brien said. "I can't go chasing the end of the rainbow forever, can I?"

"I suppose not," she replied. Although he did not describe it, she knew with total certainty the image that filled his mind. He saw a home, children, sitting on the porch in the evenings with Katherine beside him, a vision of domestic bliss. He would be a different O'Brien, responsible, content to be with the woman he loved. She wondered if it would be possible, but as he had said, stranger things had happened.

They came to a ridge and Shandu, now fully in command of himself, took his bearings. "It is time to descend now," he said. "If we go down these hills a few more miles we should come to the cut at the end of the valley. By riding down the other side, we shall come outside the valley and begin to track Wohlman."

Kokolo pointed down the hill and said something to Shandu, who grunted and nodded. "Kokolo thinks that Nkupu will have men waiting at the road that leads from the valley," he said. "He knows we seek the German and if we escape the warriors he sent after us, he would send men here also to wait for us."

"He's a cunning old bastard," O'Brien said, "and he knows Wohlman will be after him if he lets us get away."

"We go quietly then," Shandu said. "We must use what cover we can, and then near the bottom of the hill we must dismount and go forward with more care still."

They moved down the hillside in single file with

Shandu in front. The vegetation grew thinner still here, and soon the woods gave way to open areas of tall grass, interspersed with thickets of trees and tall shrubs. They could see only a mile or so ahead of them where the hill descended sharply before lifting up again. That was the pass out of the valley that they had seen from a distance earlier.

"Which side of the pass do you think they'd be guarding?" O'Brien asked.

"On this side, or inside where we could not see them as we came," Shandu replied.

"Well, why don't we just ride on and leave them waiting for us until kingdom come?" Katherine suggested.

"It is more open land on this side. They could see us too easily and come after us," Shandu said. He dismounted and gave Katherine the reins of his horse. "I shall go forward alone now and see if they are there."

"And if they are?" she asked. "What do we do then?"

"We take them," Shandu said with a grin. "We shall hunt the hunters then."

"You'll come back before doing anything?" O'Brien said.

Shandu nodded. He took his long *assegai* and loped off into the grass. They watched his progress for about a minute, and then he disappeared into a long line of trees.

Fifteen minutes passed.

"Do you think he's all right?" Katherine asked uneasily.

"I think we would hear something if he was in trouble," O'Brien replied.

Ten minutes later, Kokolo said something and pointed at the trees below them. They glimpsed movement first and then saw Shandu come out into the open grass.

"Are they there?" Katherine asked when he reached them.

"Six of them," Shandu said. "They sit behind a big rock, waiting for us to come. They sit with their backs to us, facing south. They do not know that we come like a storm from the north."

"And now?" Katherine asked.

"Now comes the storm," Shandu said.

Chapter Thirteen

THEY TIED THE HORSES to tree trunks and followed
Shandu down the hill. The land here was dotted with
huge boulders, some almost as big as houses, and
they darted between them as they advanced. They
came to a particularly large boulder and Shandu signaled for them to stop. They pressed their cheeks
against the smooth warm rock and looked down.

The road into the valley was a dirt path as wide as
two men. The six warriors sat behind a heap of rocks.
Two of them were playing a game with stones, one
was sleeping, and the other three nervously kept
their eyes on the trail, hoping, no doubt, that nothing
more dangerous than a cow would come out of the
pass.

There was another mound of rocks only about
twenty yards from the men, and Shandu motioned
for them to go to it. They swung around, keeping the
rocks between the men and themselves, and ran in a
crouch to the barrier. The lazy voices of the guards
drifted back to them. O'Brien and Katherine held
their revolvers ready, and Kokolo grasped Shandu's
small spear. Shandu motioned for Katherine and
Kokolo to go around the other side of the rocks while
he pulled at O'Brien's sleeve to come with him.
Slowly they moved around the huge stones.

They leaped out suddenly, two to each side, star-
tling the guards into complete immobility. O'Brien
and Katherine leveled their revolvers at the bewil-

dered men while Shandu roared out a command, telling them not to move or they would be shot. The men
apparently had no intention of moving. They stood as
still as the rocks around them, except for their swiv-
eling, frightened eyes. Shandu ordered them to drop
their weapons and they did so, allowing their spears
and shields to fall to the ground. Kokolo scooped
them up quickly and said something to the men.

"He tells them they are lucky they are facing lions
and not jackals. A lion does not kill mice when there
is large game on the veldt," Shandu said with a
pleased smile.

"What shall we do with them?" Katherine asked.

"We shall send them back to the village," Shandu
said.

"They won't turn around and follow us?" O'Brien
asked.

"These?" Shandu asked with a contemptuous gesture of his *assegai.* "They will run like hares. Perhaps
if they meet the other band they will get their courage back and come after us. By then we will be far
away."

Shandu and Kokolo whispered to each other while
O'Brien kept his gun pointed at the men. Kokolo then
pranced back to the men and harangued them for
almost five minutes. Their reactions were written on
their faces for everyone to see, ranging from relief,
through fear and horror, and back to relief again.

"He is telling them that we will send them back
without killing them," Shandu explained. "He also
tells them that their Chief Nkupu will die for his
treachery against Kokolo, even though Kokolo is no
longer there. Soon—today, tomorrow—Nkupu will
die. He says that even though we are not their enemies we cannot let attacks on us go unpunished."

"He is saying just that with all those words?"
Katherine asked.

Shandu smiled. "Kokolo is like a bag of wind.

Where one word will do, he will tell a long story. But
no matter the words he uses, when those men go back
to the village and Nkupu dies, word of his power will
spread. We will have no further trouble from those
people."

With one last shriek and a wave of the hand, Kokolo sent the men on their way. They turned and
walked down to the path. When they reached it, they
broke into a trot, not once looking back.

Shandu shook his head sadly. "The chief's son
wishes me to train these men to be warriors," he
muttered.

Kokolo picked up the *assegais* and held them under
his arm. "We will drop those in the bush when we
leave," Shandu said. He turned to O'Brien. "Let us go
and get the horses while the others wait here."

Katherine and Kokolo stood in the shade of a rock
while Shandu and O'Brien went back up the hill to
get the animals. The sky was clear and the sun hot,
but over on the eastern horizon Katherine could see
the beginnings of clouds.

"Rain?" she said to Kokolo. She pointed at the
clouds, at the sky above them, and wiggled her fingers to mimic falling drops.

Kokolo nodded, pointing up. That was the extent of
their conversation.

When the men returned with the horses, Katherine mounted and they continued along the path. Kokolo walked and jogged in the grass beside it,
oblivious of the thorns and stones.

The land ahead was flatter and slightly drier than
the area they had just passed through. About ten
miles farther along, and a few miles to the east,
smoke in the sky indicated another village. Far
ahead to the west, twenty miles perhaps, another
mountain range filled the horizon. It looked higher
than the one they had come through, but it was difficult to tell at that distance.

"Are we following their tracks along this path?" Katherine asked. The hard ground carried no tale for her.

"I will show you," Shandu said. He got off his horse and crouched above the sand, pointing to some marks in the softer soil to the side of the path.

"These are the marks of feet, many feet," he said. "Here you can see half the mark of a horse's foot. It is only half because it is covered by a foot. This shows that the men rode ahead, while the warriors ran behind. The horse mark was made a day, two days ago. You can see where it has crumbled and then hardened."

O'Brien was fascinated. "I don't understand the part about crumbling," he said.

Shandu got back on his horse and talked as they rode. "When the hunter rises in the morning and follows the track of the antelope and sees that the footprint is a dark color, this shows that the morning dew fell on the mark. He knows then that the animal passed in the night, before the dew fell. If the edge of the print is sharp, the animal passed in the early morning when the sand was moist and firm. If the edges have crumbled, it shows that the animal passed at noon. One can also look at the depth of the footprint. It is deeper if made after the dew has fallen, when the earth is softer. These footprints have crumbled and then been hardened by the sun baking on one or two dews."

He pointed ahead to a mound of horse manure. "That is hard on the outside, baked by the sun, so it looks old." He leaned down without dismounting and poked it with the point of his spear. "See. It is still soft inside. A day, two days old, that is all. This is the way they came."

"The American Indians. They also can track like this," O'Brien said.

"All who hunt must be able to track, or they will soon starve," Shandu said.

Katherine pointed over to the clouds on the horizon. They seemed to have moved closer since she had last examined them. "If those bring rain, what will it do to your tracks?"

Shandu frowned. "They will be washed away," he said. "We must go faster now, I think."

Thirty minutes later the path split. The larger, more well-traveled portion curved down toward the village they had seen. The other continued roughly in the direction of the mountains.

"They are going either to the mountains or alongside them," Shandu said after examining the tracks.

"It will be the mountains," O'Brien said. "If they are looking for gold, it will be there. Though we risk losing the tracks, I think if we head for the mountains we will find them."

"It is not good," Shandu said. "The mountains are big."

"If we go wandering through there, hoping to come across them, it's likely that they'll find us first," Katherine said.

"You are right. It is not good, Lionheart. We must try to keep following the tracks," Shandu said.

Once again Katherine experienced a feeling of helplessness. The unexpected kept threatening. Perhaps that was the one thing that could be planned upon. Wohlman should have been at the village when they arrived; he wasn't. Their approach should have been a secret; it wasn't. They should not have had to deal with the added burden of Nkupu's enmity; but they had to. Now even the weather seemed to be turning against them. Well, she thought, gritting her teeth, if the gods were testing her, they had found worthy materials. She would persist in spite of it all.

Thirty minutes later, Kokolo suddenly shouted something. Shandu reined his horse and looked into the distance. He asked the old man a question and Kokolo pointed. They all saw it then, the great bird circling an area about three miles ahead. As they watched, another bird rose from the ground and joined its mate.

"Vultures," Shandu said. "We must look."

As they came closer, two more birds rose, and then another. They rose high on the drafts of air, but still circled the area, as if waiting for the intruders to leave.

The ground was gouged by *dongas*, some twenty or thirty feet deep, created by the annual onslaught of rainwater from the hills.

"Whatever it is, it must be in one of these *dongas*," O'Brien said.

"We are still following Wohlman's tracks," Shandu said. "They will lead us to it, I think."

He rode slowly, following the trail to a lip of earth. He dismounted and went closer to the edge.

"It is here," he said softly.

They all went to the edge of dry earth and looked into the hole. The body looked as if it had been thrown thoughtlessly down. It lay crumpled and twisted on the bottom, not ten feet away from them.

The vultures had been feeding for some time. Whoever was down there was now unrecognizable. His face, or what had once been a face, was now pulp and bone. Katherine turned white and fought the compulsion to retch.

"First they take the eyes, then the flesh," Shandu said.

"It's Koos," O'Brien said, and walked away.

"You are certain?" Shandu asked.

"I can tell by the clothes, the boots. It's Koos, the poor bastard," O'Brien said.

"It is as Kokolo said," Shandu noted, his voice awed.

Katherine went back to her horse and leaned her head against its shoulder. She smelled dust. Blood and dust, she thought. It's the story of this country.

Countless bones scattered throughout the land, walked over, built over, unremembered. That bastard, she said to herself, thinking of Wohlman, her hate bubbling up again until it thickened her throat and pricked her eyes. So much for Koos. He had betrayed them, and now he had been betrayed himself.

"Koos was a fool," she said harshly. "Wohlman had no further use for him."

O'Brien didn't bother replying. His face was mottled red and white.

"They did not want to kill him in the village. It would not have been proper for people to see white men fight among themselves," Shandu said.

"Shall we bury him?" Katherine asked.

O'Brien looked up at the waiting birds in the sky. "No, leave him," he said. "Let the vultures finish the job. They're experts. Whatever kind of fool he was, Koos loved this country in his way. Let him lie in it openly like the hunter he was. He was a damned good hunter, that man."

As they rode away, they watched the vultures wheel down in smaller and smaller circles.

Wohlman's trail led almost to the foothills of the mountain range, then turned north.

"He's following the range north," O'Brien said. "That means that anywhere in the next fifty miles of mountain he could have cut in."

The mountains were much like those they had passed through earlier, although, as they had guessed from a distance, these were higher. There were stark rocky cliffs inhabited only by baboons and eagles, and everywhere else a superfluity of vegetation suffocating the mountain. A small army could hide unseen in there for weeks.

It was almost evening, and the distant clouds had marched west until now they filled the sky, pregnant with moisture.

"It will rain soon," Shandu said.

"Within the hour," O'Brien agreed. "The trail could go on for a day, or it could turn into the mountain just a mile farther on. What do you think we should do?"

"We need to fill our bellies," Shandu said. "A man cannot travel or fight on an empty stomach."

"I'll go see if I can get an antelope, while you make camp around here," O'Brien volunteered.

"If Wohlman is close he may hear the shot," Katherine said.

"I will go with my *assegai*," Shandu said. "It will make no noise."

"You can kill an antelope with just that?" Katherine asked.

Shandu looked affronted. "How do you think we lived before the white man came with his guns?"

"If Wohlman is close we won't even be able to light a fire," O'Brien said. "Why don't you continue following the trail as you hunt, at least for a couple of miles. That way we'll know at least that he isn't near."

"That is good," Shandu said. "I shall go on foot. If I am seen by chance, they will think that I am just a hunter from the village on the plain." He pointed to a cleft in the hill. "Move back and make camp there. Do not light a fire until I return. If they are not close, the smoke from the fire will not be seen."

O'Brien took Shandu's horse, and they rode back into the hill to an area under some trees. Flat rocks sat like saucers on the grass.

"No water," Katherine said.

"There's probably a stream nearby, but why bother?" O'Brien said. "It's going to be pouring out of the sky soon enough."

While they unsaddled the horses, Kokolo began to gather wood and place it on one of the rocks. Through the diligent use of sign language he managed to get

O'Brien to part with his groundsheet and spread it over the wood to keep it dry when it rained. If they got wet they would at least have a fire to dry them off.

There was nothing to do then but sit and wait for Shandu, their stomachs growling at the thought of food.

O'Brien still brooded about the fate of Koos. "To kill someone that coldly and thoughtlessly . . . murder. Those men can be little better than animals," he said gloomily.

"They are evil men—very evil men," Katherine said. "I don't think evil can be understood properly by normal people. It's hard to face up to, let alone understand. I warned you about them."

O'Brien dug a stick into the dirt. "I know. And I've seen men callously kill others before, but it's not something I can grow used to."

Again, Katherine thought of Wohlman's sharp, crooked teeth and the night at the camp. How pathetic Alan's body had looked, sprawled on the ground, how lonely and lifeless. And what of Timothy? He had hardly begun to taste the fruits of life when life had been snatched away from him. How could evil like that be understood? At least Colin was safe, thank God. She wished suddenly that she was with him. Soon now, she told herself fervently. Soon. It would not be long before this was over and they were back together again as they should be. Would O'Brien like him? It was a strange thought. She looked over at him, at the sensitive mouth and strong hands. Could she be falling in love with him, after all? It was not unlikely. He was such a complex man, romantic, adventurer, hero. Attractive, gentle, a man of many parts. She looked at the way his mouth curved into the angular cheek.

O'Brien suddenly turned his head and met her eyes. She could feel herself blush. The thoughts were so unlike her. Why was this happening? He smiled and held her gaze with his. She looked away, embarrassed.

She remembered how his arms had felt around her down at the river, the touch of his lips on hers, even the masculine smell of his body. Stop, she commanded herself. Not now. This wasn't the time. His gaze was still on her; she knew it without looking up. She could feel the burning in her cheeks.

Kokolo grabbed her arm then. He pointed down the hill with his hand.

"What? Is it Shandu?" she blurted out, relieved at the interruption of her thoughts.

Kokolo placed his fingers to his lips urgently, and this time she heard. It was a horse, a single horse coming up the hill. She looked at O'Brien's alarmed eyes. Shandu had gone on foot.

"Come on!" O'Brien said, getting quickly to his feet.

They ran behind the trees and pressed against the trunks, revolvers in hand.

The horse came closer. Peering around the trunk of the tree, Katherine caught a glimpse of a man before she jerked her head back. A white man.

The form came closer still, almost to where they had been sitting, and stopped. There was the sound of a man clearing his throat.

The man called out something in the Boer language.

O'Brien and Katherine swung out simultaneously from behind their trees, revolvers pointed at the man.

"Don't move!" O'Brien shouted out. He held his gun steadily with both hands.

The man looked at them in astonishment. He had a brown goatee and wore a broad-brimmed hat and khaki pants and jacket. There was a rifle at his side.

"I've never seen him before," Katherine said to O'Brien.

"State your name and your business. And don't move," O'Brien said.

"What kind of welcome is this?" the man asked in English.

"Name?" O'Brien barked, waving the pistol slightly.

"I am Jan de Wet," the man said stiffly.

"Business?" O'Brien asked.

"No business. I'm just riding this part of the country. A little bit of hunting and exploring."

"Where are you from?"

"From the Klerksdorp area. I know you. You're O'Brien, the American. I've seen you in Potchefstroom. My father is Piet de Wet."

O'Brien lowered his gun. "It's all right," he said to Katherine. "He'll do us no harm."

She kept her revolver pointed at the man. "Koos could have told them your name. He could have joined them after I met with them."

"No, it's all right, I tell you," O'Brien said. "I know the family. They live just a bit south of Potchefstroom."

She lowered her gun reluctantly and looked more closely at the man. He was about twenty-five, well tanned, with gray eyes, keen and wrinkled from the sun like all these Boers. His mouth twitched under her appraisal.

"May I move?" he said ironically.

"I'm sorry, please get down," O'Brien said.

The man dismounted smoothly. "I was riding south along the trail and saw you ride up to the mountain. I thought I would come and see who it was. I never expected to see a lady up here."

"This is Katherine Carson," O'Brien said. Kokolo stood alongside the tree behind which he had been hiding. "That is Kokolo."

"There were four of you, I thought?"

"Shandu. He has gone to get us food. Zulu."

De Wet raised his eyebrows at the mention of a Zulu in this region, but he did not question it.

"May I join you?" de Wet asked. "It will rain soon. There is no point in traveling on tonight."

"Of course," O'Brien said. "If our hunter is successful, we may even soon have food to offer you."

De Wet unsaddled his horse and then came and sat beside the other three. The sky began to spit out the first warning drops of rain.

"How far have you been traveling, Mr. de Wet?" asked Katherine.

"I've been going in almost a circle," he said. "I went first to the Lydenburg district in the east, and then north up to the Soutpansberg Mountains, and then across this way."

"Have you seen other white people in this area?" she asked casually.

"Not within fifty miles," he said. "I met one other hunter about three days' ride away, and a couple of families who are farming a little to the east." His mouth twitched into the beginnings of a smile again. "Your questions have a purpose. You were expecting someone else when I rode up, someone not as friendly as I."

O'Brien looked at Katherine and lifted a shoulder. "Yes," he said to the man. "We're looking for some other Europeans in this area."

"You mentioned Koos. Is that by any chance Koos du Toit from Potchefstroom? Is he also up in this country?"

"He was," Katherine said grimly.

"His body is lying in a *donga* not more than half a day's ride from here," O'Brien explained.

"*Ach*, that is terrible," de Wet said. "He may not have been much of a man, but he was a good hunter. What happened to him?"

"He was murdered by the men we're looking for," Katherine said.

"Murdered?"

"Yes. He was shot and thrown into a *donga* for the vultures to feed upon," she said.

"And you seek the men who killed him?"

"Not for that reason," she said. "They have killed before."

De Wet shifted to a more relaxed stance. "You have a story to tell. Why not tell me?"

She looked at O'Brien, who nodded. De Wet waited patiently, his eyes on her face, while she gathered her thoughts.

"It's a long story," she said.

He opened his palms. "We have nothing to do but sit here and get wet," he said, smiling.

He was unlike most of the other Boers she had met, she realized as she began her narrative. Certainly not as stiff and unyielding as Pretorius, for instance. There was something of O'Brien in him, she thought. A touch of the adventurer.

He did not interrupt with comment or sympathy. When she had finished, he said only, "You are a woman of great courage, *mevrouw*."

Lightning tore at the sky, and a peal of thunder bounced off the mountains above them.

"We had better get under the trees," O'Brien said. "It's going to come down now."

They moved back a little and sat close to the trunk of a giant tree, its leafy branches outstretched like an umbrella over their heads.

"You haven't heard anything of these men?" Katherine asked.

De Wet shook his head. "Nothing. I was at a Kaffir village not far from here, and although I asked many questions about the area, they did not say anything of other white men. It seems your men did not want to be seen. If they had been seen, the Kaffirs would have told me."

The rain came down hard then, obscuring the

country around them like a fog. In spite of the large tree under which they sat, they began to get wet. Shandu suddenly appeared out of the gray wall like a ghost. He carried a small antelope over his shoulders.

He stopped when he saw de Wet, but O'Brien shouted out that he was a friend and Shandu came running on. He threw the antelope proudly down in front of them and then sat, panting from exertion.

"Where did you get it?" O'Brien asked.

"There is a stream not far from here where the animals water. I killed him there, as he was drinking," Shandu said.

"And the trail?" Katherine asked.

"It goes on," Shandu replied. "I went for maybe three, four miles and still it goes on. They have not turned into the mountains near here."

"You heard nothing of them?" O'Brien asked.

"Nothing."

Katherine remembered de Wet and her manners. "Shandu. This is Jan de Wet. He happened upon us."

De Wet leaned forward and made a sign of greeting to Shandu, saying something to him in Zulu. Shandu smiled and spoke back.

"You speak Zulu?" O'Brien asked.

"Yes, I speak about three of the native languages," de Wet said. "It helps you turn enemies into friends when you travel around as much as I do."

"What about your father's farm? Doesn't he expect you to work it?" O'Brien asked.

"I have two brothers who are better helpers than I am," de Wet said with a smile. "My father does not like it, but he understands my temperament."

"And what is this temperament?"

De Wet knitted his hands together. "There are too many people in Klerksdorp already. I have an urge to see this country, to see places that few men have seen before. To see something new each day. There is nothing like it. As I travel I look at the land and the people that live on it, and I grow to understand it. My father has his life and I have mine. Somewhere out there is my farm, the land that I will claim."

"You have not found the place for you yet?" Katherine asked.

De Wet chuckled at himself. "I think I have, but when there is this much, it is hard to choose. I like the Magaliesberg the most of what I have seen. I think it will be there."

He got up then and took a long knife from the sheath at his hip. "If I am to be your guest for dinner, will you let me butcher the animal for you?"

Shandu, whose prize it was, agreed, and de Wet got to work on the antelope. Quickly, skillfully, he skinned the animal, cleaned it out, and cut meat for the meal.

The rain had moved on, its thunder a faint echo in the distance. Water still dripped from the leaves of the trees, and Katherine moved into the center of the clearing, hugging herself. She was wet and beginning to grow cold.

The Magaliesberg was where Alan had wanted to settle. Perhaps if everything had happened as planned they would have one day been de Wet's neighbors. They might have even had a roof over their heads by now. Alan, having done all the research before they left Cape Town, had explained how easy it was to construct a rudimentary dwelling of mud walls and thatched roof, much like the native huts, although rectangular instead of round. They would have built it in two weeks and moved out of the wagon. In the months that followed Alan would dig the foundations and quarry the stone for the big family house he had planned. So much for dreams.

The light was fading, the veldt silvery with water. Birds darted from the trees seeking the earthworms that had risen to the earth's surface.

"I think it will be all right to build a fire now,"
O'Brien said, noticing Katherine's discomfort. "First
we get warm and then we feast on fresh meat."

Soon a small fire glowed in the clearing. At first
they huddled around it like refugees. Then, as they
became dry, they moved back and sat in a comfortable circle while de Wet cooked the meat on long
sticks over the flames, for they were all too hungry to
wait for coals. The second round would be cooked
more slowly over the pit, de Wet said.

The meat was delicious, with the strong distinctive
taste of wild game. They ate it like savages, tearing it
apart, blood dripping from their fingers.

When they finished, O'Brien loosened his belt.
"Oh, God, that was good," he said.

De Wet and Shandu talked together in Zulu. Kokolo joined in, and soon the three of them were
laughing uproariously. Katherine and O'Brien felt
quite left out.

"How is it you speak the native languages as you
do, Mr. de Wet?" Katherine asked. "I thought most
Europeans did not bother and expected their servants to learn English or the Taal."

"Most servants do," de Wet said. "But these men
are not servants, nor are most Kaffirs in this country. How can I learn from them if I do not speak their
language? Much I now know about this country
would never have been discovered otherwise. Also, it
seems to me that if you can talk to a man, it is more
likely that you will not fight with him. There is too
much fighting as it is."

"You like these people?" Katherine asked.

"Of course," he said. "Some of the best times of my
life have been spent sitting around fires such as this
in villages or on the veldt. It is different when you
speak the language, you see. Most people hear these
people struggle with English and they appear slow
and dim-witted, without humor or character. But you

should hear them talk in their own language. They are eloquent, these people. *Ach*, the stories they tell!"

"You are different from other Boers," Katherine said.

"How many Boers have you met?" he asked with a smile.

Katherine looked embarrassed. "Not many, I'm afraid. But those I have met are different from you."

"*Ach*, we are like all people. There are many different men among us. We are not all Bible-bound and stuck in the mud of righteousness. There are some things we have in common. Most of us love this country and hate the English, no offense to you. But even there we differ. Many of us want to conquer this country and bend it to our desires. Not I. It is an Eden already. I just want the peace to enjoy it."

"Do you think there can be peace?" O'Brien asked.

"No, I do not," de Wet said.

"The time of my people has been and gone," Shandu said. "It is the time of the white men now. We are like a lion that has been speared. It has one more great breath to let out before it dies. We had our time, long before the father of my father's father. We had great cities then, and we were a great people. The cities have long crumbled to dust and now there is only a memory."

"Ask Kokolo what he thinks the future holds for his people," Katherine said.

De Wet translated Kokolo's reply. "He says, 'I am no longer human like others and I have no people. The idea of a people is not a thing of the spirit. I am of the spirit. I will say this: It is now the time of the white men here. But compared to the times that have gone before, his time will be short, like a small spark lost in the stars. He has forgotten the spirit that is in him, and no people can survive for long without that truth.' That is as true a translation as I can give," de Wet concluded. He shook his head reflectively. "He is a wise man, this one. I fear that he is right."

De Wet looked down at the ground as if grappling for words. Then he spoke. "I would like to help you," he said. "To go with you. Men such as those you seek despoil everything they touch. They are the serpents in our Eden and must be destroyed."

"We certainly could use the help," O'Brien said. "The numbers are not exactly—"

"No!" Katherine interrupted sharply.

Everybody looked at her, startled by the intensity in her voice. "No," she said more softly. "There is no need for any more help. We'll manage."

"There are three well-armed men, maybe more," O'Brien said. "What's more, they're probably waiting for us. How can you say that?"

"I cannot be responsible for any more lives," Katherine said. "No more. You, Shandu, Kokolo, I have grown to love you all. For all I know, I'm leading you all to your deaths. It's my responsibility and I do not want more."

"My life is my own," de Wet said. "The choice is mine."

"No," she said, shaking her head. "The choice is mine. And I say no."

"As you wish," de Wet said. "My offer to help still stands if you change your mind."

"I thank you, but I shall not change my mind," she said.

Shandu laughed and said something in Zulu to de Wet.

"What did he say?" Katherine asked.

"He says that you have the heart of a lion, and the day you change your mind the sun will rise in the west."

The men talked then of hunting and places they had been, and the mood lightened.

"How did you learn to speak English so well, Shandu?" O'Brien asked later.

Katherine remembered asking the same question

when she had first met him, and she remembered his
evasive reply that he had learned from a friend.
This time, however, he was more generous with his
answer.

"First, I learned at a mission near to where I lived.
The Inanda School, from a Reverend Lindley."

"You were brought up a Christian?" O'Brien
asked.

"He was a good man and he tried, but no. I learned
only the language, not the religion. It is no religion
for a warrior. After that I learned much more from a
white man, a hunter who lived near to there. He was
an Englishman and we called him Joji. In English his
name was George. He spoke Zulu well and he taught
me many things. Sometimes we would go into the
bush for weeks, inland, up the coast and down, and
we would talk. For my help, he taught me English.
Ai, he could shoot, that man. He was a great hunter."

"He taught you how to shoot?" O'Brien asked.

"Yes."

"Why didn't you tell me? When the time comes you
can use my rifle. That will help even up the odds."

"I was going to tell you when it was time," Shandu
said simply.

Katherine lay on her side with her back to the fire,
staring into the darkness. The dancing shadows of
the flames melted into the greater blackness beyond.
All was quiet out there, the voices of the men, who
were still sitting around the fire, a soft murmur behind her.

Wohlman was out there somewhere. He was waiting for her and she could sense his presence. It was
evil, and soon she would face it. How would they find
him? she wondered. There was little doubt that the
trail had been washed away, and apparently no one
in the area had seen them arrive. It could take weeks
to comb the mountains, searching for traces. It was

dangerous as well. If they stumbled unprepared onto Wohlman it could be disastrous. Something would happen. It would have to. It was time for a little luck.

She sensed another presence too. It was struggling to reach her, swimming past the barriers of her preoccupied thoughts.

Alan? she thought.

Her mind grew as still as a pool then, and she knew it was Alan. It was almost as if she were communicating in pure concepts instead of words. She sensed that he was trying to repeat something he had told her previously. Then there was a rush of affection that seemed to fill her body and warm it.

She opened her eyes and it was morning.

Chapter Fourteen

GRAY CLOUDS filled the sky. The insipid morning light dropped past the leaves above Katherine's head. There was a croak and she stiffened slightly, narrowing her eyes. A large black crow sat on a branch, not ten feet overhead. The bird was looking directly at her, its gold-ringed eyes glittering. The sleek feathers were not really black, she noticed. They contained a spectrum of colors.

"Hello, crow," she said softly.

The bird croaked again, then hopped into the air and flew off with a flap of wings.

Shandu stirred, then de Wet. O'Brien and Kokolo slept on.

Katherine got up and splashed her face with water from one of the bottles, wiping it on the tattered tail of her shirt.

What had Alan been trying to tell her in her dream, if it was a dream? What was it that he had said before that would help her now? She thought back to their other conversation and cursed herself. "Dammit!" she said aloud. How could she have forgotten? North, she had remembered. They are going north. But that was not the totality of Alan's message. They are going north to a mountain of caves, he had said. A mountain of caves. That was it.

"De Wet!" she cried. He turned and looked at her, his eyes still dimmed by sleep. "Tell me something. Have you seen or, in talking to the people around here, heard anything of a mountain of caves?"

"*Ja, ja,*" he said, his voice still thick. "There is a place in this range that the local Kaffirs call the Mountain of Caves. They will not go near it, though. Too many bad spirits."

"Where? Where is it?"

The sound of their voices woke O'Brien and Kokolo. O'Brien got up, as stiff as an old man, his blanket wrapped around his shoulders.

De Wet scratched his head. The intensity of Katherine's expression told him that this was no casual question. "Well, it sounded interesting and I asked a man to take me there, but he would not. As I said, they are afraid of the place. He did point it out to me, however. It's about fifteen miles on, and then you go into a fold in the mountains, west. It is one of the mountains on the right as you travel in, I do not know which one. Apparently it is riddled with caves, though, and you should be able to see it."

"That's it! That's it!" Katherine exclaimed excitedly.

Shandu and O'Brien had come over to them while de Wet was talking. They both looked curiously at her.

"What? What are you talking about?" O'Brien asked.

"That's where Wohlman is," she said. "The Mountain of Caves."

"Now wait a minute," O'Brien said. "How can you know that? What the hell are you talking about, Katie?"

"I know," she said emphatically. "I know that Wohlman is here in this range at the place called the Mountain of Caves. I just know it."

"How?" he persisted. "How can you know that?"

Kokolo now joined the circle as well. He stood and looked at each speaker, not understanding what was said, but drawn by the tone of the conversation.

What could she say, Katherine thought wildly. She had faced the same problem with Pretorius when she had tried to tell him that Wohlman had gone north. I dreamed it. The spirit of my dead husband told me. How could she say that and expect to be believed? The exultation seeped out of her and she shook her head.

They all watched her, concern in their eyes, as she went through her mental struggle. For God's sake, she thought, looking back at them. These are my friends. I can say what I like.

"I dreamed it," she said, her voice tremulous. "My husband Alan came to me in a dream and told me Wohlman was going to a mountain of caves."

"You dreamed it?" O'Brien said blandly.

She nodded. Shandu was talking to Kokolo, telling him what she had said.

O'Brien began to laugh, then he stopped himself. "I'm sorry, Katie. I just don't know what to say. Now we follow a dream!" He smiled, chuckled, and held his hands out. "What the hell! What else do we have to go on? Let's go on to the Mountain of Caves. It's as good a start as any and it may even be right."

"Kokolo says it is good," Shandu said seriously. "He says you must accept the help of the ancestor-god."

De Wet said, "You cannot scoff at dreams. Three times my mother has dreamed that relatives have died, and three times she was proved right."

"Well, then it's settled?" Katherine said uncertainly, unable to believe their prompt acceptance of her notion.

"Hell, yes," O'Brien said. "We're off to the Mountain of Caves to find Wohlman."

Shandu nodded his agreement.

"First a quick fire and a warm cup of coffee and another piece of venison for breakfast," O'Brien said, rubbing his hands together cheerfully. "Then we'll be on our way."

"You still have not changed your mind, *mevrouw*?" de Wet asked. "I still would like to ride with you."

"No," she said. "I could think of few better men to be at our side, but I still do not want to involve you in this now."

"It is your decision," he said.

As they sat and drank their coffee, Katherine looked at her friends and thought how lucky she was. Kokolo with his guile and wisdom, Shandu with his courage, and O'Brien with his loyalty. What more could she ask for? Jan de Wet, too, was a unique man. He had forced her to revise her opinion of the Boers. She had said herself that generalities were seldom true. It was time that she practiced what she preached, she chided herself. It was tempting to allow him to join them. There was no doubt that he would be an asset. Perhaps it was irrational of her to maintain this attitude, but she could not change her mind. Shandu was here for his own vengeance, Kokolo for his own reasons, unfathomable to her, and O'Brien because of his own free will and his love for her. On some level she did not understand, all these men were her responsibility. She could not add another to the load. Would not.

Later, after they had eaten and prepared to go their separate ways, she almost relented.

De Wet mounted his horse and waved. "Good-bye, my friends," he said. "I hope we will all meet again."

The urge to tell him to stay was strong then, but she restrained it and waved instead.

"Good-bye," she said. "*Totsiens.*"

Even though it was slower, they hugged the wooded slopes of the mountain range as they traveled north. They had no desire to be seen by passing travelers on the plain, and there was always the possibility that Wohlman or one of his men could come out of the hills for supplies. Far off to the east they could see another native village, but other than that there was no sign of people.

"That de Wet was a good man," O'Brien said as he

rode beside Katherine. "I wish I had met him before
and gone on some of his treks with him. That's one of
the consolations of traveling in this country: you
meet men like that—individualists all of them. They
want nothing more than to experience this place in
all its fullness. They love solitude, but they are not
hermits, you understand. They just prefer the company of their own kind of people."

"And are you one of that kind?" Katherine asked.

O'Brien smiled sheepishly. "I suppose in a way I
am. There's not much I love more than steering my
horse in some direction I have not been before and
simply riding. The petty politics and social chitchat
of town people bore me to tears. There is so much else
to see and do. Life can be such a glorious adventure. I
understand people like de Wet and feel close to them.
I cannot understand the man who fritters his life
away day after day in inconsequential acts that he
has no liking for."

"You're talking about most people," she said.

"I know," he said. "Isn't it sad?"

"Maybe. Perhaps people live the kind of lives they
are equipped to deal with."

"Perhaps they just never get the chance to find out
what they are equipped to deal with," he said. "Look
at you. Could you have predicted these turns in your
road? Did you know just how much courage and for-
titude and persistence you really had? I'll bet not. It
took a twist of fate to place you in this position. Because of that you have learned to know yourself and
your capabilities."

"If everybody wandered off on adventures like you
and me, where would the world be?" she said with a
smile. "There would be no banks and shops and
towns, no progress as we know it. You have to admire
the people that see their duty and stay with it."

"If everybody followed their dream, the world
would be a better place," O'Brien said.

"And you, O'Brien, would just spend your life riding around wherever your fancy led you."

"Ah, Katie, don't take that tone with me. I take care of the obligations I consider important. I am what I am, and I doubt I'd ever change."

"I know, Jim. If you were any other way, I probably would not love you as I do," she said.

"Love?" O'Brien said loudly. "Do I hear the lady talk of love? Is all not yet lost?"

"Why, I was speaking of brotherly, platonic love of course, Jim," she said, but then she smiled.

He brought his horse closer. "And I, dear Katie, am speaking of passionate, erotic, definitely not brotherly love," he said. "Do you think the two can meet?"

She felt her cheeks tingle. O'Brien was looking at her unabashedly and smiling at her discomfort.

"Nothing is impossible," she said. Her horse moved smartly forward as she kicked it. She heard O'Brien laugh behind her. She turned to see him riding a few yards behind her. Still smiling, he doffed his hat mockingly.

She smiled back at him, warmly, then turned and continued riding on.

At midday they reached the fold in the mountain that de Wet had described. They stopped in the trees to one side and dismounted to examine it. The fold was actually a valley, and it went deep into the range, with peaks rising on either side of it. A river flowed down its center and thick vegetation obscured the sides.

"The bush is good cover for us," O'Brien said. "It will be hard going through there, but at least it's not open country."

"Kokolo and I should go down and look," Shandu suggested. "Let us see where the paths go and also if there are tracks of these men down there."

"Good idea," O'Brien said. "Katie and I will wait up here with the horses."

"Be careful," Katherine cautioned. "We don't know

how far up he is. There may be guards posted. Do not forget the warriors he brought up with him."

O'Brien and Katherine settled with their backs against a tree while the other two disappeared into the bush.

They drank water from O'Brien's bottle and talked desultorily. Katherine's thoughts were too chaotic. Wohlman was here! She knew it. Somewhere in this valley, Wohlman, Dieter, and Tommy were doing whatever it was they were doing. The end of her quest was here, right here, in this place. What was more, Wohlman would not be expecting them, she was sure of that. Alan and Timothy had been the victims of surprise. This time, surprise would be on her side.

Almost an hour passed and then O'Brien said, "Here they come."

Katherine stood as Shandu and Kokolo came up the hill toward them.

"They are here," Shandu said, suppressed excitement in his deep voice, and Katherine suddenly remembered that he had been following Wohlman for even longer than she had. "This is the place," he added.

"What did you see?" O'Brien asked.

"There is a path on the other side of the river. Their tracks are there. The tracks of both horses and men. They lead up into the hills."

"Did you see anything else?" Katherine asked.

"No. Only the tracks. We followed them only a short distance," Shandu said. He crouched down and picked up a stick. Drawing in the sand, he said, "The river goes up the valley. Like this. The path the men took is on the north side of the river. This means that their destination is on that side, I think, because there is also a path on the other side. Like this."

"Is the path on this side covered enough for us to take it?" O'Brien asked.

"In the beginning, it is. It is possible that farther

on it can be seen, but if we go slowly and with care I think we can take it."

"You saw no sign of the mountain we are looking for?" Katherine asked.

"There are peaks on each side of the valley. Like this," Shandu said, marking his map in the sand. "At the end of the valley, it rises into another mountain. I could see that it was rocky, but it was too distant to see if there are caves. We shall just have to watch as we go."

"This is it! I knew it!" Katherine said, unable to restrain herself.

"Led by a dream and a ghost," O'Brien said with a rueful shake of the head. He smiled at Katherine. "Well, there's no point in waiting. Let's go."

They dodged through the trees down the steep hill to the valley floor, leading their horses by the reins. The earth was muddy from the rain and it was a slippery, dirty descent. The river was swollen and brown, fed by the downpour and numerous springs and streams farther up in the hills.

Katherine stopped to wash the mud from her boots, and Shandu cautioned her to hurry. "This is not a good place to stop," he said. He pointed to a narrow trail in the bush on the other side. "That is where their trail comes out."

She looked over, half-expecting to see Wohlman step out of the trees. Hastily she splashed water over the mud and hurried after the others.

The trail they followed was like most others in the dense bush. Originally it had been a game trail, and then it was discovered by hunters who widened and flattened it further. It was only wide enough for one rider. At times they had to lie flat on the mounts' necks to avoid being toppled by low branches or whipped in the face by bushes.

As they went deeper into the valley, the foliage grew more luxuriantly dense. Flowers bloomed on bushes and trees and fruit hung heavily on low branches. Although beautiful, it slowed them down, and at times they had to walk, followed by their horses. In places the path was completely overgrown, and they pushed their way through thickets of verdant brush that left its residue of seeds and thorns on their legs. The river, slightly below them, was a constant presence, its tumbling roar a part of the background noise, together with the hum and chirp of insects, the call of birds, and the incessant chattering of monkeys. At times they saw the muddy, angry water through the trees as it rushed past.

It was arduous and tiring and soon Katherine's shirt stuck to her body like glue. They moved on silently, for they had no energy to waste in talk. Every now and again they stopped at a relatively clear place in order to view the hills around them. They saw one cave in a gray cliff, but that was hardly enough to qualify as the site of the Mountain of Caves.

Once they saw a leopard bound off into the bush, and once an antelope was surprised while feeding and looked up at them with the startled, innocent eyes of a child. Soon after that they passed through the territory of a troop of huge baboons. The irate animals, as large as men, jumped up and down, threw fruit at them, barked out warnings, and fiercely pounded their chests.

For a while, the path led away from the river, where the bush was apparently too thick to allow passage, and took them up the slope of a hill. The roar became a whisper, but soon the path descended nearer to the river again, then led over clear, unsheltered rock at the base of a cliff. To avoid being seen they took cover in the forest, stumbling along for a few hundred yards before returning to the trail.

They reached the Mountain of Caves late in the afternoon. For the previous hour, the path had been climbing remorselessly, taking its toll on them. There was a sudden descent, another steep climb, and then they were there.

The valley widened unexpectedly here. Tall peaks surrounded it on three sides, but within it were six smaller hills, ranging from one to two thousand feet in height. Three were on their side of the river, and three on the other. Almost directly across the river from where they stood was their unmistakable destination: the Mountain of Caves.

It was a grim peak of pockmarked rock faces to which gnarled, twisted trees clung like leeches. It looked as if it had been riddled by cannon fire. The gaping mouths of at least twenty caves faced them.

"My God," O'Brien said. "No wonder it's called the Mountain of Caves. We're just looking at one side of it. God knows how many there are on the other side."

"Look," Shandu said.

It was Wohlman's camp. There was an enormous cave directly at the base of the hill, and Wohlman had made his camp just outside it in a clearing. They saw four horses, which no doubt included the animal of the murdered Koos, blankets, pots, and debris. There was no sign of people.

"They must all be inside the cave," Katherine said.

"Either that one or another above it," O'Brien guessed. "We need to find a site from which we can watch."

"Higher or lower, which would be best?" Katherine asked.

"A little behind them, I think," O'Brien said.

Shandu pointed to a small rise ahead of them. "Let us continue on the path. We can make camp behind that hill and climb up to watch them. There is good cover there."

Taking every precaution now, they followed the long route around the hill so that they would not be seen. They chose as their own camp a small hollow on the other side of the rise that Shandu had pointed out.

"They will not hear our horses?" Katherine asked anxiously.

"Too far," O'Brien said. "Also, we're in a hollow and the brush will muffle the sound."

"Can we light a fire here?" she asked.

"Well, they'll have their own fire filling their noses and probably won't be able to smell it," he said thoughtfully. "What do you think, Shandu?"

The big Zulu shook his head. "You are right, I think. But it is a risk, and I do not think we need to take a risk at this time. It will be cold for us, but we will not die."

Katherine agreed regretfully, thinking of the chilly night ahead. Already shadows filled the valley. In an hour or two it would be dark, and an hour after that, cold.

They unsaddled their horses, then went up to the crest to look at Wohlman's camp. They were separated only by the river and an additional distance of about three hundred yards. They lay in the brush and watched.

Ten minutes passed and then Shandu whispered, "There!"

A black man walked out of the cave. A minute later three more straggled out, and then the rest came, followed by the three white men.

Katherine's stomach turned. It was Wohlman. There was no doubt about it. Although it was too far to make out his features, she could see the dark shadow of his goatee. Behind him was Dieter, tall and thin, with the walk of a snake. The red-haired boy was last.

She realized that she was shaking. There they were! Finally. Nausea began to overtake her, but after a minute the sensation passed.

One of the Kaffirs gathered wood for a fire. Wohlman sat down and pulled his boots off.

She had seen enough. She slid back below the crest of the hill, then turned and almost tumbled down to their camp. She sat there, willing her body to stop its shaking.

"Are you all right?" O'Brien asked softly. The others had come down after her.

She nodded, unable to trust the sound of her voice.

"These are the ones?" he asked.

Again she nodded. Slowly her body regained its equilibrium and she felt her strength return.

"We must make a plan," Shandu said.

"Can we get them as they come out of the cave?" Katherine asked. Her voice sounded strange, cracked.

O'Brien thought about it. "Too risky, I think. They don't all come out at once. We would just drive them back in if we fire on them. There might be another exit from the cave and then the tables would be turned on us. I don't think it's a good idea." He looked questioningly at Shandu.

"I think not," Shandu said. "If it was our only choice, it would be worth the chance, but there must be another way."

"We need to watch them for a time and learn their patterns," O'Brien said. "See what they do tonight and tomorrow. If we know what their routine is, we'll be able to make a better plan."

"That is wise," Shandu said. "One of us can go on the hill and watch until it is dark. Then again early in the morning."

Katherine loathed the thought of more waiting, and it must have showed on her face.

"We are so close," O'Brien said to her. "All we need is a little patience now and we can do it right."

"Yes," she said. It was true. They couldn't go rushing in like fools. They were liable to get themselves killed. All they needed was a good plan, one that would enable them to strike quickly and accurately.

Kokolo went up the hill to take the first watch. Shandu sat down with his back against a tree and began to whittle on a piece of wood. O'Brien whistled tonelessly through his teeth. Katherine stared at the bush surrounding them.

"I'm going for a walk," she announced, standing up. At this moment she wanted to be alone more than anything.

"It is not wise," Shandu said.

"I won't go far. I'll take that path." She pointed to a small game trail leading into the bush behind them.

Shandu shrugged. "Take this," he said, handing her his *assegai*. "If you meet some animal you must not use your gun."

"I'll be back soon," she said, taking the spear from him.

It was a rough path, not yet battered into shape by men. She walked along it, oblivious of her surroundings at first. The sight of Wohlman had unlocked a scrambled mixture of sensations inside her, both physical and mental. Her body was still in a state of upheaval and her thoughts buzzed like infuriated wasps. In a sense she was ashamed of her violent reaction, but this was soon submerged in waves of anger. That too passed, and by the time she had gone a hundred yards through the brush she was calmer.

She stopped at a bare, sandy patch and saw the hoofprints of a small deer. A little farther on were the soft pad marks of some cat animal, and beside them the smudge of a human footprint indicating that she was not the first to use this path. Small gray monkeys chuckled at her from the trees, more curious than afraid. A long green snake inspected her from a branch not two feet away. They regarded each other calmly for a minute, and then she moved on.

Soon she reached a small clearing where the trees locked overhead to form a roof. She estimated that she was about three hundred yards from the others. She sat on a moss-covered log, uprooted ages ago by the elements. Ants scurried about in the dirt at her feet in apparently aimless circles.

It was peaceful here. She thought that she could sit in this spot forever in a cloud of calm and forget about Wohlman and the past. From what she could see of the sky it was getting darker. She told herself that she should return to the others, or they would begin to worry about her and come looking. Instead, she sat where she was, unwilling to leave for some unexplained reason.

There was a noise in the bush. At first she thought that it might have been one of the others, but then she realized that it had come from the opposite direction. She listened intently. More noises. Branches cracking, twigs underfoot. Something was coming and, whatever it was, it was no small animal.

She got up quickly and stepped behind a tree, pressing against the trunk. Most likely it was a buck. If she were still enough it would walk right past her.

Another sound. A voice. A man. A man singing to himself.

She clutched the *assegai* in her right hand, her heart leaping. What should she do? Shandu had said she should not use her pistol. The sound would give them away. Perhaps if she stayed hidden he would just pass and go on to wherever it was he was going. No! The path would take him out at the clearing where the others waited, and he would see them. Would they take care of him? Probably not. More likely he would see them first and circle the camp and continue on to the village on the plain. Possibly he was with Wohlman. That would be even worse. He could be one of the Kaffirs that Wohlman had brought from the village. No, it was on her shoulders. She would have to handle it here and now. Could she use the gun to force him to surrender? Then she could take him to the camp and decide with the others what to do with him. It was too risky. If he attacked her she would be forced to use the gun.

The thoughts flew through her mind in a few seconds. The man was nearer now, just yards away.

She took a deep breath and gripped the *assegai* firmly in both hands. She waited until the last moment and stepped from behind the tree into the path.

There was only one man, thank God. He was about her height and carried a small antelope over his shoulders. He held a short spear in one hand.

The man's face was a picture of surprise and fear. His mouth hung open, his eyes bulged, white against his black skin, his breath stopped somewhere in his throat. They faced each other for no more than a second, and then Katherine brandished the *assegai* above her shoulder.

"God of the Bush!" she cried for no particular reason, and drove the spear into the man's bare chest.

She was surprised at how easy it was, like a knife into bread: a moment's resistance at the crust and then unhindered passage.

The man's cry strangled in his chest. Blood spurted from his wound like a small fountain. She quickly stepped back a few feet, not wanting it to touch her. The man's knees buckled, his mouth finally closed, and he fell.

Katherine looked away from the body on the ground. She swallowed twice and took a deep breath, but the overpowering smell of blood clogged her nostrils. A kernel of nausea in her stomach uncurled and rushed up into her mouth. She bent over and retched, her muscles stiff.

When it was over she straightened up and turned back, forcing herself to look at the man to see if he was still alive. Not a flutter. The body had to be moved in case anyone came looking for him, but it was too heavy for her. If she attempted to drag it she would leave a mess nobody could overlook. She would have to get the men to dispose of it, she decided.

The spear had entered near the heart, directly into it, for all she knew. She reached for it and pulled, not looking at the man's face. It did not move. She took it with both hands and pulled again. Stuck. Finally she overcame her repulsion, placed one foot on the man's shoulder, and pulled the spear free. She wiped the blade in grass and leaves to clean it, but they stuck to it instead. Better to get back to the others and not worry about that now, she told herself. Turning, she went back down the path, walking rapidly.

She reached the clearing in ten minutes. The others were exactly as she had left them, as though nothing had happened.

"Did you enjoy your walk?" O'Brien asked genially.

She walked over to Shandu and handed him his spear.

"Thank you," he said absentmindedly. Then he looked at it. He stood up quickly, asking something in Zulu. He corrected himself and said, "What has happened?"

O'Brien looked up alertly then, aware that something was wrong.

Katherine's legs suddenly began to shake and she sat down.

"There was a man in the bush," she said. "He was coming this way on the path I had taken. I have killed him."

"Are you all right?" O'Brien asked anxiously. He came and kneeled beside her, placing his arm around her shoulder.

"Yes. I'm not hurt," she said.

"The man. Where is he?" Shandu asked.

She waved a limp hand at the bush. "I left him there. Up the path a few hundred yards. You'll have to go and hide the body. It was too heavy for me."

"I shall take Kokolo with me. He may know the man," Shandu said. He frowned. "We must know if he will be missed."

"He was a hunter," Katherine said. "He carried game with him."

"That is good. Many things can happen to hunters," Shandu said.

He went up the hill to get Kokolo, and then the two of them went back up the path.

O'Brien was looking at Katherine with a worried

expression. "Are you really all right, Katie?" he asked.

Was she? She held her hand out in front of her and saw the fingers tremble. She tried to speak but no words emerged.

"You killed him with the spear?"

"Yes," she said at last, and added almost in apology, "I surprised him."

"My God! I should have walked with you. You could have been killed."

She forced a grim smile. "Not until I get Wohlman," she said.

She stood up and looked absently around the camp. The last vestiges of light were fading, and the evening chill was settling in, creeping up from the ground.

"I'll take Kokolo's post until he returns," she said.

She walked up the hill, leaving O'Brien down at the camp. At the top she stopped and crouched in the bushes. As her eyes grew accustomed to the mingled shades, she made out the thin curl of smoke from Wohlman's evening fire. There were men sitting around the fire, but it had grown too dark to allow her to make out any detail. They looked comfortable and relaxed, settling in for the night.

She breathed deeply again, and this time there was no stench. The air was clean here, except for the musky trace of smoke.

The paralysis began to leave her and her thoughts slowly gained momentum like a wagon cresting the peak of a hill. *God*, she thought, *I have killed a man!* There was no pleasure in it, no pride. She had thought about killing Wohlman, and in her visions the moment was filled with a fierce pleasure. This had been nothing like that, and now she wondered if Wohlman's death would satisfy her. This was different, she assured herself. This had been an innocent, someone who just happened to be in the wrong place at the wrong time. It etched her deed in bitterness.

She focused on Wohlman's camp again. Nothing had changed. The men still sat around the fire. They would be there for the night now. She turned and went back down the hill.

O'Brien put a blanket around her shoulders and they sat silently together. The clouds still hung low in the sky, but they had dropped their load and were barren now. Soon the depleted masses would drift across the mountains to the desert, unable to relieve that parched land.

Shandu and Kokolo came back, their faces stoic.

"The man? Did Kokolo know him?" Katherine asked.

"Yes. He is one of the warriors that the white men took from the village. He is known as a hunter," Shandu said, sitting down beside them.

"What did you do with the body?" she asked.

"We moved it away from the path and buried it under rocks," he said. He added approvingly, "Your thrust with the *assegai* was as good as any warrior I have seen."

"Will they come looking for him?" O'Brien asked.

Shandu grimaced. "I think not. I hope not. In the morning we must watch carefully. If they send men up to look for him, we must move quickly to another place."

"No one will come," Katherine said confidently. She knew the men they were dealing with. "Wohlman will decide either that he's dead in an accident, or that he has deserted. Whatever he's doing there, it's too important for him to waste time searching for a man he cares nothing about."

"I think you are right," Shandu said, nodding. "Have you looked again at their camp?"

"They're settling for the night," she said. "They will not move now."

O'Brien had cooked extra meat that morning. Now he unpacked it and handed it out.

"I can just smell the smoke of their fire," he said

enviously between mouthfuls. "Right now I would
give my life for a cup of coffee."

"You should have seen how she speared that warrior," Shandu said proudly. He shook his head.
"Shoom! Through the heart!"

"God of the Bush," Katherine said quietly.

"What?" O'Brien said.

Katherine did not answer. O'Brien noticed her in-
trospection and spoke softly to her. "Katie, don't be
too hard on yourself," he said. "You did what had to
be done. You must know that."

She began to cry then, silently, her hands over her
face, her shoulders shaking. O'Brien pulled her head
against his chest and she felt her escaping tears wet
his shirt. He stroked her hair and kissed the top of
her head.

Katherine stopped crying and rested her head on
him. "Jim," she said against his throat. "Will you
sleep with me tonight?"

She felt a jolt as he pressed his body against hers.
There was a brief silence and then he said, "Will I?
Of course I will. God, yes!"

They were deliberately ignored by the knowing
Shandu and Kokolo as they walked away from the
camp, their blankets draped around them. O'Brien
held her hand at first and then put his arm around
her shoulders, hugging her closer. They did not
speak. Katherine felt an acute sense of relief, as if finally doing something she had put off too long.

They came to a small clearing of soft grass. Katherine turned and faced him, still not speaking. They
looked at each other silently in the darkness.

Slowly she unbuttoned her shirt and unbound her
breasts. The shirt slipped from her shoulders as she
rolled the tight pants from her legs. She stood naked
in front of him, her arms at her sides.

"You are more beautiful than I had ever imagined," O'Brien said in a whisper.

Her cheeks were flushed and her hair, golden in the gloom, hung softly to her shoulders. Her large brown nipples hardened as he watched.

He took his clothes off quickly and let them drop to the ground. Naked, he stood there as still as she.

His body was taut and wiry. Fair hair covered his chest, darkening around his genitals.

She looked at him without embarrassment and then reached out her hand and heard his breath hiss.

"You are beautiful," she said.

They held each other and the cold retreated from their bodies. Falling to the blankets on the ground, they joined their mouths and breathed life into each other, discovering with their hands the secrets that they alone could share.

They went into each other then, their features as soft as petals, transformed by their unity, and their bodies began the ascent, entering a rhythm as ancient and enduring as the land upon which they lay.

An owl hooted mournfully in a tree above their heads, but they did not hear it.

Chapter Fifteen

WHEN KATHERINE AWOKE, the sun had already risen. O'Brien stood beside her, buttoning his shirt. He dropped to his knees and kissed her.

"I didn't want to wake you," he said. "You looked so beautiful lying there like that, it would have been sacrilegious."

She stretched her arms behind her head, arching her body up and yawning luxuriously. She felt wonderfully content and satiated, a feeling that had long existed only in memory.

"Katie," O'Brien warned, his voice suddenly thick. "We must get back to the others. They'll be wondering where we are."

She was tempted to pull him down on top of her, to enter again into that all-encompassing passion, but she knew he was right.

He watched her as she dressed, savoring the movements of her body, the soft femininity that he now knew.

When she had dressed she stood up and kissed him, and her lips, soft yet demanding, said more than words ever could.

"I shall never forget this night," she said into the hollow of his neck. "Never."

"Nor I, as long as I live."

They walked back to the camp. Shandu smiled when he saw them and nodded his head a few times, his sign of approval.

"Where is Kokolo?" she asked.

"He has been watching the camp since before the sun rose," Shandu said. He handed them each a piece of meat and some fruit he had picked from the surrounding trees.

"Everything all right?" O'Brien asked.

"They have eaten and all entered the cave a short time ago," Shandu said.

Katherine and O'Brien wolfed the food down ravenously.

"You are hungry," Shandu noted. "That is good."

They smiled at each other and Shandu laughed out loud at them. "That is good," he repeated.

"They sent no one to look for their hunter?" O'Brien asked as he finished eating.

"There was talk among the warriors and they pointed their fingers into the hills, but the white men shouted at them and they all went into the cave."

"Just as I thought," Katherine said. "Wohlman is not concerned."

"Have you thought of a plan?" O'Brien asked Shandu.

"Kokolo and I have talked. We both think that we must find a way into the cave. From inside we can surprise them, or even lure them after us and trap them. But we do not know how to get in without being seen."

"I agree," O'Brien said. "It would be ideal to take them inside, but . . the problem would be in finding a back way in."

"Let us go and look at it," Katherine suggested.

They went up the hill and joined Kokolo, who was lying comfortably on his stomach and watching the caves.

"It has been quiet. They are all inside," Shandu said after speaking to him.

"Look," Katherine said. "There's another smaller cave directly above the one they're in. Do you think they might be connected by a passage?"

O'Brien frowned. "It's possible, Katie. There's just

no way of knowing until we look, though. It's an aw-
ful chance to take. If we got trapped in there . . ."

"We could go in while they're working in the other
cave during the day. Have a look around quickly and
be out before they came back out," she said. "What
do you think, Shandu?"

"I do not know, Lionheart. You are a bold one, that
much I know. One thing, we must not do it now. First
we must watch and see what times they come out.
Think what would happen if we went into the top
cave and came out the same time as they came from
the other."

"We can see the mouth of the cave from here,"
Katherine said. "That means we can see this spot
from the cave. If Kokolo stayed here, he could signal
us if there was any danger below."

"We'd have to get up from the side anyway,"
O'Brien said. He pointed to a ledge that ran like a
ring to the mouth of the cave. "We'd have to get up to
that ledge over there, about fifty yards away, then go
along the ledge to the cave mouth."

"It looks as if it can be done," Katherine said.

"Yes, it can be done," O'Brien said. "It also means
that we don't get up or down right at Wohlman's
cave. Lessens the chance of discovery if they surprise
us by coming out. It's fifty feet above them and people seldom look up."

"Well, what do you think?" she asked.

"I think it's worth a try. Shandu?"

The Zulu nodded. "I think we must wait until tomorrow to do it."

"We don't even know that Wohlman will be here
tomorrow," Katherine said. "We cannot afford to
wait any longer. The more we stay here watching, the
more we risk being discovered ourselves. Who knows
when the next hunter is going to come this way? I
think we have to do it now."

"It makes sense, Shandu," O'Brien said.

Shandu still looked uncertain. He had no wish to
be discovered halfway up a cliff.

"Tell Kokolo the plan and ask him what he thinks," Katherine said.

The two black men talked to each other and then Shandu turned back to the others. "He says that some battles can be won by waiting, but not this one. He thinks that now is the time for us to move."

"And you? What do you think?" she asked.

"I still think we should wait, but I am cautious. We will do as you wish."

Kokolo spoke to Shandu. "He says that he will be in this exact spot, to the right of the tall tree with the red flowers. He will lie as still as death itself. If anyone comes from the cave, he cannot risk shining the sun on his spear or any signal like that. We must just look for movement. They will not see it from below, but if we look at the exact spot we will be able to see it."

"Good," Katherine said. "The horses will also be in his charge. Tell him not to expect us until tomorrow. If we find a passage we will not be able to go into Wohlman's cave until tonight when they are outside. When they go back in tomorrow morning, he will hear us."

"Also, in the morning the horses should be saddled and ready to go in case we have to leave in a hurry," O'Brien added.

Shandu relayed the orders to Kokolo, who nodded.

"Let's go back to the camp," O'Brien said. "I have to make some torches, and we're going to need to take rope with us."

When they got back down the hill O'Brien began work on his torches. First he found two sturdy pieces of hard wood, and then he ripped one of the blankets and tied the pieces lightly around the wood with a spare pair of shoelaces.

"I really should have wire for this," he complained.

"You have some," Katherine said mysteriously.

He stopped what he was doing, smiling at her expression. "Where?"

She pointed to his saddle. "There. On the cooking cans."

"The handles! Of course! You are an angel," he said.

After securing the rags he took a small bottle from his medicine kit and sprinkled drops of liquid on the cloth. "That'll burn as well as anything," he said. "We only use the torches when we have to, and only one at a time."

Lastly, he got a length of rope he always carried on his saddle and slung it over his shoulder.

"We tie this each to the other while we move along the ledge and inside the cave," he said. "I'm in charge of this part of the expedition. Remember that. I'm the prospector here, and I've been in caves before. You both have to do what I tell you, all right?"

They both agreed.

"Now check your revolver, Katie," he said.

"The rifle," Shandu said.

"Oh, right." O'Brien had forgotten that Shandu could use it. The Zulu took the rifle and his short stabbing spear.

Katherine's stomach tightened as she checked her equipment. There was no turning back now. This was the moment she had worked for, prayed for. Now it was only a matter of marching forward. She tied her hair up and put the hat on, wondering if her face was dirty. Well, she thought, when they crossed the river she would stop long enough to splash some water on her face. She had heard that soldiers were like this before a battle, their minds fixing on trivialities to avoid preoccupation with what lay ahead.

"Ready?" O'Brien said.

"Yes," she replied, pleased to note that her voice betrayed none of her nervousness.

They took off through the brush with O'Brien in the lead. The brush grew thicker as they neared the water, and they had to zigzag down the hill to find a passage through. They heard the river before they saw it and then, without further warning, found themselves standing on a thin bank.

Katherine knelt down and washed her face as she had promised herself. The water had gone down after the previous day's rain, but it was still muddy. She drank some anyway and filled the canteen at her waist. It was fresher than the water they had.

"I think we had better cross up there," O'Brien said, pointing about twenty yards away where the river narrowed. Stones formed a crossway there. They were about a yard apart, and the one in the center was submerged under an inch or so of water. It was the last leap that concerned Katherine, however. It looked slightly over four feet, and if she missed, the water below her would be deep and cold.

"Can you do it?" O'Brien asked, noticing her apprehension.

"There's only one way to find out."

"There's my girl," he said. "I think Shandu should go first. He's stronger than I am and he can catch you if you fall. I'll come behind you."

They started across, stepping from one rock to another. Shandu did it without difficulty in his bare feet, but Katherine wavered in the center as her boots slipped on the wet surface. She hesitated at the last leap. It was over four feet, as she had guessed, and the distance looked immense.

Shandu held his hand out for her to grab. "Jump!" he said.

She held her breath and jumped. Her right toe reached the rock, but that gave her no footing. As she fell back, she swung her hand toward Shandu. His hand closed around her wrist and he gave a hard tug, lifting her up before she hit the water. She scrambled up the rock as Shandu gave another pull. She stood breathlessly beside him on the rock. They moved back to the bank to give O'Brien room, and he made his jump easily.

Ten yards from the river the vegetation began to

thin again. The ground rose almost immediately toward the hill. Katherine looked back for Kokolo, but
from this angle he was obscured by trees. They were
a hundred yards up from the mountain at this point
and they had to cut down through the brush, parallel
to the river. They moved quietly, staying in the
thicker bush, sacrificing speed for secrecy. In ten
minutes they reached the base of the mountain. The
curve of the hill hid the mouth of Wohlman's cave,
but they saw the horses and the southern edge of the
campsite. Now, looking back, they could see the tree
beside which Kokolo lay.

The ledge to the second cave began almost immediately. It curved around the hill at a forty-five-degree
angle, culminating at the mouth of the cavern above
Wohlman's.

"Time for the rope," O'Brien whispered.

He tied it securely around his waist and then
deftly slipped it around Katherine and then Shandu,
who would come last.

"Now we take it slowly along the ledge," he said.
"I'm going to set the pace, so just keep up with me.
Ignore the rope around your waist. Use your hands
for balance and to hold onto the rock face if need be."

The ledge was about eighteen inches wide at first.
O'Brien moved slowly, always keeping a grip on the
wall facing him. Katherine thought he was being too
careful until there was a clatter of falling rock as a
portion of the stone directly beneath him gave way.
From that point on, she carefully emulated everything he did.

About thirty feet above the ground, the ledge narrowed to less than a foot. A bush, tenaciously growing from a thin fissure in the rock, stuck out there
and they had to inch around it, bodies bent precariously back into space. It was tempting to use the
bush for balance, but she saw that O'Brien kept his
hands off it and she did the same.

Ten yards from the mouth of the cave the ledge

suddenly ended; they had not noticed this from the ground. There was a gap of about three feet before it began again. As O'Brien stretched his way across, Katherine looked at the hill over the river to see if she could spot Kokolo. She saw the red-flowered tree opposite them and lowered her eyes. There was a blur of movement.

O'Brien made his way safely across the gap and then turned to her, his hand outstretched.

"Okay, Katie," he began to whisper.

She put her fingers to her lips and pointed down with her other hand.

A man stood at the edge of Wohlman's camp, a little ahead of them, about fifteen yards out from the cliff. They froze in their positions and watched.

He was one of the Kaffirs from the village, a tall thin black man wearing only a loincloth. He looked around for a moment and then walked directly ahead to a bushy area. When he reached the cover he dropped into a crouch, flipped his loincloth up, and began to relieve himself.

He faced the cliff, his arms resting on his knees, his head down. All he needed to do was grow bored with the view at his feet and look up; he would certainly see them.

O'Brien shuffled slightly to reach his revolver. If the man looked up, he would die. He pulled the gun free from his belt and moved his feet. A small rock rolled down the incline of the ledge to the gap. They watched, horrified, unable to do anything. The stone seemed to move in slow motion. It almost stopped at the edge of the ledge and then toppled over. It hit the wall once on the way down and then landed on the ground. It was a small rock and it only made a small sound, but they heard it from a height of thirty feet.

The man on the ground lifted his head quickly, scanning the bushes around him. They waited for him to look up, O'Brien with his revolver cocked and ready, but the man's gaze settled on the horses instead. At the same time, he stood up and walked back to the mouth of the cave, eyes still cast downward. He disappeared below the lip of the ledge, and they assumed he had re-entered the cave. They looked up at Kokolo and all was still at his position.

Katherine breathed an enormous sigh, and then O'Brien reached out his hand again, Katherine took it and, with the help of a little tug, made it safely across.

"That was close," O'Brien whispered.

She touched her forehead and realized she was sweating. If the man had looked up . . . Well, at least luck was on their side for a change, she told herself.

Shandu leaped nimbly across the gap and grinned at them. The ledge widened again, and in two minutes they had reached their destination.

The opening was smaller than the one below, about six feet high and eight feet across. They peered into the forbidding darkness. There was light the strength of twilight for about ten yards, and then it swiftly faded to blackness.

"Come on," O'Brien said, leading the way in.

It was bigger than it appeared from the outside, immediately ballooning in size, with a ceiling at least twelve feet above their heads.

"Look!" Katherine said. She pointed at the largest wall on their right.

A series of faded paintings covered the space, stretching for about twelve feet. There were figures of curiously tall and elongated men wielding spears. They appeared to be chasing a herd of about twenty long-horned antelope, the animals leaping high in the air. The lines were fluid and delicate, depicting both human and animal figures in a remarkably loose and lifelike manner.

"Bushman paintings," O'Brien said. "They were the best artists in Africa. These paintings can be found in caves all over South Africa. Truly remarkable."

"Could they still be around the area?" Katherine asked.

O'Brien laughed softly. "I don't think so, Katie. These paintings could be hundreds, even thousands, of years old. They last forever. Look how true the colors still are."

"They're beautiful," Katherine said. The details were so lovingly done, so natural in spirit, she felt an acute admiration. How close to the land this artist must have been.

"We must go," Shandu said impatiently.

"Right," O'Brien agreed. He took one of the torches from where it hung around his waist and lighted it. Holding it over his head, he looked more closely at the cave.

"This is a dolomite cave, I think," he said, sounding like a guide. "It could have once been a subterranean water course. It could go for miles into the mountain for all we know. We'll have to be careful in case there is still water here."

The air quickly became cool and damp. O'Brien's voice was flat in the enclosed space, not the booming echo Katherine had expected.

They walked forward and saw that the cave divided into three forks.

"How do we choose?" she asked.

O'Brien pointed to the one at the right. "We try that one first. We're looking for a passage down to the next cave, so we have to watch the slope. See, it goes down slightly. It may go back up again immediately and we may just have to try them all."

After only five yards the passage did indeed go up, sharply.

"The roof is getting lower now," O'Brien said. "But let's go on for a bit."

It was about ten feet high at this point and the cave had narrowed to a width of about six feet. Katherine began to feel closed in.

"Will it go much lower?" she asked.

"Hard to tell. It could, or it could even go higher than it was. Open up into an entirely new cavern. We'll just have to see as we go."

Another tunnel went off at a ninety-degree angle. O'Brien bent lower to look at it, his face crimson in the flickering torchlight. The entrance was only a yard high, but they could see that inside it widened slightly.

"I had better see what this one is," he said to the two of them. "Why don't you wait here. It'll be easier and faster that way. I'll give you this extra torch and some matches, in case anything happens, but don't light it unless you have to. We may really need it later."

"You mean we should just wait here in the dark?" Katherine asked dubiously. Shandu didn't look too happy about the idea either.

"You'll be all right," O'Brien said reassuringly. "I'm not going too far. I'll be back in a few minutes."

He took the rope from around his waist and went into the hole. They watched the light for half a minute and then it abruptly disappeared.

They sat in complete darkness, connected by a rope. "He must have turned a corner," Katherine said. "I wonder why the natives are afraid of this place?"

Shandu laughed. "Why should they be any braver than we are?" he said.

O'Brien's light appeared then, and he came out of the tunnel shaking his head. "That one is a dead end. Solid rock. Let's go back to the beginning and test the others."

"Shouldn't we go farther along this main passage?" Katherine said.

"We can come back to it if we have to," O'Brien said. "I'd rather check the other passages first."

They went back to the fork and tried the middle passage. For the next two hours they explored more holes than Katherine cared to count. The passage was punctured with holes. Every few yards it seemed another tunnel went off to one side or the other. O'Brien went into the smaller ones by himself; all three trooped down the larger passages. Some rose, some sloped, some rose and then sloped, others ended in rock walls. O'Brien went alone down one that opened into a passage larger than the main cavern and extended almost a mile into the mountain. Some caves were wet and others were dry, with a thin, powdery dust that fogged their eyes and clogged their nostrils. None of the passages offered an entrance to the cavern below them where Wohlman was.

Katherine grew frustrated. "It could take days to explore this damned mountain," she said disgustedly. "There may not even be a connecting tunnel, and then what? We're back where we started."

"That's possible," O'Brien said blithely. "But it's also possible that the next tunnel could be the one we're looking for. We just have to keep going."

"Spoken like a gambler," Katherine said. "No wonder you were happy prospecting for gold. But this is different. Time is our enemy."

"Tell you what," O'Brien said. "Let's go back to the main cavern, rest for a bit. Have a drink and a bite to eat. We'll all feel better for it."

Katherine and Shandu agreed. They were more tired than they cared to admit. O'Brien alone seemed to retain his good temper.

He proved to be right. After a fifteen-minute rest and some food, Katherine felt less desperate.

O'Brien got up after a final swig at the water bottle. "Just sit here for a few minutes," he said to the others. "I'll go ahead and see what this other passage looks like."

Ten minutes passed and the American did not return. Katherine began to drum her fingers on the floor where she sat. Another five minutes and still no O'Brien.

"Do you think something might have happened to him?" she said finally to Shandu.

He shrugged. "Let us wait a few more minutes and then we will go and see."

A few minutes later, O'Brien popped out of the passage, brandishing his torch like a banner, a big grin on his face.

"I've found it," he said excitedly. "I've found a way in. A hole that drops right through the ceiling onto your Mr. Wohlman's head."

"Where? Where?" Katherine asked in excitement.

"It's about forty yards in. A small passage. It drops down suddenly in a funnel and ends as a hole in the roof of Wohlman's cave. It's not easy, though," he warned. "There are ledges that make it possible to climb down, but the wall is about twenty feet high. Quite a drop."

"Can we do it?" Katherine asked.

"Yes, we can do it."

"Did you hear anything, see anything of what is going on down there?"

"No," he said. "I didn't want to go down the funnel too far. It's like a chimney. If I kicked a rock, down it would go. I didn't want to try our luck twice in a row. I heard the sound of voices, though. Couldn't make out whose they were or what they were saying, but I could hear people down there."

Shandu got up and began to walk to the entrance of the cave. "I told Kokolo I would signal him if we found the way through. He does not like not to know what is going on."

He moved close to the opening and waved his arms up at the hill. Satisfied that Kokolo had seen, he came back to where they were and lay down with his hands behind his head.

"What are you doing?" Katherine asked.

"I am going to sleep," he said. "We can do nothing until night when they all leave the cave. Now is the time to rest."

"He's right," O'Brien said. "There's nothing else to do for the remainder of the afternoon."

"We could plan," Katherine said. "We still don't know what we're going to do once we are inside that cave."

"And we won't until we see exactly what is there," O'Brien said. "Like it or not, we are going to have to improvise. You can't plan in the face of a mystery, and what is going on down there is a mystery until we investigate it."

"I suppose you're right," she said.

"Of course I am," O'Brien said. He patted the ground beside him. "Now sit a little closer to me and—"

He was interrupted by a noise, a dull boom. It came from within the mountain and the floor beneath them trembled. Shandu bolted up, and they all looked around, as if expecting the explanation to appear on the cave walls.

"What in God's name was that?" Katherine said.

O'Brien looked shaken. "It was an explosion," he said. "The bloody idiot! He's blasting down there."

"Is there danger?" she asked.

"You've seen how many caves there are in this hill. One charge in the wrong place, or too heavy, and the whole thing could come tumbling down. I hope to God he knows what he's doing. If not, we won't have to bother with him, he'll kill himself."

"Well, it seems safe enough now," she said.

"Let's hope so," O'Brien said dubiously. "I don't mind him killing himself, but we're in here too, you know."

Shandu lay back down again and closed his eyes, apparently satisfied that death was not imminent. To Katherine, it seemed the most intelligent approach.

"Now, what is it you were saying?" she asked O'Brien.

"Me? I . . . oh . . ." He patted the ground again. "Come a little closer."

* * *

O'Brien and Katherine slept like the exhausted lovers they were; they had not had much rest the previous night. When they woke with their hands entwined, Shandu sat in the center of the cave with his back to them. He was looking out at the twilight, his body as still as a rock, silhouetted against the darkening sky.

O'Brien stretched. "It's unfortunate we were not alone," he said. "I had more than sleep on my mind."

"At a time like this?" Katherine said, shaking her head mockingly.

"What better time? You are about to die . . ." he intoned.

"Do not talk like that," she said sharply.

He rubbed his forehead.

"Has something happened?" she asked, watching his face.

"No. Nothing. I just had a dream, that's all. It was upsetting. I dreamed I was killed."

She placed her palms tenderly on either side of his face. "Jim, there are dreams and there are dreams," she said. "A dream like that is just a trick of the mind."

"Yes, I suppose you're right," he said. He forced a smile. "It was just a child's nightmare."

"Come on," she said, pulling at his arm. "Let's go and see what Shandu has to report."

They went over to Shandu, and Katherine asked him if anything had been happening while they slept.

"They are outside now," Shandu said in a low voice. "If you listen, you can hear the sounds they make. It is the end of their workday. Soon we shall be able to go down."

"Not until well after dark," O'Brien said.

"I want to see what they are doing," Katherine said.

"It's not a good idea," O'Brien said. "We're safe

here. They can't see us or hear us. Go out toward the cave opening and you're taking a risk. What if one of the men left the camp for a walk. If he was at a high enough elevation he would just have to look directly across and he'd see you."

"They'd have to cross the river and go up the hill toward Kokolo to do that," she argued.

"It's a risk," he said.

"I'll crawl," she said impatiently. "All I want to do is hear what is happening. I'll stay away from the edge. I won't be seen."

"All right," he said resignedly. "If you must."

Shandu smiled. He had never doubted the outcome of the argument.

Katherine walked a few steps toward the opening and then fell to her knees and crawled, as she had promised O'Brien. It was growing dark quickly. Only the rim of the horizon still showed light, and as she looked up she saw a bat fly over the treetops. The smell of Wohlman's evening fire drifted up to the cave. There was the muted sound of voices from below, but she could see nothing. If she moved farther forward she would be on bare, uncovered ledge. She debated doing it. For some reason she wanted to see Wohlman close up, perhaps to reassure herself that he was really there, but O'Brien's warning helped her resist the temptation.

There was a hoarse shout, a command, and then some laughter. Her teeth clamped together automatically. That had been Wohlman's voice. There was no doubt about it; she would recognize it anywhere, anytime. She realized that her muscles had tensed up and she consciously relaxed. How easy it would be to go to the ledge, lean over, and put a bullet through Wohlman's head. How stupid, another voice in her head told her. He was forty or fifty feet away, and it was growing dark. Even if she was lucky enough to hit Wohlman, the others would scatter.

She moved back, still on all fours. Safe in the darkness of the cave, she stood up and walked back to the others.

"So, what did you see?" O'Brien said.

"Nothing to be seen, but I heard Wohlman," she replied.

They sat in the dark then and waited. O'Brien had extinguished the torch before they slept, and it was too dangerous to light it until they were well back in the passage. An hour passed, then another. After another half hour Shandu silently moved to the mouth of the cave. Then he came back, appearing just as silently beside them.

"It is very quiet," he said. "I think some are asleep and the others just sit."

"Another hour and they'll all be asleep," O'Brien said.

"Shall we wait?" Katherine asked.

"I don't think it's necessary," O'Brien said. "As long as we move quietly I don't think there's a chance of being heard. The funnel goes off the main passage about forty yards in. Then there's another ten yards before it drops into their cavern. That's at least fifty yards into the mountain. Unless we do something stupid, they won't hear us."

"What if someone goes in to check the cave while we're coming down?" she asked.

"Why would they do that? They're guarding the front. There's nothing to check on."

"Let us go, then," Shandu said.

"Let's just wait another half hour," Katherine said, suddenly feeling cautious. "It can't do any harm. We have ample time to get down there; we have all night. I would feel better if I knew they were all sleeping."

Shandu grunted, surprised by the reversal of roles.

"It's fine with me," O'Brien said. "There's no point in taking chances if we don't have to."

They sat in silence, and then O'Brien took Katherine's hand in the darkness. "How are you feeling now?" he asked.

"Fine," she said glibly. "No, I'm lying. I'm nervous, even scared," she said.

The sound of Wohlman's voice had made it all real. This was no game now. There was no denying the fear deep inside her stomach.

O'Brien squeezed her hand comfortingly.

"Listen to me, Lionheart," Shandu said quietly. "There is no warrior who is not afraid on the night of a battle, no matter how brave or honorable. It is good, this fear. It gives energy to the body, strength to the limbs. It helps a warrior move faster and be more nimble on his feet. It helps the warrior stay alive to fight another day, because he who has no fear is careless and walks into the flying spear. Do not try to deny your fear, for then it can grip you tightly and distort your mind. Just feel your fear for what it is and be thankful that it is there."

He spoke calmly, in a kindly manner, and Katherine felt a sense of relief at his words. She had been denying her fear. She had been feeling guilty for having it. Somehow it seemed to invalidate the rightness of her cause. As soon as she realized this it subsided and became more manageable.

"Thank you, Shandu," she said.

They sat quietly then, almost patiently. After a while, Shandu got to his feet.

"Let us put the rope on, it is time to go," he said.

Katherine rose too. Her body felt aflame with emotion, but ice flowed in her veins.

Chapter Sixteen

THE PASSAGE WAS WIDER, higher, and straighter than the others. O'Brien led the way with steady intensity, holding his fiery torch high above his head. Dust powdered his face, his hair was in chaotic disarray, and his eyes glowed with a reddish light. He walked with certain steps into the bowels of the mountain.

They could have been leading a vast army, Katherine thought as she followed, equally purposeful. She would not have been surprised to hear the clank of armor, the rattle of sabers, the flap of unfurled banners, the stamp of a thousand marching men behind them. This was an ancient battle, the cause of good against evil. Marching as to war. Soon weapons would meet and blood would flow. Resolution would come. The balancing.

Shandu hummed behind her, his tune matching the rhythm of their steps. His body gleamed like black gold. With spear in one hand and rifle in the other, he was vengeance personified.

O'Brien stopped and pointed. "There," he said.

It was a small passage, no more than four feet high, and seeing it brought Katherine down to earth. In her frame of mind she had expected something much more impressive.

"Does it stay that height all the way?" she asked.

"Pretty much," O'Brien said. "Just after we enter, it veers sharply to the right and almost parallels this passage. Then it drops down, very steeply."

He stooped to go in, then stopped and turned. "We have to be quiet now. Very quiet. No talking. If there's a chance that someone is in there . . ."

The passage was not only low but narrow. Stooped into a crouch, Katherine felt one shoulder rub the wall, then the other as she moved to compensate. Shandu would be having difficulty, particularly with both hands full. She felt her revolver dig into her stomach and pushed it aside.

"Let me take your spear," she whispered to Shandu, reaching back with one hand.

"Ssh!" O'Brien said.

Shandu handed her the spear, grateful to have one hand free. It was still hard for him, however. She heard him grunt as he twisted his body.

O'Brien stopped ahead of them and beckoned for Katherine to catch up. The passage continued straight on, but just in front of him was a hole about three feet wide. By twisting their bodies sideways, she was able to draw equal with him and look down. It was a funnel, as he had described it. It went down for about fifteen feet and then opened into the cavern below. Alongside the end of the funnel there was a wall about twenty feet high. Katherine was somewhat relieved to see that the wall was rough and had a few crevices, for they would have to climb down this wall to get into the cave. A dim light came from the cavern; Wohlman must have left a torch burning.

O'Brien put his finger to his lips and they listened for about a minute. There was no sound from the cave except the soft thunder of falling water.

"All right now," he whispered softly. "I am going to go first. We have about eight feet of rope between us, so when it starts to tighten you come down. Do exactly as I do. Watch me all the way so you can see where I find holds. Got that?"

"Yes," she said. The smoke from their torch was starting to hurt her eyes. "What about the torch?"

"Shandu can carry it." He craned his neck around.

Shandu's head was at their feet. "You carry the torch. As soon as I reach the ground drop it and I will catch it," he said.

He reached across the space of the hole and put the torch on the opposite ledge to free his hands. Gripping that ledge, he pulled his body forward and gradually lowered it into the tunnel. He moved from side to side, bracing himself against the walls with his arms and legs. When a foot of slack remained on the rope, Katherine gave a small tug to indicate that she was coming down after him. O'Brien stopped and waited for her to get into position. She could see the pale blur of his face looking up.

She lowered herself into the hole and began to emulate his movements. It had looked easier than it was. Every now and again there were ledges upon which she rested her feet, but when they were absent the strain of holding her body up with simple pressure against the sides began to tell. First her legs and then her arms started to ache.

She felt a pull at her waist and looked up to see Shandu getting into position. She pulled her rope to let O'Brien know. They waited until Shandu got into position and then began again.

Looking up once, she saw that Shandu held the torch and rifle above his head with one hand. At least with the spear she was still able to use her arm as a brace; he was at a greater disadvantage. O'Brien reached the end of the hole and began to tackle the wall. She went down a little faster to catch up. This was the part she needed to watch.

He clung to the wall like a spider, finding cracks and ledges she was unable to see from her angle. It looked difficult. She would need both hands and both feet to hold on. He stopped and looked around, twisting his body to see as much as possible.

"It's safe," he whispered loudly up at her. "Empty."

"Untie your rope," she said.

"What?"

"Untie your rope and go down first. I'm going to have to drop this spear down to you. I need my hands."

O'Brien nodded and fumbled at the rope around his waist with one hand. Finally he got it loose and it dangled against the wall. She waited until he reached the ground. It seemed to take an interminable time and the pain in her legs bit at her. As soon as he touched the ground and looked up, she let the spear slide between her legs. It clattered once against the wall and bounced, but he caught it before it hit the ground again.

Slowly Katherine moved out of the hole, her body plastered against the wall. She did not look down, knowing it would seem an immense distance. They could do it, O'Brien had said, and he had done it. But to her it seemed the most difficult feat she had ever attempted. The footholds were minuscule, the cracks and ledges barely large enough to hold onto with her fingers, let alone her thick boots. But she moved, inch by painful inch, her fingers feeling as if they would leave their sockets at any second.

She had gone about five feet when she fell. Shandu was ready for her, thank God. She felt the rope jerk at her waist and heard him grunt as he took her weight. For a second she swung, and then she scrambled madly for the wall, finally getting one hand in a fissure and pulling herself back to the surface with all the strength at her command, groaning and sweating until at last her right foot found a ledge to rest on. She clung to the wall like a wet rag until she regained her breath, and then continued down again.

A pull on the rope by Shandu told her it was time to untie; he too would have to drop his load in order to have his hands free. She tried to reach the rope around her waist, but she was in a precarious position and had to keep grabbing at the wall for support.

"Wait," Shandu ordered.

There was a noise and then the rope went swishing past her. Shandu had untied his end. There was no support now and the thought of the remaining ten-foot drop filled her with apprehension. There was no point in just staying stuck to the wall, however, and she continued down an inch at a time with no idea whatsoever of time or distance until she heard O'Brien's humorous voice almost beside her.

"You're here," he said. "You can let go now."

She moved her left foot down about two inches and it rested on the solid rock floor. She left her hands where they were and leaned her head against the wall, a feeling of grateful relief surging through her.

She heard O'Brien catch Shandu's rifle and then the torch. Her legs felt boneless; she was sure if she tried to move them they would collapse under her like soft mud.

"Come on, Katie," O'Brien said. "Shandu is almost on your head."

He took her shoulders and pulled her back a few paces. She looked up and saw Shandu descending easily, bare feet and hands discovering holds without hesitation. A minute later he dropped lightly in front of her.

"That was a good catch there, Shandu," O'Brien said, grasping him by the shoulder.

"Thank you," Katherine said. She surprised herself by sounding normal. She shook her hands then, and bent her knees. Everything seemed to work.

Only then did Katherine turn to look at the cave.

"My God!" she exclaimed.

It was a huge subterranean chamber, about a hundred yards long and fifty feet high, with an enormous domed ceiling. In the flickering light of O'Brien's torch it flashed and sparkled like the inside of a ball of crystal. Remarkably complex formations hung from the roof and rose like scintillating towers from the floor. As O'Brien moved his torch above his head, the entire room blazed like an enormous precious jewel.

The hole had dropped them near the entrance. Far to their right, they saw the two torches left by Wohlman. This was the light they had seen from above. They moved forward slowly, awed by the splendor. In the center of the room was a small, perfectly circular lake that gleamed with reflections. A waterfall tumbled into its far side, filling the space with a gentle murmur.

Among the twisted formations that filled the room they saw lightning frozen in motion, moonbeams captured in time, starlight and sunlight sculpted in eternal brilliance. Although the shapes were bizarre in form, the brilliant light filled the entire cave with a life and a beauty that left them speechless. It was as if all the sublime radiance of Earth had been gathered here in this cave for them to view. For the first time in her life, Katherine felt the urge to drop to her knees, not to pray but somehow to pay homage to this prodigious masterpiece of nature.

Shandu was the first to break the silence. "It is a room for the gods," he said. "But now we must deal not with gods but with men."

"I've never seen or heard of anything like it," O'Brien said in an awed voice.

Katherine felt suddenly drained by the devastating display of splendor. "Well, one thing is certain," she said wearily. "Wohlman is not here to enjoy the beauty. We had better discover what he is doing."

Shandu pointed to the lights on the far wall to the right of the lake. "That must be where they are working," he said, and he began to pick his way around to the site.

"This is the place," he said. The torches were wedged between some rocks, about fifteen feet apart. There were boxes, picks, and shovels scattered untidily about in piles of rubble in the intervening space.

O'Brien bent over and opened the lid of one of the boxes. He whistled to himself. "Look," he said. "They've enough explosive powder here to blow up the whole mountain range."

He replaced the lid carefully and looked around. A passage led into the wall on their right. O'Brien held the torch ahead of him and peered in.

"Only the first twelve or fifteen feet of this was a natural cave," he said. "See how the rock changes there. The rest of it was blasted out. This is where they have been working."

They walked quickly down to the end of the passage, another thirty or forty feet into the mountain, until they came to a wall of rock.

O'Brien took his revolver from his belt and tapped the butt against the wall. The sound was dull. "Solid rock all the way," he said.

He kneeled down at a fissure in the floor and dug into it with his knife, pulling out a dozen stones.

"Here, hold these," he said, giving them to Katherine. He picked at the hole some more and came up with another three or four stones.

"Let's go back out," he said thoughtfully.

They went back to the work area and O'Brien sat on one of the boxes. He scraped at one of the stones with his knife, an intent expression on his face.

"Ah," he said presently. "Now I know exactly why our Mr. Wohlman is here."

"Why?" Katherine asked. "What have you found? What are these stones?"

O'Brien grinned widely. "It is more a matter of what *he* has found, the cunning devil," he said mysteriously.

"Well?" she said.

He held his hands up, a stone gripped between thumb and forefinger of each. "These little stones that you see here, these dusty, grime-coated insignificant little stones that you see, these have been the cause of wars, assassinations, and suicides. Women have wept for them and men have killed." He stopped, the grin still on his face, teasing her.

Katherine could not stand it. "For God's sake, Jim. What are they?"

The smile left his face, replaced by a brittle look. He tossed one of the stones in the air and casually caught it.

"Diamonds!" he said. "What we have here is probably the richest discovery of diamonds on Earth."

"Diamonds? Here in Africa?"

O'Brien smiled. "There are not supposed to be diamonds in Africa," he said. "Oh, there have been rumors, of course. Occasionally someone comes in from the bush and says he's seen a Kaffir wearing a diamond, or heard talk of them, but it's never been substantiated."

"And Wohlman found it," she said.

"That Kaffir in the village, the one with the stone beads on his necklace. As sure as hell, one of them must have been a diamond. And Wohlman recognized it somehow. Got the man to lead him to the place he found it and then killed him. Now he has these warriors slaving away here for him. He'll kill them too when he's done. He probably plans to keep this place a secret and gradually sell the rough stones overseas. If he's half as cunning as you seem to think he is, that's what he'd be doing. Once news of this got out, it would be a month, at the most two, before there were ten thousand tents spreading across that plain below."

O'Brien began to laugh, "God! These Boers have been so worried I'd find gold in their country, gold that would bring the English and other foreigners into their precious lives. Here I am, sitting on the richest diamond mine in the world, right in their backyard."

Shandu was not interested in the Boers. "We must make a plan now," he said.

Katherine agreed. "How do they work? I mean, how is Wohlman likely to proceed once they come in here?" she asked.

"Probably quite simple," O'Brien said, looking around the work area. "I imagine they come here in the morning and lay some explosives at the end of that passage, blow it up, and send the Kaffirs in to dig out the rock. The rock is brought out here and the men sift through it for the diamonds."

"Well, the first thing we could do is hide in one of the caves leading off the side, perhaps on the other side of the lake," she said.

"I suppose it would be all right," O'Brien said dubiously. "As long as no one came exploring. But then what?"

"If only there was some way we could trap them in the mining passage. There is no way out of it," she said thoughtfully.

"We might be able to blast it so the front collapses," O'Brien said.

"You know how to use explosives?"

"Oh, yes. I've used explosives quite a bit in my time. They're sure taking a chance blasting in here, though. God knows what could happen."

"But you feel you could do blasting in here?"

"The idea scares the hell out of me, but I think I could do it without killing us all."

Katherine shook her head. "Of course, if we did that we would also trap the villagers in there. That would not do."

"Do I detect a note of compassion?"

"I have already killed one man, an innocent man, and I find that I have little taste for it."

"Well, what about Wohlman? How will you feel killing him?"

"Different," she said emphatically. "He and the other two are not innocent. I have no hesitation about it at all."

"Good," Shandu said, cutting into the conversation. "I wish to kill those men and I wish to kill them with my spear, so that I can see their blood drip from its point. I do not want them to die like rats in a cave."

"Look, I know you're both spoiling for a fight, but

we have to be a little clever about this," O'Brien argued. "After all, we are outnumbered, you know."

"Only the white men will fight us. The others will turn and run away," Shandu said.

"Perhaps," O'Brien said. "We cannot count on it happening that way, however. At the very least, we have to find a method that gives us the advantage of surprise."

Katherine snapped her fingers. "What if we managed a blast that trapped the natives in the cave and the others out here alone?" she suggested. "After disposing of Wohlman we can dig them out."

O'Brien smiled tolerantly. "Aren't you starting to grab at straws, Katie? There are too many variables. That all the Kaffirs are working in the cave at the same time. That all the white men are out here at the same time. That the explosion provides just the right amount of force so that they aren't killed in there. It's too risky. Besides, how would I light the fuse without being seen by Wohlman out here?"

"I think we should try it—at least set it up," Katherine said. "First, it would serve as a good diversion if we need it. Second, there might be an opportunity to trap them in the cave, and I think we should be ready for it, if it arises. If we think of something better, fine. But let's be ready with that."

She stood up and went to a large pile of rubble that ran parallel to the wall to the passage entrance. "If you ran a fuse behind this rubble, it would not be seen," she said. She pointed to a spot about twenty-five feet away. "You could run it into the darkness there. You would be able to light it from there."

"It would have to be fast-burning," O'Brien said. "If they spot the flame, it has to be burning too fast for them to stop it."

"Can you do it?"

"I can give it a shot," he said resignedly. "We had better find some holes in the rock around the entrance for the explosives now. We can't chisel it in; it would make too much noise. We need some existing holes we can just dig a little bigger if need be. You can help with this, Shandu."

He found some cracks in the rock and showed Shandu where they were. "You do this while I fix the fuses. Make them about this big." He formed a ring with thumb and forefinger.

"Katie, I don't know if this is going to work," he said as he measured the explosive. "A wrong calculation and I could bring this whole place down on our heads."

"I trust you completely," she said.

He stopped what he was doing and looked up. "And I love you," he said.

She smiled and squeezed his hand with hers.

"Is this what you want?" Shandu asked, standing near the wall.

O'Brien went to look. "That's good. Do the one on the other side just like that."

When Shandu finished, O'Brien plugged the holes with powder, attached the fuses, and ran them back behind the rubble, hiding the string behind rocks wherever possible. He finished and went down the line again with the torch held high above his head.

"With a little luck they won't see it," he said. "And with a little luck it will work. Add that up and it comes to more than a little luck."

"Don't worry," Katherine said. "The spirits are on our side."

Shandu pointed over to a large formation of stalagmites near the waterfall. "We can hide there," he said.

"What about the fuse? I have to be near here so I can light it," O'Brien complained.

"Can you lengthen it and run it over there?" Katherine asked.

"It would just increase the chances of its being seen," O'Brien said. He walked over to the area where Shandu had pointed and then back a few yards to the rear wall. "Look," he said. "Running next to the wall is what almost amounts to another wall of stalagmite. It's like a road in here. If I crawl along it, I think I'll be able to get to the fuse without being seen."

Katherine looked at it carefully. It was not ideal. There were gaps in the "wall" where he could be seen passing, but it was beyond the glow of the torches and unless someone happened to be looking directly at the spot, he would probably be able to pass unseen. "I suppose it will have to do," she said. The place Shandu had indicated had stalagmites about four feet high. If they crouched behind them they would not be seen unless someone walked over and looked.

They put their weapons down at the chosen site and sat with their backs to the wall, their feet against the stalagmite.

"It's a long wait we have," O'Brien said. "They won't be here till morning. If anyone wants to sleep, that'll be okay as long as one of us is awake and keeping watch. Meanwhile we had better douse our torch."

He rubbed the torch in the dust until it went out. The light from Wohlman's torches barely reached them. If it wasn't for the reflections in the cave it would have been totally dark.

O'Brien fidgeted some more and then stood. "That waterfall is mighty inviting," he muttered. "I'm going to have a quick wash."

Two minutes later he was back, still buttoning his pants, his bare chest dripping, and his face flushed.

"I've found it!" he announced excitedly. "The place for us to hide. There's a cave behind the waterfall! You can't see it unless you're standing right in the water. It's the perfect place for us."

"Can we get out of there to light the fuse without being seen?" Katherine asked.

"I told you, it's perfect. There's a small entrance on the side, right next to the wall. You can walk right by

MADEMOISELLE

MADEMOISELLE wants YOU to save $9.03

GET YOUR MADEMOISELLE BY MAIL

12 ISSUES FOR JUST **$11⁹⁷**

and save $9.03 off the cover price of $21.00—$1.75 each!

ORDER NOW, WITH THIS POSTAGE-PAID FORM ☐ PAYMENT ENCLOSED ☐ PLEASE BILL ME

NAME

          (please print)

ADDRESS   APT.

CITY   STATE   ZIP

The first issue of a new subscription mails within 8 weeks of receipt of order—watch for it!

This rate limited to the U.S.A. and its Possessions. For Canada add $8.50 for additional postage.

4553

it and not see it, but it's big enough for a body to get through with a little wriggling. You can also get in the front way by going under the waterfall, in through the side. You don't even have to get wet. Come on, I'll show you."

They followed him and soon found themselves inside a large comfortable cave. The waterfall was like a curtain over the entrance.

O'Brien lit their torch again and held it behind them.

"It goes way back—miles, for all we know," he said.

He stooped down and ran his hand across the pebbled floor. An exclamation burst out of him like a bubble and then he began to laugh, a boisterous sound that filled the cave.

Katherine's first urge was to tell him to keep quiet, but then she realized that the waterfall would deaden the sound.

"What is it?" she asked, smiling helplessly.

O'Brien handed her an oily, milk-colored stone almost half the size of her fist. "For you, my lady," he said with a graceful bow.

She turned it in her hand, puzzled. There seemed nothing special about it; the floor of the cave was littered with similar stones.

"Should I thank you?" she asked.

"I think you should," O'Brien said. Then he shouted exultantly. "It is only the biggest diamond I have ever seen! This cave is full of them! They're lying here to be picked up. Hundreds. Diamonds by the hundreds. Poor Wohlman. He's been blasting and digging and sifting through the rubble and the real treasure has been lying only a few yards away, in the open, waiting to be found!"

Katherine began to laugh at the irony. Wohlman thirsted for wealth like a drunkard for whiskey, and how he had to work for it. She had never wanted wealth, never sought it, yet here she sat, surrounded by wealth beyond imagining.

"Look at the size of this," he said, holding up another stone. "It's worth thousands and thousands. Just this one, this random choice. It's unbelievable, impossible, yet here it is. Bejesus, I can't believe it!"

Only Shandu was silent. He stared morosely ahead at the waterfall, ignoring O'Brien's jubilation.

"What's troubling you, Shandu?" Katherine asked.

He clenched his fist and let it waver in the air, as if it contained the words he wanted to use. "This, this wealth you speak of." He opened his hand and the words gushed out. "It will mean the end of my country, the end of my people. I am not a fool. I have seen that the end is here already, no matter how we struggle against it. But this! This will bring it sooner, like a wind brings a fire closer. The white men will come here on their ships by the thousands. Their wagons will reach in a line from here to Cape Town. First their tents will fill the veldt, and then their towns. My people will be conquered and will become as beasts of burden. I have seen it coming, but now I know that it will be sooner than I thought."

It was a long speech for Shandu, and he delivered it with a tragic intensity, not looking at his companions, his eyes blinded by this image of the future. Katherine felt she was reading his mind, for she saw exactly as he saw, understood it as he did, felt the sadness he felt at the inevitable destruction of a people and a culture. She saw too that in the wisdom of future times man might mourn this loss, but it could never be recreated, for man does not have the ability to go back.

"It is exactly what the Boers have feared," O'Brien said. "Even though your people fight them, you are closer than you know. Sooner or later it will come to pass. There is no avoiding it."

Katherine gripped Shandu's arm tightly. "Shandu, I swear to you. On my honor. No one will ever learn of this from us. I swear it."

"I too," O'Brien said. "We shall take some of these

stones with us when we leave, but we shall tell no one where they came from, and we shall never return for more."

Shandu reached back and patted Katherine's hand. "I thank you," he said. "Still, you are right. One day it will happen. This land is filled with things precious. One day they will be found and that will bring the end. We cannot change what will be. Still, with this secret between us, we can add some time. I thank you, my friends."

"It's not only for you," Katherine said. "I too wish to live in this land. I have no wish to see its ruin."

A moment later she realized what she had said and it startled her. At least one decision had been made: she did want to stay in South Africa. The possibility of returning to England when this was over had remained an alternative in her mind. Now England was abhorrent. How dull it would be. How snug and suffocating and mindless after the limitless space and potential of this land.

The thought surprised her and she examined it more closely. Yes, it was true. In the past weeks she had grown to admire, even to love, this magnificent land with all of its mystery and barbarism and beauty. The very contradictions it contained were a part of its lure. They represented life and growth as opposed to that stultifying sameness that passed for life in some places. There was no place on earth like it that she knew of, no place she would rather be than here, for all its dangers and hardships.

In the past weeks, despite all the disappointments, she had discovered the taste of freedom, and it was like no other feeling in the world. There was no other place she could be so free, where she could be whatever she wished, and become whatever she was able to become. America? South America? Perhaps. It was indeed the new countries of the world that carried its future. England had a great empire now, but the decline had unmistakably set in. She could see it.

These new countries, these were the vital lands, where the true advances of mankind would take place. This was the future. And this was her choice.

O'Brien shifted the torch, and it cast a rainbow of reflections against the waterfall. The sparkling reflections danced in front of their eyes as if to some hidden music. The music of Africa.

Chapter Seventeen

KATHERINE OPENED HER EYES and saw only blackness. There was a brief burst of terror, and then she
realized that she was not dead, but alive in the womb
of the earth. She had finally fallen asleep, early in
the morning by her reckoning.

Slowly she allowed her eyes to grow accustomed to
the darkness. O'Brien had extinguished the torch
hours before. The cave was not completely dark, however. Weak traces of light filtered through the waterfall. Soon she was able to make out a figure near the
mouth of the cave. It was Shandu. He was staring
into the waterfall, or through it to the mysteries
beyond.

O'Brien lay beside her. He breathed lightly as he
slept, his brow as calm as a baby's.

She got up and went to Shandu. "Anything?" she
asked, touching his shoulder. She ignored the urge to
whisper. The water would drown any sound they
made and prevent it from reaching the large
chamber.

"No, but they will be here in an hour," he said.

She did not ask how he was able to know the time
without any normal reference points, but she ac-
cepted it as true. For all she knew, it could have been
noon. "I had better waken O'Brien," she said.

The American was hard to wake. He ignored her
voice and she had to pull roughly on his arm. He sat
up in sudden confusion. "What?"

"It's I, Katherine," she said. "It's morning. Time to
awaken."

They chewed on small portions of meat and washed it down with water from their doorway, a delicious drink with a soft, effervescent taste.

Once again, there was nothing to do but wait. Katherine hated waiting, now as always. There had been times in her life when waiting had seemed a part of the natural order of things—when she was pregnant, for instance—but even then she had not relished it. The analogy was farfetched, but she found herself thinking it anyway. Here she sat in the womb of the earth, waiting to be reborn.

"Doesn't it seem funny," O'Brien said.

"What?"

"Well, here we are, the three of us, sitting and waiting to kill three men. I would never in all my days have predicted it. I still can't figure it out, how things have come to this pass. What a strange assortment of people we are to be here together at this time. Have you ever thought of that? An Englishwoman, a Zulu, and an American. It's preposterous."

He lapsed into silence and she put her hand on his.

"O'Brien."

"Yes?"

"You are a wonderful man."

"I lied," he said.

"About what?"

"I do know how this situation came about. I fell in love with you, that's what happened."

"You should have chosen some simple Boer girl," she teased.

"There are no simple women," O'Brien said. He hesitated. "Katherine, when this is all over, I want you to marry me. Consider it. I know you can't answer now. It isn't the time. All I ask is that you consider it. Will you do that?"

"Yes," she said. "I shall. I'm honored that you've asked." She held his hand tighter.

"I had to ask," he said.

Would she marry O'Brien, she asked herself. She

still did not know, in spite of what had happened between them. The memory of Alan blocked out everything else like a wall. No, she corrected herself. It was not his memory, it was the blood debt she had taken upon herself to avenge what had been done to Alan and Timothy. Until that was repaid she did not want to make a decision about anything else.

While Alan was alive she had never wanted any other man. Some found it curious, for Alan was by no stretch of the imagination a romantic Lothario; but their relationship had been steady, comfortable, and fulfilling. They had attained a simple ease with each other, almost a merging, in which each knew instinctively the intimate thoughts and feelings of the other. Completeness. That was the key to their relationship. Well, now the chain had been broken. Soon it would be time to forge a new link. It could not happen, however, until she had completed her mission.

Her thoughts turned to Colin. She hoped so much that he was happy with his temporary guardians. Every time she thought of him, her heart skipped a beat. How she missed him! How she missed his avid curiosity, the smile that bubbled from him like sweet water, even the cries when he needed her. She would make this up to him as soon as they were reunited. She would never leave him again, she resolved. When next they separated it would be years in the future and it would be his choice. All the love she had divided between him and Timothy would now be his alone. He would never lack love, she swore.

They are coming, the voice in her head told her suddenly.

"They are coming," said Shandu.

She released O'Brien's hand and took her pistol from her belt.

Lights appeared on the far end of the cave, tiny vague balls like the ghostly will-o'-the wisps on the English moors.

Now! she thought. Now! She was seized with exhilaration. It was coming. Soon her mission would be fulfilled. Soon she would be free of this tragic burden.

The lights moved slowly closer. A large group of men clumped together. She strained her eyes to pick out individuals from the mass. Where were the men she wanted to see?

A hiss of breath escaped from between Shandu's teeth, and at the same moment she also saw Wohlman. He was leading the way, a torch in one hand. She recognized his bulky body immediately. Behind him loomed the tall Dieter, and then came the slight English boy, Tommy.

The muscles in her stomach contracted. For a moment she had the urge to vomit, but she subdued the sensation and concentrated on what was happening before her. They were close enough now for her to see the goatee on Wohlman's face. There were about half a dozen black men following him, dragging their heels and being goaded on by Dieter and Tommy. Wohlman had his pistol strapped to his side and Dieter carried a rifle. She could not see if Tommy was armed but assumed he was. As far as she could see, none of the Kaffirs carried spears or any other weapons.

Wohlman began to shout orders, his unmistakable voice carrying over the sound of the waterfall. Still holding his torch, he went with one black man into the mining passage, leaving the others outside. A few seconds later he came out alone, got something from one of the boxes, and went back into the mine.

"He's gone in to lay the explosive," O'Brien said. "This is when the others could spot the fuse. They have nothing to do."

"They will not see that you have taken anything?" she asked.

"Only if they look very hard, and why would they do that?"

Dieter walked to the wall along which the fuse ran

and leaned casually against it. Tommy came and stood beside him and the two men talked. O'Brien held his breath and Katherine bit her lip, but neither man noticed the fuse.

Wohlman strutted from the passage and gesticulated for everyone to move back toward the entrance. A moment later there was the clap of an explosion. Dust poured out of the mine and the floor shook. They all came slowly back. Wohlman shouted out more orders, and the natives picked up their tools and went back into the mining passage, together with the three white men. The entire area was now deserted.

"We could blow it now and they'd all be trapped," O'Brien said, his voice shaking slightly.

"There's no point in trapping the natives," Katherine said.

"I do not want the dynamite to kill them," Shandu said. "I, Shandu, and Lionheart—we must kill them with our own hands."

"It's probably just as well," O'Brien said, changing his mind. "I don't know if we should even use it as a diversion. I'm not really sure how much powder I should have used on that rock. I could have used too much and that makes it dangerous for us as well as them."

Katherine sighed. Doubts were filling her mind now as well. What an inept and pathetic group of ambushers they were proving to be! Here they sat, after days of travel, within sight of their victims, and they had no idea what to do. What were they doing in here, anyway? Perhaps they should be waiting outside to shoot Wohlman down when he came out at the end of the day. She yearned for action, but she had no idea what it should be.

Shandu did not share her quandary, however. "Now it is time to fight," he said assertively.

"What do you mean?" Katherine asked.

His teeth were abnormally white in the dark. "We

are warriors, are we not? Then let us be warriors, Lionheart. We have surprise with us now. Let us go along the wall near to where they are working. We can light the fuse if we must for an added surprise. Then we will leap out and attack. We will overcome them."

"Can it work?" Katherine asked aloud. But she had already made up her mind that it could. She wanted nothing more than to get this over with quickly now. No more waiting. They had not come this far to sit and wait for inspiration to strike.

"Provided the other Kaffirs don't attack us as well," O'Brien said.

"They will run," Shandu said.

"Then let us do it," Katherine said. She smiled. Deep inside, she had known all along that it would come to this. Even as her mind searched for ingenious plans she had known that it must end with her facing Wohlman with a gun in her hand.

"Look," O'Brien said, touching her shoulder. "We could not light the fuse now if we wanted to."

Dieter and Tommy were moving the boxes against the wall, directly beside the fuse.

"They must be making space for more rubble from the cave," O'Brien said. "Those boxes contain powder. If we lit that fuse now, the whole place could blow up in our faces. It would be suicide."

"Well, that's settled then," Katherine said.

O'Brien checked his revolver and then Katherine's. Shandu picked up the rifle and examined it, then he lifted his spear. Faced with the prospect of action, he was now a different man. He began to hum to himself, and the whites of his eyes glittered with reflected light. He too had known that this was how it would be, Katherine suspected.

"Come," Shandu said, leading the way.

They squeezed their bodies through the hole at the side of the cave and moved behind the barrier in a crouch, Katherine behind the two men. It was an uneven barrier, and where it was short or ended altogether, they lay on their stomachs and crawled. They moved as quietly as possible. There was no waterfall now to smother their sound. They reached the point of cover closest to the mine and stopped, breathing hard. They sat with their backs to the wall.

Shandu lifted himself up slowly and peered over the top of the barrier. The light from the torches barely reached them. Dieter and Tommy stood ten or fifteen yards away, and the mouth of the mine was five yards farther on. Shandu lowered himself slowly, holding the wall in front of him for support. A piece of stalagmite broke off in his hand with a loud snap.

"What was that?" It was Dieter's voice.

"I didn't 'ear nothin'," they heard Tommy say.

"I heard a noise, I tell you."

Dieter's footsteps grew closer to them as he moved to investigate. O'Brien pointed his revolver up. If the German stuck his face over the wall he would blow it off.

"Don't waste your energy. It was probably a bat," Tommy said. "There's nothin' else in 'ere."

The German murmured something in reply and his footsteps receded. O'Brien lowered his pistol and let loose a sigh. He hadn't realized he had been holding his breath for almost a minute.

"We must wait until they are all out of the mine," Shandu whispered.

Katherine hated the thought of further waiting, but Shandu was undeniably right. They had to have everyone out in the open where they could be seen, and they also needed to leave an avenue of escape open to the unarmed workers who, according to Shandu, would want nothing more than to flee the cave. Her mouth was dry, the palms of her hands clammy. She forced herself to relax, but she couldn't help fixing her eyes on the stalagmite barrier in front of her, as though expecting a face to peer over without warning.

* * *

Thirty minutes passed. Katherine's legs began to stiffen. She felt O'Brien wriggle around beside her, trying to loosen up and get more comfortable. Only Shandu was still. He did not move a muscle, keeping his eyes directly ahead, a weapon in each hand.

Another thirty minutes. Her muscles wanted to scream. She tried to change her position by crossing her legs, and something made a snapping noise in one knee. It sounded as loud as thunder to her, but nobody else seemed to notice.

While they waited, men had been going in and out of the mining passage, hauling rubble and piling it outside. There, Dieter and Tommy sorted through it, exclaiming loudly whenever they found a particularly choice stone.

There was no sign of Wohlman, though. He stayed in the cave and apparently supervised matters there. Shandu looked over the top again and saw the workers come out of the passage in a group. They milled around and then went down to the water to drink.

"They are all coming out now," he whispered.

Katherine bobbed up and then ducked down again. There was still no sign of Wohlman.

Shandu slid up with his back against the wall, his eyes almost level with the top of the barrier. He stayed in that position and watched. Wohlman still did not appear. The other two white men stood near the mouth of the cave and stared down at the natives as they drank from the lake.

Minutes passed and Wohlman did not come out. Dieter went into the passage, probably to see what Wohlman was doing. Tommy moved back from the entrance and sat on one of the powder boxes.

Shandu shot down suddenly. "He has found it!" he whispered urgently.

Katherine looked over slowly. Sure enough, Tommy was gazing at the fuse on the wall behind him. The boy stood up and followed it to the entrance of the passage, peered into the holes where it led, and scratched his head. If he followed it back now, it would lead close to where they were hiding. Luckily he did not, but looked again at the powder holes instead. He rubbed his chin and then went into the passage.

"He's gone to ask Wohlman about the charges," Katherine said. "It's now or never."

"We could light the fuse now and catch them all in there," O'Brien said quickly.

"No!" Shandu protested. "I want to see them. We get them when they come out. They will not be prepared for anything."

They slid up against the wall and waited for the three men to appear. The villagers at the pool were enjoying their break and did not look back at them. Some were drinking, some washing, some just sitting on the ground resting.

The front of the cave lightened and Dieter appeared with a torch in his hand. Wohlman and Tommy were behind him. The English youth pointed, and Wohlman walked over to the fuse, a puzzled expression on his face.

"Now!" Katherine said.

They vaulted the barrier, firing as they moved toward the men. O'Brien's shot caught Tommy in the shoulder. Katherine aimed at Wohlman and missed. Shandu's shot with the rifle appeared to take Dieter in the arm, but not before the tall German took his pistol from his belt and fired, hitting O'Brien in the leg. Out of the corner of her eye, as she continued to move forward, Katherine saw the American fall. She stopped in her tracks and looked back at him. He was holding his leg with one hand and struggling to stand up.

When she turned back, a split second later, Wohlman had disappeared.

"He has gone back into the mine!" Shandu shouted.

Dieter too had turned. She caught a glimpse of him running toward the entrance to the cave. "Take him," she shouted at Shandu, but he was already occupied.

Two of the natives that Shandu had said would never fight ran up from the pool, picks raised above their heads. Shandu let out a fearsome scream and turned to meet them, his spear held low with both hands. One of the men swung his pick down at Shandu's head, but the big Zulu jumped nimbly to one side and thrust his spear in and then out, faster than the eye could follow. The other was more formidable and kept his distance, circling Shandu, his pick held in front of him as a shield. Katherine wanted to shoot, but she was afraid of hitting Shandu. He needed no assistance. He feinted once to the right with his right hand. As the man moved to cover, he quickly transferred the spear to his left hand and stabbed, all in one smooth motion. The weapon went into the man's side. It came out, dripping with blood, and the man fell.

There was no fight left in the remaining villagers. They ran for the exit, voices raised in terror.

Shandu came up to Katherine, not even breathing hard. "I shall go in after him," he said, pointing at the mine where Wohlman was.

"No!" Katherine said. "He'll shoot you down."

O'Brien hobbled over, still holding his leg.

"Are you all right?" Katherine asked.

"Fine," he said tersely. "The tall one escaped. Ran out the main exit."

"Wohlman is in the cave," she said. She went to the mine entrance and stood to one side.

"Wohlman!" she shouted. "This is Katherine Carson. Come out or we blow up the mine."

There was a flash from inside the cave and a bullet ricocheted off a nearby rock. They all ducked back, and a second later a dark shape hurtled from the passage. It was Wohlman. Shandu threw his assegai, but it missed and went clattering off into the darkness. There was another flash from Wohlman's pistol and Katherine let out a cry. She fell back, her hand on her shoulder where the bullet had entered.

O'Brien limped off after Wohlman, firing his revolver. Shandu knelt beside Katherine and looked at her shoulder.

"You will be all right," he said.

"Don't worry about me," she said. "Get after Wohlman. We can't let him escape."

Only two torches still burned. Both lay on the ground and gave off only a weak light. They were surrounded by a ring of darkness.

"O'Brien? Where is he?" Katherine shouted. Her voice sounded weak.

"I have him!"

She was confused, dizzy. At first she was elated to hear it, but then she realized with a shock that the voice was not O'Brien's. It was Wohlman speaking.

Her revolver felt as heavy as a rifle. She leveled it in the direction of the sound.

Wohlman appeared at the far edge of light. He had one arm around O'Brien's neck. With the other he pointed his revolver at the American's head. Using O'Brien's body as a shield, he offered no target to Katherine.

"Drop your gun!" he called to Katherine, wearing that wolfish grimace she remembered so well.

Shandu stood helpless and unarmed beside her. She kept the gun pointed at Wohlman. It couldn't end this way, she told herself furiously. It couldn't. Wohlman couldn't win this one too. Yet she remained frozen, not knowing what to do.

"Drop it, or I will kill him," Wohlman said again.

The hate welled up in her like a wave. For a moment she considered firing, willing the bullet through O'Brien's body into the German, but she could not bring herself to do that and instead she began to lower the revolver, blinking at the tears that filled her eyes, tasting their bitterness in her mouth.

"No!" O'Brien shouted.

He bit into the arm Wohlman held around his neck with an animal growl and kicked at the German's legs. Wohlman yelled in pain.

Katherine understood with dreadful clarity what O'Brien was doing. The thought flew through her mind in a fraction of a second. If she dropped her revolver, Wohlman would kill them all. She knew it and so did O'Brien. He was sacrificing himself to give her a chance!

"No!" she screamed as Wohlman, off balance, still managed to fire point blank into O'Brien's head.

"No!" Katherine screamed again, lifting her revolver, watching the barrel waver like a candle in the wind, grimacing with pain, and pulling the trigger.

The bullet took Wohlman in the side. His legs wobbled and he sat down neatly beside the body of O'Brien. There was an expression of incredulity on his face.

Shandu ran over and picked up the revolver. Then he bent over and looked at O'Brien. He shook his head at Katherine, telling her what she knew already.

She got to her feet and stumbled forward, ignoring the pain that burned her shoulder. This was her triumph, bitter though it was, and she could not allow her own pain to cheat her further. A foot away from Wohlman she stopped.

He looked back at her, his eyes blank with an animal fear. Powerless, he seemed smaller and less imposing. She remembered Kokolo's words and saw the truth of them. The man cringing before her was impotent except when imposing his will upon others who were weaker. Now, as he faced her, he was little more than a man of straw.

"I made a pledge to my husband and child, and now I will fulfill it," she said resolutely.

Wohlman saw his death in her eyes and held up a hand. "No!" he cried. "Do not do this. I will make you the richest woman in the world. I will do anything. I will—"

She lifted the revolver up with both hands and pointed it at his head. He stopped speaking and watched the gun with mesmerized eyes.

"You are a monster, Wohlman," she said. "And you are also a fool. You never had to steal and kill to live, but you did—and now you will pay for it with your life."

As she pulled the trigger, a sudden twinge of pain in her shoulder caused her to lower the gun. The bullet hit his right kneecap and he screamed in agony with the pain of it.

Shandu grunted beside her. He had retrieved his spear and was leaning on it, watching them.

Wohlman began to sob. She raised the gun again, pointing it carefully at Wohlman's head.

"Look!" Shandu cried urgently.

He was pointing at the mine. She looked over and saw a spark traveling along the wall. At first her mind did not register what was happening, but then she knew what it was.

"The fuse!" she cried. "The fuse is alight!"

She noticed now that Dieter's torch had fallen a few inches away from the fuse. The heat had finally ignited it. Now the fuse was burning in both directions.

She stood there, torn. She did not know whether to run for the fuse to try to stop it, or head for the exit. She touched her shoulder with her hand and felt the viscous flow of blood.

Shandu made up his mind. He took her good arm and began to pull her toward the passage out of the mountain. She glanced back at the helpless, immobile Wohlman, then at the fuse. It was burning its way straight to the dynamite.

And then the earth moved.

The sound of the explosion was magnified ten times over by the acoustics in the giant cavern. There was no doubt now that O'Brien had misjudged the charges. The entire face of rock surrounding the mining passage buckled and then flew out.

A rock the size of an apple hit Shandu on the head and Katherine saw him fall. At the same time, she realized that her feet were not on the ground. She was flying through the air. For a second every crystal in the cave glowed crimson. Then there was nothing.

Katherine opened her eyes, but found it difficult to focus on anything. Her shoulder felt as if it had been hit by a falling tree, and tendrils of pain extended from it to grip the rest of her body.

The walls of the cavern rumbled and groaned. The thunder of falling rock filled her ears every few seconds as some new section caved in. Miraculously, one of the torches still burned. It glowed like a ghost in the swirling clouds of dust.

There was a cough, and a shape loomed beside her. It was Shandu.

"Are you all right?" she asked.

"Yes," he said. He pulled her to her feet. "How is your wound?"

"It's nothing." She knew it was a lie, even as she spoke. She was losing blood and growing weaker by the minute.

"It does not look good," Shandu said, his voice concerned. "Wait."

He ran off and came back shortly with the torch and a piece of cloth. Quickly he bandaged the wound. "At least that will stop the blood," he said, pulling it tight and tying a knot. "Kokolo will do more when we get out."

There was a loud groan from about ten yards away. Katherine bent down painfully and picked up the pistol where it had fallen. Shandu led the way to the noise, holding the torch up.

It was the young Englishman, Tommy. Rock covered his legs. There was a circle of blood on his shoulder where O'Brien had shot him. He was sweating and his lips moved with unintelligible sounds. Katherine lifted the pistol.

"No. You cannot kill me," Tommy whimpered. "I spared your life. I could have killed you and I spared your life."

"You killed my child," she said.

"I didn't mean to, I swear. I spared your life."

His fish eyes bulged and spittle ran down his chin. She lowered the revolver and turned her back.

She heard Shandu move beside her. Tommy screamed once as the *assegai* entered his heart.

It was done. She moved a few yards away from the body to find O'Brien. Slowly, she walked over to him and looked down.

Shandu lit another torch from the one he was holding and handed it to her. He moved away toward the exit.

Katherine had never felt so exhausted. Her legs had no strength. She sank to the ground beside O'Brien and took his hand in hers. She found herself rubbing his fingers, as if to bring life back to them. The fact of his death suddenly became real. It hit her like a blow to the heart. O'Brien had given his life for her. She gasped for air and lifted O'Brien's hand to her cheek, anointing it with her tears.

Her emotional dam burst then. The torrent of feelings that she had denied for weeks poured out unrestrainedly. Grief engulfed her. She wailed then, the wail of a woman who had lost more than she could bear to lose. She cried for Alan and Timothy and Jim O'Brien, and she cried for herself. She felt Shandu put his arm around her shoulder, and still she cried, purging herself of all the hate that had imprisoned her soul. It felt as if she cried for a lifetime, but it was only a minute or two, and when she was done, she knew that she was done with grief, that she was finally free of the past, that the balancing had been accomplished.

Shandu read the signs in her face and finally spoke.

"You are ready?" he asked.

"Yes, I'm ready," she said.

"There is much rock there," he said, pointing to the exit passage. "We cannot get out."

"We can't dig?" she asked.

"Too much," he said. "I think the passage has all fallen. It would take months."

"What about the way we came in?"

"That has gone too," he said soberly.

There was a roar as another part of the ceiling caved in. The entire mountain seemed to rumble and move. Katherine began to cough as dust rose into her nostrils.

Well, she thought, at least some of the villagers have escaped. Dieter as well, no doubt.

"Wohlman?" she asked.

"He is dead, I think," Shandu said. "If not, he soon will be, as we will be if we cannot leave here."

"There is a way out," Katherine said. "At least, there is a chance." She pointed at the lake, wincing as she lifted her arm. "The waterfall. It's bringing in a tremendous amount of water. But, you see, the level of the lake does not rise. Where is it going?"

Shandu began to understand. "It must go out somewhere," he said.

"Look over there," she said, pointing again. "The water moves in circles. It is almost like a whirlpool. There's the hole through which the water is leaving."

She felt more like lying down than continuing, but she forced herself on. "It might be a small hole, or it might be big. It could lead farther into the mountain, but I think it must lead out to the river. It's our only chance."

"Yes," Shandu said. "I have looked at all the passages and they are blocked."

More rock fell around them. Dust particles filled the air. Katherine reached into her pocket and pulled out the diamonds she had collected, including the large one they had found behind the waterfall. She handed them to Shandu.

"These are for my son. I want you to give them to him," she said. "You must hurry now. The roof will fall in completely soon."

Shandu pushed her hand away. "Give them to him yourself, Lionheart. You will come with me."

"I cannot," she said. "My shoulder, I can't even move this arm. I won't be able to swim."

"I will not leave you," Shandu said stubbornly. "You will come with me."

"What sense is there in your dying with me?" Katherine said angrily. "To satisfy your honor? Life is all that has purpose and meaning. What have we gained if we both die in the heart of this mountain? You must go. I don't want you to stay and watch me die."

"Woman, that scratch is not enough to kill you," Shandu said with a smile. "I shall carry you through the water. I shall place you on my back and swim with you."

Katherine shook her head. "No, Shandu. I don't wish to die by drowning. Leave me and go."

Shandu drew up to his full height, and now his voice became angry. "You will come with me, Lionheart, and stop this talking. I will hear no more. If you do not come now, I shall knock you out and carry you unconscious."

She did not doubt that he meant what he said. She put the diamonds back into her pocket, then she touched O'Brien's hand and said good-bye to him. She stood up, holding on to Shandu's arm. "Let us go, my friend," she said.

They stood together at the edge of the water. "You must get on my back and place both your arms around my neck," he said. "It will hurt your wound, but you must hold tightly and not let go. We do not know what we will find, so there must be a signal.

Listen for my voice. When I say *now*, you must breathe as deeply as you can and hold it. You must do it fast. Do you understand?"

Shandu crouched down in front of her and she clambered onto his broad back. She put her arms around his neck and held the wrist of her wounded left arm with her right hand so that she would not crush his neck. The pain was almost unbearable and she ground her teeth. He stepped in and began to wade toward the area where the hole was.

The water deepened quickly, and soon Shandu was swimming.

They felt the suction from the hole before they even saw it. It grabbed them like a rough hand and began to pull them down.

"Now," Shandu cried, and under they went.

The rush of water carried them into a passage that led sharply down through rock and then leveled slightly, although the incline was still downward. The water gathered still more force, as if joined by tributaries, and their bodies crashed against the walls surrounding them. Shandu fought the current, using one hand as a rudder and the other as a shield above their heads. Katherine felt her lungs begin to ache. She fought against the overwhelming urge to open her mouth.

Suddenly there was noise and she realized her head was above the water. She gulped for air, allowing it to flood her lungs. Shandu lifted his hand and felt the rock of the roof; it was at least a foot above their heads. He allowed the water to carry them forward.

The river seemed wider now, but no slower. She wondered how long they would have enough room above their heads to be able to breathe. Where would the current take them? Did it lead out of the mountain, or deeper into the ground? The questions filled her mind with fear, but there was no answer in the blackness around them.

The roof moved sharply down. Shandu shouted a warning, and she had just enough time to take another quick breath before they went under again.

This time it seemed endless. Her lungs ached and then began to burn as though aflame. She thought of Timothy, of Alan, and of her lover, O'Brien. She thought also of Colin, waiting for her return. She had a vision of him playing in a mound of sand and knew then that she would not die, could not die. Somehow she would survive this ordeal and meet with him again.

Their bodies bounced off the rocks, but they were both past the point of pain. Katherine opened her eyes under the water and saw nothing. She felt Shandu swimming beneath her now and clung to him for dear life.

And then she saw light. At first she thought that her mind was playing tricks on her in the final moments before she lost consciousness, but no, it was growing lighter around them. She forced herself not to open her mouth, feeling the blood thunder in her ears.

In seconds, they were out in the open, but swirled around so violently that they were sucking in water as well as air. A roaring noise filled their ears. For a wild moment, Katherine thought she had died. Then they were flying!

She looked up and then down, saw the sky above and the water rushing to meet them. They had come out of the mountain on a waterfall. They fell twenty more feet, and then they hit the water. Katherine lost her hold on Shandu's neck and felt herself go down. She kicked her legs furiously and felt herself rise again to bob on the water. She kept kicking her legs to stay afloat, and then Shandu came from behind and grasped her around the chest.

With powerful strokes of his free arm, Shandu propelled them toward the greensward edging the pool. They pulled themselves out of the water and lay spread-eagled on the ground. Katherine saw that both of their bodies were bleeding from cuts and scrapes. No one place hurt; pain was everywhere.

Katherine did not know how long she lay there, but finally she sat up and looked around. The mountain was perhaps a hundred and fifty yards above them. It appeared to be engulfed by fog, but as she looked she saw that it was dust rising from places where there had once been caves. The entire mountain had changed its shape and crumpled in like dough.

Shandu stood up and began to shout, a joyful, boisterous sound. "We are alive!" he cried. "We are alive!"

He helped Katherine stand and slowly they began to walk back up to the mountain to where the entrance cave had been. But there was no cave now, just a pile of rock where once there had been a hole. There was no sign of Kokolo either.

Katherine leaned against a tree trunk and willed herself to carry on.

"Where do you think Kokolo is?" she asked.

Shandu shrugged.

There was a movement in the trees to their left, and Katherine suddenly froze, her heart missing a beat with the reminder that Dieter had escaped from the cave and was probably still alive.

A white man stepped out. It was Jan de Wet, the Boer they had met a couple of days earlier.

"Are you all right?" he said anxiously to Katherine.

"What are you doing here?" she asked, not answering his question.

De Wet grinned. "I came back," he said. "I traveled on for a day and a half, but the feeling that you would need help grew too strong for me to deny. I turned around and came back, too late to be much help I see."

"You turned around?" she repeated stupidly.

He nodded and looked at her shoulder. "You have been wounded. We must attend to that."

"Kokolo. Where is Kokolo?" she asked.

"Look. Sit down for a minute," he said, taking her arm and tugging her gently. "You seem all in."

"I'm all right," she said. "What of Kokolo?"

"He went off after one of the white men," de Wet said, gesturing toward the hill where they had camped. "I was coming up the trail when I heard the explosion. This white man began to run back up into the mountain. The way down was blocked by me, of course. Kokolo went after him. He told me to stay here and help you."

"And you let him go by himself?" Katherine said.

"I was worried about you," de Wet said. "That old fox can look after himself."

"We must go after him," Katherine said, looking at Shandu.

The Zulu nodded wearily, but de Wet protested. "You are in no shape to go anywhere, either of you."

"He will need our help," she said. "Can you bandage my shoulder?"

De Wet restrained himself from speaking and hurried to his horse in the trees. A moment later he returned with a bandage and began to work on her shoulder.

"This will only do for a short while. You need medicine on that wound," he said.

"Kokolo will be able to take care of it," she said.

"What about the American?" de Wet asked. "What happened to O'Brien?"

"O'Brien is dead," she said tonelessly.

"*Ach,* that is a shame. He was a good man. I liked him," de Wet said sadly.

"Yes. I too," she said.

"And the others?"

"Wohlman is dead. So is the young Englishman. The third man is Dieter, the one you saw. He ran out just before the cave collapsed."

She winced as de Wet tugged the bandage tight.

"There," he said. "That will do you for a short time."

Katherine pursed her mouth as she stood and repressed the groan that rose to her lips. The recognition of pain was a luxury now. It would have to wait.

With Shandu leading, they crossed the river and went past their camp and into the bush beyond it. Shandu had no difficulty following the tracks and they made good time. After an hour they stopped to rest on a ridge.

"They must be down in that valley," Shandu said, pointing.

It was a small circular valley with a grass-covered clearing in its center mysteriously devoid of trees and bush.

"They could both be dead," Katherine said morosely.

"More likely Kokolo is chasing him somewhere in that bush," de Wet said.

Sitting on the ground, they stared down into the valley as if concentration alone would bring something into view.

"Tell me, what happened in the mountain . . . Wohlman . . . O'Brien?" de Wet asked.

Katherine stood. Events in the mine were still a tumble of confusion in her mind. "I shall tell you later," she said. "We had best go down into the valley."

Suddenly the air reverberated with the sound of a shot. A flock of birds rose from trees near the grassy edge.

Katherine held her breath as she gazed down, trying to see some further movement.

"There he is!" de Wet said first.

Kokolo ran from the grass into the stand of trees, followed a minute later by the tall German. The grass was high, up to the black man's chest; he ran in a crouch, stopping every few yards and turning to look back at Dieter.

"The tables have been turned," Katherine said.

"Kokolo had a spear when he left the cave. He must have lost it," de Wet said.

"Perhaps he threw it and missed," Katherine said. The men looked like midgets in the distance. "Is there anything we can do?"

De Wet hefted his rifle. "It is a long distance, but I can try," he said.

Shandu placed his hand on the Boer's gun. "No. It will not be needed," he said. "He is cunning, that one. He is leading the white man where he wants him to go. Look!"

They watched Kokolo zig-zag through the grass. Every ten or fifteen yards he stopped to look back. The maneuver cost him valuable time, but now they realized that Kokolo was deliberately preventing the German from losing him.

There was the sound of another shot, and they saw Kokolo fling himself to the ground. A moment later he bobbed up ten yards away and the chase continued.

"Now!" Shandu said. "See how he moved around."

Indeed, Kokolo had moved in a half-circle to avoid a particular area of grass. Now he stood on the other side, looking back at the running white man for longer than before.

The German ran forward, waving his pistol. And then, without warning, the earth gave way beneath him. A black hole opened in the ground and he disappeared from view.

There was one high, piercing scream, and then silence from the valley below.

"What happened?" Katherine asked in a half-whisper.

"It was a hunter's trap," Shandu said. "The German will be dead."

"They dig a pit in these parts," de Wet explained. "In the bottom are spears, pointing upwards. They cover the pit with branches and straw and the animals fall in, pierced on the spears."

They saw Kokolo walk to the end of the trap and gaze down. Shandu raised himself up and let out a resounding shout. The black man in the valley looked up and then raised both arms triumphantly.

Katherine rubbed her eyes. Everything around her seemed insubstantial, as if she could almost see through it. Dizziness engulfed her.

"So it is . . . finally over," she mumbled. She wanted to sit down, but she was not sure she could bend her legs without falling.

"It is done," she said.

De Wet caught her as she fell.

There was blackness, and in the distance a faint light. She waited and watched, without thought and without fear. Slowly the light grew brighter. It was coming toward her.

It grew closer, and soon she saw that it was a star, a burning ball of fire, a sparkling jewel of life. It hovered in front of her as if waiting for an invitation, and then a figure stepped from its center and stood before her.

He was dressed in white and he stood there with his hand outstretched. It was Alan, a different, more glorious Alan than the one she had known.

"I have come to say good-bye now," he said tenderly. "You have done what had to be done and we thank you and wish you well. I say farewell for Timothy and for Jim."

"I love you, Alan," she said.

"And I you," he said. "That will always exist. It will never change."

"Where are you going?" she asked, wanting to understand.

"We go to seek new life, as we must," he said, his eyes luminous. "There are no endings, only new beginnings."

"And what of me?"

"You said it yourself, 'Life is all that has purpose and meaning.' You spoke the truth. You will live, Katherine, and your life will have purpose and meaning. You will love again and you will teach our son what you have learned. I am happy for you."

"Yes," she said.

"Good-bye," he said. "Good-bye."

The star came forward then and engulfed Alan in its center, its light too brilliant to behold.

"Good-bye," she said, and the blackness came again.

She heard the soft voices of the men around her. Slowly she opened her eyes and saw a fringe of leaves outlined against the turquoise sky. She heard the calls of birds and the soft rush of the river.

Jan de Wet's face appeared above her. His eyes were gentle and concerned.

"You are going to be all right," he said. "Kokolo did a fine job on your shoulder."

"Can you help me sit up?" she asked.

He put his arm around her and shifted her so that her back was propped against a tree. There was a fire burning and Shandu and Kokolo sat near it. A delicious smell rose from a bubbling pit.

"I've made a stew from the meat of a buck," de Wet said. "Do you want some?"

"Yes," she said. "I am very hungry."

"That's good," de Wet beamed. "I'll get you some."

"How do you feel?" Shandu asked.

Her shoulder still hurt, but it was now only a dull ache. Her body was stiff and sore, but she knew it would soon recover. "Good," she said. "And you?"

Shandu shrugged. "A few scratches. I have known worse than that."

"And Kokolo?"

Shandu grinned. "He is happy that this is over. He wants me to come back to Nkupu's village with him. He says that there is the milk and honey he saw at the end of the journey when he joined me."

De Wet handed her a cup of stew. "Kokolo says that he will take the wives and cattle that are owed to him. He will not be too busy, although he will heal the sick and make rain when it is needed. The rest of the time, he plans to frolic with pretty maidens, drink beer, eat honey, and grow fat."

"And what of you?" she asked of Shandu again. "Will you do that?"

"I have nothing to return to. Here, I could make a new family. We shall see. I think I shall try it for a time."

"Are you happy now that you have done what you set out to do?" de Wet asked.

It was a searching question, and she thought before answering. Was she happy? She had accomplished her goal. She had done more in a few weeks than most women did in a lifetime, and she would never be the same again. She had become herself, grown to know herself, her strengths and her weaknesses, more intimately and honestly than most people ever did.

"Yes," she said finally. "I am happy now."

"Good. Good," de Wet said, pleased by her answer.

He spoke with Kokolo for a minute and then turned to her again. "We have tried to find out from Shandu what happened in the mountain, but he wouldn't speak of it until you awoke. Tell me, did O'Brien die well!"

"Yes," Katherine said without hesitation. "He died well. He died like a great warrior. He gave his life so that Shandu and I could live."

"And what were those men doing in the mountain?"

"They were looking for gold," she said.

"Did they find it? Is there gold there?" he asked.

She felt Shandu's eyes on her and the diamonds in her pocket pressing against her thigh.

"No," she said. "There was nothing. O'Brien said it was not even worth mining."

De Wet slapped his leg. "That is good. We can do without gold here."

"Yes," she said. "We do not need it."

She looked over at Shandu and saw that he was smiling.

"Did you bring Jim's horse?" she asked.

"Yes. All his belongings."

"There's a journal in his saddlebag. Would you bring it to me, please."

A short time later, de Wet returned with the small, leather-bound book. He handed it to her and then began to prepare a can of coffee. She held the journal in her hand without opening it and watched the smoke rise from the fire. The sun was dropping to warm the other side of the world. A nearby troop of monkeys burst into passionate conversation. Life was all around her. Its purpose was survival, and it continued in spite of everything. There was also life of a kind in the pages of the book she was holding. It was a thing of the spirit and she could feel its presence.

She opened the book and turned to the last entry. O'Brien's handwriting was large and bold; he wrote with a flourish, as he had lived. She read the words before her.

I know now that I will die here, in this Africa I love so deeply. I suppose I have always known it. There was never any other way but the way that was to be. I am sad because I want more, but I am happy because I have had so much.

This woman has given me more than I ever knew I wanted. She is bold and gentle, cold and warm, a magnificent contradiction, and I love her for it. To have known her is enough.

She may not know it, but she is now a woman of Africa. They are so alike, this woman and this land. Both have an unquenchable spirit and both have a savage splendor that is beyond the understanding of men. I have known and loved both, which is more than most can say, and I am happy for it.

Yes, I now know that I will die here. I have lived my life with a smile. I have tried, in my way, to live it well. My only remaining hope is that I leave it well. Perhaps not with a smile, but at least with courage. Strange, I do not feel that this is the end, but more like the beginning of a great new adventure. So be it.

Katherine closed the book and placed it in her lap. She felt the tears on her cheeks. He need not have questioned his courage. He gave as much as any man could ever give.

She lifted her eyes and looked into the sky. Yes, she thought, now she was a woman of Africa. She had been forged in the fire of this land, and now it was a part of her and would always be so.

High above the mountains, so high it was only a speck in the sky, an eagle glided, gazing at the beautiful land below with hot, yellow eyes. She wondered what it saw.

TREVOR MELDAL-JOHNSEN

THIS CRUEL BEAUTY

In this romantic adventure, Katherine Carson, a resolute young English settler journeys into the wilds of South Africa to avenge the brutal murder of her husband and son, and discovers constant danger, a rich store of diamonds, and an unexpected love which binds her to this cruel yet beautiful land.

81851-5/$3.50

ALWAYS

This is the story of Gregory Thomas, a rising young screenwriter, whose fascination with Brooke Ashley, an old Hollywood movie star, turns to obsession when he realizes that he is her reincarnated lover. Thirty years ago Brooke and her lover died in a blazing fire. And as Gregory begins a desperate search to find her again, he encounters a malevolent force determined to keep them apart...forever.

41897-5/$2.50

Available wherever paperbacks are sold, or directly from the publisher. Include 50¢ per copy for postage and handling: allow 6–8 weeks for delivery. Avon Books, Mail Order Dept., 224 W. 57th St., N.Y., N.Y. 10019

Meldal-Johnsen 3-83